Books by Ian Gouge

Novels and Novellas

An Infinity of Mirrors - Coverstory books, 2018

Losing Moby Dick and Other Stories - Coverstory books, 2017; Kindle, 2018

Losing Moby Dick - Kindle 2015 (individual edition)

Writing to Gisella - Kindle 2015

Riding the Escalators - Kindle

Short Stories

Degrees of Separation - Coverstory books & Kindle, 2018

Secrets & Wisdom - Coverstory books, 2017; Kindle, 2018

Poetry

After the Rehearsals - Coverstory books, 2018

Punctuations from History - Coverstory books, 2018

Human Archaeology - Paperback, 2017

Collected Poems (1979-2016) - Paperback, 2017; Kindle, 2018

Ian Gouge

The Big Frog Theory

Coverstory
books

First published in paperback format, 2012;
this version published by Coverstory books,
2018

ISBN 978-1-9993027-3-3

Copyright © Ian Gouge 2018

www.coverstorybooks.com

ONE

In a Malvern tea-shop he sat, watching the steam from his coffee filter rise unevenly above the rim of a faded white cup. Beneath the porous surface of the filter, he could imagine the liquid dripping slowly - drip, drip, drip - and adding to the volume of the dark fluid beneath. Despite his present preoccupation (or perhaps because of it) he allowed the diversion of his coffee to tug at his mind, and he sniffed, searching for a distinctive aroma. One of the women on the next table - a large, well-coiffured, Conservative kind of woman - looked coldly across at him, eyes betraying her reaction to an interruption. Perhaps he had sniffed a little too loudly or intrusively - though given the nature of the offence, it was something he could not permit himself to dwell upon. He returned her stare without emotion and, seeming to have failed in her challenge of him, she resumed her conversation.

The tea shop - a tired establishment which, he imagined, owed more to the past than the present - was mostly empty. Apart from the Conservative lady and her companion, there were only two other patrons present: a younger couple in muddied walking boots sitting against the back wall, their bright waterproofs a marked contrast to the plain and drab decor. When they had entered, Neville, drawn to their arrival by the weary "ping" of the door's bell, had watched as the Proprietress - a large lady who looked as if she might have personally sampled every meal ever served there - had stared warningly at their boots, almost as if the intensity of her gaze alone might physically clean them. To the credit of the boots' owners, they had, in consequence, been almost over-zealous in the vigorous attention they bestowed upon the doormat, which seemed momentarily to groan under the pressure of their scrapings and rubbings.

Neville, having relived that recent memory, glanced back down at his coffee. The filter appeared to somehow contain more water than it had a few moments before, as if the drip, drip, drip had ceased and the cup, in some kind of rebellion, had started to force the liquid back from whence it had come. He felt too tired to respond to the evidence of his own eyes, and, ignoring the impossibility of the happenings on the table in front of him, looked out of the window by which he sat as if, in doing so, he might remind himself of his situation, of his relation to the outside world, and of the reason he was there.

'So why *are* you here?'

The voice had come suddenly to him from nearby; it was a quick, shrill, impatient voice, carrying with it a not insignificant air of menace. He hesitated a fraction then turned, expecting to find himself confronted by either the Conservative lady or the establishment's owner; but the former was still in conversation and the latter nowhere to be seen. The smell from his cup - that which he had been seeking just a few moments earlier - now forced him to look down at his coffee again. The filter was now empty. Lifting it away, he revealed a cup full of dark coffee. Outside an old bus rumbled slowly passed the window, coughing from its exhaust like an old man about to expire.

Was it an accident that he now found himself here, sitting alone in this quiet and somehow forgotten tea-shop? And of all places, that it should be here in Malvern! Unable to give up the past, he recalled how he had left his office quietly and without fuss, collecting his briefcase on the way to the lift. His Boss had been as humane as the situation and his own humanity allowed; which meant precious little considering his not undeserved reputation for being a complete bastard.

'Neville, my boy' - he had tried his most wheedling, ingratiating, and "I hate doing this to you, Old Son, please believe me" type voice - 'Neville, this company's going down the toilet, and something's got to be done about it. Something, indeed. No doubt you'll have heard the rumours and seen the stories in the local press - and the national press, come to that. The place is rife with rumours, I know. Scaremongering, I call it! Nothing but scaremongering. Of course, given the present difficulties we do have to look at our costs. The shareholders are concerned: poor dividends, poor exports, poor forecasts. So we do need to make one or two' - he hesitated over the next word - 'economies. You understand?'

Had he understood? Did he understand now? He wondered if he had said anything, but could not recall.

'So - as part of a whole raft of measures, you understand - we've decided to restructure your department; we're going for a leaner, fitter approach. Fighting fit for the future! That's it! We're giving Brian a broader brief, Colin the challenging clients, and David the difficult decisions. So, I'm afraid that makes you redundant. Sorry. Lovely working with you. See Celia on your way out, she's got your cheque.'

And that had been that; with a sudden rush of words his career was in ruins.

'You should have punched him on the nose!'

Again the disembodied voice. Neville, struggling with the thought as to how he should respond - and even, if he was honest with himself, whether or not he had actually heard anything at all - sat and looked out of the window, trying to ignore the unwanted intrusion. Returning to his interrupted recollection, he vaguely remembered standing up - probably without saying anything, though he couldn't be sure - and just leaving. Briefcase, coat, door, lift, car, motorway. It had been as simple as that. From the centre of Birmingham he had been on some form of automatic pilot - which, without any conscious design on his part, had brought him here. It was probably two years since he had last been in Malvern; since he and Mirelle had walked the hills together. With a stab, he remembered happiness.

He picked up his coffee and, in doing so, noticed that the Conservative lady was now alone, the walkers had gone, and there were now two waitresses tending the vacant tables. He checked his watch - the watch that one year had been a reward for "exceptional service and loyalty to the company" - and wondered if, despite all external appearances, at 3:21 in the afternoon they might be expecting some kind of rush.

Two years seemed a long way away. Two weeks even further. He had propelled his most recent scenes with Mirelle towards ancient history with such force that they had overtaken more distant events in their headlong rush for oblivion. The sharp tang of the coffee on his palette brought them back. Mirelle's coffee always tasted like that; sharp and bitter. Perhaps because she was half-French. Perhaps because she made fucking awful coffee.

Luckily the last cup he had seen in her hand had been empty - or at least it was empty by the time it flew past his head and crashed into the dining room wall. He had seen it late, and, without time to calculate trajectory, simply ducked. Instinctive self-preservation. When he looked up again she was gone; the door open, the room empty.

'She was a bitch anyway! What did she ever do for you?'

There was no-one near him. The Conservative lady was now talking to the owner by the counter - about him, perhaps? - and the waitresses were busy re-laying the walkers' table. He had put his coffee down. As he did so, it seemed as if the discarded filter gave him a muddy grin. He rubbed his eyes. He was suddenly tired.

Outside, the old bus he had seen a few moments before had now reappeared, this time going slowly and noisily the other way. He watched it as it stopped. The driver, having switched off the engine and re-established silence, got up from his seat and opened the door. He looked as old as the bus, and Neville wondered if, somehow, he and the bus had been inexorably linked since the former's birth and the latter's construction. The driver's uniform finished abruptly at his waist where vaguely shabby corduroy trousers took over from a serge jacket to look after his legs. Without concern, the man stepped into the road, evidently heading for the tea-shop.

Mirelle had hated his own cords. In fact, she had hated his entire wardrobe. She used to moan -

'Constantly!

- about how she herself had so little to wear, and how everything she did have was either old or cheap. How Theresa from number seventeen - the one with the silicone implants and the stock-broking husband - went to Paris every year to buy her underwear; Marks & Spencer just wasn't the same! And if it wasn't clothes or underwear, then it was the car they didn't have, or the holidays they never took, the dinner parties they never gave, or the cannabis they never smoked. She was obsessed with the things they didn't do or didn't have. And all because **they** could never afford anything as a result of **him** choosing to work in a "shabby office" for a pittance, rather than better himself in the world.

He had tried. If he could say anything in his defence it was that. He feigned ambition to see where that would get him (it got him the watch), but ran out of steam. In a brief excursion to the opposite pole, he had even tried gambling for a while, such was his desire to satisfy her. But, after losing three hundred pounds on six consecutive Epsom favourites - something unheard of, the Bookmaker had told him as he relieved him of his last fifty quid - he gave that up too. The beginning of the end came when Mirelle, in her quest for fortune, started charging him for sex.

'She was a tramp; forget her! You're well rid of the frog bitch!'

Despite his resolute attempts to ignore its unwanted intrusions, the voice - which was now becoming strangely comforting - was, Neville knew, unquestionably right. He had been well and truly shafted - even before he started paying for it. And where was he now? What did he have? He had been completely usurped on all fronts, and was now sitting alone in a Malvern tea-shop cradling an empty coffee cup.

The bell above the door rang as the bus driver entered. He gave a slight "old boy" kind of nod to Neville (the sort one might expect to receive from a stranger one recognised) then made his way over to the counter. Neville put his cup down on the yellow tablecloth, noticing, as he did so, a large slice of Black Forest Gateau on a blue and white plate before him. He couldn't remember ordering it; and, if he had, it would certainly have been to accompany - rather than follow - the coffee which he had so recently finished. Replacing the old filter on top of the cup, he made to pick up the cake.

'Forget it, brother!'

That shrill, angry voice again. From the top of the cake, two eyes of cream and glacé cherry stared back at him.

'Eat me and I'll give you gut rot so bad, you won't be able to stand up for a week!'

Neville, with an acute sense of embarrassment, glanced up. No-one was looking his way, and his sudden discomfort seemed to have gone unnoticed. Indeed, despite the presence of the Conservative Lady, the Waitresses and now, the Bus Driver, he felt strangely alone. He looked down at the cake again.

'I mean, do you have any idea how old I am?!'

He fought the desire to respond; fought the instinct that was attempting to persuade him to give in and to enter into conversation with this rather tired slice of Black Forest gateau - tired, despite its attempts to appear alluring. He didn't even like Black Forest gateau; not really.

'OK Neville, I know what you're thinking: you're thinking "what the hell's going on?" Right? "What am I doing talking to a slice of cake?" Right? Shit, forget it, man! I understand! Just relax, OK? I know what you're going through.'

'You know...?'

It was involuntary, but he had opened the door - and the cake slid a crumb right in there to keep it open.

'See, that was easy wasn't it? My name's Hans. Black Forest. Germany. Get it? Mind you, this is a piss awful place to end up after that - those are **real** mountains, man! - but there you have it. Don't really get too much say in the matter, not when you're like me.'

'Like you? What's going on?'

Neville, suddenly feeling very warm, heard the sound of geese. He looked out of the window, expecting to see a small flock flying low-level along the street outside.

'Forget them, that's nothing. Hey, Nev. Hey!'

Hans was insistent. Neville looked back at the cake, which proceeded to roll its cream and cherry eyes upwards.

'On the wall, there.'

Between the counter and the door, about six feet from the floor, three china geese hung on the wall, line abreast, largest at the front, smallest bringing up the rear. Now animated, their beaks worked angrily as they cried, flying as hard as they could but getting nowhere.

'They're pissed too. They feel hard done by. They don't want to be stuck in here; they want to be somewhere else; **out there**.'

He loaded the last two words with such meaning, that Neville forgot the geese and looked back at Hans.

'Where?'

'Out there. In the Real World, Nev. Where you've just come from. Or from where you've just been thrown. That shitty little experience you call existence. Those dummies on the wall think it's all pond weed and stale bread out there; know what I mean? So they're bitter about being stuck in here. *I* know the Real World's not so hot; I mean, look at you.'

Neville tried to understand what Hans was getting at. From his coffee cup he saw steam rising again, the filter half full of water, and the drip, drip, drip beginning again. The Real World? In the last two weeks, the "Real World" had dumped on him in a major way; it had ripped the guts out of his life, and trampled them into the mud.

'But you're not alone.'

'Sorry?'

'You. You're not alone, even though you think you are. Shit, you're sitting here talking to me aren't you?'

'But...'

'I know what you're going to say. People always say the same thing; "But you're just a cake", they say. I've heard it all before, so just don't, OK? Don't, and we'll get along just fine. I'm just trying to help, that's all.'

Neville struggled vaguely with the notion of being aided by a stale slice of chocolate gateau.

'Help?'

'Just drink your coffee, Nev, and shut up for a minute.'

The filter was empty again, and when he lifted it away, there was another brew of coffee. He sipped it gently, almost cautiously. It tasted better this time.

On the wall, the geese had stopped their cawing and seemed a little more contented. The sun had broken through the clouds outside, and a shaft of light - reflecting off one of the windows of the bus - bathed them in a small patch of warmth. The Bus Driver was sitting down talking to the Conservative lady at the table next to Neville's, and the Proprietress - who seemed to be growing ever larger - had taken a stool by the counter. The two waitresses were still re-laying the walkers' table.

'Nev, you're in the pits, OK? There's no easy way for me to break this to you - not that you don't know it anyway - but really, you've fucked up in a major way. Your life's going down the toilet and, quite frankly, the whole thing's a great big sodding mess. Sorry, but there it is.'

Neville, who had the very real sense that he was being lectured, kept dutifully silent, sipping his coffee and looking at Hans - who, despite his physical limitations, had taken on a kind of professorial aspect.

'So, what do you do? You're stuffed - and you're sitting in a tea shop talking to a slice of cake. Can't go any lower really. I mean, I've been there myself. I used to be a fresh young thing, full of life and get up and go. But if you miss the bus, the bastards somehow manage to just beat all of that out of you. Know what I mean? So, when it happened to me, I took a long look at myself and decided to try and do something about it; to salvage something.'

'And?'

'And, now I do this. It's my job. Sitting here, talking to guys like you. Mostly guys, anyway. I can't understand women, you know? I always try and leave the women to Maurice, he's better at it.'

'Maurice?'

'Yeah, the croissant.'

Slowly, Neville replaced the cup on the table and, with an involuntary sob, dropped his head into his hands. The room was silent.

TWO

He was unsure how long he remained there, motionless in the silence. Eventually - his eyes still closed - he raised his head until he was confident that, on opening them, he would be looking high above the table. After a pause, he let the world in. On the far wall, the three geese were rigid. The patch of sunlight that had illuminated them was no more, and in their lack of motion they seemed reassuringly dull. Perhaps he had been dreaming; perhaps it was all some kind of mistake, or an elaborate joke.

He began to lower his head, gradually, as slowly as he could. So slowly in fact, that for a moment he doubted if he were moving it at all. Then the first glow of the yellow table cloth; the definite edge of the table; the tired flowers; the faded menu. And then the top of his coffee cup, the discarded filter. So far, so good.

'Feeling better?'

Hans. He dropped his eyes. There was the blue and white plate, and on it the Black Forest gateau. He stared at it without comprehension, and without feeling. Trampled and beaten, at that moment he would have given in to anything. And then, from his right, a new voice.

'Are you all right, dear?'

It was the Conservative lady, now sitting close by. Except that she wasn't. That hard, blue-rinse bossiness had gone; its superiority replaced by something softer. And in her face he caught the warmth and familiarity of his old grandmother.

'You had quite a turn there. We were worried.'

'We?' he echoed. Glancing up, he saw the driver and the Proprietress silently looking his way. The bus driver gave him another of his nods (perhaps he had legion), and in the corner, the waitresses continued noiselessly relaying the walkers' table.

'You'll be fine; you're in good hands.'

'"Hans"?'

'One of the best.' And with that she rose, then slid - as if on a cushion of air - across the tea shop and out through the door. The bell failed to ring.

'It gets people like that; the suddenness of it. Anger, self-pity, confusion; the works. I should know. I've seen them all. The way they take it.'

'It?'

'It, yeah. The "situation". Shitsville. Where you are. See what I'm saying?'

Neville said nothing. He knew, somehow, that his coffee cup would be filling itself again, and when he checked, sure enough the steam had begun once more to rise.

'Hey! You're getting the hang of this!'

'But I don't know what "this" is. I don't know who you are. **What** you are.'

'You're pissed, right? Confused too. I understand, Nev. Hey, when I first came here I was so fucking angry no one could talk to me for a week! Really! But it's OK for you; at least you can get out.'

'Out? Out from what?'

'From here; this tea shop. Back out into the Real World. Back into the sodding rat race that you laughingly call your life. Back to your petty...'

'OK, OK', Neville cut him short. He didn't need a semi-arbitrary mixture of butter, eggs, flour and cocoa powder telling him how depressing his existence had become.

Something had changed however. For the first time he began to understand that there might be something to get "out" of - or back to. He looked round. The bus driver was reading a paper - from a picture on the front page, a politician winked at him - and the ever-larger Proprietress cleaning behind the counter, seemed in danger of becoming permanently wedged there.

He expected Hans to say something again. Expected more words of wisdom; but nothing came. He took the filter from the cup and tasted the coffee. Was this his third or fourth cup? He couldn't remember, and did it matter anyway? Back at his office Brian, Colin and David would have already forgotten about him; in fact, they were probably taking a trip to the pub to celebrate their good fortune. Brian would be coming up with a new scheme to organise his files; Colin would be talking about the latest pub quiz he had entered; and David would be contemplating his next political coup. "Poor old Neville" someone might say as they stood at the bar, and then everyone would laugh. And somewhere else, Mirelle would be arching that French back of hers to allow her latest beau entrance to the Tunnel of Love; "Ride of a lifetime! £100 round-trip!"

'So?' He couldn't take the silence from Hans; it seemed unnatural. Then, as he waited, he caught himself having the somewhat absurd thought that an *inanimate* Black Forest gateau might actually be considered "unnatural". From somewhere inside him the beginnings of a smile stirred.

'"So"?' Responded Hans after a pause.

'Oh, there you are. I thought you might be asleep - or whatever cakes do.'

'Right, Nev. Very funny. And don't forget I'm not just a "cake", OK?'

Neville said nothing. Suddenly a little more buoyant, he thought about lifting his hand and flicking one of Hans' eyes from his "head" - if he could call it that - to see if he could hit the geese on the far wall.

'Forget it, buster!'

'But if this is a game...'

'Game? Who the hell said anything about a game? Don't you get it, what's going on here? We're talking about your **life** and you want to start playing stupid juvenile games!'

'Sorry. Really.'

Neville could tell that Hans was experienced at this. He'd been on interviewing courses at work and knew bits of theory about Subject Manipulation; but that was all it was to him, theory. Here was a master at work.

'Thanks. It's nice to be appreciated.'

'You read minds too, of course.'

'Of course.'

To their right, the bus driver put down his paper and looked across. Another nod.

'OK, let's get moving!'

Hans sudden outburst - implying the need for energy and action - took Neville by surprise.

'Sorry?'

'Time, Nev; time! You can't sit here all day. We've got to get you sorted.'

'To get me "out"?'

'Exactly! To get you out, yes! Which means, of course, that there is a need for something to happen.' Hans waited for a moment. 'So, any idea what are you going to do?'

'Do?'

'Shit, yes; "**Do**"! You have to **do** something don't you? Can't hang around on your butt forever. What are your options?'

Despite the turn the conversation was taking, Neville could still feel the smile brewing. It was buried a long way beneath the surface, but it was there, somewhere. It gave him a hint that some of his humanity remained.

'Why don't you tell me. It'll save time.'

'Good idea! OK, let's go!' Hans paused for a moment, apparently organising his thoughts. 'There are choices, OK? One. There's a nice deep river not far from here. Plenty cold enough. And enough big stones handy, so you could easily fill your pockets. Wouldn't take long, you know.'

'You mean...'

'Yeah, I know. Not my favourite option either, but some guys like it. Strange how it's always the angry ones who choose the quick exit. I don't reckon that's for you though. You're not really the type.'

'Thanks.'

'Option Two - another easy one. Just go back. Get a new job with another company that's destined for the toilet - the "Armitage Shanks" principle we call it. Which means, of course, that one day they'll sack you. And get yourself another woman who may look a bit different and be called something else, but will just be Mirelle all over again. Go back like that, and when you've lost your job and your woman again I'll see you here in a couple of years - if you're lucky.'

'If I'm lucky?'

'Sure. Most people just slide off the rails, go completely nuts, or kill themselves. Or kill someone else, come to that. Ever thought of topping the old frog bitch? Yeah, I bet you have! Well, you didn't, so be grateful. Anyway, number Two's just more of the same, more of what you've already got - because it's just more of the same old you.'

'And Three?'

'Did I say there was a Three?'

'No. But, I got the impression...'

Neville's words failed him. Hans let the plea hang unanswered for a second.

'Well, lucky for you there is, see? Number Three; it's a bit tougher than the other two, 'cos the other two are just running away, right? Yellowville city, Arizona. You may be a bit thin, Nev - guts-wise - but you're not completely lily-livered; know what I mean?'

'Thanks.'

'You're welcome. So, Three.' Across the room, the bus driver stood up. Alarm crept into Hans' sense of urgency. 'Shit, is that the time! OK, OK!' - he shouted to some unseen voice - 'Three is where you face it head-on, go for the balls. Try and sort out the "big problem", hear what I'm saying? It ain't easy, and there's no guarantees.'

'OK.'

'And there's a big risk too. See, there's Three "A", and there's Three "B"; and you don't get control over the ending.'

'The ending?'

'"A"; everyone lives happily ever after - just like James Stewart's movies, OK? What a guy!! "B"; you....you don't. That's it. The risk.'

'And I don't get any choice, even though one ending is...?'

'Sorry, pal. I don't make the rules.'

A grunt from the far corner distracted them. The bus driver was trying to pull the owner from behind the counter where she now seemed firmly wedged. Both were red with the struggling. Neville was amazed at the woman's increasing girth.

'She must be...'

'Forget her, Nev! Decide! What's it to be?'

He stared back at Hans, trying to focus on the question before him.

'Not One; I don't have the guts.'

'Debatable, but OK.'

'And Two doesn't sound so great, either.'

'Terrific; so it's Three then?'

'I guess so.'

Hans whistled.

'More commission for me.'

'Commission?'

'Don't you worry about that, you've got other things to sort out; like deciding what you're running from. What is it that you need to face up to, that causes you the greatest problems?'

'Don't you know?'

'Sure, I know! But if this is going to work then you need to see it too. That's the first big step. So come on, pal. Tell me!'

Neville, drawn in by Hans' sense of urgency, thought hard. The goings-on behind the counter now seemed more threatening than comical, and there was an embryonic air of danger in the room. The waitresses had stopped laying the walkers' table and were watching as the Proprietress grew still larger. On the wall, the geese seemed restless again.

'Come on, Nev! Why are you here? What brought you here?'

'The job. Today it was the job.'

'OK. And? Is there more?'

'More? Mirelle, I guess. That's why I came here too. Malvern and Mirelle. And...'

'And? Shit, that's enough! OK, pal; now what's the connection? What's one thing joins them together? What one thing has dominated the last ten years of your miserable little life, ruled you, and made you subservient? Think!'

Neville looked to the counter, the geese. He looked out of the window, searching. There was the old bus. "Don't miss the bus" - Hans had said something like that. From inside the cafe there came a the crash as the bus driver flew backwards having finally released the Proprietress who was now floating in the air by the baked potato machine. Neville, making an obscure connection somewhere in the depths of his mind, had an idea.

'Money?'

'Money!' Hans was triumphant.

'Mirelle wanted money. Always! I worked for it. Gambled to try and get it. I kept up a job I hated because if it. Because of her.' Animated, he remembered his watch. 'And this.'

He pulled the watch from his wrist and threw it across the room. One of the waitresses caught it between her teeth, then swallowed it whole.

'Great Nev, great! So what are you going to do? How can you free yourself from it? How are you going to get out?'

'Get it all, every last penny I have; then use it to do the things *I* always wanted to do, but never did. Because of the job; because of her.'

'Use your money to free yourself; the very stuff that's held you back! Fuck, that's poetic! I'm proud of you pal!'

'I'll sell everything I have; change it all into money. Then I'll do things! And if it's three "B" in the end, then I've nothing to lose anyway. Right?'

'Right!'

Neville had now warmed to the task, feeling as if he were about to embark on some great Crusade.

'I need to make a list.'

'Hey Sister, Give this guy something to write with!'

From the far side of the room, one of the waitresses - her prim black and white uniform billowing - rose into the air and flew towards them. In her hand she carried an oblong piece of card. As she gathered pace, she began to imitate the roar of a Lancaster bomber before dropping the card on the table in front of Neville. It was white, with the word

MENU

printed at the top. Immediately she had had flown her first sortie, the other waitress took off and flew towards him. From her pocket she pulled a cheese straw and from six yards away, launched it towards him like a torpedo. It bounced once on the table then landed straight in his hand.

'What..?'

'A list, Nev. Make your list!'

The bus driver, who had now risen from the floor and dusted himself down (though with little external effect) coughed meaningfully in their general direction.

'Shit! Look, at least start the list! A list of your money, of the things you are going to sell; you know? You need to get your enemy out into the open; flush him out. What have you got on you now?'

Neville pulled out his wallet and emptied the contents on the table.

'Trash the plastic, Nev. What's left?'

Neville counted.

'Three pounds forty seven.'

'OK. Write it down.'

And Neville, using the cheese straw, wrote

Cash: Three pounds forty seven pence

on his Menu. Then there was the cheque.

Redundancy: Two thousand Five Hundred pounds

'Now, what else?'

'My car. The house. I've got some shares.'

From his right he was aware of the Proprietress who had grown so large that she now filled half the shop. There was a ring from the doorbell. The driver was standing on the threshold and looking his way.

'OK, OK! Nev, get the idea? Nev! Finish the list. Later, but do it! Turn your life into money, then burn it. It's the only way! OK? OK?!'

'Yes, but...'

'Now, **GET OUT**!'

Neville rose and, with the huge bulk of the owner towering above him, made a dash beneath her apron for the door. He felt the swoop of her arm and a draft of air rush past him, then suddenly he was out into the street clutching his list and the cheese straw he had used as a pen.

The driver, now at the door of the vehicle, waited for him to step onto the bus. It was not until he was on board that he looked back into the tea shop.

Through the window he could see nothing but the pattern of the owner's apron pressed hard against the glass. His table, the coffee cup - all was hidden from view. From beneath his feet he felt the rumble of the engine as the driver started the old bus up. The gears groaned as they were forced into action once more; then, slowly, they pulled away.

Neville twisted in his seat to look behind, back towards the shop; and, just as they were turning the corner, he witnessed the entire front of the building explode into the street, the road instantly covered in a shower of apron fragments, table cloth, and Black Forest gateau.

THREE

'Where to, Sir?'

The driver's voice roused Neville from a general state of suspension induced by the fleeting sight of the tea shop exploding into the road. He looked along the aisle of the bus (he was sitting about half-way down) and saw the old driver wrestling with the ancient controls.

'Sorry, what did you say?'

'Where to, Sir?'

There was some attempt at cheerfulness in the literal repeat, but Neville thought - despite this - he detected a fading note of enthusiasm in the voice of the speaker. He wondered how long the Old Boy had been ferrying people around like this. In his pocket he could feel the firm edge of the now-folded menu, and - lifting them to his nose - from his hands came the smell of the cheese straw. Those last few moments came quickly back to him.

'Where do you usually go? I mean, what's your route?'

Conveniently the traffic lights ahead turned red with a sly wink. The bus stopped, and the driver shifted in his seat to face his solitary passenger.

'Route, Sir? I don't "usually go" anywhere. I mean it's entirely up to you; begging your pardon.'

Neville marked the contrast with Hans; the subservient tone, the deferential air. Despite his still undetermined situation, now that he was out of the Tea Shop he felt a little more in control.

'Well, I need to go back to my car.'

'Your car, Sir?'

'My car, yes. I parked it in that pay and display place down by the station. Take me there. That'll be fine.'

The driver hesitated.

'Sorry, Sir; but I don't think you quite understand...'

'Lights.'

The green glowed clearly and Neville's observation forced the driver to return to his duty and press on. The bus swung unsteadily left, then gradually downhill (a little right all the time) until it came to the car park. As they pulled in, Neville notice two things: the first was that someone appeared to be examining his car; the second, that his was the only car there. This latter fact seemed strange as he distinctly recalled there had been just a few spaces left when he had originally parked. Indeed, he now realised that, apart from the old bus in which he was now riding, he had not seen another vehicle of any type since he had left the tea shop.

'How much to do I owe you?'

The driver looked quizzically at him as he prepared to disembark.

'Owe me? Nothing, Sir. Really.'

Neville, a little exasperated at the seemingly constant repetition of every question he posed, shrugged his shoulders and stepped down onto the tarmac.

'I'll wait,' the driver called after him.

'There's no need; I've got my car.'

'I'll wait anyway, Sir; if you don't mind.'

As he walked towards his car, Neville realised that he was beginning to feel a little better; a little more "normal". Perhaps it was the fresh air, or the coffee he had drunk in the shop. He remembered again the Menu in his pocket, and the cheese straw; and he remembered his conversation with Hans, and the three options. But here, out in the open, he now felt much less inclined to believe what had happened to him. The notion that he might have been hallucinating came back to him - but unfortunately this was only partially satisfactory as an explanation; there were too many unanswered questions. Like, where were all the other cars?

Ahead of him, the figure - cloaked in a long fawn raincoat - was bent over the bonnet of his car: he appeared to be rubbing the headlights. As Neville approached, he straightened and turned towards him.

'Your car?'

Neville was confronted by a well-built man who, he guessed, was in his early fifties. He was smartly dressed beneath the raincoat (from what Neville could see) and carried himself with a remarkably upright stance. On his face, he boasted a stunning handlebar moustache that was so long, it seemed to leave his face and disappear behind his ears. Neville guessed he might once have been a military man.

'My car? Yes, it is.'

'Um.' The man paused. 'Fine machine.'

'Not really. I mean, it's only a bulk standard Ford. There's nothing spectacular about it.'

'Nothing spectacular?' The man stared at Neville as if he was verging on insanity. 'Nothing spectacular?! I'll have you know that this is one of the finest vehicles ever made.'

'Really?' Neville felt he could only humour the other man.

'A superb example of British craftsmanship. Magnificent! And such a wonderful colour!'

Neville looked at his maroon Sierra (which he suspected had been manufactured in Spain) and wondered exactly how long the old soldier had been drinking. He moved towards the driver's door. The man tried to block his way.

Neville, whose sense of perception seemed to be somehow recently heightened, shouted **'ATTENTION!'** as loud as he could, and while the other drew himself to his full height, clamped his feet firmly to the tarmac, and straightened his back even more, Neville slid round him and opened the door.

'I say,' a hand landed firmly on the open door frame, 'that was rather cunning, you know. Still, I admire a man with a little guile.'

'Thank you. Just a hunch, you know. Now, do you mind?'

'Look. How would it be if I offered to buy the car off you?'

'Buy it?' Neville felt the stab of the cheese straw - which was suddenly awfully firm - in his side. 'But it's only an old Sierra. It's not even worth very much.'

'Perhaps not; but all the same...'

Neville hesitated.

'I need to get back to Birmingham.'

'To where?'

'Birmingham. I've got things to do.'

'Yes; of course.'

Slowly, the old Soldier unbuttoned his raincoat. For a moment, Neville expected to see a sawn-off shotgun or some semi-automatic weapon of Eastern European extraction hanging from an inside belt loop. Instead, the coat was held open to reveal eight pockets - four on either side - with bundles of cash exposed from the top of each.

'I can pay.'

'Yes, evidently.'

'What would you want for it?'

Now it was Neville's turn to straighten. He faced the man, eye to eye.

'What's it worth to you?'

'Five thousand?'

The car was, at best, worth no more than fifteen hundred pounds. He would never expect to get two thousand for it, let alone five. Was there a catch? He eyed the soldier cautiously; the offer seemed genuine enough. He remembered his deal with Hans. If it wasn't true, if he had imagined the whole affair and there was no such thing as "3A" or "3B", then selling the car would still net him a cool three and a half grand profit. He could not lose.

'OK, OK. I can see you drive a hard bargain,' - Neville had said nothing - 'I'll make it six thousand, and throw in two thousand for the lights.'

The man extended his hand. Neville paused but a moment, then took it. Seconds later, the Soldier was divesting himself of the cash from his pockets - a thousand pounds from each - and depositing the money into Neville's hands.

'Any idea how I might get back to Birmingham?'

'To where?'

'Home?'

The Soldier turned and glanced at the bus. The driver was standing by the door, watching the conclusion of the transaction. Neville nodded. The driver nodded back.

'Yes; of course.'

A few minutes later, Neville was once again back on the bus. He had removed the Menu and the cheese straw from his pockets and was writing

Car: Eight Thousand Pounds

under the previous entry. As the bus jolted into life again, he could see the old Soldier standing by the car, stroking its lights.

'You know' - this time Neville had chosen to sit at the front of the bus, almost alongside the driver - 'that guy gave me about five times what the car was worth.'

'To you, Sir.'

'What do you mean, to me?'

'Five times what it was worth to you, Sir; or what you might have paid for it yourself. He simply paid you what it was worth to him.'

'But it was only an old Sierra.' Neville was inclined to debate, but sensed that this might be futile. He changed tack. 'Did you see the way he stroked the headlights?'

'Always does, Sir.'

'Always does?'

'The Colonel; that's what we call him. Loves cars. Always buying them - though he can't drive of course.'

'Of course!'

'He had a son who used to work in the Rover factory just down the road. He died when a two litre Vitesse fell from the overhead conveyor. Squashed him flat. It was his job to put the lights in you see; but he never quite managed it in that Vitesse.'

'But that was a Rover, not a Ford.'

'Ah well, Sir; the poor old Colonel can't tell the difference. He just loves cars because they remind him of his Son; that's all. So you see, your car was really worth much more to him than it was to you.'

Neville looked away from the driver and out of the front window of the bus. They were, to his surprise, already out in open country, rattling along an open - and empty - road. The speedometer showed twenty seven miles an hour.

'Oh Sir, almost forgot. You had a phone call.'

'A what?'

'A phone call, Sir.' The Driver pulled a mobile phone from a recess in the dashboard and offered it to Neville. 'Someone calling himself "Your Broker". Could you call him back, please.'

'Richie? How did he know where I was? I mean...'

Neville took the handset. It was incredibly light, and appeared not to possess an aerial. Undaunted, he rang Richard Robinson Associates (Stock Brokers) on their office number. The purr of the phone, then loudly - 'Nev!'

'Richie. How did you know it was me?'

'Expecting your call, Old Boy. Chap said you'd phone back.'

Neville glanced at the driver who seemed intent enough on the road ahead.

'How did you get hold of me?'

'Got a message. Look, can't explain; we're in a flap here! Bloody shit's hitting the proverbial, and I've got a tip that the whole bleedin' market's just about to collapse. Nev, you've got to sell everything! Get out!'

'Get out? What do you mean? I thought things were pretty stable at the minute?'

'Didn't we all, Chum! My source - bloody reliable chap - says there's a major disaster on the stocks' - pause - 'in about seventeen minutes actually. So you've got to sell. And fast!'

Richie sounded a little different; perhaps it was the pressure. Perhaps he too was going bananas. But, despite the odd eccentricity or two, Neville had never known him to be wrong. He may not have invested much over the years nor had much at stake, but Richie had never let him down. All this - along with some vague sense that he was riding some unstoppable roller-coaster - meant that his hesitation was minimal.

'OK, do it.' There was silence at the other end. 'Richie?'

'Yep?'

'Do it, Richie.'

'In the pipeline, Chum!'

'What's it worth - all of it?'

'Hang on.' Another pause. 'After tax?'

'Forget the tax; what's it worth?'

'Well, couldn't get top dollar for the Utilities, but we've cleared three two seven five. OK?'

It was a little less than Neville had expected which - given his recent experience with the car - came as something of a surprise to him. Richie sensed his disappointment.

'OK, I know it's less than four - but in about ten minutes you wouldn't even get two. Trust me!'

'Thanks Richie.'

'OK. Must dash; more Suckers to save! Money's on its way to the bank. Ciao!'

The phone seemed to go limp in Neville's hand as Richie rang off. He handed it back to the driver.

'Everything all right, Sir?'

'Yes, I guess so.'

'You sound a little disappointed, Sir.'

Neville said nothing.

'Funny how things can change their worth isn't it, Sir? Depending on how you look at them, I mean.'

Neville had withdrawn his Menu and was already writing

Shares: Three thousand two hundred and Seventy Five pounds

For a short while there was nothing but the sound of the tired old engine breaking the silence. Outside, the hedges rolled by (at twenty seven miles per hour) and occasionally Neville thought he could see Birmingham skyscrapers in the distance. But then a hill would rise and the image would be lost.

'What's your name?'

'My name, Sir?'

The driver seemed slightly thrown by such a personal question. He glanced at Neville, then back to the road.

'Samuel, Sir. That's my name.' It sounded more like an impromptu decision than a fact.

'And how long have you been doing this - whatever "this" is?'

Slowly the bus decelerated from its standard speed. Ahead there was a lay-by, and it was evident that Samuel was making for this.

'We're stopping?'

Neville's question remained unanswered as Samuel concentrated on grinding down through the gears and slowing the complaining bus to a halt. The rumble changed in tone once they were stationery, then, as the engine was turned off, spluttered and coughed like a dying man fading to silence.

'Now then Sir, what was it you said?'

'How long have you been doing this?'

'And what do you mean by "this", Sir, if I might be so bold?'

'Driving this bus. Looking after people like me; people in my "situation". I don't know. Any of it.'

'Ah, I see Sir.' Samuel paused. 'Not sure I could rightly say to be honest. A long time, I suppose. It must be.'

'And all of this - Hans, the car, Richie. What exactly is happening Samuel?'

Samuel coughed, and was then silent. Having stopped the bus, he now seemed intent on giving the impression that he was reluctant to say anything.

'Would you like to go on, Sir?'

It was a feeble attempt, and Neville resisted it. Samuel had obviously chosen to stop in order to allow them to talk, and Neville was determined to get some sort of answer from him.

'Not yet; not until you tell me - something, anything.'

'I see.'

'Please?'

And then, in an instant, Neville got the distinct impression that all this had been rehearsed; that Samuel went through these same motions every time; and that there was nothing unique about this situation whatsoever. But before he could interject, to protest about something - maybe the vague sense that he was little more than a specimen in a vast and sophisticated laboratory experiment - Samuel had started.

FOUR

'Of course, at this precise moment in time - where we are, here and now - you aren't really sure what's going on, are you? So far you have had a rather bizarre experience in a tea shop, a man has bought your car for a vastly inflated sum of money, and you suddenly get a phone call telling you to sell all your shares - which, had you kept them, would now be worth two thousand pounds, if that.

'In addition to all of this, you find yourself sitting in a rather old bus - but a faithful old bus, I must say - talking to the driver (myself) who is probably at least old enough to be your grandfather.'

He paused to offer a slight smile. Since Samuel had begun to speak, Neville had perceived something of a change in him. The smile was the same as the first he had given Neville in the shop, but the man who delivered it now seemed much more than a shuffling old bus driver.

'I am here to help you, Sir. That's my job; that's all I do. You are actually a very lucky man. You have been given a rare opportunity. Hans helped of course; but even Hans - despite his rather wonderful qualities, and that abrasive style of his! - isn't able to help everyone. Do you realise Sir, that some people never actually make it out of the Tea Shop? (I say Tea Shop in this instance, but it needn't be of course.)'

Neville marked the "of course" again, as if what were happening was so self-evident as to make explanation redundant.

'In any event, you have been given a chance to see your life. Do you mark my words, Sir? To **"see"** your life. Most people simply live their lives, don't they? They have a pattern, a plan if they're lucky - most often drawn out for them by some force or other - and they live to that plan, that formula. They rarely see their lives, see what they are living. Do you understand, Sir?

'You have been given a special chance; the chance to see your life for what it is. Perhaps it is too late, perhaps not. I cannot tell you. Hans certainly could not either. At least you have begun to see something of it yourself, and that is a good beginning.'

'Money?' It was Neville's first offering in the conversation. Samuel smiled. It was an old smile; lips parting with the tired wisdom of many journeys.

'Indeed, Sir. That was a very good start, but it is not enough, not on its own. You must realise - in both senses - the goal you have set for yourself.'

'The third option?'

'And make no mistake Sir, there is nothing unreal about that. All of this may seem very strange, but there is nothing fantastic about what awaits you. You have - unwittingly or not - set out on your quest, and you must endeavour to succeed. You must, Sir, you must.'

There was, in Samuel's delivery of those words, a quiet insistence that Neville found absolutely unnerving. For a moment he seemed unable to control his voice.

'Or else?' he said, in a whisper that was not his own.

Samuel raised his right arm, and slowly extended it to point out of the windows on Neville's side of the bus. There, beyond the hedge and as far as the eye could see, were row upon row of white tombstones.

'Hundreds and thousands of fading monuments to anonymous people; millions of forgotten and unfulfilled lives.'

And as Neville looked, from amongst the gravestones, a sudden wind raised a moan that encompassed all that could be said and felt about loss in a single note. It lingered but a moment, and then was gone.

Neville looked back at Samuel who was lost in his own private reverie. He waited. Eventually Samuel turned to him again.

'There.'

Neville did not know what to say, or even if he was expected to say anything. He was struggling with the sense that he might be lucky; that he might be on borrowed time; that he might, in some unusual way, have a purpose to fulfil or a chance to take. His eyes, he suddenly realised, had filled with tears.

'Please look at your menu, Sir.'

Neville pulled the menu from his pocket and looked at it. There was a new entry at the bottom of the page:

House: Five thousand three hundred and Seven Pounds 53 pence

and beneath it the final line

Total: Nineteen thousand and Eighty Six pounds

Although he had written neither, both were in his hand.

'I'm afraid we couldn't get as much as you might have liked for the house; they charge so much for fees and legal expenses these days, and by the time we paid off the mortgage... But at least it has been sold and so you don't have to worry.'

'Yes, of course.' Neville, unconsciously adopting the literal acceptance of the obvious, wondered again who Samuel might be referring to when he said "we".

'So you see, Sir, you now know that your life is worth just a little under twenty thousand pounds. That's what it translates to; the bottom line, if I might be so bold.'

Neville found himself focusing on that single line - the bottom line indeed - and the words began to slowly blur into a single scrawl that was nothing more than a meaningless smudge.

After a short while, Samuel cleared his throat. Neville had been given enough time for reflection. He looked up and sensed - now, as in the tea-shop - the need to get on; that, even in this strange new world, time was passing and waiting for no-one - least of all a temporary visitor like himself.

'Yes. Yes, I see. So, what happens now?'

'Well Sir, it is really up to you. Perhaps you should consider what you have.'

'Apart from the money, you mean?'

Samuel nodded, and from within his pocket Neville felt the cheese straw dig him in the leg. He had never considered cheese straws to be sharp, either physically or intellectually, but this one appeared to be the exception.

'My Menu, I guess. I can't think of anything else.'

'Indeed, but perhaps it is only half a menu; only half of the equation. The first half. The means, perhaps.'

'To the end?' Neville offered, having been led towards that inevitable conclusion.

Samuel seemed pleased, and his face broke into another reassuring, grand-fatherly kind of smile. Neville reflected for a moment how he had been seeing echoes of ancient relatives: the Conservative Lady in the tea-shop; now Samuel...

'So I need to decide what the end might be?'

'Indeed.'

'To write down what I want to do with the money?'

'You need to think about how you might like to "see" your life; what you would like to experience in order to put it into context.'

Neville was beginning to get a picture of how the game might be played.

'A frame of reference?' It had been an expression he had first heard on a late-night Channel Four talk show, and had, since then, kept it in the wardrobe of his vocabulary where it hung, nicely ironed and ready for use.

'Ah.'

'Another list.' Neville imagined how, at the end of all of this - and how soon that might be he could not tell - the two sides of his menu would probably need to either balance or cancel each other out. He suspected that he may have little or no control over what he would be left with. Indeed, he failed to conceive how there could possibly be a judgement, or on what would his future be decided.

'I'm sorry, Sir. I'm afraid I can't help you; I don't know.'

Neville smiled. Of course Samuel could read minds too.

'Thanks Samuel. I'll just try my best.'

He looked out of the window. In the fields, crops swayed gently in the breeze where the solid tombstones had been, and across the hedge, four Friesian cows, dressed as a Barber Shop Quartet, began to gently harmonise an accompaniment to the rhythm of the wind.

The reverse side of the menu was completely blank. Neville hesitated, thinking for a moment of scrawling his own heading "Menu" at the top. The cheese straw was shorter than it had been originally. The writing had evidently worn some of it away. The numbers from his "bottom line" played, rearranging themselves into ever less meaningful combinations, distracting him from the task in hand.

'Samuel?'

'Sir.'

'How do I know how much things cost? For my list.'

'For example?'

'Paris. I've always wanted to visit Paris - despite Mirelle being French. Or perhaps because of it. How do I know how much it will cost me, or how much I will have left afterwards?'

'How much would you expect it to cost you?'

'I don't know. Maybe a thousand pounds; maybe two.'

Samuel smiled.

'Yes, I would guess you might not be far off there. It does, of course, depend on what you decide to do while you are there. And what the visit might be worth to you.' Samuel paused for a moment. 'But for the moment, don't worry about that. We'll look after the costs for you. That's the way it is, and I'm afraid you'll just have to trust us, Sir.'

Neville was tempted to ask about the reference to the "we" again, but decided to let it pass. He turned to the menu and entered

Visit Paris

at the top of the blank side. He paused.

Samuel sensed the hesitation.

'If it's any consolation, Sir, this bit is often the most difficult. You should try and think of the things you have always wanted to do but never have because money held you back; because you couldn't afford to do them.'

'And nothing else?'

'For example?'

'To be honest...' He paused, uncertain whether honesty was prudent - never mind unavoidable - in his new circumstance. 'Well, to be honest I'd quite like to fall in love again. After Mirelle, you know. Just once more.'

Samuel shook his head. The lilt from the cows had a distinctly Parisian air, and from somewhere Neville could hear an accordion playing.

'If you can't buy it, Sir...'

Neville nodded. Samuel would read his resigned, but unspoken "OK".

The task seemed immeasurably difficult. Perhaps he didn't have that much money to play with after all; perhaps - and this was something of a shock - that maybe the lack of money was not the issue he had imagined it to be. He tried not to analyse. What had he always wanted to do? He wrote:

Eat a really expensive meal

Fly an aeroplane

and then stopped. He could certainly buy all of those, but it did not seem to be much of a list. And how much of his twenty thousand had he allocated so far? He wondered about a cruise. It might be too expensive; it might denude his reserves too much.

Neville told himself that there must be other things; there certainly would have been with Mirelle around. Indeed, he would have needed pages and pages to include all of her ideas! Thinking of Mirelle led him again to thoughts about holidays away from Birmingham, and in consequence

Go on a Cruise

was added to the list.

'How am I doing, Samuel?'

Samuel had been watching him all this time, saying nothing. Neville had the sensation that the old boy had been mentally calculating as each item was added to the list.

'Fine, Sir. Presumably you were only thinking of a short cruise; nothing too elaborate?'

Neville smiled, pointing to the last entry with the ever-shortening cheese straw.

'I guess am now!'

'Indeed. And I should warn you that, just because you put something on your list, there is no guarantee that you will be able to fulfil that wish.' Samuel paused. 'Might I suggest, Sir; is there anything you would like to possess? Some little extravagance, perhaps?'

'I had assumed that having something material was out of the question.'

'Not necessarily. For example, have you ever wanted to buy yourself an expensive hat, or a half-hunter watch? Such things might be acceptable, I'm sure. And you could take them with you on your trips if you wished.'

'And after?'

His question found no response.

Neville thought about a hat and discarded the idea. Yet he had always fancied owning his own tuxedo; something that might be appropriate for the expensive meal. With his scope thus broadened, he continued

Tuxedo

then stopped again.

Neville looked at the remains of the cheese straw which was now so short he was having difficulty holding it. He might have only one choice left.

He thought again of Mirelle and how she had nagged him constantly to do things, to take her places. "Nagged". She had wanted him to take her horse riding, and had once pestered him for weeks on end. He did not like horses; indeed, he did not trust them. But having thought of the idea, he remembered how he had occasionally talked about going to the Derby.

Despite his failed flutters on the ponies, was this to be it? Determined, he gripped the cheese straw for one final time and wrote

Go to the Derby

finishing the last word just as it vanished from his hand. He sniffed his fingers; only the trace of its smell was left.

There was almost instantly a rumble from beneath his feet. Samuel had started up the bus.

'Is that it?' Neville asked.

'It?'

'The end of my list? Can I add nothing else? Is my money all gone?'

Samuel smiled.

'I think you have enough on your list to cater for most of the money you have. Perhaps you will get the opportunity to add something later, Sir. Who can say?'

Neville caught a glint of playfulness in Samuel's eyes as he said this, as if he knew all too well who could say; as if he could already see the future and was keeping its secrets hidden.

For the first time in a long while Neville suddenly laughed. Perhaps it was the same laugh that had begun to brew back in the tea shop. It was enough, however, to signal the departure of the bus which Samuel now swung back onto the road. Sedately - at twenty seven miles per hour - they began again their journey forwards. Neville, preparing to sit back and enjoy the ride, was amazed when, after only a few moments, Samuel pulled the bus round a corner in the road and revealed Paris stretching out below them in the distance.

FIVE

Despite the impossibility of its sudden appearance, there could be no mistaking that the city beneath them was, indeed, Paris; a Paris almost devoid of suburbs. Neville recognised first the snaking shape of the island-bearing Seine, and then - as if any further confirmation were necessary - the unique frame of the Eiffel Tower standing proudly against the skyline.

Even from this distance, he could make out some of the more prominent landmarks as the old bus made its way down the hill and closer to the city. Occasionally the sun - which had now broken through the clouds - reflected brightly upon an ornate, gilt-encrusted roofing, sending Morse-like greetings towards him.

For those first few seconds Neville was spellbound; not owing to the fact that he was suddenly here (he was beginning to feel as if nothing could surprise him now) but simply in the bewitching beauty of the place.

Samuel had said nothing since he had re-started the engine.

'Paris,' Neville observed with a kind of naive uncertainty.

'Indeed, Sir.'

'Because it's first on my list? Is that why we're here?'

'Not necessarily. Perhaps it is simply the best place to start.'

This was a little too cryptic for Neville to pursue. Indeed, he had decided that Samuel's inclination to stray into obscurity - like the open-ended references to "we" - would be left unchallenged if possible; partly due to the fact that he sensed the futility of embarking on any literal challenge, but also in the hope that such a double-bluff might tempt Samuel to gradually lower his guard.

'Where would you like to stay, Sir?'

'I have a choice?' The open question had not been expected.

'Of course.'

'But it will be a question of money?'

'Partly, yes – although again I am unable to say at this point exactly how much things might cost.'

Neville smiled. He had begun to get a sense of the game that Samuel was playing; the test almost, revolving around the notion of "worth" that the Colonel had already so ably demonstrated.

'Nothing too grand then. Comfortable perhaps, and certainly where I will fit in.'

'As a visitor?'

'An English visitor, yes.'

They were nearing the bottom of the hill and had come upon the outskirts of the city. Four-storey apartment blocks lined the road on either side. Not particularly attractive, they somehow still seemed to possess an air of the Parisian about them. Perhaps it was the cream coloured concrete or the preponderance of shutters.

'I know a nice place just south of the river, not far from the military academy. It should suit you fine, Sir.'

Through the window, Neville could see Parisians going about their daily business. It seemed for the first time in - how long? - that he might be amongst ordinary people again; about to return to a world which shared his own reality. Since the tea-shop, Neville had lost a fundamental part of his grip on this and what he expected of it; and it had been loosened further with his unruly temporal travel.

Cars whistled passed them, often tooting as they did so, and Neville realised that Samuel, now sitting immediately in front of him, was driving - quite correctly - on the right side of the road.

More than that, the steering wheel and all other controls had moved with him. Above the dashboard, Neville noticed the logo of the Citroen motor vehicle company, and wondered if - again without his being aware - the whole bus had changed too. The only thing that seemed to remain constant was the speed, though even that had been translated into kilometres per hour.

'Perhaps you would like to check your wallet, Sir.'

Neville pulled his wallet from his back trouser pocket and opened it. Inside was a collection of French bank notes.

'A few hundred euros, I believe. The hotel has been part-paid for in advance, so you should really only need spending money.'

'Can I keep track of the money I spend, Samuel, just in case?'

'Check your watch, Sir.'

'My watch?'

Neville looked at his wrist. The watch - that testament to loyalty from his former employer which had been swallowed by the tea shop waitress - was strapped to him once again, and now boasted a small crystal display tastefully inset into the face. The numbers 18558 stared back at him.

'My balance?'

'Not counting what you have in your wallet. We have booked you into the hotel for three nights. Is that enough? If you want to stay longer, there will be no problem.'

'No; three nights should be fine.' He allowed himself a moment of mental arithmetic. 'But isn't a little over five hundred pounds a bit much for such a short stay?'

As Neville might have guessed, Samuel declined to say anything. With the somewhat arbitrary relationship between monetary value and worth already established, he gave up the enquiry.

Despite the fact that he was on the verge of a mission of self-discovery, Neville could not help but feel that there might actually be little true exploration to be undertaken. How much, for example, had been laid out for him already? He had the utmost confidence in Samuel's decision that three days at the hotel was the precise amount of time he needed to spend there, in spite of anything he might suggest himself.

'Thank you for your faith, Sir,' Samuel had been mind-reading again, 'but I do assure you that our skills are really only organisational; I think in the modern world of business, you might call us "facilitators".'

'Yes, perhaps we might.'

By now they were in the heart of the city. Occasionally Neville caught glimpses of the Eiffel Tower between buildings, across open spaces, or at the end of long tree-lined avenues. Although it had represented little more than a marker for him up to this point - a geographical stake in the ground as it were - he now began to feel as if it might hold some greater significance within his overall visit.

Samuel pulled the bus round a corner and came to an almost immediate halt - accompanied by the obligatory tooting of other road users - outside a large and impressive hotel. It looked expensive.

'Not too pricey, Sir. We have found it very reasonable in the past for the service it offers.'

'Of course.'

Samuel turned and smiled.

'Your bags are on the seat behind you. Just a few things for your visit: toiletries, changes of clothes, that sort of thing.' The door opened with a moan that was, quite noticeably, Gallic. 'I'll be here in three days to pick you up.'

'But if I need you before then?'

'Don't worry about that, Sir. You just make the most of it.'

The journey was evidently at an end. Samuel had made his last statement and now, smiling but tight-lipped, waited for his passenger to disembark. Neville rose. Two bags - taupe canvass ones he had owned for some years now - awaited his attention. He lifted them up and made for the steps.

'Thank you, Samuel.'

Samuel nodded, and Neville climbed down from the bus.

With a complaining hiss, the door of the vehicle - now a rather dirty yellow Citroen that had certainly seen better and brighter days - closed behind him; then, accompanied by a chorus of car horns, Samuel swung the bus out into the speeding throng. Neville stood and watched it become submerged in the stream of traffic, and then turn suddenly out of sight.

The hotel facade, when he turned his attention to it, proved to be even more impressive than he had first thought. Either side of the large revolving entrance doors, two majestic stone lions stood guard, growling menacingly at passers-by who strayed too close. The doorman, surprisingly rugged despite the elegance of his uniform, looked more like a lion-tamer than a member of a noble service industry. Indeed, the rather gruff "Good day" he bestowed on Neville - with one eye firmly fixed on his stone charges - did little to dispel the notion.

Inside, the foyer offered both warmth and intimacy. Its decor, once presumably the height of fashion, had lost a degree of its lustre, and its plushness seemed slightly warn. It was a hotel on the way out, but still tenaciously clinging to the best traditions of a more glorious past.

Neville rested his bags at his feet when he reached the unattended desk. He raised his palm to press the bell provided for those seeking attention, but before he could complete the action, the bell rang itself.

'Pardon monsieur, but I am - how you say – "pissed off" with being banged all the time.'

Neville, now feeling quite unfazed by such animated interruptions, nodded and lowered his hand. When he looked up, he was faced by a middle-aged woman dressed in a neat, if somewhat prim, suit.

'Monsieur?'

He was uncertain whether or not to try out his rather rusty schoolboy French at this point, but then he realised that both the Doorman and the Bell had already addressed him in their own interpretation of English. He decided to stick with his native tongue.

'Good day. I believe you have a room booked for me.'

The woman smiled professionally, and nodded.

'Of course - and may I say, Monsieur's French is most excellent.'

Neville had spoken in English - yet this had been instantly translated into fluent conversational French. He decided to try something a little more elaborate.

'I must say I am impressed by your welcoming vestibule. It retains the character of a bygone era expressing all that is quintessential in elegance and style.'

Again, perfect French.

'Monsieur is too kind.' Again the smile and the nod.

A young man had appeared at Neville's side, and was already holding a taupe bag in each hand.

'Room 206, Sir.' She looked at the boy. 'Chambrés deux cent six, Albert. Allez, vite!'

Neville followed the boy to the far end of the hall. Stairs swung upwards in a wide sweeping spiral enveloping as they did so the open lift that rose in their centre. The boy pulled back the lift's trellis door and Neville stepped in. As they rose to the second floor, Neville watched the hotel foyer disappear beneath his feet and the first floor pass before his eyes. Somehow the lift - which reminded him of one he had ridden in Foyle's London bookshop - seemed typically French. He would have expected nothing less.

Room 206 was a few yards along the corridor. The boy opened the door and led Neville into a large room. That feeling of a more luxurious past he had sensed in the entrance hall was echoed here too: the slightly fading wallpaper; the slightly tired curtains; the slightly worn fabric of the arm chairs. There was comfort here too, but amidst that a sense of sorrow and regret.

Neville turned to tip the boy, but he had already left; the door was closed and the two bags now resident on the large double bed. Neville walked to the window, drew back the curtains, and opened the shutters onto the street below. There was a table near the chairs, and on the table some hotel stationery. He thought of the Eiffel Tower again, and wondered if, in order to make the most of his visit, he ought to plan an itinerary for himself.

He pulled off his jacket, laid it across the back of one of the chairs, then sat in the other. The stationery, not surprisingly off-white (though this time presumably by design), bore the name of the hotel and its rather elaborate leonine crest, as did the ball-point pen that had been placed nearby.

Neville picked up the pen - no cheese straw this time! - and reflected how he seemed at present to be doing nothing but making lists. From outside the tooting of the car horns was joined by the shouts of street vendors who had stalls across the road, and the combination of the two began to take on something of a rhythmical quality. In the corner of the room, a water dispenser bubbled in time, and from the vase on the dresser, Neville noticed the aroma of the fresh flowers for the first time.

'Ambiance.'

He looked behind him to where an antique grand-mother clock tick-tocked quietly with the rhythm.

'Ambiance, we call it. A very French word, you do not think, Monsieur?'

'Indeed. And thank you. I am quite relaxed.'

The clock tick-tocked on. Neville turned his attention to the paper again.

'Not everyone appreciates it you know; the ambiance,' the clock interrupted again, 'especially - if I might be so bold - the English.'

'Ah.' Neville resisted the temptation to turn round; he wanted to work on his list. On the dresser, the flowers appeared to be leaning in his direction, listening to the conversation. He wondered where he should start.

'A list. That is good, Monsieur. And La Tour Eiffel; of course you must go there.'

Neville turned to the clock. A small moon-like hand, popped from side to side in an aperture in the face, keeping time with a pendulum that swung out of sight within.

'Should I go there first, do you think?'

'Monsieur?'

'After all, you are a local; an expert in these matters.'

'Oh, you are too kind.' The clock tick-tocked slightly louder, as if with pride. 'But you are correct; I have helped people in the past. It is not my job of course, but then if one can be of assistance...'

There was now the faint sound of dripping behind him, and Neville turned to find a fresh filter coffee brewing on the table in front of him.

'Déjà vu?' The clock asked, and then chimed the quarter hour with such relish that it was almost a laugh.

'Déjà vu, indeed.'

'Now, La Tour. I would suggest that you leave her to last. She will give you a view of all you have seen here; it will be a memory to take away with you. Do you not agree?'

'Sounds very sensible. So, apart from the tower, what else should I see?'

'Monsieur, in Paris where does one start?!'

Neville picked up the pen and divided the page into three, one part for each day. At the very bottom he made a note of his final rendezvous.

'I would start with the city. Just to drink her in, to feel her. That is how to start your visit, Monsieur.'

'And you would suggest?'

'A walk down Le Champs Elysées; a cognac on the terrace, watching the city pass you by. Magnifique! Then perhaps to simple stroll through the streets; perhaps a little shopping. That is the way to start your visit.'

Neville wrote almost as if he were taking dictation.

'And then?'

'Then you must do two things: see our history, and see our art. I would suggest Sacré-Cœur, Montmartre, Notre Dame. And for our art you should see the Louvre, and the Musée d'Orsay.'

The visitor continued to write.

'Monsieur?'

'Yes?' Neville looked up. This time the interruption was a little more hesitant.

'The evenings; les nuit. Do you wish to see Paris - at night?'

To Neville, this question seemed a little loaded, as if it carried with it some special challenges for him.

'If I have come to see Paris, then should I not see all of her I can?'

'Bravo! Bien sûr! So, to your list you must add a visit to La Pigalle - you may take in a show if you choose - and, perhaps, La Rue St Denis.'

'Rue St Denis?'

'I offer it to you, Monsieur, simplement. I say nothing further.' And with that the clock stopped.

From the dresser, Neville thought he could make out the sound of whispering, but when he looked round, the flowers were still and silent. On the table in front of him the paper revealed

Day One: The Champs Elysées - Shopping

Day Two: Montmartre - Notre Dame

Day Three: Louvre - Musée d'Orsay

The Eiffel Tower

As he re-read his list and pondered its appropriateness, there came a knock at the door.

SIX

He opened the door to find the Doorman facing him. Instinctively, Neville looked down, half-expecting to see his visitor accompanied by the two stone lions from the hotel's entrance.

'Monsieur,' the doorman was alone, 'your taxi is 'ere.'

'My taxi? I wasn't aware that I had ordered a taxi.'

The Doorman said nothing, standing motionless and with the air of a man who was determined to take his charge - however unwilling - down through the hotel and to the waiting cab. Neville recalled his earlier image of the man complete with whip, and decided not to argue the point.

'Just a minute.'

He left the man at the door and walked into the en suite bathroom. Again he found an air of faded glory: the fixtures were a little worn and ornate, attractive in their own way yet somewhat over-elaborate for his time.

Sitting on the porcelain toilet, Neville heard a hiss from his right. At the head of the bath, the taps boasted a hand-shower attachment, and it was this that was now moving slowly snake-like in the bottom of the bath. A small amount of water dribbled from the steel shower head, which sounded a sly hiss.

The shower head stopped moving and looked hard at him, its spray holes combining to form a curious one-eyed stare.

'Off out?'

'Apparently so.'

'You pay good money for facilities like this, yet no sooner do you arrive than you go out! And when will we see you next, eh? Tonight, when you come back - drunk, probably - you'll come in here for a quick piss and then go straight to bed. Have you any idea how neglected that makes us feel? Have you?'

Neville stood and pulled up his trousers. He took objection to being nagged - especially as he might have expected his status as "visitor" to demand a little respect to be shown towards him - but could not deny that the shower head might have a point.

'I'll make full use of you tomorrow. Really.'

'They all say that!'

'Promise. OK?'

The shower head hissed again and turned away from him. Neville expected to find the Doorman still waiting for him, but although the door to the room was still open, there was no-one there. Picking his coat from the chair, he left the room. There was no-one in the hallway outside either, so - ignoring the lift - he made his way down the stairs.

The lobby was also deserted, except for a small figure standing by the entrance, looking through the window onto the street outside. Neville looked behind the desk to see if he could locate the Concierge, but failing to do so decided to take his key with him.

As he walked towards the exit, he could see a bright yellow taxi outside. It had been badly parked, with its two near side wheels up onto the pavement.

Neville had one hand on the revolving door when a voice to his side said, 'Taxi?' It was strange guttural voice, almost as if it had been encumbered with years of prolonged coughing or chest infections. He turned. The voice had come from the figure at the window, and the figure belonged to a frog.

'Sorry?'

'Taxi? You wanted a taxi?'

Again the strange voice. Neville expected the last question to be followed by a croak but it was not; he sensed that it might have been suppressed, the only trace a vague and almost inaudible "hic".

'Yes. Thanks.'

He let the frog leave first. He was wearing a bomber jacket with the collar turned right up, and a faded baseball cap with the letters "N" and "Y" stitched in white. His legs were adorned by silky track suit bottoms with the legend "St. Etienne" embossed in green down the sides. From a distance, there could be no telling that the owner of the clothes was an amphibian; not from behind at any rate.

Neville followed the frog's odd gait to the car, where a green, three-fingered hand fumbled with the door.

'Great. Thanks.'

The cab had a strange, distinctly saline odour to it. And on the back shelf behind Neville, was a model of a plastic newt with a nodding head. It nodded caustically at him as he got in.

'Bonjour.'

'Morning.'

By now the driver had managed to get himself into the car and was fiddling with the controls. His apparent lack of dexterity gave Neville little confidence; a concern that was redoubled as the taxi suddenly lurched off the pavement with a bang, and sped out into the traffic. They did not appear to be following too straight a line.

'Champs Elysées, oui?'

'Yes, please.'

The driver looked at Neville in his rear view mirror.

'You OK?'

'Fine, yes.'

They were racing along the street with the driver still looking at Neville rather than at the road. He gave a slight toad-like grin.

'Surprised?'

'At what? Sorry.'

'Me.' And with that the car suddenly lurched around to the left and began to career down another avenue. 'I am a frog, yes?'

'It would appear so, yes.'

'And you are a little surprised, no?'

'A little,' though not as much as he might once have been, Neville thought.

'Special treat for the English. Frog taxi drivers. Get it? Sophisticated French joke, non?'

And with that the frog gave a sudden laugh that sounded like all the plumbing in the entire city had suddenly ceased to function and was belching water and sewage everywhere. Neville smiled politely, but was, by now, too nervous to laugh. From behind him he heard the newt whimper "Oh, shit" and when he turned he found its head had been withdrawn into its hollow body and was nowhere to be seen.

It now appeared that they were travelling at least twice as fast as any other vehicle on the road, and the driver seemed determined not to change his style - if it might be called that - to accommodate anyone. Neville thought about saying something, complaining even, but felt that to distract the frog now might actually end up being his last ever action; "3B" a little prematurely perhaps.

Within a short while - though it seemed like a period of torture - the Arc de Triomphe was in sight and the frog spun the taxi out onto its mesmerising roundabout without a moment's hesitation. Suddenly the Champs Elysées stretched before them. The taxi bounded on for a hundred yards or so then suddenly dived to the right and came to a screeching halt on the pavement. Neville could smell the burnt rubber. He handed over some cash, uncertain of its value or the amount actually required. The frog checked it and seemed satisfied.

'OK. Get out.'

'Thanks.'

'I should have a cognac if I were you,' and with those words of advice hardly out, the frog rammed the taxi into gear and speed out into the traffic again, the door from which Neville had exited flapping and banging against the side of the cab where he had not even had the time to close it.

Conveniently, the taxi had dropped him immediately outside a cafe. Even though its pavement tables were very busy, it appeared that the rather alarming manner of his arrival had gone unnoticed. There was a table free near the front of the terrace area and as Neville made his way to it and sat down, he decided that if the frog's driving might not be much to write home about, then his advice could well prove worth taking.

The waiter - a stiff individual who gave every impression of having an ironing board shoved down the back of his jacket - was at his side in an instant, offering him a napkin and some cutlery. Neville raised his hand and smiled politely.

'No thank you. Just a coffee - and a cognac, please.'

'Au lait?'

'Thank you, yes.'

Leaving the napkin, the waiter removed the cutlery and disappeared into the cafe.

Relaxing a little in anticipation of the cognac, Neville eased himself a little further back in his chair and began to take in the scenery. As he did so, he realised that the occupants of the table to this left - two suited businessmen - had indeed taken an interest in his arrival and were evidently talking about him.

'Poor English Bastard! That old Frog-driver stunt gets them every time!'

'Bet his pissed his little white panties, don't you?'

Both men laughed.

'Now watch the waiter sting him for his drinks. Here he comes!'

Neville was considering speaking to the men - though what he would have said was unclear, especially as doubts about his command of the language were returning - when the waiter reappeared with his coffee and brandy. He pulled a note from his wallet and handed it to the waiter, who nodded, then disappeared.

'Told you! That's the last he'll see of that!'

The two men laughed heartily again then rose. They exchanged pleasantries with another couple nearby and then moved away. As they did so, one of them brushed Neville's shoulder.

'Excuse me. Terribly sorry.'

The accent was perfect English.

'That's quite all right, really.'

Once the two men had gone - they lingered on the pavement for a moment, shook hands, then went their separate ways - Neville took up his coffee and scanned the scene.

The avenue was, of course, busy and bustling. The six lanes of traffic pulsated in that stop-go way that major arteries do, punctuated all the while by the tell-tale repetition of yellow taxis. For a few moments Neville concentrated on these, to see if he could count the number of frog drivers there were; or indeed, if there were any other members of the animal kingdom who had taken up the hackney carriage as an occupation. He gave up after a while, a little disappointed to find his search unfulfilled.

People moved about the pavement in seemingly ever greater numbers; a pavement which might well have benefited from the kind of markings that attempted to impose some modest discipline upon the traffic. In just in a few seconds, he witnessed numerous bumps and near things, and soon picked out the many phrases of "Excuse me" or "Pardon" which accompanied them.

It was obviously a wealthy street in a wealthy city. Many of the women were wearing fur coats, and such a large proportion of the men were adorned in sharp and fashionable casual clothes that he might have been forgiven for mistaking half the population as members of the modelling profession.

The coffee tasted wonderful - "really French", Neville thought - and half way through this he took his first sip of the cognac, which warmed him even more than the coffee. He felt himself sigh internally. Yes, he had imagined Paris to be like this.

After a few minutes, a pony and trap pulled to a temporary halt outside the cafe. It was a ride for tourists, taking them for a one-way trip along the Champs Elysées. The driver had dismounted from the trap and was now collecting his fare from two middle-aged American ladies who were struggling with their French and, in consequence, offering the man less than half the standard tariff. The driver simply spoke slower and louder. Neville had thought it was only English people who did that.

The horse, which had for a brief moment shown some interest in the negotiations, now turned his attention to Neville.

'Having a nice time?'

'Yes, thanks. You?'

'Oh, so so.' The horse attempted to shrug his harnessed shoulders - presumably much in the manner of his master - and simply succeeded in rattling his hooves on the tarmac. 'You know; up and down, up and down. Still, I suppose it's better than being sliced up and served to voracious Italians.'

'So I would imagine.'

The horse looked back at the driver. Negotiations were coming to a conclusion.

'Fancy a ride? Down to the Louvre, perhaps?'

'Not today. But thanks anyway.'

'Sure. It's nothing.' And with that, the horse and trap moved sedately off, the driver looking for their next customers.

Neville finished the last of his coffee and chased it down with the remainder of the cognac. Remembering the bill, he looked around for the waiter who had served him. He could not see him. He waited for a few moments then, with casual resignation, gave up his change, stood up, and walked onto the pavement proper.

To his left, the Arc de Triomphe stood large and proud against the skyline, with the heads of visitors who had climbed the monument just visible at the very top. To his right was the long stretch of the tree-lined avenue, and it was in this direction he decided to go.

SEVEN

He had not gone very far when he decided to cross the road. There appeared to be a greater variety of things to see on the other side of the avenue, and so - with this in mind - he walked to the edge of the pavement and came to a halt.

The traffic roared past him at ever increasing speeds such that crossing on foot began to look nothing short of suicidal. He waited for a few seconds, trying to catch a break in the onrushing wave of cars, but still they came like an unstoppable tide.

'Monsieur! Monsieur!'

From somewhere above his head a voice called down to him, and Neville looked up to discover a tiny man in the cage-like bucket of a small mobile crane suspended some twenty feet off the ground.

'Yes?'

'You wish to cross the road, no?'

'Actually I do, yes. But it's very busy.'

'Eh! It is always busy. People have died trying to cross here. Morte, n'est pas? Perhaps I can help you.'

With this the man signalled to his partner sitting in the cab parked in the centre of the road. Immediately the basket began to descend. Once at pavement level, the man opened the gate and beckoned Neville on-board.

'We are checking the street lights, and this little machine' - he tapped the cage - 'means that we don't have to climb the ladders all day long!'

'Very useful.'

By this time they were already off the ground and swinging out over the speeding traffic.

'They drive very fast,' Neville offered to his host, keeping a special eye on the taxis.

'Fast? Bien sûr; they are French, monsieur!'

Within a few moments they were out across the centre of the road (Neville remembering a wave of gratitude to the man in the cab) and on their way to the other side. As they began their descent, Neville noticed that the pavement they had just left now seemed the more bustling and attractive. However, it was too late to go back.

With a bump they hit ground.

'That was very kind of you,' Neville said, as he stepped from the cradle.

'My pleasure. Always happy to help an American.' And with that the workman was up again, once more aloft and brushing the branches of the trees.

Neville continued his walk away from the Arc de Triomphe. He strolled slowly, relaxing as the cognac took effect, not a little hopeful that the drama of this extraordinary day might be over.

The shops promised a variety of delights: clothes shops with immaculately turned out mannequins offering chic beyond most people's wildest dreams; music shops pumping out popular sounds of fame and stardom; jewellery shops, glittering in the mid-afternoon sun. And punctuated between these, the terrace cafes where occasionally all three - chic, jewellery and fame - would come together as the rich and famous paraded themselves as if they too were all part of one gigantic shopping experience.

Neville only browsed in the windows of the shops. He had no desire to go into any of the clothes shops - he had not forgotten his tuxedo, but Paris he had decided, was not the place - and the music shops held little fascination for him, especially as their sounds were either English or American and somehow much too familiar.

After a short while, he came to the entrance to an arcade which seemed to offer something of more interest. Inside he discovered a plaza populated by small shops of myriad variety, and a number of mobile stalls selling everything from perfume to parasols. He thought of Covent Garden. Perhaps every capital city had its own version.

He had been looking at some silk handkerchiefs on one of the stalls, when a voice called to him from the barrow alongside.

'Psst! Over here!'

Following the instruction, he found himself looking at a display of earrings, brooches, and general ornamental trinkets. He smiled noncommittally at the stall holder, who smiled back. The voice had not been hers.

'Hey! Here!'

Neville was beginning to gain some experience in locating disembodied voices by now, and his semi-trained gaze turned to a small tray of brooches and badges. Apart from the standard jewelled offerings, there were a number of slightly more unusual objects on offer; one of these was a small brooch boasting the white painted face of a Pierrot.

'Monsieur; how are you?'

'Very well, thank you.'

Neville looked up at the stall holder and smiled again, just to affirm his expectation that she would not be concerned over his conversing with an item of her stock. She nodded back with a little more conviction than before, perhaps entertaining the idea that she might soon have a sale.

'How has your day been so far?'

'My day? Pretty eventful, I guess.'

'You like Paris?'

'It's my first visit, and this is my first day, so it's a bit early to say - but yes, I think I do.'

'Sure you do! That is good.'

Neville began to glance at some of the other items when the Pierrot called him back.

'Hey! Need a guide?'

'A guide?'

'To Paris; while you are here. Can't do worse than ask a native!'

There was something about the Pierrot's accent which suggested that its birthplace might well be called into question; the lilt, if it could be called that, was more American than French.

'Are you offering?'

'Hey! I'm your man! I know this city inside out; you just tell me what you want to see and I'll show it to you. I'll even show you some things you don't know you want to see!'

'May I?' Neville put his hand forward to pick the brooch from the tray.

'Sure.' And the badge winked at him as he lifted him in his palm. 'Not so heavy am I? And you could wear me on your lapel; that way I'd be nice and close to give you a running commentary whenever you wanted.'

The lady behind the stall had now risen and was smiling hopefully at Neville.

'Deal?' The Pierrot asked hopefully.

'Deal,' Neville said, and asked the woman the price. He pulled some notes from his wallet and handed them over. She smiled again.

'Thank you, Monsieur.'

Neville eased the pin from the Pierrot's fastening and attached it to his collar.

'Hey! Thanks man, that's great!'

Neville thanked the stall holder again, and continued to wander around the stalls in the arcade, all the while the pierrot chattering excitedly and full of generally useless information. Neville stopped walking.

'Look...'

'Pierre. Can you believe it?! Pierre the Pierrot. Some people have no imagination!'

'OK Pierre, do me a favour; I know you're pretty excited, but can you keep the chatter down - maybe to giving me advice when it's obvious that I need it, or if I ask you something. Is that OK?'

'Sure, that's fine. But...' Pierre paused.

'My name's Neville.'

'Neville, we will just chat sometimes, yeah?'

'Of course.'

'Good,' Pierre paused again. 'Neville; that's not a French name is it?'

'Pierre.'

'Yes, Neville?'

'Shut up.'

'Oops!' And in the reflection of a shop window full of cheap imported T-shirts, Neville saw Pierre smile a little.

Within a few minutes Neville completed his tour of the arcade and made his way back to the street. To his surprise it was now dark, and the Champs Elysées was already brightly lit by the shops, cars, and street lamps. The suddenness of the vision took Neville a little aback and he came to a halt on the pavement.

'Pretty, n'est pas?' Pierre offered.

'Yes, very.'

There was something magical about the place. People still thronged the pavements, cars still raced up and down the avenue; yet the myriad of lights against the darkness gave the whole experience a different tone.

'Where too, Monsieur?'

'Any thoughts, Pierre?'

'A little night life perhaps?'

'Why not?'

A bright yellow cab pulled up in response to Neville's raised arm. Once bitten, he bent low to get a good look at the driver before opening the rear passenger door. This time all seemed normal.

When seated, the driver looked at him in the mirror and uttered a low guttural grunt rather than anything as intelligible as an enquiry about his destination.

'Rue St. Dennis', Pierre whispered, and Neville echoed this back to the driver.

Again there was nothing more than a grunt in response. Neville wondered if he might now be receiving the treatment normally reserved for Parisian natives; he could certainly equate the attitude with a number of Birmingham taxi drivers he had encountered.

Briefly they headed up the Champs Elysées towards the Triomphe, then pulled right and headed off into the city. Pierre - as good as his word - was dutifully silent, except when his role as guide demanded he make a little professional interjection to point out some feature or other to his client. Thus, as they drove passed the brightly lit Opera, Pierre offered a potted guide to the building that took all of seven seconds, yet seemed to Neville as if he had been told all he would ever need to know about the place.

'Boulevard Haussmann', Pierre offered as they entered a broad street, lined on both sides by more shops and more cafes, each with their own particular illumination of the scene. Neville tried to recollect an image of Paris that he had locked away somewhere in his memory.

'I know the painting you mean, but that is of another avenue on the south of the river.' Evidently, Pierre could read minds too.

After a few more minutes the taxi pulled to a halt and Neville handed his fare to the less than monosyllabic driver. As he stood and watched the taxi pull away, he felt disappointed by the ride, as if it had offered him little and added nothing to his experience. Perhaps he was simply beginning to expect too much.

'So, what now? What is this "Rue St Dennis"?'

'What or where?' Pierre clarified. 'Where? It is just there, fifty metres ahead on the right. What? It is Paris!'

Neville walked on, allowing Pierre his little cryptic indulgence because he was so boastfully a Parisian, and because he professed to love his city so much. They passed a small shop, which was in darkness, and a cafe that was less lustrous than those he had seen earlier. Indeed, he began to realise that they were now in a markedly less fashionable area of that particular thoroughfare.

On the corner of Rue St Dennis, Neville stopped. Their destination appeared to be nothing more than a narrow side street; indeed, it was sufficiently narrow for it to be one-way only to traffic, though this did not deny it a steady, if somewhat subdued, flow of vehicles along it. Also, there were still a number of evening strollers promenading on its narrow pavements. The whole picture was of a darker and slower Paris that he had seen thus far.

Without waiting for the prompt he sensed was on the verge of Pierre's lips, Neville began to walk down the street, adjusting his pace in concord with his fellow pedestrians. After a few yards, he had seen nothing at all inspiring.

'Pierre.'

'Monsieur?'

'What am I supposed to be doing here?'

Pierre laughed quietly.

'For now Monsieur, just looking.'

'Looking? At what?'

'Across the street, now; what do you see?'

'People walking. A couple of girls talking in a doorway. That's about it.'

'And the girls?' Pierre's whispered glee betrayed him as almost revelling in some kind of private game. 'What do you notice about the girls?'

Neville glanced across again.

'They are quite young, I suppose. Attractive, too. What of that?'

'And their clothes?'

Both were wearing short skirts and skimpy blouses that seemed a little risqué.

'A little provocative perhaps.'

'Now Monsieur; watch!'

And as Neville slowed his gait a little, he saw a man approach the two girls. After a few seconds talking, the man and one of the girls disappeared through the door outside of which they had been standing.

'Perhaps in two or three minutes he will be out - and with a smile on his face too!' - and with that, Pierre gave a low whistle.

Neville's recognition of the situation came as suddenly to him as the night had come to the Champs Elysées. The girls were of course prostitutes, and the street was full of them. He looked back over his shoulder: he had already walked past at least four doorways with two or three girls standing in each. Ahead - no more than ten yards ahead - there was another.

'Ah!,' Pierre exclaimed with hushed professional enthusiasm, 'the centime has dropped, n'est pas? Now, do not appear interested Monsieur; a casual glance. Remember you are a tourist, not a customer!'

And with that advice - and he had asked Pierre for advice - they approached the next group. Neville glanced, for the briefest of seconds, to see three girls again dressed in very little (hot pants appeared to vie with miniskirts for favouritism here) and all appearing to be disinterested in the passers-by. Without exception, all appeared young and attractive.

'Amazing,' Neville confessed as soon as they were passed.

'Magnifique, yes?'

'Compared to England; the girls here appear so beautiful, and so disinterested.'

'That is their skill, Monsieur; because they are Parisienne. They can all make themselves attractive, it is their magic. And disinterested? Non! They have a kind of radar, yes? They can sense a customer, always. And when they fish, they never fail. You understand?'

'I think so, Pierre.'

There was a brief pause. Neville noticed a policeman controlling traffic a little further down the street.

'Ah yes. The government is also Parisienne. It knows that she cannot stop this, so she looks after it, takes care of the girls; there is no trouble here. It is very safe. And for the customer too.'

Had Pierre been able to, Neville felt certain that at this point he would have felt an elbow dig into his ribs. Pierre had made a distinction between tourist and customer, and perhaps had Neville decided to "trade up" then the Pierrot's secret project might have been a complete success. But Pierre had no arms, and in any event, at this precise moment Neville would not have felt him prod anyway.

He had come to a complete halt on the pavement and was staring, quite blatantly, across to the other side of the road. Walking in his direction - but separated by some twelve feet of tarmac - was the most stunning woman Neville had ever seen in his life. She was quite tall and slim, with long dark hair. Her face was not classically beautiful, but simply captivating, and she walked with a confidence and pride that added to her aura. He could see little else - apart from exquisite ankles above small boots - as she was wearing a long flowing coat. Indeed, in the half light of this particular street, even the colour of the coat was denied him.

'Monsieur. Neville!'

Neville was roused by Pierre's voice and a bump delivered by a passing pedestrian. He was in the way. He apologised automatically. When he looked across again, the woman was nowhere to be seen.

'Monsieur!'

'Did you see her, Pierre?'

'Who?'

'You know who I mean! You can read my mind can't you?'

'Unfortunately at this time, yes I can.'

'Who is she?'

'Who is she?' Pierre paused for a split second. 'Do you mean, do I know her? Or does she "work" here?' He paused again. 'Perhaps. But we should go, yes?'

Neville did not want to go, but he could see no sign of her and he sensed that his dithering might be rousing a degree of interest in the other girls there.

'If you would like a little more night life, we could try La Pigalle. More wonderful Paris!'

Pierre's enthusiasm was suddenly no longer infectious.

'Not tonight. Perhaps tomorrow. I think I would just like to go back to the hotel.'

'Very well. Perhaps it is for the best.'

And accompanying those words, another yellow taxi pulled to Neville's side and he got in.

EIGHT

Neville awoke to the sound of the telephone from the side of his bed. It rang three times and was then silent. He had arranged an alarm call the previous evening on his return to the hotel, and that triple chime was, he assumed, the result.

The room was still dark, the heavy curtains keeping out most of the early morning light. It seemed quiet too, so perhaps they kept noise at bay as well. For a few moments he lay still, allowing his mind to retrace through the events of the previous day. He remembered the Champs Elysées and Pierre - his jacket hung on a hook at the back of the door - and he remembered the Rue St Dennis and the raven-haired woman he had briefly glimpsed there.

He smiled to himself. Appropriate, was it not? After all, Paris was supposed to be a romantic city, full of chance encounters? Not that the girl had been any kind of 'encounter' at all really; an encounter assumes some kind of contact, rather than a one-way stare across a one-way street. Still it was a memory for Neville to lock away for the future, whatever that might be - and however long it might last.

Getting out of bed, he went into the bathroom and began to run a bath.

From his room came a knock at the door. He grabbed a complementary bath robe, donned it, and answered the door. A young maid stood there with a small tray: his breakfast. He had not ordered breakfast in bed, but perhaps the service was standard here.

'Good morning, Monsieur.'

'Morning. Could you put it on the bed please?'

And he watched the girl as she walked in, placed the tray on the bed, then left. He wondered, as he took a bite out of a warm chocolate-filled croissant, how often the maid - a pretty, if slight young thing - had been propositioned in the line of duty; her job could take her into dangerous territory. Then - more abstractly - he wondered if he might not be chewing on a chunk of one of Maurice's "relatives".

The coffee - which was piping hot - brought back a memory of the cafe he had visited the previous day, and also - for a fleeting moment - an image of Mirelle. From the sublime to the ridiculous.

Neville carried the coffee and the remains of his first croissant into the bathroom. The bath was nearly full. He checked the temperature of the water, stuffed the last of the croissant into his mouth, slipped out of the bath robe and into the bath. The shower head, which had been motionless a few moments before, began to unwind as soon as Neville turned off the water.

'Made it then?' the shower head said, as it joined Neville in the bath, lying along one side, fixing him with its one-eyed stare.

'Apparently.'

'Good time last night? Didn't hear you come in.'

Neville choose to ignore this rather grumpy line of enquiry and looked around for the soap and shampoo.

'Behind you; small green bottle.'

'Thanks.'

'Not as good as the stuff they used to give guests here, but then I suppose it's a sign of the times.'

Neville cupped some water in his hands and doused his hair. The shower head wriggled uncomfortably.

'Hey, what's wrong with me? That's my job.'

'Really.' And again Neville poured water on his hair from his cupped hands. He couldn't be certain why, but he was in no mood to be nagged at; he wanted to be in control.

He unscrewed the cap from the small green bottle and poured some of the shampoo into his hair. As the cold gel began to run against his scalp he started to massage it in, creating a reasonable rather than luxurious lather. By this time the shower head was beginning to get excited, and its originally rather relaxed movements had begun to get more and more exaggerated.

'OK, OK!' it hissed, 'Now you have to use me!'

'"Have to"?' And Neville made to fill his cupped hands with water again.

'I'll give your scalp a really healthy massage too. Pulsating jets; no extra cost. Come on!'

Neville pulled the shower head from the water, turned the knob on the tap unit, and opened the taps. After a slight splutter, water gushed out of the shower head with a satisfied hiss.

True to its word, the shower head delivered pulsating jets of water firmly into Neville's scalp as he rubbed. The soap suds flew away, and Neville could feel his head tingle under the refreshing barrage. After a few seconds the rinsing was over, and Neville was able to turn the water off and return the shower head to its resting position.

'Hey, wasn't that good', it dripped enthusiastically. 'Best shower head this side of the river.'

Neville slipped down in the bath - which was actually very long - so that only his head remained above the surface of the water.

'So what's on the agenda today, Monsieur?'

'Today?' Neville remembered his itinerary. 'Montmartre and Notre Dame I believe; but I'll have to check with my guide.'

'Your guide?'

'Yes. A little badge; called Pierre. Picked him up yesterday.'

'No a pierrot by any chance?'

Neville was a little surprised.

'Yes. Why?'

'You know what a pierrot is, Monsieur?'

'A clown, of sorts.'

'Of sorts, yes. But from a pantomime. And sometimes these pierrot are not what they seem.'

'Meaning?'

'Just be careful, Monsieur. In French pantomime, the clown often makes others look the fool, rather than himself. You understand? I don't know about your Pierre, but I have heard stories; that is all.' And with a final dribble, the shower head uttered its last hiss and was suddenly motionless.

Neville remained in the bath a little while longer, and then pulled the plug and rose. Within a few minutes he had demolished the remains of the breakfast and was dressed for the day ahead. It was only this morning, as he prepared for his second day in Paris, that he noticed how well prepared his suitcases had been and how appropriate the clothes chosen.

Having consulted one or two of the free pamphlets left in the room for the average tourist, Neville pulled his jacket from the door. The badge was still in place and the movement seemed to have awoken Pierre. The pierrot gave a long yawn.

'Bonjour, Monsieur. Did you sleep well?'

'The sleep of the just.'

'Pardon?'

'Sorry; English saying.'

'That's OK.'

'Tell me,' the shower head's words were fresh in his mind, 'I've been wondering; what kind of role does the pierrot have in French theatre?'

'Role, Monsieur?'

'What do you actually do?'

'Do?' Pierre paused. 'We are clowns - I think that is your English word. We make people laugh, enjoy themselves; that is the point of pantomime.'

'And who do they laugh at, you?'

Pierre paused slightly.

'I understand in your English theatre the clown is something of an idiot, non? Ridiculous, comical. In French we are a little more subtle, with a little - excuse moi - "savoir faire".'

Neville said nothing further, but walked to his bedside table to pick up his wallet.

'Why do you ask, Monsieur?'

'Oh, just interested.'

Five minutes later they were walking through the foyer of the hotel. A bell boy came over.

'Can I get you a taxi, Monsieur?'

'No thank you. I'll walk a little first.'

The boy nodded, and disappeared behind the Concierge's desk.

'Walk?' Pierre seemed a little surprised.

'For some fresh air,' Neville explained, as they left the building, 'It's good for me. Now, which way?'

'Left, Monsieur. But where are we going?'

'I thought history was on the list today; Montmartre, Notre Dame...'

'And later?'

'Pierre; one thing at a time. Now, are we going in the right direction?'

'Bien sur.'

Neville walked on. It was relatively early and the city was, to a large extent, still waking up. Shutters rolled up on shop windows as he passed them, and buses rolled by full of people on their way to work. Always there was the sound of car horns, and the flash of speeding taxis. Neville suddenly thought of Samuel, and wondered what he would be doing during his three days here.

At the next junction Neville waited for the traffic lights to change so that he might cross safely. He noticed a MacDonald's restaurant on the far corner, and heard the rumble of the metro as it passed nearby. He closed his eyes for a moment and remembered his six years in London. He had met Mirelle at a party in Hammersmith.

'Monsieur, the lights.'

Neville crossed on command, then paused.

'OK Pierre; Notre Dame or Montmartre first?'

'That depends Monsieur on a number of things, but given the general time of day and the weather etc. etc. I would suggest Notre Dame.'

'Taxi?'

'Bien sur.'

Within minutes he was once again ensconced in a yellow Renault heading across town.

When they reached Notre Dame, large and looming against the skyline, Neville was surprised to find only a few tourists loitering in its precincts.

'It is early, Monsieur. In Paris we are a little more enthusiastic for the late nights rather than the early mornings.'

He had read a little about the cathedral from one of the guides in his hotel room, and expected much from the Rose windows, the vaulting architecture, and the view from the top of the tower - especially after the five hundred steps it took to get there. Each of these expectations was met with a little disappointment. He had visited Chartres once with Mirelle and remembered the glory of the Rose windows there. Now, he found nothing awesome in the architecture and the view could in no way match that initial sighting from the rickety old bus when they rounded the road on the hill.

When he left the cathedral and found himself in the bright sunlight again, he wondered if the day was due to be a day of disappointment, anti-climax.

'That is up to you, Monsieur,' Pierre offered. The pierrot had been a dutiful, if somewhat subdued guide during their tour of Notre Dame, and Neville had sensed his boredom. Where Pierre's passion lay was evident.

'So.' Neville said, open-endedly.

'Monsieur?'

'And now? What shall we do now?'

'You are a little bored, non?'

'A little.'

'And Montmartre? She is still on your list?'

Neville nodded.

'But perhaps a coffee first.'

Pierre directed him to a small cafe nearby where Neville, sitting inside rather than on the pavement this time, ordered a coffee and a small pastry described by his guide as "one of the best in all Paris". In the event, that was a little of an exaggeration too; but at least the coffee did not let him down.

He was preparing to leave - the coffee was finished and he had begun to address himself mentally to the prospect of Montmartre - when he saw a woman across the far side of the cafe who looked vaguely familiar. She had just risen from her table (where she had been sitting alone) and was chatting to the waiter who had served her.

'Pierre?'

'Monsieur?'

'That woman; over there, walking to the door.'

'Oui?'

'Do I know her?'

It seemed a ridiculous question, and he had no time to retrieve it.

'Do you know anyone in Paris, Monsieur?'

Neville ignored the rhetorical nature of Pierre's reply. There seemed something about the woman as she moved, in her attitude. For a moment, although she appeared very different - almost blonde hair, for instance - he was certain it was the same woman from the Rue St. Dennis.

'Pierre. Is it her again? The woman from last night?'

'How can I say, Monsieur?' And Neville felt the word "perhaps" form on Pierre's lips but then fall silently away, unspoken.

He rose sharply from the table, pulling a note from his wallet as he did so, and walked to the door. Once outside he looked around, knowing as he did so, his search would be in vain.

And so it proved. The crowds had thickened since he had been in the cafe, and finding someone amongst this new, animated throng would have been impossible. Neville thought briefly about Pierre's attitude to the woman, his lack of assistance, the warning he had received in his bathroom just a couple of hours ago... He was suddenly not happy.

'Taxi,' he said, almost as a command, and turned his back on the cathedral and the crowd in the square.

NINE

By the time he reached Montmartre, Neville had calmed down and was in possession of a more even temper. The journey across the city had not been particularly quick, which under the circumstances, had probably been a good thing. Pierre had been noticeably silent throughout, not even offering the shortest of guide-book commentary.

The taxi dropped Neville off at the foot of a long hill that led up to the white church that dominated the summit. Ahead were two parallel chains of steps that zigzagged in a mirror image to the top. He was struck by the whiteness of the whole scene, and, as he placed his foot upon the first of the steps, the strangely solid nature of the stone.

At various stages, the steps were broken by large plateaux. These were populated with bench seats, boys playing impromptu games of football, and North Africans selling trinkets from brightly coloured blankets. Neville paused at one selling necklaces made from various natural materials; coral, ivory, wood. As their owner chattered away, the necklaces writhed in time with the music from a nearby ghetto blaster whose owner was busy showing off his break-dancing skills for money.

As they left the necklaces to move on, Neville detected a sound from Pierre that appeared less than approving.

'Something wrong, Pierre?'

'Monsieur?'

'You don't approve of these people selling things here?'

'The selling,? Mais oui. The people, perhaps non.'

'Why? Because they are not French?'

Pierre said nothing. Neville assumed an affirmative answer.

'But I thought Paris was proud of her multi-cultural background; of the variety it brought to the city.'

'But these people are scum - pardonnez moi, but I have to say it. They turn areas of our city into slums. They do not know how to live - like Parisians!' Pierre paused. 'But is it not the same in England?'

'The same?'

'Do you not have ethnics too? Are there not problems?'

'Yes. And there are problems. But we must try to overcome them.'

Neville realised that he was in danger of sounding like a trite politician, and almost forgave Pierre the Gallic sigh that closed the conversation. The thump in the back Neville received from a football at that moment, also helped to terminate the debate. He turned to seek out the offending footballer, only to find the area deserted - except for the football which was trying to slink away unnoticed. From somewhere in the bushes Neville heard someone say "Gazza", and then muffled laughter.

Suddenly taken by a desire for boyish revenge, he set his sights on the football, took one stride forward, then aimed at the bushes. With a strange "crack!", he sent the ball flying towards the undergrowth where it arrived with such velocity that immediately there came the sounds of breaking branches and the faint smell of singed wood.

'Very good, Monsieur!' Pierre was impressed.

Neville - resisting the temptation to try an inflated tale of his schoolboy soccer prowess - resumed his climb to the top of the hill. As he neared Sacré-Coeur, it seemed to grow ever larger before his eyes, its whiteness becoming brighter all the time.

Pierre had obviously relaxed a little thanks to the incident with the football, and was once again offering stories about Saints and Martyrs - and after whom there was, somewhere in the city, at least one avenue named to commemorate them.

The cathedral was quiet and peaceful. Neville noticed the difference between his first impression here, and those from Note Dame just an hour or so previously.

'We are lucky, Monsieur,' Pierre offered, 'there is a service.'

In the body of the church, a few dozen people sat listening to a priest talking to them quietly. Neville remarked the lack of microphones which seemed to dominate modern English churches.

He made his way round the side, glancing alternately between the service - to which he was getting closer - and the statues and figures set within the fabric of the walls. By a large pillar he paused.

'What kind of service is it, Pierre; a wedding?'

'Non, Monsieur. I believe it is the taking of vows by some novices from a Monastery in the country. Sometimes they come here, just for this purpose.'

'Tourists too?' Neville added a little facetiously.

'Non. They are more than that, n'est pas?'

'Yes; sorry.'

Neville resumed his walk which had now taken him a little ahead of the front row of pews. As he glanced back he saw seven young men, each dressed in brown, intently listening to the words of the Priest. He tried to interpret himself, but could understand little of the ecclesiastic litany. Strangely, however, he felt a sense of peace in the voice of the older man, as if he were imparting years of experience upon his young charges.

Then, as he finished speaking, the young men rose as one and began to hum a Gregorian chant. The melody was taken up by those sitting behind them, with strange harmonies being added from all around the church. Even the statues seemed to be contributing their voices. Standing silently, Neville became enveloped in a wave of emotion transmitted through sound and the echoes and harmonics of the building.

This lasted for a few minutes, and then the young men sat down - their habits now changed to a radiant and peaceful blue - and the priest began speaking again.

'Magnifique, n'est pas?' Said Pierre, who had obviously been affected by the spectacle too.

'Marvellous, yes.'

'And only in Paris, Monsieur; only in Paris.'

Neville wandered for a little longer, his visit punctuated by the occasional burst of song, or the deep bass of the organ. By the time he regained the sunlight outside, he found himself in a much more relaxed mood.

'And now?'

'Maintenant, la Place du Tertre!'

'Where the painters are?'

'Oui, Monsieur. Another famous Parisian institution.'

'But,' Neville paused, leaning against a balustrade and looking down the steps to the base of the hill and the city below, 'there is Art tomorrow, isn't there? The Louvre...'

'The Musée d'Orsay,' Pierre prompted.

'Yes. Of course. So more paintings today?'

'But Monsieur, one does not go to the Place du Tertre for the paintings; one goes for the atmosphere, for the spectacle. And I know a small cafe...'

'Where they do a fantastic pastry, n'est pas?'

Pierre said nothing for a moment, and Neville sensed a degree of embarrassment in his guide.

'Where is it?'

'Ah, nearby. Ten minutes, no more! Just down the hill, to the far side of Sacré-Coeur.'

He left the Cathedral behind and made his way down a small side street. Pierre's instruction took him down a small cobbled lane where the houses seemed suddenly to belong to a different age, their slightly misshapen windows and doors giving him an echo of Charles Dickens, of all things - something he dared not mention to Pierre for fear of offence.

After a few minutes, the crowd began to thicken perceptibly, and suddenly Neville came out into a small vibrantly coloured square full of people. At its centre was an inner rectangle defined by trees and lined by Artist after Artist working at their easels and surrounded by examples of their work. In the centre of the square - and all around its outskirts - dozens of cafe tables. Between Artists and cafes, two streams of voyeurs made their respective clockwise and anticlockwise progress around the square, watching the craftsmen in action and, in turn, being watched by those at the cafe tables.

Apart from the colour of the scene - which was quite unlike anything Neville had experienced before - he was struck by the volume of noise, which seemed quite extraordinary. It was the sound of conversation multiplied a hundred-fold, and backed by wave upon wave of music as one circumnavigated the square.

There were many different styles of work on display; many undoubtedly honed to meet the market place they were in. Certain styles seemed to appeal to the visitors, and the instant portrait in charcoal was a popular attraction. It did not take

Neville long to realise that he was not looking at "great art", and the last thing he wanted to do was to spoil the day he had planned for tomorrow.

'Where's this cafe, Pierre?'

When no immediate response came, he looked to his lapel to see Pierre in conversation with the portrait of a pierrot resident on an easel by which he was standing. It could almost have been Pierre looking in a mirror.

'Pierre.'

'Pardon, Monsieur. An old friend.'

Neville accepted the apology, and though he did not quite understand it, decided not to push for an explanation.

'The cafe?'

'We are here, voila!'

The establishment Pierre was referring to appeared, to Neville, to be the oldest and shabbiest on the square. For a moment he thought to question his guide's judgement, but just then a little old man appeared from inside the cafe and ushered Neville to one of the empty tables. He sat down facing the painters, ordered a coffee and pastry (again according to Pierre's suggestion) and settled to watch the crowds.

His time in Paris seemed punctuated by cafes, coffee and food, and he wondered if this were a reflection on him or on the city. When it came the coffee was as reliably French as always and - this time - the pastry remarkably good. Pierre chatted for a little, but gradually became silent. Neville, relaxing in the warmth of the day, began to soak in the atmosphere.

Almost directly in front of him sat one of the charcoal portrait Artists. He was busy at a new piece, but had no customers at present. Neville glanced over the examples of the artist's work on display and was suddenly surprised to notice a drawing of

Mirelle staring back at him. It was not a recent work - she looked a little too young for that, a little too much how he would have liked to remember her - but there could be no doubt that it was indeed her. With a start, he suddenly realised that there were other people there whom he knew; there was even a drawing of Samuel (who until this moment had slipped from his mind) sporting a natty French beret and Breton shirt.

Neville took another sip of coffee and wondered if he should ask Pierre what was going on. And then he remembered that Pierre could read his mind so there was little point. Presumably, as he had volunteered nothing, Pierre had nothing to offer. Or chose to offer nothing.

In front of him, the Artist rose from his small seat. As he did so, Neville saw the face of the woman from the Rue St Dennis staring back at him from a drawing that had been, until that moment, obscured from his view. He felt an arrow slice through him. She was indeed, truly amazing. For a second he froze.

'Magnifique!'

Pierre's voice interrupted him, and Neville looked up to suddenly find himself focusing on his own face, there in charcoal, being presented to him by the Artist. It was his face, but it was a strange face too. There was something about it Neville failed to recognise, as if it were him from another time; past or future he was uncertain.

'Every visitor should have one,' Pierre extolled, 'and such value!'

Neville went to his wallet and offered the Artist some cash, which he took with a slight smile and handed over the portrait in return.

'I thought you might like that, as a souvenir,' Pierre said.

'You asked him to do this?'

'Monsieur; it is my city, this cafe and this seat was my choice. I wanted you to have this.'

And Neville looked up to see that the Artist - and all his works - had vanished, and now someone else occupied his place. He was not surprised, but began to wonder again exactly how much control Pierre had over him.

Neville rolled up the portrait carefully and slid it inside the cardboard tube he had also been given. Dusk was falling, and for the first time that day, Neville felt a slight chill in the breeze. The crowds had begun to thin, and one by one the artists were packing up their wares. Things seemed to disappear rather than be put away, their owners more like magicians.

He watched two portraits conversing in front of him: one was of an attractive, bare-torsoed young man; the other a young woman, tears welling in her eyes. The styles were different, and they were obviously about to be parted.

'Good night, my Darling', said the woman, stifling a sniffle.

'Tomorrow, perhaps,' came the reply.

'Can you persuade him to stand here again?'

'I can't be sure; today we took very little money. He may want to try somewhere else.'

A woman appeared; evidently she was the owner of the female portrait, which she lifted from the ground.

'A bientôt, my sweet,' and in a moment the portrait had gone, gathered up in an armful of others.

'Monsieur?'

The familiar voice of Pierre broke into the closing of the scene. Neville rose, and threw some money on the cafe table.

'Monsieur?'

'Yes, Pierre?'

'She we go to la Pigalle now? There is much to see there?'

Neville walked into the centre of the now deserted square. All the artists had gone, all the cafe tables were empty, the lights hung in the trees were dim. Without the magic, there was nothing. He felt the portrait in his hand.

'No, Pierre. I just want to go back to the hotel.'

Pierre remained silent, knowing how tired Neville felt, and recognising the sense of doubt - about Paris, about his future - that had suddenly come upon him.

Neville looked up, hopeful of seeing a battered old yellow bus waiting for him on the street corner, Samuel standing by its door. But there was no bus; and Neville felt strangely alone with memories of the past and doubtful premonitions of the future.

TEN

At breakfast the next morning, Pierre began to harangue Neville over their failure to visit La Pigalle the previous evening. There was nothing venomous in Pierre's nagging, but Neville did begin to wonder if the visit Pierre envisaged - or perhaps had already planned - was more for his own gratification rather than Neville's. In any event, this morning Neville did not feel disposed to consider the wants and wishes of his porcelain companion.

Inclined to something a little different - and regretting his rather meagre intake of food the previous day - Neville ignored Pierre's advice and requested some form of cooked breakfast. He presumed that this request was not too unusual for a hotel catering for English tourists, but when the feast arrived Neville found himself staring at a single, rather wizened sausage, and three fried eggs. Accompanied by two slices of rather under-done toast, the whole appeared indecorously arranged on a willow pattern plate.

With a slight sigh - 'Not what you had in mind, eh?' was all Pierre offered - Neville picked up his knife and fork and made for the sausage. As he did so, the sausage rolled out from under the knife as if to avoid any incision. Two small figures within the pattern on the plate - a "typical" Japanese scene common on willow-patterned plates – also visibly moved just as Neville's knife made contact with the china.

He stared hard at his breakfast, then listened, waiting the inevitable voices. There was nothing. The restaurant was virtually empty, and the only background noise came from the slurping of coffee at a table hosting two Germans. Neville prepared for another attack.

As his knife and fork made for the sausage again, in an echo of Malvern he heard the distinctive roar of an aeroplane -

presumably some kind of dive bomber - and then, unmistakably, the sound of anti-aircraft fire. Again the sausage rolled away, this time managing to get underneath one of the eggs, and the two figures - who had been standing on open ground - disappeared into the willow patterned house. His knife hit the plate again (another unsuccessful raid) and he noticed, on his hands, small splatters of tomato ketchup.

Frustrated, he dropped the knife and fork and grabbed one of the soft slices of toast, biting hard before it too could escape.

A waiter appeared at his side holding a small plate containing two hot croissants. He placed the plate in front of Neville, removing the virtually untouched "English" breakfast with his other hand. Then - again unbidden - he topped up Neville's coffee. As he went away with the willow plate, the sound of an "all clear" siren wailed. Neville took up one of the croissants. It was warm and moist and the first bite melted in his mouth.

At this particular moment in time, Neville's desire was to talk about the things that he had seen over the past two days, but the only person he could confide in he presumed he would not see until sometime the next day. Whatever he was, Pierre could in no way be considered a confidant. Fundamentally, Neville did not trust him. It was hard to say why, or whether his suspicions had been initially aroused by the shower head, but he could not help but question the course events seemed to be taking.

'Monsieur?' Pierre prompted, the tone of his voice showing no concern for Neville's present state of mind. Indeed, there appeared no recognition that his present master might be in the process of rebelling.

'Yes, Pierre?'

'The croissants; they are good?'

'Of course. And the coffee.'

Neville sensed his small friend wanted praise or thanks, but he was in no mood to offer either. He wondered what today might have in store for him; where his Parisian roller-coaster might take him.

'Where should we start today? The Louvre or the other one?'

'The Musée d'Orsay, Monsieur. Bien sûr, the Louvre is the more famous, but she is - how shall I put it? - not so "moderne". I think you will find d'Orsay more immediate.'

'You mean accessible?'

Pierre paused, weighing Neville's choice of word.

'Accessible, perhaps. But I think immediate is a better word.'

From somewhere in his past, Neville remembered a rare trip to a circus. He had seen a clown there, face painted white, tall conical hat. This clown proved to be more of a ring master than a fool, directing those about him into situations which brought them nothing but humiliation or pain. He rose.

'Shall we go?'

'The Musée does not open for another demi-heure; but perhaps a short walk along the Seine then would be good. The weather is very fine.'

Outside, Neville waited in the hotel doorway for a taxi. The two lions eyed him with a degree of suspicion, but without imparting any sense of danger. There was another doorman in attendance, though to Neville's eye it appeared the same person despite earlier assurances to the contrary.

A yellow cab rolled to a halt and Neville, without regard for its driver, opened the rear door and got in.

As he watched the streets roll by, he was aware that he had managed to cultivate an undeniably fatalistic attitude towards the remainder of his visit; perhaps even beyond that. He could not say if it had come to him out of choice or as a result of his recent experiences; all he was aware of was the sense that he just wanted to get it - whatever "it" was - over and done with.

The taxi spun round a corner and headed towards the river. Pierre was silent (as seemed his want now) and Neville in no particular mood to talk. Outside, the weather seemed a little less bright that previously, with an intermittent layer of cloud partially blocking out the sun.

They came to a halt by one of the many bridges over the river. Neville paid and found himself once again heading off under Pierre's direction. Ahead in the distance, he could make out Notre Dame, and his mind flitted back to the scene at the cafe and the disappointment the whole experience had given him.

Across the river, Neville saw a glimpse of the giant pyramid that was the remarkable entrance to the Louvre; an edifice strangely out of context with the solid and historic building to which it offered itself as gateway.

After a short while, Pierre pointed out the Musée d'Orsay; a large rectangular building on the other side of the road.

'It looks like a railway station,' Neville said, immediately unimpressed with its exterior appearance.

'Monsieur!' Pierre was pleased, 'Bien sûr! It **was** a railway station! Only in Paris would you find such a thing transformed into a palace of wonder.'

Neville thought "palace of wonder" a little strong, and, despite the tone of Pierre's voice being reminiscent of their initial few hours together, he was not entirely convinced of its authenticity.

Having crossed the road, he joined the short queue that had begun to form. In the window, a poster proclaimed a special exhibition of works by a group of artists whose movement was known as Fauvism. Neville considered asking Pierre for a little background, but decided against it.

In the small square in front of the building, pigeons fluttered amongst the few tourists who were waiting on the seats, begging as they perched and hopped for the crumbs of late breakfasts nibbled from anonymous paper bags. The sound of bolts being pulled back and keys being turned, drew Neville's attention to the doors which were now being opened.

The queue shuffled forwards and in through the glazed entrance hall. Once inside, they filed through one of two booths collecting entrance fees. Having paid, Neville loitered for a moment looking for a guide to the museum written in English, then, suitably armed, moved into the core of the building.

He was greeted by a large and remarkably bright open space. The roof had been generously panelled with glass, and the day's light flooded in. Much of the interior of the building had been refurbished with white marble. The centre of the museum was dedicated to sculpture, and on this floor numerous alcoves opened off the central atrium, each boasting its own small collection of paintings dedicated to individual artists or schools.

Standing quietly, absorbing the breath-taking quality of the place, Neville found himself as thrilled by its interior as he had been non-plussed by its exterior.

Gradually he made his way from alcove to alcove. The ground floor seemed dedicated to Realists and Romantics, and wall upon wall greeted him with both the famous and the unfamiliar. He was pleased he had come early as the gallery was still not busy, and he was able to relax as he toured in relative silence.

At the end of the building, an escalator rose to the first floor. Open to the body of the building, he was able to see others as they wandered below him, in and out of the alcoves as he himself had just done.

He consulted his guide. Each level seemed to exist as a ring about the central space, with balconies and walkways looking out across the museum and down to the sculptures below. The first floor was dedicated to more Realists and the early Impressionists; the second offered the great works of the Impressionists and the Fauvism exhibition. Neville decided to try the special exhibition and work back down.

As he made his way up to the top floor, he pulled off his jacket and swung it over his shoulder, supporting it with his finger in the collar. Pierre, who had once again returned to silence, became lost amidst the folds of the cloth. 'Out of sight...' thought Neville.

Turning left at the top of the escalator, he found himself confronted by more of the posters he had seen at the entrance, then, turning right into the exhibition area, came face-to-face with the pictures themselves. There was a display on the wall offering a general introduction to the exhibition and the artists whose works were on show. Despite the paucity of Neville's knowledge about Art, he recognised a couple of the names.

As he wandered slowly to the first display, his eye was caught by a number of paintings by Andre Derain. They were landscapes; bright, attractive pieces that Neville found instantly appealing. Here was the quality missing from the Place du Tertre! One piece in particular drew him. It depicted a number of trees in the foreground of a brightly coloured landscape. According to the display, it was painted in 1906 and called - appropriately enough - "Les Arbres".

He walked up to it and stopped three feet from the canvas. The trees were bright, wiry things in mauve and bold reds, and the landscape danced before his eyes with its bold brush strokes.

'Enticing, isn't it?'

Pierre had emerged somehow from the folds of Neville's jacket and appeared to be admiring the work too.

'Derain has a certain vitality,' he continued, 'a certain rawness, perhaps. As if he is in touch with - something.'

Not bothering to reply, Neville leaned a little forwards and took one single step closer.

His foot came to rest on a surface that felt entirely different from the hardness of the museum's polished tiles. He looked down and found it softly embedded between great tufts of grass. But the grass was not green; it was amber and ochre. And looking up, he saw four trees immediately in front of him. The one nearest, to his left, was light purple deepening to a dark blue base; the others, various rusts and reds. He pushed out his hand and felt the firmness of the trunk.

About his body, he sensed the heat of a summer's day; the sun shone brightly in the pale blue and yellow sky, and there was a breeze which carried with it the hint of water. In the distance rose mountains of blue and indigo.

He took a another step and moved further into the field. Just beyond the clump of trees - in whose midst he now stood - the land slipped away slightly, down to a yellow field. Beyond this field, and some more trees - was that the green of figs or dates? - the river.

Lured on by the shape of the land, its invitation to explore, Neville continued walking, down through the yellow field and across the pale blue shadows cast by the dark trees with their solid fruits, pink in the sun.

The river flowed in blocks of solid colour, purple, blue. Away in the distance, riding on a mass of red, the ferry - little more than a splash of brown - plied its trade to the far bank. Neville looked down. His shoes had become misshapen rectangles of blue, now supporting legs apparently suffering from years of exaggerated rickets. He felt fine.

Over his shoulder, the four trees he had first encountered were now away across the field and up the hill. Ahead, beyond the river, the mountains; and to either side, stretching away, the strange mosaic of the landscape.

As he reached the river, the ferry was making preparations to leave. The ferryman - a misshapen man of black and blue - beckoned him facelessly, and with confident steps, Neville climbed on board the strange vessel. It seemed to have no definite sides or edges to it, just layer upon layer of reds and fleshy pinks. He could make out no definite hull or waist, but managed to find a seat (a spotted white oblong) on which to sit. Silently the ferryman pulled on his oars, and with the assistance of the wind pushing at the magenta and cobalt sail, they moved out onto the river.

The journey to the far bank was over in moments. Neville had hardly time to take in the sensation of travelling across a rippling surface of blue and leaving a wake of green and yellow, when they arrived. Immediately in front of him, the mountains rose ever higher, their mass darker and more solid now. A road - strangely white - beckoned him towards the mountain pass, and effortlessly he carried on.

As he moved further into the hillside, he noticed that the colours had become more solid, larger; they had begun to be defined by black lines around their perimeter, as if to hold the colours in. Gone was the freedom and the flowing beauty from the other side of the river; now things seemed a little darker. The yellow had gone from the sky which was a deeper blue; the lightness of the fields had moved towards orange; and Neville noticed that in one or two places, deeper shadows had begun to appear. Where there had been nothing but colour before - the blue shadows of the green fruit trees - now came shade.

The road began to sweep downhill, and Neville was carried onwards by it. He tried to look behind, to check his progress, but to no avail. His legs were no longer random, but solid more exact things; and on the white road, he had begun to cast a shadow.

Down through the mountain pass the road swept, and as he moved onwards he moved further into a darker landscape. He had begun to feel a little cold, and had donned and buttoned his jacket against a chill breeze that had sprung up. The sky menaced before him; now ivory, it bore nothing but the promise of storm.

He turned a corner and was suddenly out of the landscape and into a bleak monotone flatness. The earth was a dull grey now, and large rectangular shapes of buildings loomed on either side. Their black windows offered nothing, and their long shadows cast a deep cloth in front of him. On the wall of one building, a plain clock began to dissolve under his gaze, its numbers melting down the brown brickwork. Ahead on the horizon - and how far was that? - strange creatures appeared to be moving in his direction.

The empty space became suddenly swallowed up the shadows of the building, and he found himself in an ever darker alleyway. Ahead was a single door through which he seemed compelled to go.

From one place of desolation, he entered another. Now there was no sky, and no walls. All seemed to blend together. Even the definitions between things had begun to blur in a monotony of tones. He suddenly longed for a splash of yellow; for a hint of green. He looked to his lapel, but Pierre was invisible in this light.

Ahead, from what appeared to be some kind of kitchen, came the throbbing sounds of a boiler as it beat against an invisible wall. Neville tried to stop, to turn back, but his progress was remorseless. Suddenly the boiler wrenched itself from the wall, spewing black water in his path. Steam poured from its pipes as it lowered itself to the ground, then, uncertainly at first, began to walk towards him.

Neville could see the flames from within it burn ferociously; but even these possessed little colour. The boiler began to make better progress, growing larger before his eyes. The noise it was generating had become almost deafening, and Neville began to wince at the intrusion. He looked for help, for an exit, stairway, anything; but there was nothing he could distinguish, nothing remained.

The boiler stretched out its pipe-like hands, spraying water and steam towards him. It roared monstrously, and all Neville could do was to find his voice and scream.

ELEVEN

When Neville awoke, he found himself lying on his bed. Judging by the light filtering through the faded curtains, it was probably morning. Moving, he discovered not only that was he not beneath the covers of the bed, but also that he was fully dressed - and in clothes he had not been wearing when he went out the previous day.

He sat up slightly, leaning on his elbows. At the foot of his bed his two bags sat neatly side by side. In the far corner of the room, one of the doors of the wardrobe was open, revealing emptiness inside. Apparently his bags had been packed.

'Bon jour, Monsieur!'

Neville's jacket was lying across the back of a chair, and Pierre had been in a position to watch his first stirrings.

'Your last day in Paris, and you must not be late!'

'Late?' Neville was now sitting on the edge of the bed, looking for his shoes. 'Late for what?'

'For la Tour Eiffel, of course! You are leaving around mid-day, n'est pas? So you do not have so much time.'

Having found his shoes neatly placed under the bedside table, Neville was pulling them on as Pierre spoke. The noon deadline was news to him, but presumably all part of the plan. He remembered that he would be seeing Samuel again, and then - only this time with a sudden chill that physically shook him - came a recall of his experience of the previous day.

'Pierre; did you say that this was my last day?'

'Oui, Monsieur.'

'Don't I have one more day to go - to visit the museums?'

'Again?!' Pierre gave a short laugh. 'Was yesterday not enough for you?'

Even though Neville could remember only part of his previous day's excursion, he decided not to press Pierre for any commentary on the remainder. Somehow he felt better not knowing what had happened – and why Pierre seemed up-beat about the whole day.

'Of course, yes,' and he stood up and went to the window.

Looking out, the view was much the same as it had been the previous two mornings; Paris awakening. It seemed slightly busier, and the clock on the wall confirmed he was some half an hour later than before.

There was a knock at the door which Neville answered with "Entree" without moving from his position. Only when he heard the door open did he look over his shoulder. The doorman - which one he could not say - filled the door frame.

'My bags?' Neville surmised out loud. The doorman nodded, and walked into the room. Turning away from the window, Neville went to pick up his jacket, but then decided that prudence demand he use the bathroom first.

Unzipping his trouser fly, he heard a familiar hiss from the bath.

'Leaving us then?' The shower head's observation sounded more like accusation than anything else.

'Apparently so.' Neville stared down into the toilet, and when he pulled the cistern chain, water began to swirl into the bowl and then away.

'Had fun?'

Considering that, at one stage, the shower head had actually tried to be helpful to Neville, he had difficulty in deciding the true nature of this particular character. Was he misanthropic or philanthropic?

Neville pulled the bathroom door closed a little further.

'What you said, the other day. What did you mean?'

'What I said?' The shower head uncoiled itself and slid into the base of the bath. 'What do you mean, "what I said"?'

'About Pierre. The pierrot.'

'Ah.'

'You warned me about him.'

'Did I?' The tone of the reply was slippery in the extreme. 'I wouldn't say I warned you about him. Perhaps simply to be cautious; observant even. But not a warning. Why should I?' A pause. 'Did I need to?'

From outside, Neville heard a call of 'Monsieur!' and a reminder about the time. He looked back into the bath. The shower head was motionless, and its hissing had stopped. Neville decided that he really did not like deliberately ambiguous characters. They thought they were so clever, but were nothing more than cowards.

'We must go!' Pierre said when Neville reappeared in the room. 'The taxi is waiting.'

'No breakfast?'

'Perhaps later.'

As he descended in the lift, watching the first floor creak passed through the trellis-work gate, Neville wondered if he shouldn't be a little more authoritative; perhaps he should put his foot down, send the taxi away, insist on breakfast. Under other circumstances he may well have done, but this particular morning found him more like a boxer the day after a fight rather than one still feeling bullish the day before.

As he walked through the hotel entrance, he saw the doorman putting his two bags in the back of a taxi parked half on the pavement. The rear passenger door was open, and he was greeted again by the unusual aroma of the taxi's interior. The frog was leaning across the back of his seat as Neville got in.

'Leaving us then?' And the frog gave his croaky laugh. 'Had fun?'

'Not so fast today, please,' was all Neville could offer.

'Fast? Man, you English got no balls!' And with that, the frog crunched the taxi into gear and pulled off the pavement with a leap.

Pierre was slightly more talkative this morning; excited even. Perhaps it was a special effort because it was Neville's last day. He pointed out minor things as the frog threw them from side to side as a result of his amazing lane-changing antics. Neville wondered what would happen to Pierre when he left, for it suddenly occurred to him that somehow the small porcelain figure could never leave Paris.

He would have asked the question but for their screeching arrival at the Eiffel tower. The frog hit the curb with a bang and the doors - all four of them - sprang open with the impact. Neville paid and made to get out.

'Come back soon - and don't forget me!' And with that, the frog slammed the taxi into gear with such force that Neville's bags bounced out of the boot and onto the pavement of their own accord. A dust trail followed the frog as he sped off into the city hubbub.

'What do I do with those?' Neville asked, looking at his bags.

'There is a small office. They will take them.'

'Good.' And with that, Neville picked up his two bags and made for the ticket office.

As he walked beneath the tower, he looked up through its centre, standing square between the four legs. All he could see was a pattern of steel repeated at each corner like some multiple mirror image. Above - and how high was that? - the first platform blotted out any residual image of the sky, and along one leg he could see the small lift making its way upward.

He walked on. It seemed that once again he was early, and because of this the queue was quite short. When he reached the booth he asked for a ticket.

'To which level?' came the rather short reply.

Neville glanced down to his lapel.

'Well?'

'Two,' said Pierre, 'there will be a long wait to get to the top.'

'Is two high enough? As I'm here...'

'Two,' said Pierre, adamantly. 'That should be fine.'

From behind the grille, the same question.

'Sorry. Second level, please,' Neville offered.

'Deuxième étage,' said the attendant.

'And can I leave my bags?'

'Of course, Monsieur. Please leave them at the door.'

Neville left his bags where he had been told and made his way to the lift. After ten yards or so, he glanced back to find the bags gone; efficiency was, to be honest, the last thing he had expected.

There was a short queue - some twenty people or so - waiting for the lift. He looked up the leg of the tower to see it on its way down, slowly descending towards them. From behind he heard the excited chatter of some Japanese tourists, and the equally exited chatter of their cameras, the latter busily exchanging advice and tips on aperture sizes, filters, and exposure speeds. He remembered that he had wanted to buy a camera. He would ask Samuel about that.

Turning his attention to the front of the queue, he noticed a figure that seemed familiar to him, a woman he could see in part-profile. She was wearing a white coat with a large grey collar, all of which contrasted with the darkness of her hair which was a mass of curls falling about her shoulders.

The sudden sound of a bell diverted his attention to the lift which was suddenly upon them. It hit the ground with a small thump and immediately opened its doors on the far side, disgorging its passengers once again on terra firma. Those arriving back seemed in good spirits, laughing and joking. He noticed one or two couples holding hands and talking half-secretively to one and other.

A nudge in the back prompted him to move forwards with the rest of the queue, and within a few strides he found himself on one side of the lift, pressed against its metal side by some of the Japanese visitors. Immediately to his left, the camera of one - slung casually across its owner's shoulder - gave him a conspiratorial wink.

'Guess what?'

'What?' Neville replied in the whisper the question was given.

'She's forgotten to load any film!' And the camera winked again, and chuckled to itself. This was obviously a tremendous joke, as a number of the other cameras nearby joined in with the merriment.

Neville thought the camera was a bit mean, but refrained from saying anything. This was partly due to his general reserve and decorum, but more so because he had now noticed that the woman in the white coat was none other than his vision from the Rue St. Dennis. She stood, here and now, no more than eight feet away from him; half-turned, her profile against the Paris skyline as the lift moved upwards. Eight feet - and completely out of Neville's range as there were two of the Japanese, three Germans and a Spaniard between them.

For two somewhat torturous minutes, the lift rose slowly towards the first level, all the while Neville trying not to stare at the woman - yet also trying to stare at her. The exit doors would open on the far side of the lift, and as they came to a halt, it occurred to him that she might get out here. If she did, he decided that he would follow. There was little else he could do.

In the event only two people got out, but a few more crammed in. The eight feet between them became squashed to around seven, and Neville faced the crawl to the second stage in the same dilemma of staring and not staring. The woman seemed to not be aware of him; at no point on their journey upwards did she look his way.

As they climbed, he allowed himself the occasional brief glance upwards to check on their progress - and outwards, in a show of interest - but there was really only one thing on his mind. Pierre had said nothing since they had stepped in the lift.

'Pierre?'

'Monsieur?'

But Neville's potential interrogation was halted by the jolt of them arriving at their destination.

The doors opened and the lift began to empty. The woman was out quite quickly and it took Neville about twenty seconds longer to exit. Once outside he went to the rail and looked about. He could not see her. The platform was not that large, so she had to be there somewhere.

Neville gave a cursory glance to the city. He could pick out Notre Dame from where he stood, and made a stab at the building that might be the Musée d'Orsay; but these were suddenly minor considerations. From the tower providing him with his memorable panorama of the city, it had now become the apparent climax of some obscure quest. Pierre had known what he was doing when he suggested that Neville leave it to last.

He moved away from where he stood, slowly walking anti-clockwise around the edge of the platform. His glance took him in towards the centre of the tower rather than away to the skyline as was the norm, and his face wore a frown rather than the smiles so abundant on the faces of others.

He had nearly completed a full circle when he turned the final corner and came across her standing immediately in front him, a slight smile on her face. It was as if she had been waiting.

He stopped instantly. She smiled.

'Bon jour, Monsieur.'

She was, without question, the most captivating woman he had ever seen in his entire life. Her greeting seemed to drop from her lips with such grace that his ears felt unworthy to receive her words. Her eyes shone with a clarity that even the purest gem stones would have envied. And her beauty, would have defied the gods themselves.

From Pierre there came a slight whistle.

'You have been looking for me, yes?'

'I'm sorry.' Pathetic.

'I saw you the other day. I think you have perhaps been looking for me.'

Neville was now standing within two feet of her. His tongue felt glued to his mouth, and his brain hundreds of feet below, grovelling among the flower beds of the park nearby.

'Yes,' then, 'no.'

She smiled.

'I mean; I recognised you. From the street, the other evening.'

'And the cafe, perhaps?' she suggested.

So.

'And what do you want of me?'

Still the smile; but this was the sort of question Neville had never expected to face - not in any normal life, let alone now.

'Want?' He could think of nothing - and everything. 'Who are you?'

'Who am I? You mean, what is my name, perhaps? Can you guess?'

Neville, for a moment lost, realised that there could be only one answer.

'Mirelle?'

'Bien sur.'

But she didn't look like Mirelle; she surpassed Mirelle in every way.

'I'm sorry,' he faltered, 'but I don't think I understand.'

He moved a step forwards. Her response was to lose the smile and to take a step away.

'Careful, Monsieur.'

'But, who **are** you?'

'I am,' she paused, 'I am all you desire. I am the embodiment of your dreams. I am all you would have me to be.' And as she spoke the smile returned to her lips, and a gleam came to her eyes. 'But I am not yours. I am mine.'

Again Neville moved forwards, this time his hands a little outstretched. Again she moved away, maintaining the distance between them. She was now more than the most beautiful woman he had ever seen; she had become the embodiment of something intangible, something he had been searching for, chasing; that elusive thing to which he could not give a name. Possession was what he desired. But he could see that she was not one to be possessed. Then, he decided, he would touch her, for suddenly even the briefest contact seemed to represent some kind of ultimate achievement.

After a moment of silence he lunged forwards. It was step into the abyss. He was leaving behind so much that he knew, and throwing himself at the mercy of the woman that stood before him now.

As fast as he moved, so she retreated. In an instant, she was standing on the railing, suddenly towering above him. And as he looked up, his hands grasping nothing, she changed into a beautiful seagull. With one magnificent flap of her wings, she leant forwards and plucked Pierre from his lapel with her beak. Then, falling back, she was away from the tower and out into the air, sailing off into the city.

'A bientôt, Monsieur' came the feint cry from Pierre as he dropped out of sight.

It was only when he felt the hand on his waist, Neville realised that he too was standing on the railing, preparing to throw himself into oblivion.

TWELVE

He had just missed him by the ticket office, Samuel explained a few minutes later as they were descending in the lift. He had seen him arrive, buy his ticket, and deposit his bags by the office.

'If I hadn't grabbed them, who knows what might have happened to them!'

Neville was a little calmer now, though he had said nothing since his encounter with "Mirelle".

'You must have been very close to... I mean; I turned around and saw the bags were gone.'

'I decided to put them in the bus and then come back for you. Unfortunately I was just too late.'

'You would have stopped me going up there?'

Samuel smiled. The lift had reached the ground with a bump and the doors rattled open.

'I think I might have come up with you, Sir. I don't think I could have stopped you.'

They walked past the refreshed queue - more Japanese, more winking cameras - and away from the tower. Neville took one last look up. He could make out one or two birds circling high above; the second stage seemed a universe away.

'I'm glad you weren't **too** late.' He tried a smile, but it proved a little difficult. Samuel squeezed his arm, and offered a silent nod of understanding.

The old bus sat waiting for them in a small lay-by just off the main road. It looked a little less battered, and now sported a bright red coat of paint. Samuel intercepted Neville's gaze.

'Thought I'd give the old girl a little treat. Well, she deserves it really.'

Neville offered nothing; he knew he wasn't supposed to. Instead, he let Samuel reach the bus first and open the door. Inside, his two bags were in their previous position, and his own seat - the one at the front alongside Samuel's - had been recovered with new fabric, and accessorised with a large soft cushion. There was a small table beside it too, and on this a fresh mug of tea steamed healthily.

'Tea,' Neville said in a rhetorical manner. 'Is that significant? I mean, it's not coffee.'

'I thought you might be just a little tired of coffee, Sir', Samuel said, and he turned the key and started the engine as if to add meaning to his words.

Neville raised the cup and took a sip.

'Where to Guv?'

Samuel had that slight mischievous smile again as he glanced back at his passenger, then, without waiting for a reply, rolled the bus gently out into the traffic.

'I don't know yet,' Neville said. 'Perhaps we should just leave the city first, then decide. Is that OK?'

'That's fine, Sir,' said Samuel. 'How's the tea?'

The bus rumbled slowly on - at twenty seven miles per hour (the coat of paint had done nothing to improve the speed) - twisting through the streets of the city. Neville sipped his tea, expecting at any moment to feel the beginning of the long drag up the incline from which they had first approached three days before. But there was no hill; instead Samuel kept steering along level and uninspiring roads, and eventually, without ceremony, Neville realised that Paris had simply slipped away behind him.

He wondered if one last look might have been in order. He had been thwarted by events at the Eiffel Tower, and that panoramic view he had promised himself - or been promised - had been at least partially denied him. Perhaps that was just as well. Samuel seemed, as ever, fully in control of the situation, and was pressing on - as much he could ever give an impression of "pressing on" - to their next destination.

'Samuel.'

'Sir.'

'Where are we going?'

'Going? Well, that's up to you Sir, of course.'

'You appear to be going **somewhere** though.'

Samuel gave him a brief glance.

'Not quite. We are going **away** from somewhere. You have to do that before you can go **to** anywhere else; if you don't mind me saying, Sir. Especially if you do not know **where** you are going.'

'That's just semantics. They are, of course, both one and the same thing - instantaneously.'

'Perhaps.'

Neville, without the appetite to pursue Samuel's philosophical theories, drained the last of his tea and realised how much he had missed its unique flavour. He wondered what other things he had missed; four days of croissants had presumably taken the place of something else. The last time he had drunk tea had been in his office - perhaps only minutes before he became a "redundant" individual. It had only been a few days, but Neville already knew that his most recent job was one thing he was never going to miss. Perhaps Brian, Colin and David were managing things a little better than he had evidently done; but quite frankly, he didn't give a shit.

After a while, Samuel slowed the bus and indicated that he was going to pull over. Ahead, was a small lay-by, vacant apart from a solitary, simple vending unit. As they came to a crawl alongside it (and in the process allowing the stream of traffic that had been behind them to race away) Neville saw that it was a fruit stall.

'Fruit, Sir?' Samuel enquired, and then continuing in a rush, 'I hope you don't mind me stopping, but I've something of a fad for bananas, and the urge has just taken me.'

The sentence trailed away into hopefulness as Samuel, the bus now stopped, turned to look at his passenger.

'Not at all.'

'May I get you anything?'

'Perhaps an apple.'

'French?'

'Whatever.'

As he watched Samuel descend and walk round the front of the bus, Neville remarked the use of his word "French". He looked on the awnings of the cabin, and craned his neck to see inside, but could find no evidence of signage of any kind. The countryside had lost some of its Gallic charm and had returned to a kind of nondescript uniformity: the gently rolling hills; the hedges; the odd stone wall. The sky - blue, but peppered with puffy while clouds - gave nothing away. Neville sniffed the air. Nothing. The fields were empty, and there was no music in the background.

'Samuel,' he was half way up the steps when Neville next addressed him, 'where are we? And don't say "between here and there".'

Samuel laughed, presuming a joke.

'Very good, Sir; very good!' And with that, handed Neville a green apple.

Neville rubbed it on his jacket - force of habit - then took a bite. It was crisp and juicy.

'Well?'

Samuel was peeling his banana. He looked up.

'You weren't joking, Sir? About being between here and there?' Neville's silence confirmed as much. 'Oh, sorry. Pity.'

For a few seconds there was a kind of silence as the two of them chomped through their respective fruits. Samuel, finishing first, consigned his banana skin to the brown paper bag from which it had been produced.

'We are, of course, between here and there. It's a shame when you didn't mean what you said, Sir, because you are absolutely correct. In our present context, "here" is Paris, and "there" is where ever you wish to go next. Of course, the saying should be "between there and there", because we are most definitely **here** - but that doesn't sound so well, does it?'

He waited for some kind of response. Neville took another bite from his apple.

'We could, of course, talk about Paris - if you wanted to? I mean, if I can help with any outstanding questions? Historical clarification, perhaps?'

Neville lobbed his apple core forwards, and Samuel caught it deftly in the brown bag. He looked at little disappointed at being called upon to perform such a facile trick; but the look lasted but a moment.

'Paris? Clarification, yes; but not so much the historical.'

Samuel nodded, smiled, placed the brown bag down by his feet, and waited. Neville weighted his words.

'What actually happened?'

A small laugh escaped - somewhat involuntarily, Neville guessed - from Samuel, though his face showed nothing but considered respect.

'I don't think I could manage anything quite so challenging, Sir. Could you be a little more specific?'

'How about what happened on the Tower for a start. Can you explain that to me?'

Samuel frowned.

'To be honest Sir, I was hoping you might do me the honour there.'

'Sorry?'

'I mean, I arrived to find you standing on the edge about to throw yourself off! If I were more demanding myself, perhaps I should ask for an explanation of that circumstance.'

'You didn't see Mirelle?'

'Your wife?!'

'No, another Mirelle. Or at least, I suppose she was.' He paused, looking for something a little less debatable. 'Or Pierre, the Pierrot.'

Samuel offered an "old boy" shake of the head, suggesting a degree of bewildered confusion.

'I'm sorry, Sir. Perhaps if you would like to explain...'

Neville considered Samuel's offer for a split second. Either he was taking the piss and knew exactly what had happened, or he was genuinely in the dark. Either way, any explanation was probably worthless.

'Forget it.'

There was an uncomfortable silence. Neville picked over the images of his visit, thinking of morsels he might offer Samuel.

'The Musée d'Orsay. Can you explain what happened to me in there?'

'What was that, Sir?'

'Samuel!'

Neville thumped the small table in frustration. And even if Samuel was in a position to explain things to him, would Neville be able to understand him, or would there be more of this phoney here-there mumbo jumbo to confuse him? And if Samuel could explain nothing, was it because he wasn't aware of what was going on, or because, for some other reason, he was prevented from doing so. Neville could resolve none of this.

'Have you checked your watch, Sir?'

'My watch? Do you need the time or something?'

'I was thinking of the additional information.'

For once Samuel's cryptic message was understood, and Neville remembered the display of his financial "balance". He looked down. The number 16738.72 greeted him. He tried to remember the initial figure.

'A little over nineteen thousand', Samuel offered.

'But that means I've spent a fortune!'

'Nearly two and a half thousand, by my calculation.'

'We said Paris would cost a few hundred; a thousand at most! This can't be right, Samuel.'

Samuel's countenance became a degree more stern, verging on the school-masterly.

'Correction, Sir; **you** said you anticipated such a sum, not I. You must remember the cost of the hotel, and the travel.'

'Travel? But I only took a few taxis.'

'I'm afraid I must include myself in your budget, Sir. The old bus may not be particularly quick, but I'm afraid she is a little expensive to run - given her particular **talents**.'

The last work hung ambiguously in the air, demanding definition; but Neville missed it, and pressed on.

'And I bought nothing.'

'There is the portrait I collected with your bags, Sir. And the Pierrot, you mentioned...?'

'But surely...' Neville lost his argument. He could not reconcile his brief visit with such vast expenditure.

Samuel waited for anything further. When nothing came, he continued.

'Do you remember the General? The gentleman who purchased your car.'

'Of course.'

'He paid what you considered to be a ridiculous amount of money for it, did he not? But he had his reasons, as I explained. I also explained that what we were dealing with there was the concept of **worth**, rather than **value**. The General paid a sum matching the car's worth to him, not one in accord with its value.'

'Are you suggesting that, somehow, my visit to Paris was "worth" nearly two and a half thousand pounds to me?'

'Perhaps.'

'How come? Explain it, Samuel; I don't understand!'

Samuel offered a smile of sympathy.

'I don't think I can, Sir. It's not that I don't want to, it is simply that I fear it is impossible. It is a lesson to be learned perhaps; nothing more nor less.'

Neville checked his watch again. Sixteen thousand. Was that how much his life was now "worth", in some vague sense? And if so, how could he possibly know how he was spending it, or when one thing might cost him more than another?

'I'm afraid you must trust us, Sir. We are, after all, on your side. I will help you all I can, but these are the rules we are playing with.'

'Option 3?'

'Indeed.'

Unable to take in exactly how things now stood, Neville looked out of Samuel's side of the bus at the fruit stall. The boxes of fruit that had stood in neat racks had now vanished, and the stall was decorated like a Punch and Judy show, with brightly coloured curtains adorning the sides of what was - to all intents and purposes - now a stage.

From within the stall (there was no-one visible) came a brief drum roll, which was followed by the appearance of a banana peeping nervously round the curtain. With a sudden lunge - as if pushed from behind - it flew out and came to a sliding halt centre stage. It bowed low. From somewhere Neville heard a small ripple of applause. The banana bowed lower, and the applause was louder.

With this second ovation, two apples - one red, one green - rolled onto the stage from the opposite direction. They appeared to be in conversation, though how Neville could actually tell this was vaguely mystifying. They stopped suddenly on seeing the banana. The red apple moved round the banana to its other side, so that the apples now flanked it. The banana tried as best it could to straighten itself. Neville sensed some tension. An orange appeared from one side of the stage, paused, the rolled quickly across and out of sight on the other side.

The apples sidled up to the banana, squeezing it between them. The banana tried to bow and failed. From either side of the stage various other fruits, evidently attracted by the drama, made their appearance; spectators rather than participants. By this time the banana was looking even more uncomfortable as the apples, both redder with their efforts, pushed against it. Neville could only watch, mesmerised by the strange show.

Gradually the banana peeled back its skin, and, as it did so, the apples backed slightly away. The audience in the wings also moved back slightly. Then, without warning, the banana spun viciously round, whipping the apples with its flailing loose skin as it did so, and sending them flying from the stage and onto the ground. With that the curtain closed.

Neville looked at Samuel, intending to ask him for some interpretation of these events, but he appeared to have dozed off.

'Samuel!'

The driver woke with a slight grunt, raising himself in his chair in embarrassment.

'Sorry, Sir. Must have just dropped off; apologies.'

'Samuel,' Neville paused,' Never mind. I think I'd like to go home.'

'Home, Sir?'

Neville sensed another discourse coming on; something he wanted to avoid at present.

'Birmingham. Let's go back to Birmingham; I need cheering up. Perhaps that meal.'

'And the tuxedo?' Samuel offered with a smile.

'The tux? Why not!'

As the bus crunched into gear, Neville felt a sudden chill breeze through his open window, and noticed that the sky had turned an angry grey. He sensed England might not be that far away, after all.

THIRTEEN

The weather broke after a few minutes' driving. The clouds Neville had seen indeed anticipated the brief deluge that was to follow. For a while, as they made their way onwards (towards Birmingham, Neville could only assume) visibility through the windows was minimal. Samuel, concentrating hard, adopted a resolute silence which seemed to carry with it a warning that, should he be forced to break it, some kind of penalty would be incurred. He had switched the bus lights on, and the windscreen wipers moaned loudly across the surface of the glass.

Occasionally, another vehicle would approach them from the opposite direction, lights blazing, and deposit a spray cloud for them to drive through. Neville could make little out. Silhouettes seemed to pass by at random moments: he detected a small wood, the odd building; it was not until a little later the realisation came that they were travelling through a built-up area. He heard Samuel sigh, and sensed a degree of relaxation that signified it was now permissible to open communications.

'Where are we, Samuel?'

'Birmingham, Sir.'

Neville peered through the window again. The rain, now held back by buildings on all sides, appeared to be lighter, and Neville was able to see more of their present environment. He had lived in Birmingham for a while and assumed that he knew much of the city, but evidently this was not so.

'You may not recognise this,' Samuel offered prior to the question being asked, 'but this area houses some of the best tailors in the city.'

'Indeed.'

Instead of discovering himself in a commercial district, Neville found that they were making leisurely progress through what appeared to be little more than residential streets. Samuel's use of the word "houses" appeared to be doubly precise, as all the buildings were indeed domestic - row upon row of terraced dwellings - and the only signs of entrepreneurial activity Neville could see was the occasional board above a door or window.

All the houses fronted directly onto the pavement, with their small square windows adorned with net curtains of various persuasions, and backed by multifarious draperies. Neville felt as if the dwellings were somehow leftovers from a previous generation; as if they should have been condemned years previously and replaced by more modern constructions.

The bus swung from one identical street into another, then Samuel pulled the vehicle to a halt.

'Here we are, Sir.'

They had come to rest outside a dark blue door whose paint had begun to concede victory to the ravages of time, and retreat in flakes to the paving stones below. Above it, a sign in a slightly different shade of blue, proclaimed "A. Bossiman – Tailor".

Samuel opened the bus door and led Neville down the steps. As he knocked at Mister Bossiman's establishment, Neville tried to peer through the front window, only to find his gaze blocked by a heavy net curtain which, judging by its off-white colour, had also seen better days. He wondered about Samuel's assertion regarding "some of the best tailors in the city", and was going to challenge this when the blue door opened. Samuel stepped to one side to reveal a small man in a blue and white striped apron. He nodded to Samuel, then offered Neville a slight bow. Neville nodded back, following the man into the building.

'Mister Bossiman,' Samuel whispered, as Neville passed him on the threshold.

'Are you coming in?'

'I'll wait on the bus, Sir; if you don't mind.'

Mister Bossiman was, to put it bluntly, incredibly small; yet, there was something about him which prevented Neville making any immediate connection between the man he now followed down the long hallway and the words "midget" or "dwarf".

At the end of the hall, Mister Bossiman turned through a door on the left and led Neville into a large and surprisingly bright room. At the far end of the room was the net-bound window which opened onto the street, in front of which two small settees were placed facing inwards. Either side of the room, rack after rack of suits, jackets and trousers hung, and near where he now stood, Neville saw an evidently well-used tailors cutting table. It was difficult to make out where the light that illuminated the room was coming from. The front window admitted next to nothing, and the bulbs hanging from the ceiling seemed so dim as to be extracting light rather than contributing to it.

Mister Bossiman turned, and smiled up at Neville.

'Pliss, your yacket.'

'I'm sorry?'

'Your yacket?'

'Yes, sorry.'

Neville pulled off his jacket and placed it across the back of a nearby chair. Mister Bossiman smiled professionally, and pulled a tape measure from his apron pocket. As he was only about three foot tall, Neville wondered how he could manage to measure him effectively. He looked towards a second door at the back of the room, expecting a slightly larger assistant to emerge and assist with the task.

'Pliss, turn about,' smiled Mister Bossiman.

Neville did so. Instantly he felt an expert hand at the nape of his neck, and a second tracing the tape measure down to the small of his back. He glanced sideways and caught a glimpse of Mister Bossiman in a mirror on the wall. It was indeed the small tailor doing the measuring, with arms that Neville could only describe as telescopic.

'Goud. Pliss, turn about', said the small tailor.

Neville turned, and Mister Bossiman extended his small arms to measure his shoulders, his chest, and then his waist in turn.

'Do you come from far away - originally, I mean?' said Neville, for some reason getting the impression that a tailor was like a hairdresser, and that small talk was demanded during a consultation.

'Yiss,' Mister Bossiman smiled, evidently pleased to make contact with his customer, 'I from Walsall.'

Neville's natural desire to laugh at the response - joke or not - was tempered by Mister Bossiman's manner, which indicated that his reply had been given in all seriousness and not without some personal meaning.

'I see,' was Neville's only possible option.

After a few more extensions of his arms, the tailor had completed the measuring exercise and - though he had committed nothing to paper - appeared ready to continue with the next stage of the process.

'Pliss, you chooce fabric?' and with a wave of his arm (now back to its normal proportions) indicated a large rack of cloth near the cutting table. The rolls of cloth showed, not unnaturally, a predominance of greys, blacks and blues. There were narrow stripes and wide stripes, but nothing as adventurous as Neville would expect to find in his local high street "man's shop". Somehow this seemed in keeping with the general tenor of the place.

'Pliss, for what you wish suit?'

'Actually, I was looking to but a tuxedo.'

'"Torpedo"? Pliss, what is "torpedo"?'

'Tuxedo', Neville corrected. 'Well, it's actually a very smart jacket; often velvety, I guess. Some kind of smooth fabric. A bit like a dinner jacket. You know; you can wear it with a bow tie and cummerbund - that kind of thing.'

'"Come-undone"? Pliss, what is this?'

Neville, amazed at Mister Bossiman's sartorial ignorance, was nonetheless disarmed by the naiveté in his professional smile. Under more conventional circumstances, he would he been inclined to storm off, but - considering Samuel had given Mister Bossiman his personal recommendation - felt such action would not only be churlish, but potentially unwise. He decided to compromise.

'A tuxedo is a very, very smart suit; and a cummerbund is a kind of wide belt made out of bright fabric. Is that OK?'

'OK, pliss,' smiled Mister Bossiman, 'smart belt. I got.'

And with another wave of his arm, once again invited Neville to choose his material. Neville had decided against any of the plain greys or blues, and had - he was surprised to discover - something of an aversion to stripes. His ex-boss had always worn suits with a stripe in them, and this had now invested such unpleasant connotations in the style, that he could not countenance wearing it himself. Towards the bottom of the rack, he noticed some material that appeared to be vaguely green, yet, on closer inspection, seemed to even possess a degree of redness about it. He heard Mister Bossiman murmur to himself as Neville bent to consider it further.

'I like this,' he said, on straightening up, 'may I see it, please?'

'Pliss, remarkable fabric,' said Mister Bossiman who then, without bending, simply extended his arms downwards, and pulled the entire roll effortlessly from the rack.

In an instant it was on the table, a metre or so unwound for Neville's closer inspection. His first impressions - of a material that suggested both green and red - were not disappointed. Neville struggled to identify exact what its base colour might be - grey? blue? something else? - but gave up almost immediately. Whatever it might be, it was certainly different enough to meet his requirements and taste.

'That's fine, thank you,' and with that offered to shake the tailor's hand and leave.

'Pliss,' suggested Mister Bossiman, and gestured to the settees by the far window, 'I make for you, suit.'

'Now?!' Neville was stunned.

'Pliss. You like tea, yes?'

'Thank you, yes.' And Neville walked to the settee where he discovered a cup of tea and small plate of biscuits awaiting him.

Mister Bossiman seemed intent on undertaking the construction there and then. Indeed, as Neville settled to his tea, he could see the tailor's arms already flying about the table, flashing scissors and tape measure amidst the folds of the material. Satisfied that his wait would not, after all, be an impossibly long one, Neville turned to look out of the window. Through the net, he could just make out the outline of the bus which was still parked outside. He felt a small flush of relief at this; knowing Samuel was on-hand gave him a feeling of security, especially after his recent escapades.

His attention was, however, almost immediately drawn back into the room by the sound of an unnatural cough. He assumed that it was Mister Bossiman endeavouring to recall his attention - presumably for further fitting measurements - but when he turned, he found, facing the settee, a dark pin-stripe suit standing to attention in front of him. The suit thrust out an arm towards its right when three other suits were now sitting, each in possession of a musical instrument. The trio, thus invited, began the introduction to a slow, drawling jazz number led by a saxophone, and backed up by a base and - of all things - a harp. Neville looked to the centre of the room again, to find the dark suit had gone and the stage was now held by a pale yellow suit and a flamingo pink ball gown - though where this latter had come from, Neville had no idea.

The trio picked up the sleazy beat of their tune and the yellow suit slid over to the ball gown and began to dance around it. For a few bars the gown feigned indifference to these advances, but then, drawn on by the hypnotic nature of the music, soon gave way, and the two of them embraced. For the next few minutes (with Mister Bossiman's arms flying about in the background) Neville watched the yellow suit and the flamingo pink gown engaged in a remarkably stunning dance routine that reminded him of the Astaire and Rodgers routines he had occasionally seen in old movies. Gradually the trio - who were also remarkably accomplished - picked up the tempo of the piece to a thumping crescendo which climaxed in the yellow suit flinging the ball gown to the ground, then collapsing in a heap alongside it. Neville's applause was automatic and unreserved. The yellow suit and pink gown rose to take their bow, and the trio stood briefly in acceptance of their guest's appreciation.

Suddenly, from the far end of the room, there came a brief crash as Mister Bossiman's scissors hit the table, and in an instant all the entertainers disappeared. Mister Bossiman now stood, hidden by the new suit his arms were proudly holding way above his head. Neville rose and walked towards him.

'Pliss, is goud?' came the disembodied voice from behind the waist of the trousers.

Neville felt the material and examined the seams. The workmanship was, without question, of the very highest quality, and the suit seemed a work of art rather than artefact.

'Very impressive.'

'Pliss, you try.'

Slipping off his shoes and trousers, Neville donned the suit. It fitted everywhere to perfection, and felt instantly comfortable. He turned to look in one of the mirrors. In this light the green in the material was emphasised, and shone lustrously. He turned to look over his other shoulder at another mirror, and discovered that the redness in the cloth now appeared dominant, and gave the suit a warmth that was remarkably attractive. Remembering that he had wanted a tuxedo, Neville, backing a hunch, closed his eyes, then turned to the mirror directly in front of him. When he opened his eyes, he found he was indeed wearing a quite remarkable tuxedo. He smiled to himself.

'Pliss, is goud?' said Mister Bossiman.

'Mister Bossiman, it is truly excellent!' And the small tailor blushed at Neville's praise.

'My fist "torpedo" I make. So pliss you like him.'

After a further glance in each mirror, Neville slipped out of the suit which then, of its own accord, folded itself and climbed into a waiting bag. Once he had restored his old trousers and jacket, Mister Bossiman offered both the bag and his hand to Neville; who took the former and shook the latter warmly.

'Thank you very much.'

'Pliss, the honner is all mine, Sur.' and the small tailor bowed low.

Samuel was waiting for Neville on the bus.

'Was your visit a successful one, Sir?'

Neville held the bag aloft.

'Yes, Samuel, it was. Thank you. Mister Bossiman is a remarkable tailor - and he has an interesting establishment.'

Samuel started the bus and began to roll it forwards.

'Indeed, Sir; as you say, a remarkable establishment. Strange how, from the outside, you would not image that such a talent could exist there.'

'But it does.'

'And has for years, as Mister Bossiman might have told you himself.'

Neville regretted he did not engage the tailor in any further discussion beyond his place of origin.

'These other houses, Samuel.'

'Sir?'

'Do they hide similar talents?'

'"Talents"? Not necessarily. But they each have something about them I suspect.'

It was one of Samuel's phrases which demanded nothing but silence and contemplation in reply, and, as usual, Neville respected it.

They drove on through one or two more similar streets - the terraced frontages, the fading signs - and then out onto open road.

'I have taken the liberty of booking a table for you at a restaurant this evening, Sir', Samuel informed him.

'What sort of restaurant, Samuel?'

'I think you had something exclusive in mind Sir, did you not? This particular establishment offers nothing but the highest quality in terms of food, service, and atmosphere. I am sure you will not be disappointed.'

'Given your most recent recommendation, I am sure I won't be.'

'You will need, of course, to wear your new suit. It is important to create the right impression.'

'Indeed.'

'And to that end, I have taken the liberty of selecting a number of bow ties for you to choose from. They are on the seat behind you.'

Neville turned and lifted a small tray containing seven ties to his lap. They varied in colour and style, but all appeared of the highest quality.

'Compliments of Mister Bossiman, Sir.'

'Ah.' Neville glanced up. 'Will we be there soon?'

'In a while, Sir. I suggest you relax; perhaps sleep a little.'

FOURTEEN

It was dark when Neville awoke; the bus was stationery. In the silence, he could hear the starlings about their early evening social activity, their chaotic cries accompanying the manic business. From somewhere at the back of the bus, he could hear Samuel whistling gently to himself. He checked his watch: it was a little before eight.

'Ah, so you're awake Sir! Good; I was worried that I might have to disturb you.'

Neville turned to discover that something of a transformation had come over the interior of the bus since he had fallen asleep. All the remaining seats had been removed and the vehicle now appeared to be compartmentalised, with a narrow passage way running down one side. Curtains separated each of the areas, but these were currently drawn back, so Neville had a full view. The first two sections contained beds, each with a small cupboard by the headboard and a lamp on a tiny shelf set into the structure of the bus. Beyond the second of these arrangements, there appeared to be what could only be described as a small galley, and it was here Samuel was currently occupied. Beyond the galley was a door - not a curtain - and Neville assumed that this could only be a lavatory. Samuel looked up from the small stove where he was tending his supper.

'I took the liberty of making a few minor adjustments while you were asleep, Sir. I thought it best to allow for any future circumstance, you see.'

'I'm impressed, Samuel; you have been busy.'

Neville left his seat and made his way towards the back of the bus. Passing the first compartment - 'That one is yours, Sir' - he felt the bed (it seemed remarkably soft) and opened the cupboard door. Inside hung his new suit, along with the remainder of his clothes. Samuel had evidently unpacked his bags too. Passing Samuel's quarters, he reached the galley which, despite its size, seemed rather well equipped. The driver was in the process of making some kind of vegetable stew which, Neville could only assume, would prove to be his dinner.

'Don't worry Sir, this isn't yours!'

Neville returned Samuel's smile.

'When will we get to the restaurant?'

'We are there already, Sir. I took the liberty of parking in their car park a little early; your table is booked for eight thirty.'

'I should be thinking about getting ready then.'

Samuel motioned to the door beyond the galley.

'The bathroom is through there, Sir. Everything should be ready for you.'

Neville opened the door. The bathroom, though compact in the extreme, still boasted a full sized bath and toilet. The bath was full, steam rising gently from the surface of the water. Above the toilet, a small mirrored cabinet stood half-open, revealing - appropriate shaving and cleansing materials.

'I'll lay out your suit, Sir; you go ahead.'

Neville closed the door behind him. Two towels waited on a rail beside the bath, and a small chair seemed provided to take his discarded clothes. He checked his face in the mirror. He would need a shave too, and was pleased to find an electric razor in the cabinet. Samuel appeared to have considered everything. He undressed quickly, then felt the bath water with his hand. The temperature seemed fine. Within seconds he was immersed. The bath was surprisingly deep, and reclining in it, Neville found his body completely covered. At the foot of the bath - where, to his surprise, there were no taps - a yellow plastic duck bobbed in the water. On a small rack to the side, a flannel, a sachet of shampoo, and some soap awaited his attention.

'Comfy, ain't it?'

The duck bobbed a little closer towards him.

'Very, yes.'

'Can't stand those bloody shallow baths.'

'Indeed.'

'Can't get enough water in 'em. Sit down, but don't get your arse wet; know what I mean?'

'Yes, I do.' Neville leant forward for the shampoo. 'Excuse me.'

'Sure; no worries. Don't splash about too much though mate; can't stand it when I gets soap in me eyes. Odd, ain't it? A duck what don't like water that much. Well, it ain't the water so much as the soap, see? Makes me eyes smart. Ain't natural, is it ; a duck and soap, I mean?'

Neville, having doused his hair, began to wash it. The duck, evidently to avoid as much discomfort as possible, bobbed away from him a little.

'What you up to then?'

'Sorry?' Neville looked at the duck through the one eye that was not covered in soap suds.

'I mean, here. In this bath. Like, I ain't seen you before, have I? You ain't like the last guy.'

'Last guy?' Neville stopped rinsing.

'Yeah. Big feller; fat, know what I mean? Hardly room for me in here with him, come to think of it. Miserable sod too. Only saw him the once.'

'You've seen lots of people have you?'

The duck gave a quacky laugh.

'Course I 'ave. Well, what do you expect; it's a bleeding 'otel, ain't it?' and the duck quacked again.

From outside, Samuel shouted through a reminder about the time. Neville's mind flashed back to the bathroom in Paris.

'OK, Samuel. Won't be long.'

'Sam. That's his name is it? The geezer who looks after the room. Sounds like an obnoxious git to me; always bossing blokes about. Can't stand that, being bossed about. Know what I mean?'

'Yes. Excuse me.' Neville stretched for the soap and began to wash.

The duck bobbed around in a circle for a few moments, attempting to whistle as he did so: something that, thanks to his anatomy, proved impossible and resulted in nothing more than a largely silent dribble.

"Ere; ain't got any bread, 'ave you? Shit, I could murder a nice crust! Bloody hotel keeps you on tight rations, know what I mean? My dad used to talk to me about rations in the war, poor bustard. But it weren't like this though; eh?'

'I expect not.'

Again Samuel shouted a reminder, and this time Neville rose and stretched for a towel.

"Ere, you're quite a big bloke aren't you? Tall, I mean. Fit are you; I mean, play football or something? Some blokes look like shit; know what I mean?'

'I'm just skinny; that's all,' replied Neville through the folds of the towel as he dried himself.

After a minute or so, he turned his attention to his chin. The razor was fully charged and was remarkably efficient. It seemed to take no time at all to remove the small amount of stubble that he had manage to accrue since Paris, and rubbing his hand across a now smooth face made him feel much more comfortable.

'Nice talking to you,' he said, turning back to the bath. But although the duck still bobbed, it bobbed lifelessly.

The door opened, and Samuel popped his head round.

'Everything OK, Sir?'

'Fine Samuel, thank you.'

'I've laid out your suit Sir, and a white shirt. The ties are there too, if you would like to choose one.'

'Thank you.'

And with a towel wrapped around his waist, Neville made his way back to his compartment through the now closed curtains. As Samuel had said, his clothes were ready for him, including a new pair of shoes and a selection of socks. Neville chose a rather flashy green patterned tie and green socks, hoping that the combination would bring out the best in Mister Bossiman's handiwork. There was a mirror on the door of the cupboard, and, within a few minutes, Neville was able to consider his overall appearance.

He was, without doubt, pleased with the final composition. He had not looked as smart as this for a considerable period of time. Indeed, he found it impossible to recall the last occasion he had needed to "dress up", but felt certain that it would have had something to do with Mirelle wanting to impress someone - and that it would have been a disaster. He checked his watch. It was nearly eight thirty. Pulling back the curtains, he was faced with Samuel who was waiting to open the bus door for him.

'I say, Sir!' he said, warmly, 'you do look just the part. Very dapper.'

'Thank you, Samuel. You think I'll do?'

'I think you will do very nicely, Sir.' And with a slight bow, Samuel opened the bus door and stood aside.

At the foot of the steps, Neville looked up to be greeted by a rather distinguished building gently illuminated by low-level exterior lights. The building was detached, and there appeared to be no other nearby. Neville felt a faint breeze on his cheek that carried with it the suggestion that they were in fact out of the city and somewhere in the country. He looked for a nameplate to identify the building, but found none. Indeed, without knowing it to be a restaurant, one might be forgiven for assuming it was a small stately home and not open to the public.

Neville made his way across the gravel car park to the front of the building, where a large well-lit porch invited him on. In the hallway, an elegant man in evening dress moved forward to greet him.

'I have a reservation for eight thirty.'

'Ah, yes Sir. Very pleased to see you this evening Sir. I trust you will enjoy your meal with us.'

'Thank you; I'm sure I shall.'

The elegant man clicked his fingers, and another dark-suited man appeared.

'Gustav; show this gentleman to table eight.'

'Eight?' said Gustav, 'certainly.'

Gustav leant forward and whispered something in the Maîtres' ear. The latter stiffened slightly.

'I'm sorry, Sir,' he said addressing Neville, 'but it appears that the last diner is just finishing her coffee at your table - which, apart from that, is of course ready for you. Would you like to follow Gustav, please.'

Neville was about to suggest that he take a different table, or that he might wait for the diner to finish, but there seemed some insistence that he follow Gustav, and this he did. The hallway opened out into a small dining area which was lit with a subtlety that matched the Maîtres' own demeanour. It was not large - perhaps containing no more than ten tables - but furnished impeccably. Around half the tables were occupied, all the remainder seemed to boast "Reserved" notices. All the diners present looked remarkably smart. He followed Gustav to a table in the far corner of the room. Its current occupant, looked up from her coffee at their arrival.

'Pardon, Madame; but this gentleman has arrived for his booking. I wonder if you would mind if he sat with you for an aperitif while you finish your coffee?'

She shot Gustav a strange look which seemed initially to display some kind of fear, though this was quickly superseded by a more relaxed demeanour and even the beginnings of a smile as she glanced at Neville.

'Of course not. I won't be very long. That is, if the gentleman doesn't mind?'

Neville returned her smile. 'My pleasure,' he said, and took the seat offered him by Gustav.

'Drink, Sir?'

'Gin and Tonic, if I may.'

Gustav nodded, and left.

As he scanned the room, Neville noticed a mural adorning the wall. From the back of his chair, it rose about two feet, and circumnavigated the whole of the room. Its theme appeared, appropriately enough, to be food. Neville was taking this in, when the woman spoke.

'I'm awfully sorry about this. Perhaps I eat slowly. They came and started relaying the table, but I didn't realise...'

'Please, there's no problem, really.'

The woman was, Neville supposed, a little younger than himself. She was just on the interesting side of plainness, with an open smile which suggested a positive outlook on life, and a bright eye confirming as much. He was surprised she was alone. Gustav returned with Neville's drink, and placed a menu on the table in front of him. He was inclined to begin his selection immediately, but the woman seemed keen to make a little conversation.

'You'll like it here; the food is excellent.'

'Good, I hope so. I have a very reliable recommendation.'

She nodded, still smiling slightly.

'I would tell you what I had to eat and recommend that, but I don't wish to influence your choice. In any event, I'm sure it is all wonderful.'

Neville smiled, raising the cold gin to his lips. The woman sipped her coffee then, after looking away, turned back to him.

'I hope you don't mind me saying this, but that is a rather fine suit.'

'Why thank you. Its new actually; the result of another recommendation.'

'Your tailor done you proud, I must say.'

The woman's dress - a vibrant pink, Neville now noticed - was also quite exceptional; and when she stood (having now finished her coffee) he could see the cut of it. The skirt was quite full, and the bodice - which was strapless - decidedly flattering. He rose to allow her to move past him. She offered her hand.

'It's been a pleasure to meet you.'

'Why, the pleasure is all mine,' he replied, a little taken aback.

And then, after a brief hand shake, and a further smile as she reached the door, he was left alone at his table. In a moment, Gustav was back at the table clearing away the coffee cup.

'Perhaps Sir would like to take the seat vacated by Madame. I think you will find it more comfortable. I will return for your order in a few minutes.' And as Neville thanked him, Gustav turned professionally on his heel, and moved away.

FIFTEEN

Neville opened the menu and was confronted by two pages, listing - in a highly stylised script - the dishes on offer. Unable to resist habit, he scanned the pages for looking for prices but found none. There was also no mention of wines, and Gustav had failed to leave him a wine list. Undeterred - and already slightly relaxed by the gin - he decided to press on with his selection.

The left hand page of the menu summarised the Entrees; the right, the main courses. As he scanned for his starter he was immediately impressed by not only the range of dishes available, but their comprehensiveness. He was not in the mood for fish, nor the more traditional starters such as pate or soup - even though these, as described, inspired selection. He expected to find making the final choice difficult, but this proved not to be the case. One dish was undeniable: Salad of Roast Duck, served on a bed of wild rice; dressed with light pepper and gherkin salad finished with a Cherry and Rose glaze. Thus decided, he turned his attention to the second page.

He had always been aware that, in certain circles, there was a kind of etiquette regarding the "construction" of a meal. Starting with duck, for example, would in theory limit the number of dishes available for a main course. Things were not, of course, subject to the "norm" at present (in almost any sense, as far as Neville could see) so he immediately decided to consider all options fair game. In Paris, Neville had seemed to take his food "on the run", as it were, and - to his present chagrin - failed to take any advantage of the city's distinct cuisine. It felt as if he should have been in this situation - sitting in a restaurant, choosing a meal - more recently, but obviously this had not been the case. He bypassed the chicken dishes - despite their temptation - and the fowl, on the basis of his Entree. This left him with meat, fish, or vegetarian.

Neville had dabbled with vegetarianism in the past, but unsuccessfully. For him it felt like something he would have to work at rather than adopt instinctively. For this reason, if none other, he was drawn to either the meat or fish. Logic having taken him this far, he took another sip from his gin, and undertook the final challenge. As before, the task seemed simpler than he imagined possible; and once again the choice was obvious: Fillet of Monkfish pan-baked in fresh cream, dressed with a subtle dill and thyme sauce, and complemented with nuggets of honey-glazed carrots, buttered mange tout, and lightly dusted mustard potatoes. Satisfied, he closed the menu.

'Great choice! "On the money", Bob!'

The voice game from his side, and he turned to find a large, bright blue fish addressing him from the mural.

'Monkfish; great! They do it so well, it's "out of this world".'

The fish had large, bulbous eyes that were slightly out of alignment, giving it a peculiar stare. In addition, the artist - whom, Neville could only assume, would not profess fish to be among his strong points - had given the creature a strange lopsided leer. Neville glanced along the rest of the mural. The style throughout was similar, but this fish a shade exceptional. Gustav returned.

'Sir?'

'Yes. The duck, followed by the monkfish, please.'

'Sir.'

'Is there a wine list?'

'We are proud that we know our wines at this establishment Sir, and it is our policy to provide our customers with precisely the correct wine for each of their courses. That way, you do not have to worry over the selection, and we ensure you get the best. Is that satisfactory, Sir?'

'Sounds fine. Thank you.'

As Gustav removed both the menu and himself, Neville was left impressed with the restaurant's efficiency.

'Really "on the ball", isn't it?' - the fish again - 'taking all the hassle out of it. And he's right, Bob; the wine's exceptional.'

'I'm sure.'

Neville glanced round the room. All the other diners were eating and drinking with an air of satisfaction that suggested there was some truth in what the fish had said. One well-dressed middle-aged lady glanced across from her table, and gave him a slight smile. She looked vaguely familiar.

'And yep, you know your onions!. The duck; wow!'

Neville glanced back at the leery fish, frozen in the mural.

'It's exactly what the woman had; duck and monkfish.'

'Woman?'

'Yes; the broad who was here before you. The one with the pink dress.'

'Really?'

The fish lowered his voice.

'If I'd had been just a few inches further that way Bob, I could have spent the entire meal looking down her cleavage!'

Neville was taken aback. Perhaps that kind of attitude went with the fish's rather lascivious look.

'"You bet your boots", she had a great pair of...'

'Enough, I think, don't you?'

'Sorry, Bob; just "passing the time of day".'

'And don't call me Bob!'

'"Keep your hair on", Bob. "Can't teach an old dog, new tricks", eh?'

Neville returned the leer with a little contempt, but refused to respond to the fish's last remark. In addition to the continual reference to "Bob", he was beginning to be annoyed by the fish's ruthless use of cliché - even where totally inappropriate. He thought about changing his seat, but recollected that at this table there was no truly attractive alternative available. Perhaps they might like to paint out the fish on the wall, if it was in danger of spoiling his meal.

'Hey, Bob; "horses for courses". I can't help being me, can I? How much choice did I get, "hear what I'm saying"? Shoot the artist if you like, but "don't shoot the messenger".'

Neville felt vaguely guilty at being hostile, and his desire to obliterate the fish altogether.

'OK; just be a little quieter, maybe.'

'Quiet, Bob? "Like the grave"!'

A few moments later, Gustav returned with a trolley on which were Neville's Entree and a half bottle of red wine. He laid the plate on the table with a slightly extravagant air.

'Your duck, Sir.'

The food presented looked nothing less than sculpted. Pure slices of duck nestling on their wild rice bed, couched within the pepper and gherkin salad, all on the shoreline of the red cherry dressing. It was - as the fish might have said - "too good to eat".

'White is normal for the Entree,' Gustav said, pouring the wine, 'but as you were having the duck followed by fish, we felt that this red - a light Beaujolais - would best suit. If Sir would care to taste...'

Neville lifted the wine to his lips. It was smooth, and skipped lightly across his palette.

'Very pleasant, thank you.'

Gustav nodded and withdrew. For a short while Neville began to delicately dismantle the food on this plate. The duck was immaculate, and the combination offered with it such a stunning mixture of flavours and textures, that his taste buds were thrown into something of a frenzy.

'A little better than you're used to, Bob? "Home cooking", eh?'

'Yes', Neville looked at the fish, deciding to be a little nicer to him. 'And you were right; the food is truly excellent.'

'The smell gets me every time. Well, the taste can't, can it?! Turns me "green with envy"'. And is if to prove it, the fish flashed from blue to green, and then back again.

Neville sipped the wine. With the remnants of duck and peppers still on his mouth, the Beaujolais tasted better than before.

'"Compliments to the chef", eh Bob?. That's exactly what the Broad said. She called Gustav over and said "Compliments to the chef". People always do.'

'I don't blame them. The food is excellent.'

Gradually the first course disappeared, and it was with some satisfaction that Neville closed the knife and fork on his plate, and poured himself the remainder of the red wine. On cue, Gustav came over to remove the plate.

'That was excellent,' Neville hesitated,' Compliments to the chef.'

'Bob!', the fish said, after Gustav had gone, 'I knew you'd say that! Didn't I say they always say that!'

'Who?'

'Customers. They are always so impressed; that's what they say.'

'Like they say other things?'

'Sorry, Bob?'

'Like "don't shoot the messenger"; like "can't teach an old dog new tricks"; like "horses for courses"?'

The fish was silent for a moment.

'OK; yes, like those things. Those are the sorts of things people say, OK? Don't take the piss out of the way I speak, Bob. How else am I supposed to learn except by listening to others; "leading by example", "hear what I'm saying?" That's all there is: "day in, day out". I listen, I learn. OK? Sure, I'm just some dumb fish, but that's it.'

'OK, sorry.'

'Sorry? Shit, you people, you've all got attitudes; "know what I mean?" That broad wasn't quite as bad as you, but I bet the next guy will be; I can tell Bob, I've seen them all.'

Gustav's arrival with the trolley once again interrupted them. Neville, who had become uncertain as to the direction the conversation with the fish was taking, found himself needing to refocus on food and the principle purpose of the evening. The waiter, having removed the red wine bottle and glass from the table, deposited a chilled bottle of white wine and fresh glass.

'A Chablis, Sir. Quite perfect for the monkfish, I think you will find.' And then, with an even grander flourish than before, he removed the silver dome from Neville's plate to reveal the glory of his main course.

The monkfish sat proudly in the centre of the plate, mange tout radiating outwards. In the segments created by the mange tout, the carrots and potatoes alternated, the whole arrangement encircled by the gentleness of the sauce. Neville simply nodded at Gustav, preferring this time to say nothing. He took a sip of the Chablis before picking up his knife and fork. Deciding where to start was not easy, as the very first invasion he made would disrupt the symmetry of the plate. He chose mange tout, and then everything followed from that. The fish kept a respectable silence for a while as Neville savoured the exquisite meal. It was difficult not to eat at a breakneck pace, and he found himself needing discipline in order to progress at an acceptable speed. The monkfish simply dissolved in his mouth, and each of the accompanying vegetables were cooked to perfection.

Movement across the room attracted his attention as one of the parties stood up to leave. This was the table containing the lady who had smiled briefly earlier on. She was a largish woman, with well tonsured hair; the kind of blue-grey perm so favoured by certain ladies of that generation. She glanced at him again as she moved away, and Neville once again had the sensation that he had seen her somewhere before.

'So it's OK then, the food?'

Neville would have expected that sort of question to come from the Maitre or Gustav, but it was the fish again.

'Superb, of course.'

He expected more from the fish but there was no follow up. He looked at the large blue body, the strange eyes and the leer, and felt vaguely sorry for him.

'What kind of fish are you anyway?'

'Me? That's tough. I've been "kept in the dark" over that one, Bob, so I'm not sure I can say. Does it matter?'

Neville paused, fork paused before his mouth.

'No, I guess it doesn't.'

'No, good. Hey, thanks.'

And Neville was sure that, had he been able to, the fish would have given him a wink of one of his bulbous eyes. He carried on eating - though there was little left now. Another couple entered the room and took up their places at one of the reserved tables, and another waiter - one Neville had not seen before - made an appearance. He checked his watch. It was nearly nine thirty; obviously they closed quite late here.

'So where are you off to next, Bob?'

'Next?'

'I mean, once you're out of here. Tomorrow, when the sun shines; what does the day have in store for you?'

Neville finished the last morsel from his plate and poured the remainder of the Chablis.

'I don't know; I guess I hadn't really thought about it.'

'See if "something turns up", maybe?'

'Maybe.'

Neville thought of Samuel outside in the bus, and wondered if there were plans for tomorrow about which he as yet knew nothing.

'What's on the schedule?'

'Schedule?'

'Yes. You guys always seem to have plans; "things to do, people to see". People always talk about their plans - to each other, to Gustav, to me even.'

Gustav came and recaptured the now empty plate.

'Take that broad who was here before you; she talked to me. She had plans, she said - though from what I could see, there was little left on her list.'

Neville began to wonder about the fish's interest in the previous occupant of his seat. Perhaps there was a little more to it than lechery.

'So where was she off too, then?'

He tried to sound as disinterested as possible, but from the tone of his reply the fish must have realised that he had hooked him.

'She said something about a Cruise; and another trip abroad, I think - though she wasn't sure about the order in which she'd do things. Why?'

'No reason.'

Neville's concentration was now taken again by Gustav, who had reappeared at his table and - having presented him with some coffee - was beginning to relay it. He showed little interest in Neville.

'What are you doing?'

'Laying the table, Sir. For the next customer.'

'But what about dessert?'

'I'm sorry Sir.' Meaning to complain, Neville looked up for the Maitre. Gustav left the table and walked away to the hallway.

'It's always the same, Bob', said the fish, attempting to console him, 'there's never enough time.'

'What?'

Gustav appeared through the door, accompanied by a large, fat man. They approached Neville's table. Gustav bowed, slightly.

'Pardon, Monsieur; but this gentleman has arrived for his booking. I wonder if you would mind if he sat with you for an aperitif while you finish your coffee?'

Neville looked hard at Gustav. Those had been the very words he had used to the woman when he himself had arrived at the table. For a moment he felt a degree of panic, of remarkable uncertainty over what exactly was going on; and then, in an instant, the waters cleared. He looked from Gustav to the new arrival.

'Of course not. I won't be very long. That is, if the gentleman doesn't mind.' He offered a smile to the newcomer, who nodded.

'See what I mean, Bob?' whispered the fish.

'Drink, Sir?', said Gustav to the man.

'Beer, ta.'

Neville smiled to himself. They were all in the same boat; him, the woman, this new chap. He could spill the beans now if he choose; let the big man know what was in store for him - even down to the leery-eyed fish - but that would not be playing the game. Hadn't the woman toyed with the idea of recommending her own choice of meal, but not done so? Had he not chosen it anyway? He looked at the suit the newcomer was wearing. Although he was a very large man, the suit managed to make the best of what was there. In doing so, Neville recognised the handiwork of a certain A. Bossiman. With this, there came a flash of memory, and Neville suddenly knew where he had previously seen the woman's pink dress.

SIXTEEN

Neville spent a short while attempting to establish some kind of rapport between himself and the newcomer. The fat man was, however, ill-disposed to this, boasting a degree of taciturnity which blocked all attempts at redundant social chit-chat. Neville wondered if he was facing another of those who had chosen Option 3; and guessed – perhaps rather unkindly – that if he had, this particular adventurer was surely destined for '3A'. He felt suddenly sorry for the big man because of this, yet things were never certain, and he could well be wrong. Who was to say how things might turn out?

He glanced at the fish. Judging by first appearances (which he knew to be an unwise move) he felt certain that the fish's words regarding the "next guy's attitude" were likely to be correct. As he left the restaurant, he wondered how 'new' the man was to the particular game they were both engaged in. How would he react to the fish, or at ten thirty, when the next customer would presumably arrive at Gustav's elbow and be invited to share the table for a short while? For his own part, Neville had tried to vary the remainder of the script a little, perhaps to put a little of his own personality on the game, perhaps in an attempt to make what was to follow a little easier for the large man. Perhaps? For all he knew, the woman - in that pink ball gown from Mister Bossiman's - might have been doing exactly the same thing to him.

Samuel was sitting on his bed reading when Neville boarded the bus. The lighting had been changed too, Neville now realised, and was a degree more practical and satisfying. Samuel looked up, then placed his book - still open - face down on the bedside cabinet.

'How was your meal, Sir?'

There was a hopeful tone in his voice, rather than the air of certainty Neville had convinced himself he would find. He wondered how best to respond. He pulled off his tie as he thought of a reply.

'The food was excellent, of course.'

'Good; I was confident it would be. Perhaps you would like a little night-cap before retiring, Sir. I have a little brandy in the galley.'

'That would be good - and please have one yourself, Samuel.'

Samuel smiled.

'Thank you Sir, I think I might.'

By the time Samuel returned with the two glasses of brandy, Neville was sitting on his bed in his dressing gown. The suit hung over the door of the cupboard, and Samuel's first move was towards this.

'Samuel, please sit down.'

'I thought I might put this away first, Sir.'

'It can wait; please.'

Samuel responded by depositing himself in the driver's seat which he swivelled round to face down the bus. He read Neville's surprise.

'Oh, just another little modification I made while you were out, Sir.'

'You are a very ingenious man, Samuel.'

'Thank you, Sir. I like to think I can turn my hand to most things.'

'I hope you are not also ingenuous.'

'Sir?'

Neville sipped his brandy, and felt its warmth contrast to the chilled Chablis he had so recently sampled. He was uncertain how to progress this conversation. There were many questions he wanted to ask; things that needed clearing up. He had his own theory about certain things too, and was looking for some form of confirmation. As he looked at Samuel, he wondered just how much the latter was in control - or knew, come to that. And how much he was still master of his own destiny.

'Samuel, I have a feeling that this evening I met two other people who are in the same situation as myself.'

'"Situation", Sir?'

'People who have chosen Option 3. You see?'

'Indeed.'

'And...'

'And?' Samuel offered a slight frown, suggesting clarification was needed.

'Is that possible?'

Samuel paused. His eyes remain fixed on Neville's as he too sipped his brandy. The image Neville had relating Samuel to his Grandfather was back again and, because of this, he felt no sense of danger or conflict in the conversation to come. Neville pulled his legs up onto the bed, and crossed them beneath him.

'Yes, it is possible. There are, of course, many people who may - at one time or another - find themselves in a similar situation to yourself. I think you might be surprised to find that it is remarkably common.'

'And do you know them all?'

'Know them, Sir? No. Some perhaps, over time; but how can I know them all when I am with you?'

'OK; what about the restaurant then? How come there were at least three of us in there this evening, sitting at the same table, eating the same food?'

'You are certain of that?'

'Yes.'

Samuel tipped his glass, and took a little more of the Brandy. He looked hard at Neville.

'What if I told you that I was not aware of that being the case? Would you suspect me of not telling the truth?'

'If you were in my shoes...?'

'Yes,' Samuel smiled, 'point taken.'

Neville finished his glass and placed it on the cupboard. Almost before his hand had left it, ruby brown liquid had filled it again. He looked at Samuel.

'Mere trickery; it is not important. Really.'

Neville nodded, prepared to let it go.

'The restaurant,' he pursued, 'you use it a lot, I assume.'

'Yes,' Samuel nodded.

'Because of the fish?'

'The fish? Well, I hear that the fish is good there - but then the whole menu is supposed to be excellent.'

'Samuel, that's not what I meant. And you probably know it!'

'I'm not sure I follow, Sir. If our clients decided - as you did - that they want to experience a high quality meal, then this is one of the restaurants we can choose to suggest to them. That is all.'

'So it has nothing to do with what happened to me inside?'

'What happens to you inside is - to be blunt - entirely of your own making. What happened to you in Paris was entirely your own doing.'

'OK, let's forget Paris for a moment. In there,' Neville nodded his head backwards to indicate the restaurant, 'I met - Bob. Bob told me that the lady who had been sitting at my table before me - and who I met - had ordered exactly the same food as me, was planning to do exactly the same sorts of things I was planning to do...There's too much coincidence.'

'I see.' Samuel paused. Outside all was quiet, the silence only broken by their conversation. '"Bob" told you this, did he? And did you believe him? Was he telling you the truth; about something that actually happened?'

Neville could not answer.

'You assume so, yes? But you cannot know, Sir. Perhaps you wanted Bob to tell you these things.'

'So what about her dress?'

'Her dress? Whose dress?'

'The lady at my table. Her dress - it was a flamingo pink ball gown; I saw the same dress at Mister Bossiman's.'

'Are you sure?'

'Positive.'

'It is true that, like the restaurant, we make full use of Mister Bossiman's services; but I think you may be overlooking one thing?'

'Yes?'

'Mister Bossiman is a gentleman's tailor. He has nothing to do with ladies' garments.'

Neville wanted to tell Samuel about the dance he had witnessed at the small tailors; about the dress, the band. But he realised quickly enough that he might suddenly be on uncertain ground. If Samuel was right - and why should he not be? - and everything that happened to him was actually in his control, then why should Samuel know about these things? What influence could he have over them? He thought back to Paris, and to Pierre. He had assumed that Pierre was something out of his control - something with a degree of power over him. If Samuel was being completely frank with him, then this might not be the case. Pierre might actually have been a manifestation of some part of himself.

This was difficult. Neville took a large swig from his brandy, and allowed it to burn slowly down the back of his throat. All the while Samuel was looking unswervingly at him.

'I'm not sure I understand, Samuel.'

There was a note in Neville's voice that caused the smile to leave Samuel's face.

'Please don't think that you are - how shall I say it? - going mad, Sir. You are not. Really.' He paused, then with a small note of relief - 'Mrs Morris.'

'Sorry?'

'Mrs Morris. I saw her leave the restaurant while you were there. Do you remember her?'

Neville tried to regroup his thoughts.

'Largish, well-dressed lady. With silvery hair?'

'Indeed. Did you recognise her?'

'Vaguely, yes.'

'She was in the tea shop the day we met.'

'The Conservative Lady.'

'Sorry, Sir?'

'Yes, Samuel, I do remember her.'

'I see her about from time to time. She's a pleasant enough character, don't you think?'

Neville nodded. He was uncertain where he should place Mrs Morris in the general scheme of things. Perhaps it was enough for now that she was there in the restaurant, and that he recognised her. As he sat pondering, he could almost feel then night descending about the bus. Samuel, for the first time in a while, took his eyes from Neville and concentrated on finishing his drink. There was a sense of an averted crisis in the air; that the reality of Mrs Morris, both in Samuel's world and his own, had anchored him somehow.

'As a matter of interest, Sir, have you consulted your watch lately?'

Neville looked to his wrist, but the watch had already been put away in the cupboard.

'No, I haven't to be honest.'

'And did you while you were in Paris?'

'I can only recall looking at it once I was back on the bus; why?'

'Do you not think it strange, Sir, that given your reasoning that your original situation arose because of money, you should be so unconcerned with how you are spending it now?'

'But you said that it had nothing to do with value, and was all about worth.'

'Indeed; but you still have a finite stock with which to play. And yet you seem unconcerned about it.'

'Is that wrong?'

Samuel smiled again.

'No, Sir; I am not saying it is wrong, I am just trying to understand your apparently more relaxed attitude.'

'Perhaps it doesn't seem so important any more. Perhaps there are other things that matter.'

Samuel's smile broadened.

'Maybe, I was wrong…'

'That it's not money that is the problem - and never was?' Samuel followed up.

'That perhaps it got in the way. Or the lack of it got in the way. Maybe that wasn't the case after all.'

He wanted to go to his cupboard and check his watch now. He wondered about the worth of his dinner, or of the brandy they were drinking now - or even the "worth" of this present conversation with Samuel. He guessed it might be expensive. A thought crossed his mind.

'If I am right, Samuel...'

'Sir?'

'Do the rules change? Does money become irrelevant?'

Samuel shook his head.

'I'm afraid not, Sir. The rules cannot change. You made your bargain with Hans, and that is the bargain you must adhere to. Your search - for whatever it is you are looking, or whatever it is you need - has already been underway for a little while. Perhaps only now are you beginning to realise just how things stand. Or how you stand. But, you have defined your limit; you cannot dishonour that.'

'Cannot?'

'Cannot.'

Finishing the remnants of his brandy, Neville nodded slowly. He was now quite tired - and, to be truthful, a little drunk. Their conversation had given him much to think about. It was like throwing away the rules of a game and being given a new set for the same game, despite what Samuel said. Perhaps he had a new goal to consider. Perhaps he had never had a real goal at all. As he slipped out of his dressing gown and into the bed, he wondered how much clearer things would be in the morning.

SEVENTEEN

He was eventually roused by Samuel's cheery 'Good Morning!' and the aroma of the cup of tea that simultaneously landed on the cupboard by his bedside. It seemed one of those unfair awakenings; being disturbed before one was well and truly ready. He had managed to get some sleep, though at what stage in the night it would have been impossible to say. All Neville knew was roughly the time he went to bed, and that it was now a little after seven.

Having checked his watch, he replaced it on the cupboard by the tea.

'Isn't this a little early, Samuel?'

His words felt blurred as he spoke them, crawling tired from him, as if they too were exhausted by a lack of sleep.

'Early, Sir? I don't think so. I suspect we might need to make an early start today.'

It was a comment which Neville failed to register. Unwittingly, he found himself returning to the cause of his disturbed night, trying to understand recent events; but he could only come up with things that seemed dream-like in themselves: "Mirelle" turning into a seagull; 'Bob', the talking fish.

'Don't let your tea get cold, Sir.'

Neville watched Samuel disappear round the edge of the curtain, and reflected on how his Mother had, for countless years, contrived to use exactly those same words at least once a day. And if you substituted 'dinner', say, for 'tea', then he had heard it more often than that. Just now, however, it seemed a reasonable command to take seriously. It forced him to sit up a little - to 'shake himself', as Bob might have offered - and think about the day ahead.

The first few sips of tea (which was actually **very** hot, anyway) somehow placed a frame around the night, parcelling it up, and allowing Neville to file it away. It was something that was over, there was nothing residual left; it was time to move on. Of course, as he half-lay there, he contemplated the inside of the bus - a mobile home which was becoming more like a home and less like anything mobile by the day!

Neville drained the tea and climbed out of bed. Pulling on his dressing gown, he made his way through the curtains and towards the smell of bacon that was, under Samuel's command, cooking on the galley stove.

'How are we this morning, Sir?' Samuel said, as Neville reached him.

'Fine, Samuel. A little tired, but fine.'

'I have taken the liberty of running your bath.'

'Thanks.'

Neville deposited the tea cup on the small sink unit, and went through into the bathroom. The bath awaited him, but this time there was no duck floating on the surface. Neville looked for it briefly, but it was not in evidence. As he slid into the water, he wondered if it might not have been quite pleasant to have spoken to it again - but then its absence perhaps suggested that it had served its purpose.

As it was, Neville emerged a few minutes later after an undisturbed and relaxing bath. Samuel was still at the stove, though now tending sausages. The bacon had disappeared, though its smell lingered.

'Everything all right, Sir?'

'Fine, Samuel; thank you.'

'I've put your clothes out, Sir; on the bed.'

Neville nodded and walked through to his small compartment.

As Samuel had promised, Neville's attire for the day awaited him: slacks, a polo shirt and light cardigan. He pulled back the curtain at the window and looked out. It seemed a little too grim outside for such light clothes, but then presumably Samuel knew what he was doing - or, indeed, what they both would be doing.

At the foot of the bed, Neville noticed the suit trousers he had worn the night before still lying there, awaiting return to the small wardrobe. He was surprised to find them, partly because he thought he could recall some form of discussion from the previous evening about putting them away, and partly because, given Samuel's faultless efficiency, it seemed something of an anathema to find them still out.

He thought about calling to Samuel, but decided that it would be simplest to just put the trousers away himself. As he lifted them from the bed, a small rectangle of white paper fell from one of the pockets to his feet. Neville, with the trousers rested over one arm, bent to pick it up. In the moments between bending and standing upright again - just about to open the folded paper - he tried to imagine what it might be: a receipt for the meal, or the bill? Had the fat man given him something? He could recall nothing.

The paper, which was of reasonable quality vellum, was folded accurately into quarters and opened easily. Neville could tell by the pristine state of the paper, that it had been folded once - firmly and with conviction - and no more; there had been no unfolding to reconsider its content. It was headed with the crest of the restaurant, but its contents were formed in free-flowing freehand. About half-way down, Neville read:

I hope you enjoyed the Duck and the Monkfish -

they were really very good, weren't they?!

I wonder if your evening turned out anything like mine;

something of a "sting in the tail"...?

I am going on a cruise - but perhaps you know

that already! S.S.Pilgrim; leaving Southampton tomorrow.

Perhaps we might meet again one day...

M.

The note could only have had one author. Neville, rather than digest its content, was instinctively interested to know how the note might have found its way into his trouser pocket. The woman - "M" - must have written the note on her way out; on that basis, at some stage did Gustav slip it into Neville's trouser pocket? Or perhaps it had been the fat man? Neville could not reconciled himself to the latter option; at least Gustav would have had the chance - and the "agility" - to perform the required operation.

He turned his thoughts to the content after a moment. They threw an interesting light on the discussions he had had with Samuel the previous evening. "M" was obviously "in the same boat" as he, and their shared experience - even down to Bob (surely "sting in the tail" was a reference?!) - patently real enough. He raised the note a little higher, as if doing so would confirm its authenticity, and prepared to call Samuel.

In the instant between raising his hand and opening his vocal chords, Neville's reaction to the note shifted from the intellectual to the emotional. Questions savaged him from all sides: why was this woman, "M", telling him where she was going? What did she mean by "perhaps we might meet again"? Was she really part of his plot, or had they somehow become entangled? And even (he was ashamed to acknowledge) was "Bob" right, and did she really have a great pair of tits?

'Samuel!'

The curtain drew back and Samuel, holding a tray containing Neville's cooked breakfast, stood before him.

'Sir?'

'Southampton, Samuel. We're taking that cruise of mine.'

'Very good, Sir. Would you like me to keep your breakfast hot for you while you dress, or will you eat it now?'

'I'll be dressed in a minute; you can leave it with me.'

Samuel put the plate by the side of the bed.

'Shall I get us underway, Sir - if you'll pardon the nautical turn of phrase.'

'Please.'

'Can I enquire the name of the ship?'

'The S.S.Pilgrim; why?'

'Just so I know where to go when we get to the docks, Sir. That's all.'

'Presumably you know where she's sailing to Samuel?'

'I believe it's the Mediterranean, Sir.'

Neville looked at the clothes laid out for him on the bed.

'And presumably, you knew we were bound to be going there?'

Samuel smiled.

'I'll get us moving, Sir; I don't think we've too much time to spare.'

EIGHTEEN

When Neville made his way to his customary seat a few minutes later, the bus was in motion. He put the plate containing his bacon, sausages and eggs down on the small table and looked along the road. They were already in the country, presumably south of Birmingham, though as he already knew, it was difficult to tell exactly where the bus might be at any one time. Samuel acknowledged his arrival with the merest glance, then returned his attention to the road ahead. Neville fell to his breakfast.

He believed he had managed to instil a degree of urgency into Samuel a few moments before: indeed, he suspected as much from Samuel's apparent willingness to get the bus immediately underway. Despite this, however, their progress was limited to the apparently mandatory twenty seven miles per hour, and as they meandered through the countryside with what appeared to be limited progress, Neville felt inclined to ask Samuel if he couldn't possibly manage to go a little faster.

History - thus far, at any rate - suggested that Samuel's judgement in terms of timing was impeccable, and Neville had no real cause to doubt the fact that they would arrive at Southampton in plenty of time to board the boat. He speared the remains of his last sausage and raised the fork to his mouth.

'I take it you have made a reservation for the voyage, Sir?'

'Reservation? I thought you took care of that sort of thing Samuel. There don't seem to have been any problems in the past.'

The sausage segment became suspended three inches from Neville's mouth.

'When I can. But you seem to have taken this decision rather suddenly.'

'You're telling me you didn't know where we were going?'

'Of course not, Sir. How could I?'

'But the clothes you laid out seemed so suitable. And your attitude. You weren't at all surprised.'

Samuel glanced round. In the brief pause, Neville pulled the sausage from the fork with his teeth.

'I like to think that I am prepared for anything, Sir.' Samuel took a breath, allowing for any potential contradiction. 'The clothes? You had talked about a cruise. Perhaps I made a lucky guess.'

'Perhaps.' Neville was doubtful. 'Does that mean the cruise is off?'

'Oh, not at all, Sir. If we can make a quick stop, perhaps I might be able to phone ahead.'

This seemed a strange departure from the ritual as Neville had experienced it thus far. Samuel seemed perfectly genuine in his manner, yet something about the situation ran contrary to the general pattern of the adventure. Neville - whose desire to make the boat had been steadily growing since the idea first struck him - was powerless to do anything except concur.

Five minutes later the bus was stationery, and Neville was watching through his window as Samuel rang Southampton docks from a roadside telephone kiosk. There was little spectacle in this, Samuel remaining motionless and non-expressive for the duration of the call apart from a slight inclination of the head at one point, and a more definite nod immediately before he put the phone down.

'All booked, Sir.' Samuel announced on his return. 'The S.S.Pilgrim sails on this afternoon's tide, which doesn't leave us too much time - but I'm sure we'll make it.'

The last remark was offered with one of his knowing winks which meant that, when they set off at their snail's pace again, questioning their progress was the last thing on Neville's mind.

Slowly they rolled through the countryside; the roads were quiet, and, apart from the occasional flock of sheep or herd of cattle, the scenery appeared quite lifeless too. Samuel had retrieved an atlas of the world from somewhere, and had presented it to Neville with the suggestion that he might like to study the islands of the Mediterranean in order to familiarise himself with them prior to their arrival.

'"Our" arrival?', Neville had echoed.

'Yes, Sir. I think it might be wise if I were on hand, don't you?' Samuel had replied – and Neville had recalled Paris, and reflected how valuable Samuel's presence might have been on at least one occasion.

As he took in details of Malta, Corsica and Sardinia, he felt the bus gradually descending downhill. It seemed a hill without a bottom, and without any adverse gradient to counter it. He could hear Samuel in his driver's seat reciting poetry -

I must go down to the seas again,

to the lonely sea and the sky,

And all I ask is a tall ship

and a star to steer her by,

and as he spoke it appeared that the bus was - quite literally - going **down** to the sea, as there, in the distance, the Solent shimmered in the early afternoon sun. There were no tall ships - at least not as John Masefield would have known them - but Neville could make out one or two large vessels and the jibs of the tall cranes working them.

The bus turned a corner and Neville lost sight of the docks. He wondered which of the two ships he had seen was the

S.S.Pilgrim - or if neither, then where on the docks she might be. Samuel would probably know, but Neville was ill disposed to disturb him as they had come as close to "racing against the clock" as they were ever likely to.

When they reached Southampton it suddenly appeared as if the entire mass of humanity has descended on the town. The roads were full of cars, and the pavements packed with people.

'Must be some kind of event, Sir,' Samuel said after they had been stationary in a traffic queue for a few minutes.

'Is there any way out of this, Samuel? How much time do we have?'

'I've been following the signs for the docks, Sir. We'll get there as soon as we can.'

Neville spotted a policeman walking their way; he was chatting with other pedestrians, apparently unconcerned by the congestion. Neville - who was by now on his feet and leaning against Samuel's seat - pointed him out. Samuel lowered his window.

'Excuse me Officer. We're trying to get to the docks, and I'm afraid we're in rather a hurry.'

'Hurry, eh?' The Policeman laughed. 'Well you won't get there through the middle of the town; there's a big "do" on, see? It's where all these people are going.'

Neville, although intrigued to know what kind of do would bring people flooding out in such numbers, had his mind firmly set on making the docks in the shortest possible time.

'Can we go some other way? Not through the centre of the town?'

'Well, Sir; let me see.' And the Policeman paused long enough to effect a professional frown before replying. 'You might try going west, and then back in from that side. I think it should be less busy that way.'

'Thank you, Officer. Now, which way's that?'

'Why, over there.'

And as the Policeman pointed, a gap appeared in the traffic to the right, just where another road branched off. Samuel swung the bus out of the main stream.

'Try a couple of miles or three,' the Policeman shouted after them, 'then head back in!'

As they headed west, cutting across the threads of traffic and people all aiming for the town centre, their progress - though still not rapid - improved. After a couple of miles, Samuel began to look out for signs that suggested "Docks" and, on finding the first one, took the designated route. The Policeman had been correct in his judgement, and, though they were now in a position where Neville would have been glad of twenty seven miles per hour, at least they were making forward progress most of the time.

When the "Docks" signs eventually drew them out of the throng and away downhill once again - and back to twenty seven miles an hour - it had been nearly an hour since they had lost sight of the Solent, the ships and the cranes. Samuel had been silent for virtually all of that time, and even now - with open road again ahead of them - remained quiet. Neville, having returned to his seat, felt a degree of tension in the air, undoubtedly caused by Samuel's unspoken concern that they might actually be late.

The first entrance they came to proclaimed **Dock Gate Twelve**. Neville looked at Samuel.

'Which one do we want, Samuel?'

'Three, Sir.'

The gates seemed impossibly far apart, and although they were no longer hampered by traffic, it was taking an age to get from one gate to the next. When they reached Four, Neville thought he could see a gentle plume of smoke rising from beyond the wharf-side sheds ahead, and wondered if that might be the Pilgrim making ready to get under way.

The S.S.Pilgrim it did indeed prove to be, as they discovered on finally pulling through Dock Gate Three and driving down to the pontoon. However, the ship was not making ready; she was actually sailing away. Perhaps by as little as ten minutes, they had missed the boat. Samuel shut down the bus engine, and the two of them sat in silence watching the S.S.Pilgrim grow ever smaller, churning a white wake with seagulls dancing in the foam. The cawing of the gulls carried back to them, mockingly almost.

'I'm sorry, Sir.' Samuel broke the silence, though without taking his eyes off the ship. 'I don't know how this happened. I don't think I have ever been late before.'

Neville wondered about the Eiffel Tower, but admonishment never occurred to him.

'You couldn't have known about the traffic or the crowds, Samuel. Otherwise we would have made it.'

Samuel choose not to reply. Again they both stared after the boat. The dockside was deserted apart from them.

'I guess that's it then,' was all Neville could offer, as he struggled with the disappointment of not making the boat, of not taking the cruise, and - most importantly – of not renewing his acquaintance with "M", whatever that might have entailed.

Samuel rose from his seat.

'Excuse me, Sir; I won't be a minute,' and with that he was off the bus and out of sight.

For some reason, Neville had a brief image of Captain Oates at the South Pole - "I may be some time" - and wondered, not without some concern, what Samuel had left the bus to do.

The minute Samuel promised actually extended to thirteen, but when he returned - boarding the bus as suddenly as he had left it - the smile on his face immediately suggested that all was not lost.

'We are in luck, Sir!' he said as he started the bus.

'Samuel?'

'The S.S.Pilgrim is making a special stop in the Channel Islands before she heads for Gibraltar. There is an airport just north of the town and I have arranged a plane for us. We can overtake the ship and board her in Guernsey.'

Neville could say nothing. He sat back in his seat as the bus moved away from Gate Three and out into the city again. Would his hopes not be dashed after all? And what should expect to find once he stepped on board the ship?

The bus began the steady incline away from the docks, occasionally offering a view of the sea and the speck the S.S.Pilgrim had now become. Samuel had taken to whistling, evidently relieved that all was not yet lost, and Neville - to take his mind off their renewed chase - had picked up the atlas again, though this time to contemplate the rather complex geography of the Caucasus Mountains.

They left the city behind and, for a few miles, travelled once again through open country. The aerodrome - signified by its tower, radar and windsock - came upon them as suddenly as the docks had gradually: one minute they weren't there, the next they were. Samuel steered the bus through the main gate, passed the car park, and out onto the fringe of the runway. As they descended the bus, Neville looked for the plane that would speed them to the Channel Islands and his longed-for rendezvous. Expecting a small jet or some such, the only plane he could see was an old World War One bi-plane which, he assumed, could not be theirs.

From the building which seemed to house the hangars and the administration section as well as the control tower, a figure emerged and began walking towards them. As the man drew closer, Neville, in recognising the portent of his leather helmet, handlebar moustache, white scarf, and flying jodhpurs, could only put two and two together. He looked back at the old bi-plane. Could that get them to Guernsey in time?

The pilot and Samuel were in conversation when Neville turned to them again. The pilot smiled and walked towards him, offering his hand.

'"Binky" Bingham's the name!' he boomed in a B-movie accent. 'Hear you chaps want a quick recce over the water, what?'

Neville smiled as he took Binky's hand, then winced politely under the pressure of the cast-iron grip.

'Have you over there in a jiffy!' Binky continued, 'No Huns about today, what?' And with that, he marched off to the plane.

Neville looked at Samuel. He refrained from articulating the questions - and the fears - that were bouncing around in his brain. Samuel's silent nod of understanding and meek smile of agreement was sufficient. They followed Binky to the plane, where, after the appropriate degree of "Boy's Own" bonhomie, they were installed in the two passenger seats. Ahead of them, Binky planted himself firmly in the pilot's seat and, pulling his goggles down, bawled "Chocks away!" to no-one in particular.

The bi-plane's archaic engine spluttered into life and, with a cavalier wave from their pilot, they began to bump roughly across the apron to the end of the runway. As they paused for the engine to work up the appropriate enthusiasm, Neville noticed another hanger near the tower outside of which numerous modern aircraft sat idle. He tapped Samuel (who was sitting in front of him) on the shoulder, ready to suggest they abort Binky for something a little more modern, when the bi-plane suddenly lurched forwards.

In pulses - rather than smoothly - they accelerated along the runway. Binky appeared to have several goes at yanking the joystick back to lift the plane into the air, but each of these met with failure. Indeed, they came within a few yards of the end of the runway - and Neville contemplating the failure of his quest in some "total" sense - when the plane's wheels hit a large bump (almost, he would reflect later, like a Sleeping Policeman) which threw the craft from the tarmac and up into the air.

For a few seconds, the plane seemed suspended, uncertain as if it would manage the rest itself; but then, roaring like a wounded lion, the single engine pulled them upwards and towards the heavens.

NINETEEN

After the initial scare, the flight began to feel a little more like a conventional excursion. They ascended to something in the order of a thousand feet, at which point the engine seemed to give up its quest for more power and insisted on levelling off. As far as Neville could tell, Binky had managed nothing as yet which suggested he had any control over their fate. Neville wanted to talk to Samuel about the arrangements for their immediate future, but was forced to abort any such plans when his first and only attempt was completely thwarted by the noise of the engine. Powerless to do anything but sit there and wait, he decided to make the most of the flight.

The plane banked over Southampton Water - though whether this was due to Binky was still impossible to say - and began to follow the Hampshire coastline west. Neville felt reassured that, for the first time since he had met Samuel, they were travelling between two relatively distant points by a means which allowed him to verify the nature of their progress. Although they were not flying particularly high, Neville soon began to feel cold as the wind rushed through his unprotected hair. Binky, at one stage, turned and gave them a "gung ho!" kind of wave, apparently oblivious to the conditions his passengers were facing. Samuel had, very soon after take-off, rummaged around in the cockpit in front of him and managed to retrieve a leather flying jacket and hat, both similar to Binky's. Within minutes, Neville found it impossible to tell the two of them apart from the rear view he had of both.

Despite Samuel leading the way, it was few minutes later - and a fair distance along the coast - before Neville decided that it might also be worth his while to see if there might be suitable clothing secreted somewhere for him. A few seconds searching around rewarded him with a rather tatty white scarf which, despite its somewhat careworn appearance, was soon adorning Neville's neck. He tried to tie it in the appropriate manner, but suspected that all he managed was a clumsy kind of knot. In any event, it was a little warmer, though still insufficient for his present needs. As he looked about, craning his neck to examine every reachable space, he discovered a small lever on the side of his seat which, when depressed, allowed him to rotate a complete 180 degrees. In doing so, he was rewarded by two things: first was the welcome sight of a sheepskin jacket in a recess by his feet; second was the realisation that the plane boasted a primitive anti-aircraft gun mounted on the fuselage just behind his seat. He pulled on the coat, wondering as he did so, how he had managed to miss the gun originally; presumably it had been the excitement - or the fear.

Warmer now, Neville looked out in a more contented frame of mind. They had progressed along the Devon coast, and ahead lay the expanse of the western end of the English Channel. It was a bright, clear day; on the horizon, Neville thought he could make out their destination. If that were the case, then surely at some stage they might also fly over the S.S.Pilgrim. He turned to the east, scanning the surface of the water, attempting to make out the cruise ship from the various other craft plying their respective trades. Tankers were easy to spot because of their bulk; yachts easy to miss because of their lack of it. The S.S.Pilgrim should, from what he could remember, reveal herself as something between the two.

He had just caught sight of a ship that met his initial requirements - right sort of size and steaming in the right direction - when his view changed instantly, and Neville found himself looking at nothing but water. Worse than that, it was water that seemed to be getting closer, and rather quickly. He looked up to find that they were in something of a steep dive. Ahead, Binky's scarf flew stiffly behind him as they sped downwards. Neville was about to tap Samuel on the shoulder when a sudden jerk from the pilot resulted in them being thrown back in their seats; all he could see now was the blue of the sky.

If the engine had roared on take-off, its complaint now was less feline and more like that of a dinosaur. Up and up it pulled them - certainly higher than before - until it they began to lose momentum. At the last minute, just as they were about to stop dead still it seemed, the plane banked and began to swoop away to the right.

Neville - who by this time had not only lost all sense of direction, but was beginning to wonder if he might not lose his breakfast too - doubted that such an extreme exhibition was part of the normal in-flight entertainment; though with Binky at the controls, anything might be possible. Indeed, he was beginning to search for other reasons for their present course when a second roar greeted his semi-deafened ears and the shape of another bi-plane appeared suddenly ahead of them, crossing their path.

Although they were not travelling particularly fast, the two planes seemed to cross in a split second, and Neville had to rotate in his chair to follow the progress of the newcomer. His tracking of this second red plane revealed the presence of a third; the latter now bearing down on them from behind and slightly above. He could not be exactly certain what first confirmed it - perhaps it was the fact that these new planes were bright red; perhaps it was their markings; or perhaps it was the flashes from the forward-mounted machine gun - but Neville knew they were in trouble.

He felt Binky begin to steer the plane into a dive again, and as they began to drop, Samuel tapped him on the shoulder.

'What!' Neville shouted, convinced Samuel could not hear him.

'The gun!'

Samuel must have made a superhuman effort to get himself heard above the din Neville decided, but hear him he did. He turned back to the gun and took its butt in his hands. It was heavy and cumbersome, and at first Neville could do little but wave it round.

As they dived, the second red plane buzzed above them. Neville could see the first turning their way, preparing to attack again. No way was this a simple drama. Remembering to aim away from the rudder, Neville tried to fire off a couple of trial shots. He pulled the trigger and nothing happened.

'Safety catch!' Came Samuel's voice again.

Glancing along the gun, Neville found a small lever that appeared might do the trick. He flicked it and tried again. The gun kicked into life, the recoil far stronger than he expected (despite its mounting), and he simply sprayed the rounds in a broad arc. This would be more difficult than he had anticipated.

As the first of the intruders swooped towards them, Neville took careful aim and fired. After a short burst, the gun ended up pointing at least twenty degrees away from the target, Neville just able to make out the fading traces of his initial attempt falling tamely away. The red plane opened fire. Neville could not see the traces of the bullets as they came towards him, yet, although he had nothing to back this up, he sensed their adversary's shooting was a little better than his own.

The planes crossed again as Binky slipped into a slight dive, then pulled up and away to the right. Considering its age, the bi-plane was performing remarkably well, and Neville was beginning to re-evaluate his opinion of Binky as an "Ace". Samuel was once again silent, watching helplessly as the drama unfolded either side of him. Neville hoped that a little instruction might come his way, but there was nothing further.

In the distance - it seemed miles away - the two red planes came briefly together then began another attack. They were faster than Binky's old crate and, it would appear, could out-manoeuvre them too. Neville flexed his hands and prepared to pick up the cudgels again. He had learnt much from his first attempt and had decided that it would undoubtedly be best not to aim directly at his target but away from it, allowing the gun's natural travel to strafe the plane's path.

From either side the red planes began their swoop. Closing in, it appeared that they would cross on completion of their attack, peel away, and come in for another run. Neville licked his lips. Fire spat from the oncoming bandits before Neville opened up - "don't fire until you see the whites of their eyes!". He aimed well to the right of the plane attacking from that side and pulled hard on the trigger. The gun swung violently around, spraying a wide array of bullets which, in his enthusiasm, peppered their own tail before coming to a glorious end by hitting the plane on their left-hand side - the one Neville had **not** been aiming at.

There was a slight puff of black smoke, a cough, and then the sight of the stricken plane beginning to fall out of the sky like a wounded bird. Neville's exhilaration was immediate and intense; he had just about enough time to imagine Samuel reciting some war poem or other, when he realised that they too were beginning to lose height. He looked about; he could see no sign of smoke. Turning to face the front of the plane once again, he failed to see the cause of their present predicament immediately - though the fact that they were in trouble was evidenced by the increasing rapidity with which they were losing height, and the slight spin that they also seemed to be taking on.

Past Samuel's shoulder, Neville noticed Binky slumped forwards. He thumped Samuel on the shoulder, and pointed ahead. He could see nothing of Samuel's face, nor hear any reply that might have been forthcoming; but what he did see was Samuel raise the thumb of his left hand. Was this reassurance or understanding? And did he have a parachute?

As his mind raced to find some kind of solution, he felt the spin steady then stop. Then he felt the plane's descent to ease. He craned his neck in an attempt to see round Samuel's body. His bus driver was now proving that he was something of a pilot too - or was it all the same thing? A second set of controls adorned the portion of the cockpit where Samuel sat, and, for a while at least, things were back under control.

Samuel's other hand jerked out over the side of the plane and upwards. There, above them, the second red devil was beginning another run. Neville swung back into his firing position and prepared himself. There was a flash, then another. He heard a strange "whing" then saw - in slow motion almost - a small hole appear in the body of the plane just by his left leg. Driven on by anger, Neville pulled the gun round and opened fire. This time it remained steady and his aim unswerving.

A puff; the tell-tale smoke; and then the beginnings of a spin. The pilot leapt from his cockpit to leave the dying craft to its own demise. Again Neville's burst of joy was short-lived as the red plane began to hurtle towards them. He spun round and thumped Samuel on the back of the head. Samuel looked round, and Neville closed his eyes.

The asthmatic cough of the dying engine was the next thing of which Neville was aware, then the rush of the red plane as it passed as they themselves fell from the sky in the opposite direction. He opened his eyes to see the second plane spinning harmlessly away like a broken toy. The two parachutes of the defeated pilots appeared as solitary flowers in a sea-green flower bed, and there, just where he would have expected it to be, the outline of the S.S.Pilgrim - oblivious of the drama being played out in the skies above it no doubt - making its way towards Guernsey.

Samuel levelled the plane and banked to head in the same direction as the liner. After a few minutes flying, the island presented itself as a welcome haven. It seemed ridiculously small, and the runway - when Neville eventually made it out - an impossibility. They circled twice before there was suddenly silence.

From ahead, Samuel shouted one word - "Fuel!" - and, as if on command, they began to lose height.

As the ground gained on them - Neville now able to make out individual houses and fields, the old fortifications and the new hotels - he closed his eyes once again. It was not lack of faith that prompted such an action, but cowardice. It seemed an age for nothing to happen. And then there was a bump. And then another. And then, in the silence, the sound of squeaking wheels on less than smooth tarmac. Neville opened his eyes; they were down.

Their arrival was greeted by a small crowd of airport staff who, to their credit, behaved as if having a slightly wounded bi-plane landing on their runway without fuel was an everyday occurrence. Once they had come to a complete halt, Neville sat motionless and silent. Samuel, flicking a lever on his own seat, turned to face him.

'Sir? Are you all right?'

Neville looked into Samuel's concerned face.

'Thank you, Samuel.'

At the front of the plane, a moan escaped from Binky.

'I didn't know you could fly.'

'I learned in the war, Sir.'

Again a moan from Binky.

'I didn't know you could shoot, Sir.'

Neville laughed.

'I can't!'

'Tally Bloody Ho!'

Binky was now standing on his seat, waving his arms and sending his scarf into spasms. Unsteadily he turned to face his two charges.

'Bloody good show! Bloody good...'

But the rest of his words were interrupted by him losing balance and falling out of the plane completely. Three airport hands prepared to scrape him from the runway.

'Is he OK?'

'Probably just a scratch, Sir. Couldn't stand all the excitement.'

Neville caught Samuel's smile.

'He wasn't the only one!'

TWENTY

There were no formalities at the airport. Neville and Samuel simply walked away from the plane and towards the waiting taxi in which Binky was already installed. Samuel had divested himself of his flying gear, returning it to its place of origin before leaving the plane, and now appeared his normal self again. As Neville watched him walk towards the car, he realised that he had forgotten that his companion was, essentially, an old man; how old it was difficult to say, but his reference to "the war" was intriguing.

Binky was sitting on the back seat of the cab, nursing a shoulder wound.

'Hah! We showed those rotten blighters, didn't we boys! Blasted the bounders from the sky!'

Neville caught the scent of medicinal brandy on Binky's breath.

'Are you all right?'

'Me? Never better, old boy! Just a spot of shrapnel in the shoulder, you know. Always gets me there. Fainted clean away! Thank God for the skipper, what!'

Binky turned to thump a congratulatory pat on Samuel's shoulder, but as he did so, the pain from his wound sent him swooning in a heap to the floor of the car. Neville bent forwards.

'I'd leave him Sir, if I were you. He's probably better resting there.'

As they pulled away, Neville wondered how close Binky's "resting" had been to some permanent heavenly abode - and how long it would be before he was plundering the skies again in his ancient machine. He looked out of the back of the cab to see the old bi-plane being pulled from the runway to a waiting hanger. Presumably it would sit there until Binky had recovered sufficiently to fly it home.

'The hospital; then the docks, please.' Samuel gave the instruction to the driver, then turned to Neville. 'Are you OK, Sir? Would you like to take that jacket off?'

Neville remembered he was still wearing the sheepskin from the plane.

'I'd like to keep it - just for a while, if that's OK.'

'Still cold?'

'The shivers. That's all.'

It was a half-lie, but sufficient to allow him to extend the lease on the garment. He was uncertain as to his exact feelings at that precise moment. There was, he suspected, still a degree of shock to emerge as a result of the flight, and he was unsure how that might manifest itself. It was certainly warmer on the ground than it had been in the air, but Neville was taking no chances.

Half-way to the hospital, Binky roused himself with a cry of "Blighters never fight fair!" followed by half a chorus of "There'll always be an England" before passing out again. Samuel pushed a cushion he had found under the pilot's head.

'Has that happened to you before, Samuel?'

'What, Sir?'

'That; the dog fight.'

'Why do you ask?'

'I don't know; you seemed quite "natural" as a pilot. And you said something about the war.'

Samuel smiled.

'Yes, I did.' He paused. 'Let us say that I have flown an aeroplane on more than one occasion - and something not dissimilar to that we flew in today.' He paused again. 'But you, Sir; you have a fine eye, if I might say so!'

Neville, buoyed by Samuel's praise, lost his line of thought.

'I was just lucky, that's all.'

'Nonsense Sir. The way you took out that second chap; most impressive. Most impressive.'

'Well, perhaps I had got the hang of it by then.'

The conversation trailed, and the journey was soon broken by their arrival at the hospital. Three porters were waiting to haul Binky from the floor of the cab and onto a waiting trolley. His cry of "Give my love to Blighty!" was the last they heard as he disappeared through the swing doors of the casualty unit.

'A fine spirit,' Samuel said quietly.

With Binky taken care of, they were off again, the taxi rolling sedately through the narrow streets of St. Peter Port. Neville had lost track of time - was it Thursday or Sunday? he had no idea - and was consequently uncertain whether or not to be surprised by the relatively small number of people out and about.

The volume increased a little as they came to the waterfront. In the marinas, dozens of boats bobbed hopefully in the water, criss-crossing their masts in animated - if silent - conversations; their owners holding forth about the state of the tides or the winds, whilst knotting ropes or sipping pink gins on deck. Further out along the quay, a large and impressive vessel was moored; the S.S.Pilgrim.

As they approached the ship, Neville could see a few people walking the various decks and hanging over the railings looking back into St. Peter Port. He tried to remember "M", but could only manage a fleeting image in pink; certainly not enough to be sufficient to locate her among those he could see now.

A couple of taxis pulled away as they drew up. There was a single walkway raised to the deck, and this was covered with a white cloth awning that flexed tautly in the breeze. Neville expected this to bear the name of the ship, but it bore the name of the port instead. At its base, a young dock hand in slightly grubby overalls stood, hands in pockets, evidently bored. He looked up at their approach, and seeing them get out of the taxi, walked over.

'You the two daft gits who missed the boat in Southampton, then?'

It was not the sort of greeting Neville would have expected. The Channel Islands had a certain reputation, a certain image in his mind; this man did not match that.

'We did miss the boat in Southampton, yes.' It was Samuel who replied.

The young man looked after the retreating taxi.

'No bags?'

'I believe everything has been taken care of. May we board?'

He shrugged his shoulders.

'Hey, Dad; it's up to you man. I mean, we've only been waiting for you, haven't we?'

Neville sensed Samuel stiffen slightly, ruffled by the abusive treatment they had received. Neville noted the man's last comment which suggested he was actually one of the ship's complement, rather than an islander.

'Come along then, Samuel,' Neville prompted, 'let's get on.' And as they walked past the dock hand, Neville managed to tread - with a deliberate degree of force - on the young man's left foot. 'Sorry; my fault.'

The look Neville received in reply was sufficient to suggest that he might not have seen the last of this particular character.

They passed under the awning, and began to walk up to the ship. At the top, one of the ship's officers was waiting for them; this time the greeting was a sharp salute.

'My name's Porter; I'm the Bursar. Glad to have you on board, Gentlemen. May I show you to your cabins?'

And with that he turned on his heel and began to walk away, safe in the knowledge that Neville and Samuel were bound to follow him. Voices now rose from somewhere else on the ship, and Neville looked back to see the insolent dock hand running onto the ship from the walkway just as a crane began to haul it away. From the jetty, men appeared to be suddenly busy with ropes, and a "whoop, whoop" from the ship's whistle set the seal on the preparations for departure.

As they followed the Bursar along the deck, a number of the passengers leaning on the rail waved towards the shore, but Neville could see no-one to wave back. Perhaps in the town and armed with binoculars, there might be relatives invisibly signalling.

Porter took a sharp turn through an open doorway that revealed a corridor.

'Mind your head, Sir,' said Samuel, indicating the slightly low lintel.

'I'm fine Samuel, thank you.'

A few yards along the corridor they came to a stairway leading upwards. Porter, this time after a brief glance behind and a slight, professional smile, took these stairs to the next deck. At this point they came across another corridor and another set of stairs. Once again Porter ascended.

At the top of the second set of stairs, the Bursar waited for his two new passengers.

'If I can explain,' he said, once they had joined him, 'you arrived on board on deck "C". We have just come through deck "B", and are now on "A" deck; this is where your cabins are.'

He began to walk along the short corridor, a little more slowly this time, talking as he did so.

'You gentlemen were quite lucky with your bookings, as it happens. I understand you arranged passage a little late? Well, we had a couple of cancellations and twenty seven and twenty eight became available.'

They had arrived at two doors, set close together, with numbers on them as Porter had indicated.

'They are adjoining cabins, with a door between them should you require such a facility.'

'Thank you', said Samuel.

'You take twenty seven, Samuel,' Neville suggested, thinking instantly of the bus. 'Is that OK?'

His question was general, and both men nodded their approval.

'Your baggage is here I believe,' the Bursar said. 'I'll let you get settled in, then arrange for Bursar, the Porter, to come and check that everything's "ship shape".'

'"Bursar"?' said Neville.

'Yes?'

'No; sorry, Bursar. I mean the Porter; his name's Bursar?'

The uniformed man smiled.

'Yes; and my name's Porter, and I'm the Bursar! Don't worry; it confuses everybody, especially the Captain!' And with that, the Bursar bowed and left them.

Samuel opened the door to his cabin to reveal a rather spacious interior that looked, for the most part, like a very expensive hotel room. Neville followed him in. The adjoining door to his own room was open and, having had a brief scan round twenty seven, Neville walked into twenty eight. This cabin was identical to Samuel's, with the sole exception of the location of the doors.

His bags were at the foot of the bed. He wondered how they had managed to get here before him; if there had been some other way of getting across the Channel, or if, at the end of the day, it was another of Samuel's "tricks". It seemed unimportant.

'Nice cabins, Samuel.'

'Very nice, Sir. We should be comfortable here, don't you think?'

Neville felt the ship begin to roll slightly underneath him as they got underway.

'Do you want to have a wander round on deck, Samuel? Wave Guernsey goodbye?'

'If you don't mind, Sir, I think I'll just have a rest. A little nap perhaps. I suspect they will be calling us for dinner in a couple of hours or so.'

'Fine. I'll see you a bit later then,' and with that Neville closed the door dividing the rooms.

His first instinct was to go searching for "M", but practicality suggested that it might be wise if he unpacked his bags first and then perhaps freshened up. It was a little after five and, as Samuel had suggested, they had no wish to be late for their first evening meal on board.

The two bags on the bed were familiar to him, though, on opening them, he discovered some items of clothing that were new. Some bright T-shirts, some shorts, and a pair of sandals had obviously been included for the Mediterranean. His suit was there (of course!) and the other items of casual wear he would have expected. There were also two new pairs of shoes: one pair were smart black leather; the second, a kind of blue canvas deck shoe.

As he toyed with the idea of slipping into the naval shoes, there came a knock at the door.

'Yes?'

The door opened to reveal an exceptionally tall man, dressed in a uniform similar to the Bursars. The first thing Neville noticed about this new man, as he bowed low in order to be seen, was the large bandage he wore around the top of his head.

'M-m-m-may I, Sir?'

'Please.'

As the man ducked to enter, he failed to duck low enough and banged his head right about where the bandage was.

'F-f-f-flaming doors,' he muttered. Neville wondered if the bandage were there to tend an old wound or prevent a new one.

'Can I help you?'

'N-n-n-no Sir; c-c-c-can I help you,' the man bowed, showing Neville the full extent of the bandage which, from this new angle, resembled nothing less than a full turban. 'I'm B-b-b-bursar; the P-p-p-p...'

'Porter,' Neville offered.

'Is there anything I can d-do for you, Sir? Would you like any d-d-d-drinks, or anything?'

'No, I'm fine thank you, Porter.'

'C-c-c-call me B-b-b-bursar, Sir, if you would. P-p-p-porter's the B-b-b-b...'

'Bursar. Yes, I've met him.'

'N-n-n-n....'

'Nice chap; yes.'

Bursar looked around a little helplessly.

'Well Sir, if that's all. J-j-j-just to t-t-t-tell you that the C-c-c-c...'

'Captain?'

'Has invited you to d-d-d-d...'

'Dine?'

'With him this evening, Sir. Eight o'clock; main b-b-b-ball room, Sir.'

Neville smiled.

'Thank you Por - Bursar; I dare say we shall see you later.'

The Porter considered replying, thought better of it, then bowed again. Neville watched him as he left, waiting for what he assumed would be the inevitable dull thud as his skull hit the door frame on the way out. Bursar paused at the door, then made a specially effort to bow low. It made no difference; "thump!".

'F-f-f-f....'

And the door closed with a naval "click".

Neville went back to his bags and completed the remainder of his unpacking. The voyage to the Mediterranean would, he assumed, take a few days; after that, there would be a few days visiting the Islands themselves. The clothes available to him would seem to be adequate to cover that period, but after that? As he sat on the bed, he recognised once again that there was no clue as to what would happen next, nor where he would be going. Had there ever been, he wondered? Presumably there would come a point where there might not even be a "next" for him to consider.

As he slipped closer to philosophy, a voice called out '"M"' at the back of his brain, and he decided to take a quick tour of the ship before dinner. He donned the canvas shoes and opened his cabin door.

TWENTY ONE

Once outside the cabin, Neville paused. He looked right to the stairwell from which he, Samuel and Porter had emerged a little earlier, then left to the end of the corridor which was defined by a single door. He decided to walk left.

The numbers on the cabins on this corridor continued ascending until forty was reached, this being the last cabin before the grey door. Neville looked back. He guessed from the length of this particular passageway that there were perhaps twenty or so rooms - presumably much like his own - leading from it. He placed his hand on the handle of the exit door and pushed it open.

He was immediately hit by fresh sea air from outside, which carried with it the hint of salt spray. The front of "A" deck was not a large affair, boasting a few recliners and deckchairs, and the odd wrought iron table welded to the superstructure. Neville walked to the front rail and leant over. Just below him he could see both "B" and "C" decks, and beyond a delimiting guard rail, the very bow of the ship complete with capstans, ropes and the like.

The two lower decks were kited out for a number of past-times; Neville could make out the markings of games courts of various kinds, including something he assumed was used for some form of curling. There were a few people milling around, fewer than he had expected, but the weather was not as brilliant as it might have been.

Despite the flying jacket, he now felt a little chilly. Turning, he noticed a second door leading back inside from "A" deck and, as he walked towards it, the bridge of the ship above it. Neville looked up. He was greeted by a sharp salute from beyond the glass which he guessed came from the Bursar, though he could not be sure.

The corridor beyond this second door was much like his own; indeed, the similarity was so great that Neville immediately remarked to himself on the enormous potential for confusion. The first door to his right bore the number one, and - as he suspected - ascended from there; the numbers proving to be the only distinguishing feature of the passage way. At fifteen there was a stairwell down to "B" deck - presumably in parallel to that he had so recently climbed on the other side of the ship - and beyond, cabins that eventually stopped at twenty.

Rather than another door at the end of the corridor, the passage bore round to the right by ninety degrees and revealed another, shorter corridor. At the end of this, another turning which completed the "U" shape of the "A" deck walkway. From the bottom of the "U", a single, much larger double staircase dropped down to the deck below. Neville checked his watch. He had enough time before he needed to prepare for dinner to push on a little further with his exploration.

The bottom of the stairs opened out into a large lobby, adorned with soft sofas and parlour palms. There were one or two notice boards, and a place specifically designed to leave messages. Neville scanned this. It was much like the pigeon hole system used in hotel lobbies. He found his own room - "A-28" - and the empty slot assigned to it. He decided to take a brief rest on one of the sofas. The lobby was, at present deserted, though he had seen a couple leave it as he descended the stairs.

From his new vantage point, Neville noticed again the remarkable degree of symmetry the ship possessed. Indeed, here it was not only left-right symmetry as he had already noticed on "A" deck, but fore-aft symmetry too. In each corner of the lobby, an archway led off in its own distinct direction, yet all possibilities appeared identical.

He had not been studying the nautical architecture for long when a voice assailed him from behind the settee.

'Bastards!'

Neville turned. An exceptionally large Venus fly trap was leaning towards him, its leaves open like a single eye complete with lashes. The leaves suddenly snapped shut with a vengeance, and became the plant's mouth too.

'Bastards!'

'I'm sorry; but who are you referring to?'

'You. Them. Everyone,' the plant snapped back, swaying slightly closer to him with the motion of the ship.

'Who is "everyone"?'

'The bastards who put me here; on a bleeding ship, miles from anywhere.'

'Is there something wrong in that?' Neville asked, moving slightly closer to the edge of the settee and relative safety.

'I suppose you'll be having dinner tonight with the Captain, won't you? Stuffing your bleeding faces, I bet!' The plant snapped open and closed again. 'And me? Starving bleeding hungry. Not a fly in slight. Stuck on board a bleeding ship; don't they know I'm supposed to be carnivorous?'

Neville was beginning to feel vaguely uneasy about his aggressive companion.

'I'm sure they must have flies here somewhere; if only to feed you.'

'And my mates.'

Neville looked nervously around, but could see no evidence of any similar species.

'Of course; and your chums.' He paused, eyeing the plant with a degree of mistrust; just how carnivorous could one of these things be? 'Look,' he said rising, 'if I find any flies, I'll keep them for you. OK?'

'Sure,' snapped the plant, 'that's what they all say!'

Without waiting for a more suitable conclusion - if there could be any such thing, indeed - Neville made a move down the nearest corridor.

There were cabins here on "B" deck too. Neville noticed that they also bore numbers in the same range as the level above, but here the doors to the cabins appeared to be slightly closer together and just along the outside of the corridor. On the inside there were other doors that bore legends such as "Staff Only" and "Laundry Room - B3". As he continued his stroll, he even came across one marked "Bursar - A.Porter". "B" deck was obviously not quite so desirable as his own. There would be more comings and goings here, more noise, and the cabins were probably less spacious.

After a few strides he came to the end of the corridor. He had evidently been walking towards the rear of the ship as the corridor now gave way to another lobby, this time with large glass doors opening out onto the aft deck. This lobby was also deserted, though out on deck a number of people were standing against the rail, wrapped up warm against a strengthening breeze, and watching the wake of the ship as it pointed back to the now invisible Channel Islands.

Neville contemplated joining them, but decided against it. Checking his watch, he decided that it was probably time for him to return to his cabin. As he walked back - exactly the way he had come to avoid getting lost - he realised he had not been given a map of the ship. This would have been useful at this present moment and, undoubtedly, in the future too, should he wish, say, to find the ship's Doctor. At some stage, he would ring for Bursar and get him to fetch one.

When he got back to the Venus lobby, there were a few people at one of the notice boards. Neville joined them and discovered that they were examining the seating plan for that evening's dinner. A large diagram, filled with circles representing tables, had been annotated in a practised hand with the names of the passengers. He found his own surname next to the Captain's on the top table. He recognised none of the others on his table, and wondered which of them - if any - belonged to Samuel. There was also - of course - nothing which said simply "M". Neville nodded politely to his fellow passengers as he left the lobby, and made his way back up the wide staircase to "A" deck.

When he reached his cabin, he found the adjoining door open and Samuel moving between the two. On his bed, a white shirt lay ready for him to wear at dinner, and Samuel was currently making sure his suit trousers had a sharp crease in them.

'Hello, Sir. Had a nice stroll?'

'Just a quick wander, that's all.' Neville took off his flying jacket and threw it on a chair. On the small table near the porthole, steam rose from a pot of tea.

'I've just made that Sir; please, help yourself.'

Neville went to the table and began to pour the tea.

'It is a nice ship, don't you think? Have you seen very much of it?'

'I just wandered down to "B" deck; had a look round the lobby, you know.'

'Porter said he saw you at the front of "A" deck, outside.'

'Porter?'

'The Bursar, Sir. He just popped in to let us know where we were sitting for dinner.' Samuel, having finished working on the trousers, placed them on the bed alongside the shirt. 'The Captain has invited us to dine with him.'

'I know,' said Neville, between sips of tea, 'I saw a plan of the tables, where everyone is sitting.' He realised that one of the names on top table had to belong to Samuel. 'There seemed to be quite a few tables too.'

'Oh, I think this is quite a large boat; probably a couple of hundred people on it.'

'It seemed very quiet when I was out, that's all. Hardly anyone about.'

'Perhaps they were all unpacking or something, Sir.'

This seemed reasonable enough. Neville caught sight of an open drawer and realised that Samuel had completed the job that he had started half-heartedly. He sat on the bed, sipped his tea, and watched Samuel as he finished brushing his suit jacket. Samuel, aware that he was being watched, offered a slight nod and smile. It was a fatherly kind of gesture, rather than that of a manservant; which is what he seemed to be half of the time. Neville felt that he was being protected almost by this old man, as if - an addition to everything else, "tricks" included - he was offering him the benefit of his wisdom.

'Is that all right, Sir?' Samuel had finished with the suit which now hung on the outside of the wardrobe along with the shirt. 'I've given your shoes a bit of a polish too, so you should be all ready.'

'Should I choose the tie?'

'Second drawer down.'

'Thank you, Samuel.'

Again the older man nodded, paused as if he wanted to respond to Neville's suddenly inquisitive gaze with something solid, but then turned silently back into his own cabin, closing the door behind him.

Almost simultaneously there came a knock at the main cabin door. It was a hesitant kind of knock, and sounded like one which had difficulty getting going; "k-k-k-knock, knock"! Neville walked to the door and opened it to reveal almost all of Bursar.

'S-s-s-sir,' the Porter said, bending his head beneath the level of the door to effect the greeting. 'I've g-g-g-got you these.'

He extended his hand, and presented Neville with a number of small pamphlets, the topmost one was entitled "Your Ship".

'I thought they m-m-m-m-'

'Might?'

'B-b-b-'

'Be?'

'Useful, S-s-s-sir.'

Neville took them and nodded.

'Thank you Bursar; just what I was looking for.' He felt as if he was patronising this tall man in some way, almost without intention; as if there was something in the other's being which sucked such an attitude out of him. There was a brief pause, during which time Neville became a little unsettled by the thought.

'Is that all?' he asked somewhat brusquely.

Bursar thought for a second, then nodded.

'Enjoy your d-d-d-dinner, S-s-s-sir.'

'Thank you.'

Neville watched the porter as he turned, straightened, then banged his head on one of the lower ceiling beams as he walked away down the corridor. Neville closed his cabin door on the sound of Bursar's "F-f-f-f-" as it came back up the corridor. Throwing the pamphlets on the bed, he decided to take a quick shower before dinner.

The bathroom was compact, boasting only a shower, a toilet, and a washbasin. Neville would have preferred at bath - indeed, at that particular moment, he had a strange desire to be back on the bus, bathing in the company of the yellow plastic duck and sharing life experiences with him. As he switched on the shower, he remembered the shower head in Paris and wondered - for the briefest of moments - if he were to be in for the same kind of experience here. There was a splutter and a hiss, but then that was it.

He got into the shower in a rather disturbed frame of mind. He felt slightly angry now, though unable to locate the root cause of this emotion; it seemed to be flapping about inside him, without a focus, looking for something to scar as it lashed around. Bursar had been an easy target, and Neville was angry with himself for that. Samuel might have been a target once too, but there was now a little too much between them to allow Neville to even consider it.

As he stood under the jets of hot water - refreshingly strong and slightly stinging - Neville tried to imagine the force of the shower cleansing the anger from within him, washing it out of his body, and away down the plug hole. He looked down at where the water swirled away and had an image of someone, somewhere - perhaps the overalled man from the quay side - waiting with a watering can to catch all his anger ready to feed it to the Venus fly trap. He smiled to himself at the picture - as if any more anger were needed there anyway! - and the tension left him.

It was replaced, without any conscious bidding on Neville's part, by the rather blurred image of "M" as she turned to wave goodbye at the restaurant. He could remember pink, the colour that dominated the image; and if he tried hard, he kidded himself that he could remember her shoulders too. This was a lie, he knew; he remembered Bob's words, and that was about it. If she could walk past him in the corridor and he not realise it, then what kind of a crusade was he embarked on?

He thought about that single, neatly folded sheet, and tried to imagine how he might fit into *her* plans; if she too were on her way to Option 3 - "A" or "B" - where did he slide into the frame?

From outside he heard Samuel open the adjoining door and walk into his cabin.

'Just coming, Samuel,' he called out, beating the other to the punch. Then, pulling the soap from its holder, he began to wash himself vigorously.

Ten minutes later, he was sitting on the edge of his bed. He could see Samuel in the other cabin looking remarkably smart in a pale grey suit with a rather magnificently patterned tie. Neville wondered what people meeting him for the first time this evening would think; of him, of what he did, of his history. And what would Samuel say, to introduce himself?

Neville, in shirt and trousers, had chosen a rather brilliant red tie from the small collection presented to him by Mister Bossiman, and had already remarked on how the suit seemed to be able to complement the colour; however, his immediate concern had become the location of his shoes.

'What did you do with my shoes, Samuel?'

'In the bottom of the wardrobe, Sir,' came the reply from the other room.

Neville checked where directed. The only suitable shoes there were the new ones he had seen earlier, and he had been looking for comfortable old shoes. As he was about to turn away, a voice called him back from the floor of the unit.

'Hey! Try us!'

'Yes,' said another, not dissimilar voice, 'try us; we're tailor made for you, honest!'

The shoes - bold and shining black leather - had a subtle brogue pattern in them which, to Neville at least, resembled something of a face; or at least, half a face in each shoe. This impression was endorsed when the left shoe - the one that had spoken first - winked knowingly at him.

'You won't regret it, will he?'

'Never!' exclaimed the right shoe, 'can't regret it, can he?'

'Ever danced, Mister?'

'Sorry?' Neville was again sitting on his bed, though with the shoes now in front of him.'

'Danced,' said the left shoe again.

'You know, the old quick step; one-two, one-two-three.'

'Ah the thrill of the ballroom!'

'Sorry,' Neville interrupted, 'but what's this got to do with me?'

The shoes winked conspiratorially at each other.

'You'll see!' they said in unison.

'Ready, Sir?' Samuel had popped his head round the door, 'I think we should be going.'

'Yes, OK; I'll be right there.'

Neville slipped on the shoes, and stood to get his jacket. As he took a pace forwards he needed to look down to check that he was indeed wearing the shoes. They felt so comfortable, it seemed as if they were not there at all.

TWENTY TWO

They reached the lobby on "B" deck almost without Neville realising it. He had been concentrating on the sensation the shoes had given him - or, more accurately, had **failed** to give him - during the brief walk along the corridor and down the double stairway. He was roused from this rather vague introspection by the sudden realisation that the lobby was now remarkably busy.

Each of the sofas was now home to a full complement of backsides of various shapes and sizes; all the notice boards were faced by people offering varying degrees of attention. Behind the settee on which he had been seated earlier, he noticed the Venus waving with the roll of the ship, snapping ferociously; if it had been ranting "Bastards!" at any passer-by, this time it would go unheard.

Neville scanned the lobby from the second step where he had paused. Everyone was dressed for dinner: the men in smart suits or tuxedos, bow ties abundant; the ladies were all finery and lace, and Neville sensed a layer of perfume about six inches deep hovering in direct competition with cigarette and cigar smoke a few inches below his nose. Samuel had pressed on into the throng, and Neville plunged through the pungent layers to follow him.

There appeared to be a general movement towards one particular corridor, although it struck him that Samuel's own course appeared to be charted with a degree more knowledge than simply following the herd would imply. He glanced over his shoulder to check on Neville's progress - he was already several bodies behind - before pressing on again. After a short while the corridor turned to the right and, as with the deck above, revealed the bottom of a "U" shape and another stairway. These stairs however, boasted not two, but three sets of steps and descended into a lobby much more grand than that on "B" deck. There was a sign indicating the ballroom, at the entrance to which - having negotiated the stairs and a 180 degree turn at the foot of them – Neville found Samuel waiting for him.

'There you are, Sir.'

The Bursar was there also.

'If you gentlemen would care to follow me, I'll introduce you to the Captain.'

Porter led the way into a large, expansive room which seemed to extend the full width of the ship and twice the same distance lengthways. At the far end, a small stage was occupied by a number of musicians evidently preparing to play some form of accompaniment through the meal. Nearest the entrance, a large number of tables were laid for dinner, with one, slightly larger than the rest and closest to the stage, evidently set slightly apart.

Some people were already seated as Porter led them towards the top table. From several tables, a number of rather elegant ladies made cooing noises to the Bursar as he walked by. He nodded professionally and courteously, even promising dances with some of the women in order to ease his progress. Neville remembered the shoes' enthusiasm for dancing, and could not fail to notice the large expanse of ballroom floor between the Captain's table and the stage.

The Master of the ship was not yet present when they reached the table. Porter showed Samuel to his seat first, then Neville to the one he would occupy next to the Captain. Neville smiled at Samuel who was virtually opposite him, then began to take in the room.

There were two other people already on their table, one either side of Samuel who, with simple ease, had already begun to enter into conversation with them. Apart from the Captain, that left three places vacant. Neville's seat placed him with his back to the stage, and thus with a full view of the rest of the ballroom. Watching people enter, he could only compare the experience with that minutes before a theatre performance where the only thing one could do whilst waiting was observe one's fellow theatre-goers and comment - mentally at least - upon them.

The general impression of his fellow travellers that he might have derived from the ladies accosting the Bursar a few moments before, proved to be as unfounded as would a general theory in relation to a cruise ship's paying company. He had expected the voyage to be populated almost entirely by wealthy, retired people who, having spent an entire lifetime working, were now out to enjoy the fruits of their labour. That there were some of these he was certain; indeed, as he sat there, he could pick out couples who might have fallen into such a category. But there were also those - of varying ages - who were obviously travelling alone; there were the young newlyweds on their honeymoons; and there were those who he felt unable to describe other than as "professionals".

Such categorisation - which had begun to take on the form of a game show to him - accounted for perhaps three quarters of the people he could now see. The remainder were made up of a mix who, although they may well have fallen into one of the previous groupings, defied immediate identification as such.

A tap on his arm pulled him from his reverie.

'Good evening. My name's Watson; please call me Audrey.'

The speaker was an elderly lady with fine grey hair and smilingly bright eyes. She had arrived at the table - as had the other two missing guests - without Neville being aware of it.

'Neville; pleased to meet you.'

'Is this your first cruise, Neville?' Audrey asked, her voice the kind of sing-song voice that he imagined all Grandmothers are supposed to possess.

'Yes, it is actually.'

'Oh, you lucky man! And the Captain's table on the first night too!'

Any reply Neville might have made was cut short by the sound - distant at first - of applause, which gradually became louder. From the entrance to the ballroom, a tall, uniformed figure was making his way towards the top table, bowing as he did so to acknowledge the applause. The smile on the man's face was restrained, cultivated, and Neville was uncertain as to the degree of pleasure or satisfaction that lay behind it.

Porter, who had stayed in the vicinity of the table, began to introduce the Captain to his dinner companions as soon as the applause had died down and normality restored. Neville - by now standing - was the last to be introduced.

'Captain Hook,' said the Bursar.

The Captain offered Neville his hand.

'My pleasure,' said the Captain cordially, taking Neville's had firmly within his own. Without breaking his smile, he turned to Porter. 'Thank you, Bursar.'

Porter, offering a sharp salute, turned and left.

'Please, be seated.'

Neville, who had been struck almost dumb by the appearance of the Captain, sat as ordered. Hook was not merely tall, he was statuesque. He boasted a dark thatch of hair and a true naval beard, mature by any standards. He had the appearance of a rugged man; a man who had seen action and lived to tell the tale. And he sported a black eye patch. For those first few seconds, Neville could think only of Peter Pan and this

Captain's namesake. How true were the parallels Neville found himself drawing? How close could this man - so apparently revered by his guests - come to being the very opposite of goodness if he were given a slight twist of attitude or inclination? Or was he already there, eye patch and all; some kind of pirate in disguise, or evil incarnate?

Looking across the table - Hook being in conversation with the lady to his right - Neville saw Samuel looking his way. There was a glass raised in his direction which, on being recognised, Samuel raised a little higher.

'Here's to you, Sir!' – and with a wink, its contents were downed in one.

Neville picked up his own glass (which had been filled without his realising it) and took a sip. It was fine white wine. He nodded back to Samuel, but Samuel was once again in conversation with his neighbours.

'So, your first cruise, Sir.'

The Captain's voice drew Neville's ear like a magnet. The face bore that same perfect "professional" smile; the inclination of the head, displayed the correct degree of interest. Neville knew that Hook had done this hundreds of times before.

'If you don't count crossing the Channel to France a few times, then yes, this is my first cruise.'

'Don't dismiss the Channel; it can be something of a vicious mistress. You can be lulled and lured in the Channel, then, in an instant, ripped asunder!'

Neville sensed a dead end in that thread of the conversation. In order to play the game - whatever it might be - he tried something of his own.

'But you must have done this hundreds of times.'

'This?'

'I don't know: crossed the Atlantic; sat down with dinner guests; docked in foreign ports.'

The Captain nodded solemnly. One or two others on the table were looking his way.

'Indeed, as you say, Sir.'

'And the Pilgrim?'

Hook stiffened slightly.

'Do you mean this ship?'

'How long have you been her Captain?'

'She,' Hook corrected with a strange emphasis, 'has been my home for several years. The S.S.Pilgrim is a fine ship, Sir; she will do for me - and, I suspect, she will do for you too.'

Although there was no change in his demeanour, Neville sensed something other than a Captain's cordiality in Hook's reply. Perhaps there was menace there, he could not be sure; but it occurred to him that much about the boat had a sense of hostility about it: the dock hand; the Venus fly trap; even its geography. Was this dark figure another?

'And what does the "S.S" stand for, Captain?'

Audrey, intruding delicately, offered the conversation a little steerage.

'It stands for "Steam Ship", ma'am,' came the prompt reply, and with it a brief history of commercial sea-borne transportation.

The completion of Hook's monologue coincided with the arrival of the first course of that evening's dinner, and within a few minutes the ballroom was filled with the general clatter of cutlery and china, glasses and bottles, and chit-chat and laughter. The Captain's table was by no means an exception to this, except perhaps in the rather restrained demeanour of the host which, though not dampening spirits, offered a degree of sobriety which was evidently not in abundance elsewhere.

Somewhere between the first two courses, a man from a far table rose, banged the table with his fist, and shouted "Here's to the Captain!" before downing a full glass of red wine. There was a general shout of approval, and Hook stood, raised his glass to the assembled throng, and sipped some wine. There was broad applause. Neville looked to Samuel who had, for the moment at any rate, ceased his conversations and was now taking in the general scene in his own quiet way. He noticed Neville looking his way.

'The food is good, isn't it?'

Neville nodded.

'Excellent.'

'Though not as good as some restaurants we know, eh?', and Samuel offered a slightly more exaggerated wink than usual as an accompaniment.

Samuel's reference brought back to Neville the reason he was actually sitting on here at all. He scanned the room in a hurried way. There were waiters moving between the tables; people getting up and sitting down; toasts being made, and toasts being answered. The general picture presented a blur of activity from within which it was pretty much impossible to distinguish anything.

Another plate of food arrived in front of him. Suddenly not hungry, he fell to eating it more as a mechanistic response to it being there than anything else.

Hook, having completed another round of the table, turned to him again.

'Have you been to the Mediterranean before, at all?'

Neville imagined him with a stock phrase book of hundreds of questions which he could trot out whenever he chose in order to wow his passengers with his concern for their well-being. Neville had decided that he didn't particularly like Hook that much - he only hoped he could do his job.

'Never, Captain. In fact, I've never been further south than - Paris.'

'Well you are further south than that already. I think you should enjoy the Mediterranean; the sea is as clear a sea as you would ever wish for. Warm and calm and blue.'

Neville waited for an anecdote about the islands, the voyage, or the people, but there was nothing else. Hook glanced away, then fell to eating again.

From the stage, the trio of musicians began to raise the volume. Neville presumed that they had been playing for some time now, but had failed to be heard above the general din. The fact that they were now insisting on being heard - and the completion of the main course - suggested that something was in-hand. Beneath the table, Neville's new shoes sensed it too. They began to tap gently to the rhythm of the band, alternating beats between them in a subtle and accomplished manner. As he was doing nothing himself, Neville felt as if his feet were getting a free massage, and so eased himself back a little in his chair, content to enjoy it.

Dessert proved to be over and done within a matter of moments, and soon all the tables were adorned by cups of coffee, bottles of Port, and the rising smoke from dozens of cigars. There was a general movement away from the tables to the lavatories and back again; ladies checking their lipstick, gentlemen emptying their bladders. From somewhere there came a crash as a waiter was sent flying by someone hastily backing out from their table.

Gradually, and without orchestration, the hubbub began to subside; the movement in and out of the ballroom diminished to a trickle; a kind of expectant calm descended. Hook rose from the table and walked slowly to the stage. By the time he reached it, the room was silent. He was handed a microphone by one of the musicians.

'Ladies and Gentlemen. May I take this opportunity, on behalf of the crew and myself, to welcome you on board the S.S.Pilgrim. There are one or two faces here I recognise from the past, and I would like to offer a special welcome to those old friends.'

From the back of the room a small cheer went up from one table. Undeterred, Hook went on.

'I trust you will all have an enjoyable and rewarding time with us. Please be assured that we will do all we can to make your time aboard as memorable as possible.'

His short bow was greeted with cheers and applause. Neville looked at Samuel who, though listening intently to Hook's words, had not joined in the approbation. The Captain raised his hand.

'Thank you. For your entertainment this evening, we have with us - to accompany our resident trio - a young lady who comes to us with the highest reputation and, I'm sure, who is already known to many of you. Please welcome, Miss Tracy Vaughan.'

And with his last words and the rising applause, the ballroom was plunged into darkness.

TWENTY THREE

For a split second, just as the applause faded, Neville sat in the darkness, his expectation heightened. Was this why he had come to this boat, for this moment? From somewhere near the stage, a woman's voice humming slightly in the blackness, picked out a rhythm which was taken up by the trio with a sleazy laziness. "Tracy Vaughan", Hook had said; but all Neville wanted to see was "M".

A light suddenly picked out a bare spot at the front of the stage and became fixed there. The woman's voice grew louder, the trio's backing more defined; then two stilettoed feet appeared in the spotlight, moving slowly forwards. Next, legs could be seen through the exaggerated split of a blue sequinned ball gown. Gradually the singer moved into the light. Neville, who had taken his napkin and was now crushing it violently in his left hand, was mesmerised by the spotlight and its contents. There seemed to be a genie about to appear in it. He thought, in a haphazard way, about magic and miracles. Then, with the rising last note of her introduction, Tracy Vaughan stepped fully into the light.

She was not "M".

As the song began, Neville realised that, even in this dim light, both Samuel and Hook were looking his way, rather than at the stage. He released the napkin from his hand and let it fall to the table. He was not aware that he had been other than silent during those last few seconds, but could not be certain. He offered Hook as casual a smile as he could muster, which, even in this light, he knew was not returned.

Sarah Vaughan was sliding through a smoky version of "Up A Lazy River", which Neville assumed, was supposed to have some reference to the fact that they were on a ship. He was trying hard to focus on the singer, on her words, on the trio behind her; indeed, almost anything to relieve him of the pressure that he had managed to heap on himself during those few brief moments of her introduction. The rest of the song passed off without incident. Vaughan's low bow at the end of the number was greeted with appreciative and enthusiastic applause. Neville, although he had not actually heard of her before - as Hook implied that perhaps he should have - recognised that she had a fine voice, and that her style was sufficiently out of the ordinary to be her own.

When the second number started, the trio led the way. This was a much more upbeat introduction which instantly had Neville's shoes tapping beneath the table. The tune was an old Fred Astaire number, and as he listened to the first few bars, he heard an echo in his head. There was something familiar about this particular tune, about the way it was being delivered. The mannerisms of the bass player reminded him of another who had played exactly that same piece.

Realisation hit him in a sudden flood which left him instantly shipwrecked: the band was playing the music he had heard at Mister Bossiman's.

If there were other parallels Neville would have been inclined to draw, the effort in doing so was not required of him. At the left of the stage, in another, softer spotlight, a figure in flamingo pink stood motionless. He had not been prepared for this; having just had his expectation crushed, he was still on the way down, still trying to regain his equilibrium. But now "M" stood - as the ball gown had stood at the tailor's - waiting.

Neville looked around, expecting to see her partner glide into view from somewhere else about the stage. As he did so, he noticed everyone on his table, as well as others nearby, staring intently at him. Samuel was smiling almost benignly; and Hook had left behind that professional study of his, and was staring at Neville with an almost malicious desire. Under the table, someone kicked him. He looked down. It was not someone, but something. The shoes, now frantic with desire, were rapping his ankles to get him to rise. It dawned on Neville that he was supposed to partner "M" for the dance, and that what he had seen at Mister Bossiman's was nothing less than a rehearsal for this moment. But he could not dance. How could he, in front of all these people, make a fool of himself?

Then, without any effort on his part, he rose from his chair. More of Mister Bossiman's handiwork. The suit had taken over.

Those initial movements were awkward, jerky. Neville's arms, uncertain of their place in all of this - as indeed was his whole being - fought the persuasive tugging of the sleeves. The shoes, demonstrating a surprising degree of power, moved him towards the edge of the stage; his efforts to simply keep his balance gave them all the edge they needed. For a brief moment, he was stationary. "M" - role-playing to a 'T' - stood, head bowed, ignoring his presence, yet waiting.

Neville knew he had no choice. He was powerless against the combination of cloth and leather; his only option, the only way he could save himself from humiliation - which was suddenly what he feared most of all - was to give in, to relax; to let the flow of things carry him forwards. He tried to recall that image from the front of Mister Bossiman's house; and then, more obscurely, he tried to imagine that he was Fred Astaire.

The next movement - a slow turn and a lazy dragging of the feet - came much easier to him. He endeavoured to concentrate on his attitude, his frame of mind, and to ignore what he body was actually going through. He suddenly found himself spinning, then stopping suddenly, as if he had just noticed "M" for the first time. He tried to look surprised, or stunned; anything which seemed to fit with this play whose script had been hidden from him.

"M" looked up. Neville thought that, in the half light, he caught a glimpse of recognition in her eyes; but it was obvious that she was playing the game too. She turned slightly from him. He wheeled across the floor until he was suddenly beside her, and, in that instant, she became his focus. Images of the rehearsal, of Fred and Ginger, fled from his mind; all he could do was to look at her.

He spun around her body, following her head as she turned it first one way then the other to avoid his stare. The music drawled out the tempo; his shoes now transmitting their exhilaration to him through his legs; the suit displaying supreme subtlety.

And then his arm was out, and he caught her hand.

She looked at him now, eye to eye. It was a play, a dance; and yet it wasn't. She made to move away, and he held her hand more tightly. This was not the suit; this was Neville, acting for himself. Whether it was the suit or his own volition that pulled her towards him he could not say; in the drama it had suddenly become impossible to distinguish. In any event, gradually, and with hesitation, she began to respond, and they began to dance.

The next few minutes passed as a blur of sensations: the brightness of the spotlights as they were caught in their rotations; the vibrant pink of her dress, as she flashed before his eyes; the heat of the trio, whose steaming rendition of the song defined the moment; the invisible eyes, drawn into the tension; the touch of her skin. Defeated, and yet victorious, Neville simply gave in and let it happen.

With the climax of the number, "M" - who, playing the role to perfection, had become more and more enmeshed in the dance - spun once, then collapsed in his arms like a puppet whose strings had been cut. There was a sublime moment of stillness and silence, and then the ballroom exploded with applause.

For an instant he was uncertain what to do. A faint movement from "M" gave him the clue to lift her into a standing position. Holding her hand, they turned to face the body of the room, and bowed. Neville could see Samuel actually on his feet applauding; the smile on his face bore the pride of a parent. Elsewhere, others stood too. Then, from the side of the stage, a young girl ran on and presented "M" with a large bouquet of flowers.

Neville glanced at his partner. She squeezed his hand slightly.

'Shall we sit down?' he offered.

'You know,' she spoke between breaths, 'I have always wanted to do that! Thank you.'

Neville kissed her hand, and led her towards the top table.

TWENTY FOUR

As they returned to the table, there was an extra chair awaiting them, set between Neville's and the Captain. Samuel, who was still standing, offered Neville his hand.

'Well done, Sir!'

Neville, having freed his right hand from "M", placed it on Samuel's shoulder.

'Thank you, Samuel.'

Having accepted the verbal approbation from those already at the table, "M" had walked round to take her chair alongside Hook. Neville, having spoken with Samuel, looked round in time to see the Captain graciously addressing himself to "M"s seat and her general comfort.

'Remarkable performance, Miss. Remarkable.'

He looked up as Neville prepared to sit down himself.

'And you too, Sir. I must say I was surprised by your elegance.'

Neville, whose euphoria at the event was still strong enough to keep him floating, was not going to allow anything negative to spoil it.

'No more that I, Captain Hook; no more than I!'

The Captain nodded at the joke, adopted his normal smile.

'And what's your name, my Dear?'

Audrey, having offered her own enthusiastic congratulations to "M", was effecting her standard introduction. Neville sat down between them. "M" glanced at him before replying.

'Mirelle,' she said, 'but I prefer Mita.'

'Mita?' Neville had hardly been surprised by her answer. Indeed, he was beginning to wonder why everyone he met wasn't called Mirelle, as if he was undergoing some form of semantic torture that would follow him throughout his life. Mirelle's qualification was, perhaps, his first break.

'It was my Grandmother's name', Mita explained. 'She was Italian, from Tuscany. My Father, who was French, was adamant that I should have a French name. Of course, I could not protest until I became old enough; but he still calls me Mirelle to this day.'

'Mita', Audrey paused, 'yes, that's quite a nice name too, isn't it Neville?'

Neville nodded.

'And didn't you dance wonderfully well too!' she carried on, placing her hand on his arm and squeezing it gently. 'Mita; didn't our Neville dance superbly?'

Mita smiled at Audrey, then Neville.

'Indeed; I could not have wished for a better partner.'

Neville smiled back. Beneath the table he felt his ankle being kicked. He looked down. The left shoe gave him a wink.

'Was that OK?'

'That was brilliant!' Neville replied in a hushed voice.

'See!' said the left shoe, 'we were brilliant!'

'Of course,' confirmed the other, 'we're always brilliant. Didn't we say you wouldn't regret it!'

A waiter appeared to replenish the wine glasses. In the background, under the umbrella of Tracy Vaughan's voice, there seemed to be a general movement of couples to the dance floor. Samuel's voice suddenly sounded nearby.

'Excuse me.'

Neville looked round, expecting to find the remark addressed to himself; however, Samuel was - with a rather fine, if discrete, bow - talking to Audrey.

'Would you care for this dance?'

Audrey, whose hand was still resting on Neville's arm, rose. She glanced at Neville.

'Is your friend to be trusted?' she said, with a mischievous note in her voice.

Neville feigned a serious expression, and glanced at Samuel.

'I think you will find Samuel to be an honourable gentleman, Audrey.'

'In that case; Samuel, I would be delighted!' and with that, she exchanged Neville's arm for Samuel's, and they walked a few steps to the edge of the throng and began to dance.

Neville watched their cautious and sedate movements for as long as he could, but soon they were subsumed into the general melee. He turned to Mita. She had been watching them too. Hook's chair was vacant.

'So, we meet again!' Mita smiled warmly. 'Something of a coincidence, though I can't say I'm really surprised.'

'You're getting used to coincidences?'

'Something like that.'

There was a code underlying all of this. Neville approached Mita as if she already knew much of his secret, and had experienced many of the same things.

'How was the monkfish?'

Neville laughed. Bob had been telling the truth, after all.

'The monkfish was fine. I don't suppose you managed dessert either? I mean, I guess I must have interrupted.'

'I was a little surprised, yes.'

There was a brief pause. Neville noticed Hook making his way towards them from the far side of the room.

'You dance remarkably well.'

Mita smiled.

'It was something I always wanted to do; something dramatic like that, ever since I was a little girl.'

'Fred Astaire and Ginger Rodgers?'

'And Cyd Charisse. She was my favourite. I remember seeing her in films with Gene Kelly. I took dancing lessons as a child because I wanted to be like her; to dance in empty ballrooms with elegant men.'

'I'm afraid that this ballroom was not particularly empty, nor your partner very elegant.'

'What nonsense!'

'If only I could take the credit.'

They were interrupted by Hook, who, on his return, immediately asked Mita if she would like to dance.

'I am afraid dancing with some of our guests is one of my chores; but before the chores begin, I should like to have a little pleasure.'

Mita took the arm he offered and, with a smile for Neville, left the table. As they walked to the dance floor, they crossed Audrey and Samuel on their way back. Audrey returned to her own seat, while Samuel took that just vacated by Mita. He followed Neville's eyes to the Captain and his partner.

'She is a very attractive woman, Sir, if I may say so.'

Neville thought how Bob - because of his lascivious leanings – had missed the whole picture and done Mita a gross injustice. Typically, Samuel had missed nothing.

'And how was your own twirl, Samuel?'

'Ah, I'm afraid I am a little rusty, Sir; but I believe that Audrey still has all her toes intact!'

Neville glanced at Audrey to confirm this, but she was now engaged in another conversation to her left and he chose not to disturb her.

The dance finished with applause for the singer and the Trio. After a few moments, the latter picked up another tune and the dancing began again. Neville expected Mita to return, but caught a glimpse of her on the far side of the ballroom, still in the custody of Hook.

'And what do you think of our Captain?'

Samuel's question came as something of a surprise. It was not that it was not a logical question to ask - indeed, just then, it was **the** most logical question to ask - it was rather the manner in which it was asked; the tone of the words; the weight behind them. Neville looked at Samuel. He was not smiling.

'He's seems popular enough, doesn't he? I mean, take the applause when he came in to dinner.'

'But what do **you** think of him?'

Neville paused, but only for a moment.

'I don't like him, Samuel. And I don't trust him. There's something about him...'

He paused. He felt a hand resting on his left arm. It was Audrey; she had been listening. She gave him a slight squeeze, but said nothing. Neville looked back to Samuel. He had the feeling that he was somehow sitting between his two guardian angels; and from their manner, he was beginning to think that there was something very definitely amiss.

'Why?'

'Sir?'

'Why do you ask, Samuel? Is there something...is there something I should know?'

'As you say Sir, Hook is a popular Captain. He steers his ship, entertains those who sail on her, and people come back. What could be wrong in that? And,' he gave Neville no time to intercept him, 'again, as you say, there is something about him, something you do not like, or do not trust. I have nothing to tell you, Sir. I think you know all you need to.'

Samuel looked out onto the dance floor; he appeared to be looking for something in particular. When he fixed his gaze, Neville knew he had found what he had been looking for. Neville followed Samuel's line of vision. There indeed was Hook; fine and upright in his uniform, dancing in the manner of a trained, professional seafaring Captain. He "cut a dash"; he was "a fine figure of a man"; and yet...and yet.

Neville could only see his back at first, but when Hook turned, he could see his partner. It was not Mita.

It was not the suit or the shoes, but Neville who propelled himself from his chair. Staring into the body of the dancers, he searched for Mita. He had no reason to panic, no reason to suspect that something might be awry. She was no longer dancing with Hook, and she had not returned to the table. Perhaps she had slipped out, to "powder her nose", to "take the air", to watch the moonlight on the sea. There could be a dozen reasons why she was not there with him and nowhere to be seen. And yet.

Samuel and Audrey remained seated. Neville glanced at each of them, but they said nothing.

As he made his way to the exit, a number of people tried to stop him to offer their congratulations on his earlier performance. He did not hear them. On his feet, his dancing shoes felt again like normal shoes; perhaps they had no liking for this kind of drama. On his body, his suit hung like dead cloth. At the door he paused to look back.

At the top table, Samuel and Audrey - both standing - occupied it alone. On the dance floor couples turned. There were officers in uniform, ladies in dresses. But there was no flash of flamingo pink, and now there was no Hook.

Out in the lobby a few people were milling. Neville had to be in a hurry to get wherever he was going (and he had not decided where that was yet) but observant enough not to miss anything. He saw the Bursar who began to prepare his sharp salute: if it was delivered, Neville missed it; he was away, up the stairs to "B" deck.

At the base of the 'U' he paused. Left or right? Both appeared the same. He decided to go left, walking quickly now towards the corner of the corridor. He turned. Ahead a long stretch of rooms. He moved on, not knowing what he was looking for. He had no idea of Mita's room, or even the deck on which her cabin was situated. Perhaps there would be something that might give him a clue. He paused briefly half way along at a stairwell leading back down to "C" deck, then made for the "B" deck lobby. Where this had been throbbing a few hours earlier, it was now deserted. Behind the sofa, the Venus fly trap stood still. He was about to move on, then remembered the pigeon holes. He checked the slot for "A-28", but it was empty.

Again he faced a decision: up to "A" deck, or along "B" deck. The corridors than ran off the lobby once again gave him no clue. In mirroring each other, they seemed only to compound the fruitlessness of his task. He decided to carry on, and aimed for one of the "B" deck corridors heading for the bow of the ship. Half way along, he came to another stairwell leading downwards. Perhaps these were the stairs that led up from "C" deck; the stairs that he and Samuel had first climbed on their arrival on board. Would it make sense to try outside? What could "B" deck offer him except closed doors to probably empty cabins?

He decided on the stairs, almost slipping half way down and grabbing the handrail to keep himself upright. At their foot, he turned out onto the deck. The night was black, darker than he had expected; and though there was a moon, the light it threw across the sea seemed reluctant to illuminate anything. There was a breeze, and the ship rolled gently as it made its way into the darkness. Ahead, a couple leaned on a handrail, looking out across the sea. No-one else was visible. He decided to push on; to do a complete circuit of the ship if necessary. If he did not find Mita here, then he would try once again inside, for he had now convinced himself that she desperately needed him to find her.

Reaching the bow of the ship - or as far as he was allowed to go - he turned and looked up. "B" and "A" decks rose above him. There were three people talking on the deck above; "A" deck appeared empty. Beyond that, in a strange white silhouette against the sky, Neville could make out the lights of the bridge. He thought he could see a figure standing at the window looking out; he imagined it might be Hook.

A couple wandered by and bade him "Good night". When he looked back to the bridge, the figure had gone.

Turning again, Neville set off for the other half of the ship. The deck was empty, and few lights were on in the outside cabins. Ignoring any stairs leading upwards, he walked the full length of the ship before finding himself at the stern. The rough white wake frothed as it left its temporary snail-like trail behind. Two men smoked cigars by the swimming pool; a young woman set on a deckchair talking to one of the ship's crew. He could hear the sound of music from the ballroom and found a door into the lobby.

At the ballroom door he stopped again. The Captain's table had been deserted, and, judging by the number of people dancing, many had left the festivities for the night. A few nodded as they passed him on their way back to their cabins. There was nothing else he could think of doing. He had walked the ship; searched as much as he was able. Could he knock on every door, hammer on every cabin? And on what pretence? Should he challenge Hook and demand - what of him?

Heavy legged, he ascended the stairs once again and made his way up, through "B" deck, towards his own cabin. When he entered, he found the adjoining door open, and Samuel waiting for him.

TWENTY FIVE

It was not until Neville had spent a few minutes explaining his recent movements to Samuel that he noticed the pamphlets that the Porter had so recently left him. He had discarded them without thought on the bed, the one titled "Your Ship" uppermost. Although his searching for Mita had been a little frantic, it had not been a complex navigation; yet, due to his ever-growing sense of urgency, he was finding it almost impossible to describe his route to Samuel. In order to outline where he had been, he had begun to wonder if there might be paper an pen in the cabin somewhere, and, in looking for this, had noticed the pamphlet.

The document was an A4 sheet of paper that had been folded twice to form a small booklet. Neville had picked it up on the assumption that it would contain a floor plan of the vessel. The front page contained the pamphlet's title and a colour picture of the ship, evidently taken in some exotic port: the sky was clear; the sea, a brilliant blue; the backdrop heavenly. Neville opened the pamphlet to the inside pages. There was no floor plan here, but instead of opening out the paper completely, he was drawn to the text via its rather enticing typeface:

WELCOME aboard the S.S.Pilgrim! The Directors of Total Leisure Incorporated would like to take this opportunity to introduce you to the ship that will be your home for the next few days as you relax on your ultimate holiday experience.

NOTHING is too much trouble for us. You will find our crew - led by the indomitable Captain Hook - only too willing to meet your every need, whatever hour of the night or day.

INDULGE yourself in your dreams, your fantasies. Our trained personnel will be on-hand to arrange and assist wherever they can.

EVER wanted that famous shipboard Romance? Or to win thousands at Roulette? Ever wanted to stumble across an impossible crime, yet solve it to the amazement of all?

TOTAL Leisure Incorporated specialises in making your wildest fantasies come true. Speak to those who have travelled with us before - they just keep coming back for more!

YOU don't have a fantasy? Nothing you want to act out? Think you're coming along for just a quiet cruise? Don't you believe it! We ALL have our hidden desires. Total Leisure Incorporated - your passage to fantasy land...

He handed the leaflet to Samuel, then walked to the porthole and looked out onto the blackness; all he could see was a reflection of himself.

'Were you aware of this?' He asked the question of Samuel, yet all the while staring at himself in the glass. Samuel said nothing. 'Was that what your warning about Hook meant. The fact that he wasn't what he seemed?'

He turned. Samuel had opened out the pamphlet to reveal the deck plan on its inner face, and this now lay on the bed. Neville glanced at it, then back to the other man.

'Samuel?'

'I wasn't sure, Sir.'

'Not sure? Since when have you been unsure of anything? Tell me that! And Mita. Is she just one of the guests acting out her fantasy with my help? If so, then what am I in all of this?'

'Mita?' Samuel seemed shocked at the suggestion. 'How could she be just a guest, Sir? You met her at the restaurant; like you, she has her own quest. That has nothing to do with this ship, has it?'

'Unless you are part of it too.'

'I'm not sure I get you, Sir.'

'"Total Leisure Incorporated".' Neville almost spat the words out. 'What if it's bigger than just this ship; if all that is happening to me is just some fucking **game**!'

Samuel moved towards him, placing an arm on his shoulder.

'No, Sir! No. I can only ask you to believe me. The fact that you are on this ship is...'

'A coincidence?'

'You are here because Mita is here; because she chose to be here. She wanted a cruise; she had her fantasy about the dance. It might have happened elsewhere, but it has happened here. And you are here because you decided that you wanted to be where she was. Is that not true?'

Neville said nothing.

'Do you think me evil, Sir?'

The question hit Neville like a slap across the face. He straightened, and looked his friend square on.

'No, Samuel; of course I do not think you evil!'

'This is a dangerous ship, Sir. Some of the things they allow to happen here... Even with some of the things I have seen elsewhere - or been party too, I have to say - even I could not condone them.'

'But Mita's dance; surely that was harmless.'

'Indeed. But where is she now; now that she has finished acting out her dream? Is she now part of someone else's fantasy? Has she herself become an innocent victim?'

Samuel's words triggered a thought in Neville's mind. If she had indeed become entangled in another's game, would it be possible for the present scenario to be his? For him to have - however subconsciously - drawn up the framework for the plot that they were all now a part of?

'I know what you are thinking, Sir; and I do not know the answer. But I think it might be possible.' There was a pause. Samuel turned away from him, and walked a little further into the room. 'My dance with Audrey, Sir.'

'What about it?'

'That was not prearranged; it was not part of my plan, or your plan, or any plan of which I was aware. Perhaps it was something that I have wanted to do for a long time. A simple dream; to dance with a lady during a moonlit cruise. Innocent I know, but although I did not will it to happen, it still happened.'

Neville walked to the foot of the bed and stared down at the map.

'I think we had better find Mita. How quickly can we be off this ship, Samuel?'

'I will find a way, Sir - if you can find Mita.'

The first three decks on the plan - "A", "B" and "C" - were much as Neville had already experienced them. It took him no time at all to outline where his initial search for Mita had led him, and, in doing so, to confirm that, without searching all the cabins and storerooms on the top three decks, he had covered as much ground as he could during that first sweep.

'Perhaps we should try elsewhere, Sir.'

'Elsewhere?'

'Higher or lower.'

Neville sat down on the bed and lifted the map in his hands. Samuel manoeuvred behind him to see.

'Higher? There's only the bridge and some officer quarters.'

'And lower?'

Neville traced an outline with his finger.

'Presumably we should call this "D" deck. There isn't too much detail here is there? These large blocks are probably the holds. And there are some storage rooms, by the look of things. These stairwells look as if they go even lower.'

'To the engine room, perhaps?'

'Probably, Samuel; yes.'

There was a "k-k-k-knock, knock" at the door.

'Sounds like Bursar,' Neville said automatically.

Samuel opened the door. The tall bandaged figure of the Porter dipped into the room.

'So **your** dreams don't come true then, Bursar?'

The Porter looked confused.

'S-s-s-sir?'

'Never mind. What do you want?'

'I was p-p-p-passing by the p-p-p-pigeon holes, Sir, in the l-l-l-l-'

'Lobby.'

'When I s-s-s-saw this in "A-28".' From behind his back, Bursar produced a lady's glove. It was flamingo pink. 'I thought you m-m-m-m-'.

Neville was off the bed in an instant, and snatched the glove from Bursar's hand without even bothering to finish his sentence for him.

'Was there anything else?'

'S-s-s-sir?'

'Any note, or anything like that,' Samuel suggested.

'N-n-n-no, Sir.'

Neville examined the glove. There was a moment of uncomfortable silence - Bursar's trademark it seemed.

'W-w-w-will there b-b-b-be anything else?'

'No.' Neville was suddenly preoccupied.

'Wait.' Samuel called the Porter back, just as he was about to leave. 'Perhaps you could explain something on this deck plan for us.'

Neville looked up, his attention back again.

'Yes,' he said, 'here.' He pointed to the plan. Bursar walked over to where he could see the map. 'Would we be right in thinking that this was "D" deck, Bursar?'

The tall man rubbed his chin, as if to indicate that he was thinking about the answer - and one which might not be perfectly straight forward at that.

'W-w-w-well, Sir.'

'Quick as you can man, if you could. Please.'

Bursar nodded.

'In that this d-d-d-deck here is called "C" d-d-d-deck; yes, Sir. B-b-b-but we don't c-c-c-call it that, Sir.'

'Why? What do you call it?'

The tall man turned and looked round the room; he seemed nervous in case someone else had joined them without him realising it. To Neville it seemed something of a theatrical gesture - but in this instance, it was perfectly appropriate.

Porter, the Bursar, stood in the doorway.

'Dismissed, Bursar! I'll help the gentlemen out.'

'S-s-s-sir.' The Porter tried a rather untidy salute, turned and left the room, banging his head on the door frame as he did so.

The Bursar, having closed the door behind him, now stood smartly at the foot of the bed. He glanced at the map.

'We call it "the Games deck", Sir. That's where many of our guests enjoy the best moments of their holidays. Those large rooms used to be holds, but they have been converted to "activity areas"; perhaps a little like stages on a film set. One is permanently set up as a Wild West Saloon; you'd be surprised how many gunfighters there are in this world!'

Neville said nothing.

'We chose not to label them on the plan Sir, for fear of giving the game away. We find the element of surprise is part of the fun.'

'So why are you telling me this?'

'Because you have lost the young lady you danced with. Is that not so? When I saw you leave the ballroom I knew that something must be the matter. The lady at your table - Audrey - told me who you were looking for.'

Neville glanced at Samuel, who said nothing.

'And I understand that you are concerned. So, I have come to see if I can be of any assistance.'

'Yes, there is something.' Samuel smiled at the Bursar, then looked at Neville to assure him that he knew exactly what he was doing. 'The one area we didn't check was the bridge.'

'You would not be allowed up there, Sir.'

'Of course not. Now it may be - and we don't know how, of course - but it may be that the young lady has found her way up there. Or,' Samuel paused, then glancing at Neville, 'I'm sorry Sir, but I have to say this. Or she may have gone to one of the Officers' cabins...'

Samuel allowed the suggestion to float in front of the Bursar. Neville knew - because he knew Samuel, and because he already had an inkling about Mita - that this could not possibly be the case; however the suggestion had to be realistic to Porter.

'I see,' said the Bursar after a moment, 'you could be right.'

'So in that case, would it be possible for you to check for us?' On Samuel's words, Neville turned away from the two men and walked back to the porthole. He hoped that this would have the desired effect. 'If she is there, shall we say "of her own accord" - if you could let us know, then we will no longer have cause to worry.'

Neville watched the Bursar in porthole. Samuel waited patiently.

'Gentlemen,' Porter said with the air of a man charged with duty, 'I'll go myself and see if I can find her. If you would care to wait here, I'll bring you news as soon as I have any.'

'Very kind,' said Samuel, 'thank you.'

Seconds later, the cabin door closed and Neville and Samuel were left alone again.

'Now Sir, I don't think we've much time.'

'Do you think she might be up there, Samuel?'

'Not a chance. If I were a betting man - and I have had the occasional flutter in the past, I must admit - I'd put money on her being down below.'

'Agreed. Are you coming?'

'I'll sort out our means of escape, Sir, if I may. We should arrange to meet somewhere.'

'How about "C" deck; where we came on board?'

Samuel thought for a moment.

'That should be fine.'

'How much time do you think we've got, Samuel?'

'I'd say it depends on the Bursar. Is he genuinely trying to help us; or if not, does he suspect anything regarding our plan?'

'Fifteen minutes?'

'It's not long, Sir - but it should be enough for me.'

Neville gave Samuel's arms a brief squeeze and, deck plan in hand, made for the door. As he reached it, Samuel called him back.

'Here, Sir.' In his arms he held Neville's flying jacket. He threw it across the room. 'You might be needing this.'

Smiling, Neville pulled the jacket on, then opened the door.

TWENTY SIX

The way down to "D" deck was concealed behind two doors on "C" deck, both inappropriately labelled "Dry Stores - Crew Only". Within moments, Neville had made his way down two flights - choosing to bypass the "B" deck lobby - and was standing outside the first of the two entrances. If they were to make good their escape as arranged, this would need to be the exit Neville had to take in order to get to the rendezvous with Samuel as quickly as he could.

The corridor was empty. He consulted the map, then slipped it into the inside pocket of his flying jacket. From the other side of the door, apart from the stairwell, the map showed him nothing and would, therefore, be virtually useless to him. He glanced along the full length of the corridor before trying the door. It opened easily.

A single bulb hung from the ceiling just beyond. Neville closed the door as quietly as he could and took stock. Immediately in front of him was a set of stairs; with bulkhead on either side, there was no room for anything else. It was darker at the foot of the stairs, and peering down them he could see nothing.

There was no time for contemplation or second thoughts. His first step echoed slightly in the stairwell. He hoped that the shoes might lend a hand, but they remained inert. Treading more carefully so as to limit the sound made by his footfall, he descended to the deck below. As he did so, he found himself counting the steps; "thirteen" greeted his arrival on the Games Deck.

He paused, wanting to be sure that no-one had heard him approach, and to allow his eyes to adjust to the somewhat subdued lighting. From the map he remembered that the passageway he was in extended both fore and aft, and with his being nearer the bow, had already decided that he was going to try aft first. He was surprised by the silence. There was nothing apart from the distant rumble and reverberations of the engine. Dim lights adorned the walls of the corridor at irregular intervals, and Neville began to wonder if he hadn't missed something; if elsewhere there might be a slightly more "passenger friendly" approach to this deck, as opposed to the dim service way he now found himself in.

Cautiously he moved forwards. He had only gone a few feet when he realised that, should anyone suddenly appear either in front or behind him, his only chance of concealment would be to throw himself through the nearest door without heed for what might lay beyond.

He came to the first door and paused, inclining his head to it, listening for any sound from within. There was none. Cautiously, he tried the handle. It moved silently, and the door opened - as the "Dry Stores" door above had done - easily and with little effort on his part.

Beyond, was a small, well lit room. In its centre was a large dentist's chair. Around the walls were various cupboards and cabinets, and in one corner a wheelchair and sink unit. He wondered what kind of a game might go on in here, and recalled Samuel's warning that dark things might happen on a ship such as this. He shivered involuntarily; this was something he had no desire to contemplate.

Back at the door, he paused long enough to check that the corridor was clear before stepping out of the room. Closing the door behind him, he flooded the passageway in darkness, and again had to wait a few seconds to allow his eyes to adjust once more. There was again the dull thumping of the engine somewhere below, and, somewhat closer, the thumping of Neville's heart.

He pushed on to the next door, a little further ahead. Again there was the pause, the listening, and then the opening of the door. This room was also lit, though less well that previously. It was also slightly larger too. There was a deep pile carpet on the floor, and the walls had been decorated in such a way as to give a warm feeling to the room. In the centre there was a long padded couch, and, along one wall, another of similar construction that resembled a bed. In the corner nearest the door, an elegant wooden cabinet stood with its top drawer slightly open. Neville pulled it towards him. Inside was a pile of soft towels, and a number of dark bottles.

He lifted one of these out. The label read "Natural Massage Oil". Any temptation he may have had to delve into any of the other drawers was rendered unnecessary by his realising the exact purpose of this particular room - which was obviously much more closely allied to conventional pleasure than the previous compartment had been.

The corridor was still quiet when he regained it. As the second room had been less bright than the first it took him little time to re-adjust to the lack of light. He knew that time was passing, and that he had spent at least four or five of the minutes allotted. He began to worry that the fifteen minute window he and Samuel had allowed themselves would be woefully inadequate for him to complete his task. Neville had got the impression that Samuel had some idea of how he would resolve his problem, yet he was still - almost literally - in the dark.

As he walked forwards, he became aware of an additional sound that had begun to echo in some vague harmony with the turbines. He paused. It was difficult to establish the exact direction from which the sound was emanating. He checked behind; all was clear. The sound became perceptibly louder. For a moment it seemed as if it was being generated above him somewhere, and Neville looked up to where the bare bulbs hung uncertainly down. What was that noise?

The realisation that it was the sound of someone's footfall as they descended the very same stairs that he had so recently traversed, hit Neville hard. Why had he not been counting? How close would the count have been to thirteen?

He had time to do nothing but react. The next door was only a few paces away. Without regard for the sound he made - and without the cautious pause he had made at the previous two rooms - he ran to the door and opened it.

Expecting to find another small room, he was surprised to find himself in a large cavern of a place. Perhaps this was one of the holds he had noticed on the map, though he could not remember where or when he was supposed to encounter the first of these. Having closed the door behind him, he pushed his back flat against it and listened. The footfall outside seemed to have ceased; there was still the sound of the engines, but now this was being embellished by another new noise.

It was difficult to make this out at first. Somewhere in the room, a dim light glowed, seeming to cast its beams upwards from the floor. He could make out the shadows of a number of objects which appeared to be crates of some kind; there appeared to be little else visible. The sound he had heard was undoubtedly metallic; not the sound of solid metal, but rather the fragmented jangling of small metal objects.

Neville looked up. Overhead, suspended from the ceiling above - which seemed remarkably and incongruously distant - were a succession of chains hanging down. They dangled loosely, having nothing suspended from them, and with the gentle rolling of the ship, sounded like crude wind chimes accompanying the vessel's progress. Given the presence of the chains and the crates, he began to wonder if this particular hold was indeed still used for the purpose which it had been designed. A image of old black and white gangster movies popped into his head; of tried and tested formulas full of old clichés.

A sudden noise echoing from beyond the crates was the first indication to him that he was not alone.

Cautiously, he left the relative security of the door, and made his way towards the first crate. It was large and, by crouching down, offered Neville a degree of shelter from the line of sight of anyone beyond. Again he heard the noise, this time the unmistakable sound of someone struggling; they were breathing heavily, and a sudden curse uttered with a degree of frustration was sufficient to persuade him that he should press on.

Peering around the edge of the crate, the remainder of the hold was open to his view. The dim light was emanating from two spot lamps that were situated on the floor by the far wall; they had been angled upwards, and thus threw a strangely diffused and shadowy light upon the contents of the space. There were a few more crates, and, quite near the lights, a figure in a chair. Even in the half-light, Neville could see enough to spot the vague glow of pink.

'Mita!'

He had not wished to reveal himself, but his relief at the sight of her escaped from him before he could contain it. She stopped struggling in the chair and looked his way, attempting to make out the origin of the voice from the deep shadows.

'Neville?'

Straightening himself, he stepped out from behind the crate and into the open.

'Are you OK?'

'What are you doing here?' Neville moved forwards in response to her question. Her shout halted his progress. 'Stop, Neville! You should get out of here!'

'Indeed; you should listen to the young lady - if only it weren't too late.'

A second voice - deeper, solid, masculine - rolled out from near where Mita sat. Frozen, Neville scanned the darkness for its owner.

'Where are you?'

It was the only thing he could think of saying. The voice responded.

'Here.'

From only a few feet behind Mita, the outline of a man appeared. He placed himself between Neville and the spotlights, casting a vast shadow the length of the hold. Neville moved forwards, then paused.

'Who are you?' he repeated.

The answer to his second question came, not in the form of a verbal response from the silhouette, but as a vicious shove in the back which, taking him by surprise, sent him sprawling to the floor.

Momentarily stunned, Neville looked up at the man towering above him. The footfalls on the steps belonged to the man from the quayside at Guernsey.

'Get up. On your knees!'

Neville did as he was told, then followed the pointing of his assailant by shuffling towards where Mita sat. As he approached, he could see that she had her hands tied behind her back and her feet tied to the chair which appeared to be fixed to the deck. The shadowy man moved a step closer.

'That's far enough!' he said. Neville was almost within touching distance of Mita; spitting distance of her captor.

A swift kick in the ribs from the quay-hand, instantly doubled Neville up, and he collapsed to the floor again. There was a brash and vengeful laugh, followed by the commencement of soft whistling.

After he had recovered his breath, he sensed one of the men standing over him. He looked up nervously, half-expecting to find himself the recipient of another blow. The first man was standing much closer now; so close, indeed, that even in the poor light, Neville could make out the features on his face. They were familiar to him; he tried to assemble a suitable image in his mind.

'Are you all right?'

Mita's voice, soothing despite its tremulous tone.

'How touching!' The first man laughed - and the laugh completed Neville's image.

'Binky?!'

There was a brief moment of silence during which Neville heard the turbines and the chains again, though seemingly for the first time. Binky had stiffened slightly, and the other man - now sitting on a nearby crate - stopped whistling.

'Is that you, Binky?'

'Why do you call me that?' There was only caution and hostility in the voice.

'"Binky" Bingham. You flew me across from Southampton. Shit, it was only this morning!'

Bingham smiled slightly.

'So the old fool's still flying, is he?'

'The old fool?'

'My twin brother. Mad as a cow. Thinks he's some fucking World War One Ace! Never could handle reality.'

Neville looked from Bingham to Mita, to the man on the crate (who had begun whistling again), and then back to Bingham. He wondered just where reality might actually reside.

'Your brother?'

'Monty. From a long line of failed war hero types. Tried it; disaster for all of us. Binky's reaction to it was to simply carry on, pretending.'

'And you?'

'Kicked out of the army. Bastards! Ungrateful sods! This country doesn't deserve the likes of me. Unwanted; cast aside; chucked out.'

Neville was struggling to put together the pieces of the jigsaw that Monty seemed to be offering him. There were clues here, but no picture to fit them to.

'So why the girl? What's she done? What's going on?'

A feint smile played briefly across Monty's face. He looked at Mita, extending an arm to touch her cheek as he did so. Neville motioned to rise, ignoring the dull pain in his chest, but the thug was off his crate in an instant. Neville became still at the threat.

'This young lady?' There was almost affection in Monty's voice. Perhaps a trace of regret too. 'She found out.'

'Found out?'

'Neville, he's mad! Get me...'

Her plea was cut short by Monty's hand across her face. He looked hard at her, now half-slumped in the chair, then turned back to Neville.

'Ever since the army rejected me, I decided that I'd work for someone who was interested in my services. Binky tried to stop me, presumably out of some misplaced loyalty. He still does. In fact, we've this little rivalry going; you could call it a family feud. He tries to stop me, and I...'

Neville picked up another piece.

'The planes that tried to shoot us down today.'

'Failed again, eh?'

'Designed to look like German aircraft, just to keep Binky's fantasy alive; and all the time...'

'And all the time they're actually working for me.'

'And you are working for "the other side".'

Monty laughed, amused that Neville had managed to put the pieces together at last.

'It's a shame about you two; considering you dance so nicely together.'

He could not be certain exactly what sparked his next action: perhaps it was the threat; or that his allotted fifteen minutes were nearly over; or even some deeply buried sense of national pride. Sensing the thug still close at hand and distracted by Monty's discourse, Neville attempted to spring to his feet.

The sudden movement, combined with the lack of grip between patent leather shoes and the metal deck, led Neville to launch himself forwards rather than upwards; the result of which was for him to bury his head in the deck hand's groin with such force that the latter collapsed on to his knees. Success brought Neville quickly to his feet, from where he followed up his initial strike by a more measured swing of his right instep into the same area.

Monty took a step back, seeing his aide now helpless on the floor.

'A lucky blow; but not lucky enough!'

From his belt, Monty pulled a small handgun. Neville had missed this in the gloom and now appeared to be completely at the other's mercy. He heard a metal rattle close to his ear. He turned to find a large chain dangling just within reach. He swayed to his right, grabbed the chain, and hurled it towards Monty.

Swinging like a heavy pendulum, it caught Monty on the side of the head on its upswing. He tottered, the gun now hanging limply in his hand. Moving forwards, Neville - still with images from thirties gangster movies resounding in his head - swung his fist, and with a "crack!" made solid contact with Monty's jaw. The body and the gun went spinning in different directions.

Neville turned to Mita.

'Come on!' he shouted, as he bent to untie the ropes, 'we've got to get out of here!'

The ropes came away after a little fussing, and soon Mita was on her feet. There was no time for a romantic embrace, just a squeeze of the hand and then Neville was running for the door with her trailing behind.

'Samuel should be waiting for us - let's hope we have time!'

The corridor was empty. Neville paused to check for sounds. There were the turbines again, and, in addition, the new sound of metal scrapping against metal.

'This way!'

Running along the corridor, their steps echoed loudly about them. It sounded as if there were twenty people running rather than two. Neville knew that there was no time for caution now. The Bursar must have completed his check of the bridge deck and would surely be heading for "A-28" - if he had not got there already.

They climbed the stairs, Neville two at a time and not bothering to count this time, bursting out onto "C" deck just as an elderly couple were walking passed the "Dry Stores" door. They froze, amazed to see two young people suddenly appear from nowhere, barge passed them without a word, and then hare off.

Outside, Neville stopped, Mita coming to a halt beside him, her hand still holding his, her quick breathing making clouds on the chill night air.

'Where is Samuel?'

Neville heard a shout from above. He looked up. Two decks above, a figure in a uniform was leaning over the rail. He had expected to see the Bursar, but he saw Hook.

'Sir; over here!'

Samuel stepped out of the shadows to join them.

'Samuel; are you OK?'

'Fine, Sir. Are you all right, Miss?'

'Mita's fine! Did you see Hook up there? How do we get out of here?'

Samuel smiled and pointed to the deck rail. A small section had been removed, and Samuel led them to the gap. Neville could see a rope ladder hanging over the side of the ship, and there, scraping against the hull as it bobbed in the water, a midget submarine.

TWENTY SEVEN

Any immediate questions Neville might have had - like "Where the hell did you get a midget submarine!" - were postponed by a cry from the bridge deck, followed by the distinct sounds of boots on steps. It was a sound Neville had heard recently enough for him not to have forgotten it.

'Samuel; you go first. Mita, follow Samuel down. And quickly!'

He had never had the chance to take control of a situation such as this, and, apart from adrenaline, was functioning on an image of how he was supposed to behave; some kind of model that had been formed from countless different experiences, just for such a situation as this.

He watched Samuel go over the side, then, when he was about a quarter of the way down, helped Mita onto the ladder. There were no histrionics; no panic. He dashed to the foot of the stairwell. There was still no sign of their pursuers, though the sounds they were making indicated that it could not be long before they appeared. Neville checked up and down the deck before lowering himself onto the rope ladder.

The last time he had tried to use one of these things had been at school. He remembered, if there was someone else climbing it at the same time as you how unstable, it could feel; he recalled he had frozen once and refused to move until he was on the ladder on his own. The experience now was similar, but not the circumstance. After a few seconds he looked down to find Samuel already at the foot of the ladder, standing on the top of the submarine waiting for Mita. As he continued his descent, Neville continued to check both upwards - for a sight of those chasing them - and downwards - to make sure Mita was safe.

Legend - gleaned from black and white movies relating wartime heroics - told him that midget submarines were craft designed for only two. However, as he watched Mita safely on board, it appeared that this particular vessel manage to cater for at least four; not only were Samuel, Mita and - soon, he hoped - himself on board, but he could also make out at least one other person already in situ.

As he placed his left foot on the submarine, Neville felt a tug on the ladder from above. He looked up to see the thuggish deck hand, Monty, and - it appeared - the Bursar, yanking at the ropes. The force with which they were able to pull it almost sent him toppling into the ocean, but luckily Samuel was still on hand to ensure a safe embarkation.

Taking his cue from Samuel, Neville lowered himself into the last place in the submarine's cockpit, a long narrow affair. Mita was already installed immediately in front of him, and - to Neville's immense surprise - Audrey in front of her. Samuel occupied the seat between them.

Suddenly the craft lurched away from the ship, and out into the churning seas, roughed up by the liner's bow as it ploughed through the water. A curtain of spray enveloped the sub, covering its occupants with a fine layer of water.

Samuel turned in his seat.

'Put on this headset,' he waved a strange helmet in the air, 'it contains an oxygen supply if we need it, and a radio so that we can talk. Then duck!'

Neville saw Mita pull her headset from the side of her chair, and found his own in the corresponding place by his left hand. He had completed Samuel's first instruction and was just about to question the second when, from the corner of his eye, he saw the submarine's canopy appear from the side of the craft. Within seconds, the perspex dome had spun over their heads and enclosed them. There was a strange kind of hissing sound as some form of seal was made, and Neville felt his ears complain at the sudden pressure.

He looked back to the S.S.Pilgrim. Already she seemed far away. He could make out a small crowd on "C" deck, some of whom appeared to be pointing in their direction.

'Samuel,' he said, having faced forwards again. He got no response. 'Samuel!' Again nothing. Not even Mita turned at his shout, and she was only inches away from him.

On the back of Mita's seat was a small panel with five lights on it. The light numbered two was flashing. Beneath the light was a button, and, assuming he was meant to, Neville pressed it.

'Are you all right, Sir?'

Samuel's voice came to him through his helmet.

'Did you hear me calling?'

'No, Sir, I didn't. We can't actually speak and be heard in this particular vessel; hence the need for the radio.'

'I see.'

'And it's only a one-to-one radio, I'm afraid. Which means you can only talk to one person at a time.'

'Where did you get this tub from? And why is Audrey here? And who's driving this thing?'

He heard Samuel give a little laugh.

'Three questions, Sir. Well, as to the first, let's say that it's just a little tr...'

Samuel's voice was cut off by the flashing of the number one light, and the corresponding voice which simply cut across the conversation.

'G-g-g-glad to have you on b-b-b-board, Sir.'

'Bursar?!'

'Of c-c-c-course!'

Neville thought of the enormously linear Porter and the general dimensions of a midget submarine.

'How did you fit into this thing? And where are you?'

'It's q-q-q-quite easy, Sir. I'm lying underneath your f-f-f-feet. There's a little glass w-w-w-window at the f-f-f-front, so I can see.'

'And you know how to steer a submarine?'

'Steer a submarine? Don't be silly dear.'

It was Audrey's voice. The third light was now showing. Neville realised that he would need to keep an eye on which light was on in order to have some idea as to who was listening in. Or talking, come to that.

'Audrey?'

'Yes, Dear?'

'How come you're here? I mean, why are you here?'

'She looks after me,' this was Mita now, 'a bit like Samuel looks after you, I guess.'

'Are you OK?'

'Me? I'm fine. What about you?'

'Sure. Never felt better.'

It sounded like a lie, but in some respects Neville knew it was the honest truth. The four light was still on.

'Was that little adventure part of your plan? Something Audrey had "arranged" for you?'

Mita laughed a little uncertainly.

'No; not me.'

'Me neither,' Neville wondered if he sounded convincing - to himself, let alone Mita.

'All I wanted was to have that one dance. That was just about the last thing on my list.'

'Your list?'

'Of things to do. Didn't you make one; at the very beginning, I mean? When you first met Samuel?'

Neville recalled the Menu, the list, and the cheese straw. And he recalled the reasons behind him drawing up the list; the motivation which, as it turned out, seemed to have been proven to be a falsehood. He glanced at his watch to check his "bank account". It showed a little over eight thousand. Neville could not remember the previous figure from the last time he had checked it, but assumed that eight-two-three-three was correct and included everything to date.

He was about to carry on his conversation with Mita when he noticed that the second hand on his watch was sweeping backwards. It was going very slowly - slower than a second-for-second sweep would normally do, but perceptibly backwards.

'Sorry, Mita; I just need to check something with Samuel.'

Neville pushed button number two.

'...and then North after that. I think that should be suitable.'

'Samuel.'

'Oh, hello, Sir. I was just giving our course to Bursar. We'll be diving in a minute; you'll hear a little bell to warn you when it is going to happen.'

'Fine.'

'What can I do for you, Sir?'

'Samuel, why is my watch going backwards?'

'Backwards, Sir?'

'Backwards, yes. The second hand is sweeping backwards, and, for all I know, the other hands are probably doing the same thing. So why? Do you know?'

There was a slight pause. Neville checked his lights to make sure that he was still connected with the right person.

'Do you recall, Sir, that you discovered that it wasn't really money that was the - how shall I put it? - the "Holy Grail" of your adventure?'

'I do.'

'And you asked if that meant that the rules of the game had changed?'

'Yes. And you said that they hadn't. I was still bound by the amount of money I had, and that I could spend no more.'

Again a pause.

'Samuel?'

'Well, Sir; I'm afraid I lied a little.'

'Lied?'

'The rules did change - not in the sense of the money, Sir; that's exactly as I suggested.'

'How then?'

'You see, you could - in theory - take as long as you wanted to spend your remaining money. You could, for example, invest it somehow and try and live off the income. If you did that, it would mean that you could go on for a long time without ever having to face up to the issues that will decide your fate.'

'Issues? What issues?'

'Those things, Sir, which decide on "A" or "B". The things you need to find or discover, that, all together, give you your answer.'

Neville had a thought. He checked the lights before his next question.

'And is Mita one of those things?'

'Mita?' Samuel paused. 'That is a difficult question, Sir. She is on her own path; your paths happened to have crossed. If she is, as you suggest, intimate to your own plan, then you would need to be so in hers. Do you see?'

'So what about the watch?'

'Yes, the watch. Given what I just said - about spending money - and the fact that there has to be some kind of limit, some target for you to reach your goal, there is a need to ration another of your limited resources.'

'My time?'

'Indeed, Sir; yes.'

Neville looked at the watch again. He could not say that he was particularly surprised. The dilemma he was now facing however, was more constrained by strict boundaries than before. Not only were his finances limited, but now his time was too - and all tied to a search for "things" about which he knew nothing, and could not readily identify. There was no list; nothing against which he could tick off any achievements.

'How long do I have, Samuel?'

'What do you mean, how long do you have?'

Light four flickered brightly. There was a note of fear in Mita's voice. Was she really one of the things for which Neville had been searching?

'Neville?'

'Sir?'

Samuel was back.

'How long, Samuel?'

'What does your watch say now?'

Neville checked.

'A little after eight.'

'If you assume that hours are days, Sir, you won't go far wrong.'

Eight days. A little bell rang, and moments later the submarine began to descend. Water soon encircled the dome, then began to flood over it. The sky became hidden by a layer of the ocean that looked like ever-thickening opaque glass. Soon there was nothing left to be seen. From the sides of the submarine, small spotlights shone as brightly as they could, challenging the darkness of the ocean to a duel they could never win.

Neville pulled off his head set and switched off his radio. Watching the darkness pass, he tried to contemplate what the next week might have in store.

TWENTY EIGHT

Having made contact with Mita again, the last thing Neville expected was to lose her again so soon.

After a few minutes watching the dark ocean and its occasional inhabitants slip by, Neville - no longer preoccupied by the radio within his helmet - simply fell asleep. When he awoke, they were once again on the surface of the water, and now within sight of land. However, the fact which gripped him the most was that the two seats immediately behind him were empty.

He shouted for Samuel before remembering the radio.

'Samuel,' button two glowed, 'where's Mita?'

'Ah, Sir. You are awake! We weren't sure whether or not we should disturb you, but considering your recent exertions, decided not to.'

'Who decided not to, Samuel?'

'Well, it was Mita, actually Sir. Though I must say, I did concur with her judgement.'

'Where has she gone?'

'She and Audrey were "put ashore" I believe the phrase is. The young lady said that she had one more thing to do; something about a list I believe. And then she was going back.'

Neville, who still imagined that he might be in a dream, rubbed his eyes and looked out of the window. Rocky cliffs passed on their left side, large tankers were ahead on the horizon, and in the distance an island loomed.

'Back? Back where?'

'To where she started. To find out.'

'Samuel, stop talking in riddles for Christ's sake! Find out what?'

There was a brief pause. The number two light went out, then, a few seconds later, was on again.

'Where were we? Oh yes, Sir, I recall. Gone back; indeed. Well, Sir; the only way to discover the outcome of the - what shall I call it - "quest", perhaps. Is that all right?'

'Do you mean "A" or "B", Samuel?'

'Indeed, Sir; "A" or "B". The only way to find out which is the route you have chosen, or for which you have prepared yourself, is to go back - in some sense or another - to where you began. To cast a fresh eye over yourself, if you will; to see how things stand.'

'That's not very clear, Samuel.'

'No Sir, I'm afraid it isn't. But it is rather difficult to explain; especially if one hasn't experienced it oneself.'

'So I will have to "go back" to somewhere, will I?'

'Or to something, Sir; yes. Or even someone.'

'And Mita? What will happen when she goes back? Does she know?'

'Know? Oh no. It is impossible to know until that one moment. Why, I have known people who believe that they have found what they were searching for, that their life has been saved; only to find out that, at the last, they were hopelessly wrong. And I have known the reverse too.'

'Does Audrey have a view, about Mita.'

Samuel paused. Neville could imagine him smiling gently to himself.

'Yes, Audrey does. She thinks Mita will do very well. But even so, she might be wrong, as I have said.'

'And do you have a view, Samuel, on how I might be doing?'

This time there was a slight laugh.

'Sir! I will have, a little nearer the time. But for the moment, let us say that I think you are progressing quite well.'

Ahead the island was growing larger, and the cliffs had given way to a flatter coastline. There were clumps of buildings here and there, and Neville made out the larger conurbation of a town.

'There is a note, Sir.'

Samuel's voice came back suddenly to him, just as he was thinking about Mita's progress - and how he was as uncertain about her future as he was about his own.

'A note?'

'Yes, Sir. the young lady left you a note. It is, I believe, in the pocket of your jacket.'

Neville felt in the side pocket of the flying jacket that he was still wearing above his suit. He pulled out two pamphlets - the top one was "Your Ship" - and an small envelope. He replaced the first two in favour of the latter, which bore no inscription. He pulled it open. Inside were several sheets of blue writing paper dressed with neat lines of blue ink.

Dear Neville,

I wasn't sure whether or not I should wake you, but then thought that if I did it might make leaving more difficult. I have one more thing that I need to do, and I'm afraid I have to do it on my own. I asked Audrey if you might be able to be there, but she said (as I knew she would) that it wasn't possible. Don't worry, it's nothing to do with you; it's something I set out to do a few days ago, and that's the end of it. I won't explain; it isn't important, and would take too long anyway.

Audrey says that she can't promise what happens after that. I've asked her of course. I guess you'll be asking Samuel the same question too someday soon. He seems like a nice old man, and I don't think he'd lie to you, not about something important. He and Audrey have a lot in common, I think, don't you?

We haven't really had much time to get to know each other have we? Just a few minutes in the restaurant, and then the dance on the ship. It was a real surprise to see you there of course - despite the "consequences"! I'm happy that it was you though; if my dream dance had a dream partner, then I think you fitted the bill very nicely.

There isn't much time really; not to tell you about why I came to be in the situation I am, or - more importantly - what I've been running away from, and what I'm going back to face. Audrey says that whatever it is - the thing that has brought us so much grief - we have to go back and face it; that's the only way of knowing really. I must confess I'm scared. I think I've taken a long hard look at myself, and that I've tried to address those things I've needed to; but I don't know, and not knowing, I can't be certain of the outcome.

Audrey says that you've only just found out about your watch. Mine says a little before one o'clock, so by the time you read this - well, it may be all over, one way or another.

I asked Samuel, if I came through OK, whether or not I would be able to see you again. He said that you still had a few days to go yet, but that he couldn't see there being a problem with me being around. I mean, apparently I can't influence things any more than I have already as far as you're concerned (I hope that's for the better!) and provided I was prepared for "the worst", then it was up to me. He wouldn't tell me what "the worst" was, or I'd tell you. Presumably he didn't want to scare me either. I've a theory that it means that one minute you're there, and the next minute you're not...Maybe we shouldn't think about it.

He said something about you going to the Derby at Epsom. Were you planning that? I said it would be nice if I could arrange to meet you somewhere; you know, something definite that we could both hang on to. (And now I'm assuming that you actually want to see me again, and that I haven't been too much trouble already!) Apparently it's not that easy. You may have said that you wanted to go there, but it wasn't definite. You said something about the Pyramids too, and he suspected that, despite it being on your list, you might not actually make it. He didn't say whether or not it would be out of choice.

Anyway, if I'm around, I'll try and get to Epsom. Who knows, although there will be millions of people there, we might just get lucky! If not, I can always ask Audrey to help me out; she seems to have lots of "little tricks"! I expect Samuel does too. Was the little submarine one of his? Actually, Audrey's been a little coy about how long she sticks around with me. If all goes well, I mean. So there's no telling, is there?

So, I guess that's about it really. Audrey says we've got a train to catch. Perhaps there will be a final surprise or two for me on there, I don't know. I'd like to be able to tell you something that would help; you know, a little tip from someone whose been a playing the game a bit longer. But I can't think of anything, and in any case, I suspect that you're pretty "street wise" yourself by now. Hopefully we'll get the chance to swap stories later...

Whatever happens, take care.

Love,

Mita xxx

When he finished reading, Neville was surprised to find that his eyes were filled with tears. There was a slight ink stain at the top of the final page, so perhaps he had been in that condition for longer than he might have imagined. Mita's note seemed sad, more like a farewell letter. He would have wished for a little more hope, a little more fight; but she was scared and unsure, and, it seemed, preparing herself for "the worst".

'Are you all right, Sir?'

Neville coughed, trying to clear the lump that had risen in his throat before replying.

'Fine, Samuel,' he said, his voice deep, hoarse, and brim-full of emotion. 'I hope she'll be OK.'

There was no reply. Neville guessed that Samuel could say nothing without sounding either patronising or morbid, so perhaps silence was the best answer of all. In any event, he chose to interpret it as "So do I, Sir; so do I".

Since he had been reading Mita's letter, the submarine had made significant progress and appeared to be heading towards a small harbour at the estuary of a river. The island Neville now recognised - thanks to the sea-bound rocks known as "The Needles" - as the Isle of Wight, and in doing so, that Samuel had brought them back to England rather than continue on to the Mediterranean.

He checked his watch. It was a little before seven thirty, so the journey in the submarine had taken them over twelve hours, most of which - it would appear - he had passed in sleep. Neville wondered if he might not have preferred a couple of days in the sun before his time ran out, but, under the circumstances, he was happy to defer to Samuel's judgement.

'Samuel.'

'Sir?'

'Where did we drop the ladies off?'

'I'm not sure I can say, Sir. You understand?'

'Yes, of course. But can you tell me if it was England? Would that be OK?'

Samuel paused.

'Let us say that we did not make it and closer to the Mediterranean. Would that be enough for you?'

'Is that all I'm getting?'

'I'm afraid so, Sir.'

'Then it will have to do.'

Samuel's light went out and then, with a loud "hiss", the submarine canopy suddenly popped off from the superstructure and tucked itself away over the side. Neville felt the fresh air stinging his face. Ahead, Samuel pulled off the helmet, then turned to him.

'That's better, isn't it?'

'Feels good, Samuel, yes.'

The quay side was now rapidly approaching, and two or three groups of people had gathered to witness the arrival of their rather unusual craft. Bursar - whom Neville had not heard from recently, though he assumed was still on board - slipped the submarine between the fishing boats and pleasure craft that bobbed gently at anchor, evidently aiming for a small jetty at the far end of the harbour.

As they approached, a man who had been sitting on a bench mending a fishing net, rose and gestured for them to throw him their mooring rope. From somewhere near the front of the sub, Samuel produced the appropriate length of hemp and threw it - with a degree of accuracy that surprised his fellow shipmate - to the man on the quay.

'Good throw, Samuel!' Neville shouted.

Samuel turned and smiled.

'Threw the odd rope or two in the war, Sir.'

'Yes, of course. How could I forget?'

With a bump, they came hard alongside the jetty. Samuel, first out of his seat, stepped up onto the hull of the submarine and then up onto the timbers of the pontoon. Neville followed suit. At the front of the submarine, from an open hatchway near what had been Samuel's seat, a bandaged head suddenly appeared, and with it the unmistakable head and shoulders of Bursar.

'Thank you Bursar,' said Samuel.

'M-m-m-my pleasure.' He looked at Neville. 'How are you, S-s-s-sir?'

'I'm fine, Bursar. Thank you very much.'

There was a brief pause, as Bursar looked around at nothing in particular.

'W-w-w-well,' he said with sudden emphasis, 'I'd b-b-b-better b-b-b-be off!'

'You take care!' Neville shouted back, as the former Porter - with his customary cry of "F-f-f-f..." dropped down through the hatchway once again.

Neville, Samuel and the man on the jetty, watched as the small submarine moved away from them and headed out towards the open sea. After a few moments, the perspex dome flipped over the cockpit once again, and gradually the craft slipped down into the water and out of sight.

'Will he be all right?' Neville asked.

'Bursar? I should think so, Sir. He seems quite a capable chap, when all's said and done.'

Samuel had the smile on his face that told Neville that he knew more than he was letting on. It was the smile of a man who had an edge, who knew the game and the way to play it. But it was a benevolent smile, and, whatever lay in store for Neville over the next seven or so days, he was pleased that the smile - and its owner - appeared to be firmly on his side.

'Shall we take the bus?'

Samuel had turned and was leading Neville towards the steps at the end of the jetty.

'The bus? Isn't it at the airport?'

The smile remained on Samuel's face as they climbed the steps. The bus - now painted a deep metallic green - was parked just a few yards from where they stood. Neville placed a hand on Samuel's shoulder, and Samuel gave a little chuckle. And as they walked to the bus, Neville suddenly wondered where Mita might be at that precise moment, and if, at some time in the future, he would ever see her again.

TWENTY NINE

Returning to the bus, Neville was expecting to find that, in addition to the colour of the exterior, things would have changed on the inside too. However, this was so much **not** the case that he noticed an old mug, still containing the dregs of his last cup of tea, resting on the small table at the front. Samuel gave a small but audible sigh as he stood by the driver's seat, with his left hand resting on the steering wheel.

'You know, Sir,' he volunteered, 'I do miss the Old Lady.'

'Prefer it to a midget submarine, eh?'

Samuel smiled.

'Just a little.'

Neville wanted to ask how the bus had found its way to this coastal inlet from the airport some ten or fifteen miles away, but he knew that the answer - although in all probability an honest one - would not actually tell him anything. He made a move towards the closed curtain that defined the boundary of his compartment.

'Well, I don't know about you Samuel, but I'm going to get changed.'

Pulling back the curtain, Neville expected to find the bags that had been with him on the ship awaiting him on the bed. This was something he had become used to; one of Samuel's "little tricks" that was entirely functional. So, when he stood facing his bed to find things exactly as he had left them prior to their departure, he was a little surprised.

'Tea, Sir?' Samuel said as he walked passed him, now carrying the empty cup he had just seen.

Neville wondered about the clothes, but refrained from asking.

'Good idea, Samuel. Why not?'

As Samuel left him, he began to wonder if the non-appearance of his clothes had something to do with the fact that the game was now timed; as if it were another aspect of the rule change which he now seemed to be facing. He had so much time, so many clothes. He pulled open the cupboard. At least there were enough clothes in there to prevent him from finishing his adventure stark naked.

Despite the not inconsiderable sleep Neville had enjoyed on the submarine, he was once again rather tired. Consequently his bed seemed quite inviting to him. He stretched and pulled off the heavy flying jacket it seemed he had been wearing for ages. He dropped it onto the bed where it landed with the sound of a garment so heavy and substantial that it had to be taken seriously. From one of the pockets, the edges of an envelope were showing. Neville bent and removed both Mita's letter and the remainder of the pocket's contents. He thought about re-reading the letter, but it felt familiar enough to him and, at the present time, it was sufficient that his thoughts should be with Mita. He needed no prompting for that.

'Souvenir, Sir?' Samuel returned just as Neville had deposited Mita's letter in his drawer, and was holding the guide to the S.S.Pilgrim.

Neville looked down at the "Your Ship" pamphlet. "Total Leisure Incorporated"; something else he was not likely to forget in a hurry.

'Should I keep it, Samuel? Or rather, can I keep it? Is that the more appropriate question?'

Samuel smiled.

'Your tea. I'll leave it here, shall I?'

Neville tapped the guide on his hand, then put it in the drawer with Mita's letter. This left him holding one other item. It was a pamphlet of similar size as that relating to the S.S.Pilgrim. He had been aware of it since Bursar had left it with him, but he had lacked the opportunity to pay it any attention since that time.

'Hey! Hey, Mister!'

A small voice of complaint rose from the floor. Neville looked down at his shoes.

'Come on! We're dog tired. Take us off!' moaned the left shoe.

'Yeah; give us a break!' added his partner.

He sat on the bed.

'OK guys, fair enough.'

Neville united the laces and slipped the shoes from his feet. Both they and his feet seemed to sigh at this freedom. He leant forwards and placed the shoes at the bottom of his cupboard, then, before sitting back to drink his tea, he also took off his suit jacket and laid it along the bed. The jacket, in so much as it seemed a barometer of his own moods and situations, looked rather grey and lifeless, and it lay, crumpled and without precision, at his side.

He picked up the second pamphlet again, and considered its title which he now noticed for the first time. The cover design was a somewhat abstract pattern. Despite the rather random character of the shapes that went to make it up, Neville had the rather definite impression that it was meant to depict something.

From the far end of the bus, he heard Samuel's voice - 'Just going to have a quick bath, Sir!' - and the sound of water running in the bath. Had he wished to consult Samuel on the pattern, or - more importantly - on the title of the pamphlet, the opportunity was to be denied him for a few minutes. Neville stared at the words now attracting his attention:

CROAK: A Guide to the Game.

It seemed a strange title for a game, "Croak"; and it was certainly one he had never come across before. He turned to the next page of the booklet.

1 - Introduction to the Game

The Board. CROAK is played without a board. If it were, however, it would be a multi-dimensional affair, with - in all probability - at least seven levels. Each level would contain either squares or hexagons which, in the full game, would need to contain in excess of twenty seven positions. With each level slightly offset from both its predecessor and its precursor, the game would offer complexities far in excess of comparable board games.

The Pieces. CROAK is played without pieces. If it were, however, the set would consist of a number of different constructs, each of which would obey its own particular set of movement rules. Although the set would need to be multi-coloured (with each colour representing a different "family" within the game) the pieces would, as a whole, form the total strength of the single side which took part in the game. As such, the struggle for control and mastery - and the ultimate goal of victory - would rival the stratagems required to complete tasks of impossible complexity.

The Dice. CROAK is played without dice. If it were, however, the dice (or die) would need to be multi-faceted, and of colours similar to both the board and the pieces (although this would not imply any strict relationship between any of the elements concerned). The faces of the die or dice would contain more than one value (though not in all cases) and the score applied when the die or dice were thrown would depend on the particular circumstance of the game at the time and would, in any event, not necessarily correspond to an equivalent move - either laterally or linearly - on the board. Given such potential variations, the use of the dice would render the most powerful computer impotent in the calculation of the variations available at any one time.

Neville turned away from the booklet for a moment and picked up his tea. As he sipped it, he tried to conjure up an image of "Croak"; the rather eccentric board, the colourful playing pieces, and the complex dice. From the description given - and this, of course, of exactly what the game was not - Neville could see a vague relationship between how the game might look and the rather abstract cover to the booklet; beyond this he was fundamentally lost. There would, he assumed, need to be some kind of rule book for the version of "Croak" described, and he could only see this as some enormous volume of ordered and numbered statements which, he suspected, would be no more than a series of "hints and tips" rather than a comprehensive set of game-playing instructions.

As he put down his tea, he tried to imagine the game without the board, its pieces, and the dice required to move them; but all that left him with was the booklet.

2 - Object of the Game

One. CROAK has a number of objectives, or goals, which the player should attempt to achieve. The first of these relates to the duration of the game. Any player of CROAK should endeavour to make the game last as long as he or she possibly can. Depending on the circumstances within the game at any one time, and any circumstantial factors relating to the player's own interpretation of the rules, the game may or may not be played beyond the point at which it ceases to be enjoyable. Indeed, many of the finest exponents of CROAK ensure a game of enormous duration by confining themselves within strict limits. If CROAK were a board game (as described above) then such a player might choose to confine his pieces (having chosen a restricted set) to a single level, and play the entire game with perhaps only one or two dice. Such a stratagem, whilst popular in that it would make the game more accessible, would not provide for a great deal of excitement or post-game analysis.

Two. The second objective of CROAK is to obtain mastery of the entire game-playing situation. This is the most difficult of the objectives of the game. The player must attempt to arrive at a position in the game where, irrespective of any move made by the player himself (or herself), or as a result of any external influence - such as an unexpected roll of the dice, or a mistake on the part of the player in the execution of a move or moves - the player must be able to retrieve the situation to such an extent that, not only is there no loss in terms of his or her overall control of the game, but that the position of the player is undeniably strengthened. If CROAK were a board game (as described above) then such a situation might occur if the player had deployed his pieces with such skill and foresight that, irrespective of any subsequent move or action, the player would have all options covered, and be able - in any situation - to move his or her pieces to such an effect that they would obtain a position of increasing irresistibility.

Three. The third objective of CROAK relates to the way the game is played, rather than the specific outcome of the game itself. CROAK is renowned as a spectator sport and, irrespective of the style of play chosen by the player, he or she should endeavour to provide some degree of entertainment to those watching. In the majority of cases, games of CROAK which are the most exciting tend to be of shorter duration than the norm; they can be quite frenetic, with the player sacrificing overall control of the game in the pursuit of this particular objective. If CROAK were a board game (as described above) the player attempting to maximise the enjoyment of those watching would be most likely to choose a game with a large sub-set of the available pieces, or to conduct the game across the full range of playing surfaces. The game would be fast, and, by utilising the majority of the dice available, the player would be accepting and taking risks, having little or no control over their outcome.

With the end of the page, Neville once again turned to his tea, this time finishing it in one swallow. From the back of the bus, he could hear faint splashing in the bath, and Samuel's rather broken tenor of as he fumbled his way through the Italian of a famous Puccini aria.

Neville wondered if Samuel might be able to shed any light on "Croak". The fact that the booklet had been given to him by Bursar, and that Bursar was - to some extent - an acquaintance of Samuel's, led him to put two and two together. This was, Neville knew, much in the way of his overall relationship with Samuel. Often there was little definition, little precision; Samuel liked to offer suggestions or remain vague as evidenced by his use of words such as "perhaps". Indeed, Neville realised, that despite the occasional chats relating to his own situation where Samuel was presumably endeavouring to pass on relevant information, in the end he often felt as much in the dark as he had been before they had started talking.

He weighed the booklet in his hand. This little document seemed to be much in this vein too; it appeared to be aiming to give information, yet as much as it gave, it seemed to take away again. Neville struggled with the concept of "Croak"; having been offered the board and all its pieces - whatever they looked like! - he was unable to remove the image from his mind and allow it to concentrate on what the game *actually* was. The rules gave nothing away, either. A picture, a diagram, or even some form of table laying out - something - would have been of use; as it was, Neville struggled with the words, lacking a suitable context within which to fit them.

Readjusting his pillows in order to allow a more comfortable sitting position - his legs, along with the rest of his body, now on the bed - he decided to press on.

3 - The Opening Position

The Set-Up. The player, on first starting a game of CROAK, finds himself confronting the opening position. It is important to note that, although there are many similar initial set-ups in the game, and that many of these could be seen to form themselves into particular groupings or styles of game, there is no standard opening to CROAK. The player enters the game as if it has already been in progress for some time, the maturity and complexity of the situation he finds himself in dependant on factors outside of his or her control yet totally relevant to the individual player. In the hypothetical case of CROAK being a board game (which it is not) the player would come to the board with a number of pieces already dispersed. The number, make-up and variety of playing pieces laid out, as well as their location in terms of not only the levels occupied but also their precise positions, remaining outside the control of the participant.

The First Move. Given the opening position, the player should first attempt to evaluate the situation he or she faces. This is important as a first step in that, by doing so, the player may make an assessment of the type of game he or she is going to play and, more specifically, which of the objectives they will pursue throughout. In order to make an accurate assessment of the situation, the player will need to spend a considerable amount of time in studying the position he or she faces. At this point in the game, the player is at his or her most vulnerable from external influences and from making mistakes in their own game-play. It is often the case that a player's assessment of the situation - and their consequent assumed direction - is proven to be incorrect, and as a result they are faced with the difficult decision of attempting to change their strategy or of making the best of the position in which they find themselves. In the hypothetical case of CROAK being a board game (which it is not) the player might choose - based on the initial position - to decrease the number of pieces they are playing with and confine themselves to a single level of the board; only to discover that during the early stages of the game additional pieces appear on the board, and in locations which undermine their overall strategy. As the first moves in such a game of CROAK would also represent something of a familiarisation period for the player, many players might choose to follow a course of plays which would suggest themselves as being safe set of opening moves, should such a thing exist. It would be important to remember that, should any such moves be available - in the hypothetical game - there is none, no matter how apparent risk-less or inoffensive, which is entirely safe and secure.

We will now go on to consider the **Method of Play**, and the **Conclusion of the Game**.

'Sir?'

Neville glanced up. Samuel, now dressed in a tweed dressing gown, stood by his curtains. He looked fresher and somehow younger after his bath.

'Hello, Samuel. Nice bath? I heard you singing.'

'Oh, sorry about that. I'm afraid I do have a minor weakness for breaking into song when in the bath.'

'It was fine - Pavarotti would have been proud!'

Samuel laughed, recognising that the very opposite was likely to be the truth.

'I just wondered if I could get you something as a night cap.'

'A night cap?'

'It is nearly midnight, Sir. I assumed that you were planning to turn in.'

Neville looked at the small clock that stood by the side of his bed. Progressing in a clockwise direction - as all sound clocks should do - it confirmed Samuel's statement. He realised that, since their escape from the S.S.Pilgrim he had lost all sense of time. There was the trip in the submarine; that had taken a few hours. And then the journey along the Solent to here; presumably that was a few hours more. It did not seem to amount to a little over a day; but then again, he had been feeling tired, and the reading had made his eyes a little sore.

He closed the booklet and placed it on the small cabinet.

'Ever heard of a game called "Croak", Samuel?'

'"Croak", Sir? No, I don't believe I recognise the name. Why?'

Neville considered explaining the pamphlet and its contents to Samuel, and - considering its origins - perhaps challenging him on his last statement. However, he decided that it might be prudent to complete the last two sections before indulging in any debate.

'Why? Oh, I'll tell you later. It isn't important right now.'

'Very well, Sir.' Samuel paused. 'And did you want anything?'

'No thank you.'

'I'll say Good Night then, Sir.' And in doing so, Samuel turned towards his own compartment.

Neville called him back.

'Sir?'

'Samuel, do you ever know what happens to other people?'

'Other people? I'm not sure I follow.'

'Mita, for example. Would you know - would Audrey tell you - what had happened to her?'

Samuel paused, tugging at the tie of his robe as he did so.

'To be honest Sir, I might never see Audrey again. If we meet in the future it will be by chance; so I have little or no prospect of Audrey telling me anything.'

'I just thought... Actually, I'm not sure what I thought. Perhaps that you saw each other regularly, somehow. I don't know.'

Samuel smiled gently.

'I'm afraid we don't belong to some kind of club; even though it might seem that way at times.'

Neville waited; and Samuel waited too.

'But will you know, Samuel?'

Samuel leant forwards and placed a consoling arm on Neville's shoulder.

'No Sir; I'm afraid I won't.'

THIRTY

'Is there anywhere you particularly wanted to go, Sir?'

This was - after the usual early morning preamble of waking up, getting dressed and eating breakfast - the first question of any real note that Samuel asked the next day. Neville sat on his stool in the galley, the empty plate that had contained his bacon, sausage and eggs, pushed to one side in front of him; his hand rested on the small breakfast bar, cradling a half empty mug of coffee. Samuel was standing by the sink.

Neville looked at the questioner. He had been staring out of the window, watching the early-morning fishermen as they returned to port. It was not a large fleet - perhaps three or four boats - but they gave the impression that the small harbour was a working one, and all the more authentic for that. He had been feeling restless since rising, and despite the opportunity to be refreshed by a bath and a hearty breakfast, was now at something of a low ebb.

'Do I have a choice, Samuel?'

'Don't you always?'

Neville chose not to reply, primarily because he was still uncertain of what the correct answer was to that particular question.

'What do I need to consider then? Given my present constraints, what parameters do I have to work within?'

Samuel put down the cup he had been drying and hung the tea cloth on a hook by the taps. He pulled his own stool a little closer and, with a small but perceptible sigh, sat down. Reaching to the side, he picked up his tea and took the first draught from it.

'You are not happy, Sir?'

'Happy?' It seemed an emotion totally out of place in the context of Neville's immediate situation, and Samuel's choice of word surprised him a little. 'No, Samuel; you could say that I am not happy. In fact I'm not sure that I can remember the last time I was.'

Samuel paused for a little more tea.

'I am not surprised you say that. I know things have been a little difficult; and especially near the end, people forget things, lose their way.'

Neville wondered exactly what "near the end" meant, but chose not to challenge Samuel on it.

'You ask when you were last happy? On the ship perhaps, when you were dancing with Mita? Or on the submarine later, once we had effected the rescue?'

Neville could only concede this, and he knew that Samuel knew it too. He checked his watch.

'Apparently I have something like six and a half days left. But "left" to what? I mean, presumably I have to go somewhere do I, at the end? Mita talked about "going back" to face something. Is that what I must do? And if so, where do I need to go? How much time do I need?'

'There are a lot of questions there, Sir, aren't there?' Samuel tried a smile to ease the tension that was beginning to build. 'I can't give you too many answers - but I do know that you are closer to answering them than you think.'

'Really?'

'Yes, really.'

Both men returned to their tea. Outside on the quay side, one of the boats was unloading its morning's haul. Crates brim-full of fish gleamed in the sun as the light reflected off the scales of the dead fish. Neville thought of Bob; and thinking of Bob thought of Mita.

'I understand, Sir,' Samuel had been watching Neville as he stared out of the window, 'but I'm afraid that all you can do is hope and have faith.'

'Faith? In what should I have faith, Samuel?'

Samuel smiled.

'You see; I told you that you were closer to finding the answers you needed.'

'How so?'

'Because you begin to know the questions to ask.'

Neville finished his tea. Perhaps there was something in what Samuel had said. Perhaps he had been approaching his situation from the wrong angle; looking for the wrong things; expecting to find **something** that was tangible and would solve the unexpressed riddle for him. Perhaps understanding was the first step. But if it was - and, come to that, understanding **what** indeed? - would that be enough, in the next six days, to save him?

'Do I go back to Malvern?' He asked the question as one might a fortune-teller.

'Why?'

'Because that's where it started. "It". All of this.' He swept his arm out in a gesture through the air, trying to encompass the bus, the harbour, all the dead fish.

Samuel shook his head slightly. He was still smiling that benign smile of his.

'Is it? Is it really?'

The last day. Neville wondered if he had that long - five and a bit days - to work out where he supposed to return to. Maybe he should aim to "go back" the day before, just in case he was wrong; just in case he might be horribly mistaken. At least then he would have a day's grace; a second chance.

So what else should he do? He tried to remember his original list.

'When's the Derby, Samuel?'

'In three days I believe, Sir.'

'Then we should go there, don't you think? I did say that I wanted to; and I told Mita that I would be there, so I have to don't I? Because...'

Samuel cut-in before he could elaborate any further.

'Indeed, yes. I would recommend that we get there the day after tomorrow; that will give us plenty of time. I wouldn't like to risk the traffic, not on Derby day.'

'And after that; do I have enough time, to "get back" to wherever I'm going - wherever that might be?'

Samuel tapped the side of the bus.

'I think that we should be able to get you wherever you wanted to go, Sir, yes.'

'Good.'

Neville, who had begun to feel a little better, returned Samuel's smile, boosted in part by the other's confidence. He wanted now to be doing something; he wanted not to be sitting idle and waiting for whatever it was that was coming his way. It was suddenly important for him to be occupied. He wanted to avoid any fear of the future, and he wanted not to think too much about Mita. To be going to the Derby was the only thing to do, and if Mita was there, and if she found him - well that could be another question answered.

'Shall we get underway then, Samuel, off in the general direction of Epsom perhaps? Maybe we could go via Winchester. I would like to see the Cathedral again; I haven't been there since I was a boy.'

'The Cathedral?' Samuel thought for a moment. 'That sounds like a good idea, Sir. Yes, let's do that, shall we?'

They both rose, and Neville handed Samuel his empty mug for washing. As Samuel busied himself at the sink, Neville replaced the two stools in their slots beneath the breakfast bar. The bus suddenly seemed a remarkable piece of engineering; everything with its own place, all fitting together remarkable well. He could think of nothing wasted, nothing extraneous.

'Will you be travelling up front, Sir, or in your compartment?'

Neville paused.

'Up front I think; mind you, there is something I need to finish reading, so I may not be much company for you.'

'Don't you worry about me, Sir; I'm happy enough just to be behind the wheel.'

A few minutes later, Neville heard the familiar sound of the old bus being persuaded into life as he stood by his bed pulling on a loose lambs' wool cardigan. The brochure that he was half way through sat at the top of the open drawer where he had left it the previous evening. In a way he was a little surprised to find it still there, as if it would have been fitting somehow for it to have disappeared before he had a chance to finish reading it. Armed with the booklet, he made his way to the front of the bus.

Samuel gave him a quick glance as he settled in his seat, but remained silent, making no reference to what he might be reading nor passing any comment on their prospective progress. Neville, having strapped himself in, took a few moments to reacquaint himself with the sensation of being driven in the bus. It seemed a long time since his last experience of Samuel's cautious twenty seven miles per hour, though he knew that it was not. Much had happened in the intervening day or two - the dog-fight, the S.S.Pilgrim, the submarine - to make that period seem to have lasted much longer than it actually had.

Outside, they had rumbled through the fringes of the tiny village and were now in open country. Inside, Neville opened the pamphlet and began to read.

4 - Method of Play

Strategy. The player of CROAK should endeavour, at the earliest opportunity, to furnish themselves with a strategy that they will choose to follow for the duration of the game. As has already been indicated, the strategy should be allied with the attainment of one or more of the game objectives. However, this is not always necessary, and the player may, if they so desire - and if the position in the game is such that the alternative is both feasible and attractive - choose to adopt a strategy which is essentially open-ended, and without allegiance to a pre-defined goal. Such a strategy, which is essentially flexible both in terms of game play and the options available to the player, is, of course, the most difficult to master. In addition to this, it has a fundamental drawback in that the player may easily find himself or herself suddenly into an end-game without having established any potential route to victory. In this case, the entire game becomes an anti-climax, and many famous games of CROAK have ended in much disappointment. Given the illustration of CROAK as a board game - evidently out of the question - the player would need to have established a wide variety of pieces across all levels of the board, and with such a balance in their strengths and mobility, that they would be in a position to easily counter any situation which may occur. The difficulty arises when the player discovers that they have an insufficient concentration in any area or level of the board, or an inappropriate mix of pieces, to deal a decisive blow at the conclusion of the game.

Levels of Play. There are numerous ways to approach the play-by-play mechanics of CROAK. The player may endeavour to plan their moves well in advance, even to the extent that they have identified a chain of perhaps dozens of moves which they plan to execute one after the other in the pursuit of their defined strategy. Alternatively, it is possible to play the game on a move-by-move basis, where the consequence of one move is never considered in terms of the move that may follow it. These two methods or levels of play - from the extremes of pre-planning and depth of thought, to the cavalier and liberated - both have weaknesses. In the first instance, certain events may force the player to deviate from his or her planned sequence of moves to such an extent that they must to take time to re-plan a new sequence of moves. A possible outcome of this is that the player may actually end up making an insufficient number of moves to achieve anything during the game. In the second example, the player may make many moves - certainly more than he or she needs to - with the problem being that, as none of the moves bear any strategic relationship to each other, the player may drift through the game aimlessly. Given the illustration of CROAK as a board game - evidently out of the question - the player will need to balance, at all times, the state of the game and their relationship with both their strategic aims and the challenges and opportunities presented to them at each turn. Dependant on the immediate situation (which could, of course, change in an instant) they will need to be able to adopt either a fully planned sequence of moves, or a number of spontaneous moves, as necessary.

Neville looked up from the booklet. Outside the countryside was passing them by as they made their casual way northwards. On both sides of the bus, large areas of forested parkland opened up, and occasionally he could see deer or ponies amidst the trees. Samuel was aware that he was now looking out of the window.

'Finished reading, Sir?'

'Nearly Samuel.'

'I was wondering if you might like to stop for a cup of coffee in a little while, before we get to Winchester.'

'Yes, that might be nice. Any idea how long it will be before we get there?'

Samuel's smile reminded Neville that, in the context of his present adventure, there could hardly be a more redundant question to ask. Had he said "How long is a piece of string" he would have been more likely to have obtained a meaningful answer. Still, the driver humoured him.

'Shouldn't be long, Sir, I expect.'

Neville checked the booklet. He had only one more section left to read, though he was - now as much as at any time before - still not sure why he was continuing to read the guide, let alone attempt to make any sense of it. "Croak" seemed to defy logic as far as he could see, though it did appear - and at every turn too - to present itself as a rational and logical exposition of a game that anyone could effectively pick up and play.

5 - Conclusion of the Game

The End-Game. At some point in the game, a position may be reached where one of a number of potential situations arise. In this event, the game comes to an end. Forewarning that the end of the game is at hand comes when CROAK enters its final phase, or end-game. The end-game - which cannot be identified by any particular occurrence, position, or manoeuvre - may last as long again as the entire game up to the point at which it is reached, or it may be over in a single move. The actual duration of the end-game will depend upon the type of game being played, the player's strategy, the position at any particular point in time, as well as any number of external factors. Once the end-game is entered, it is usual for the game to progress to its conclusion. However, under certain exceptional circumstances, it is possible for the player - either though their own efforts, or otherwise - to leave the end-game and return, quite legitimately to the game proper. Under these circumstances, the player may expect to enter another end-game phase at some stage in the future, the timing and duration of which will be no more nor less calculable than was the original. In the board game scenario - where CROAK would manifest itself in the appropriate format - the end-game may be triggered via a number of individual situations or circumstances ranging from an individual move, through a combination of pieces and their physical locations, to a particular result of a dice (or die) roll. Whichever, the player needs to recognise that they are now in the end-game phase in order for them to take any action necessary regarding the position as it stands, their strategy at that time, and their overall game objectives.

The Outcome. The result of the game will either be that the player either wins or loses. A draw is an invalid result and, in the unlikely event that such a possibility exists, the game will be extended (without the player's knowledge) until a definite result is achieved. The player wins when the fundamental aims of CROAK are met; namely that they achieve the goal (or goals) that they set out to achieve, or which are recognised as legitimate objectives for the particular game in progress. In addition, the player will have needed to demonstrate a thorough understanding of the rules, tenets and principles of the game; to have shown, at some stage (or stages) during the game that they are master of their own strategy and the application of that strategy in the pursuit of whichever goal (or goals) for which they strive; and, most importantly, that should they be required to undertake another game of CROAK, they have attained sufficient knowledge of its fundamentals for them to out-perform their previous endeavours in all respects and in all consequences. In the board game scenario - where CROAK would manifest itself in the appropriate format - the conclusion of the game would come when the player runs out of time or is unable to make any further move, or when, irrespective of any external incident - i.e. a roll of the dice (or die) or the appearance or disappearance of a piece on the board - the player needs to do nothing to maintain the position he or she has attained which, of course, would also need to coincide with the meeting of the original or revised game objective or objectives. Under these circumstances - and given any local provisos which may be in force for any game as appropriate to the player of that game - then the player may be said to have "won". In any other circumstance other than that defined as a "win", the player will be deemed to have "lost" and the game terminates.

The conclusion of the booklet coincided with a gradual deceleration of the bus, accompanied by the plaintive moan of the ancient gear box. Neville, looking up and expecting to find Samuel preparing for a coffee break in a quiet lay-by, was surprised to find the facade of Winchester Cathedral rising not three hundred yards ahead of him.

THIRTY ONE

After a brief debate, they decided to have coffee anyway. While Samuel made the coffee and opened a packet of biscuits (chocolate cookies he said he had been "saving") Neville returned the "Croak" guide to the drawer from which he had earlier removed it. Back in his seat, with the bus parked in the Cathedral square, he was able to cast his eyes over the building that, as a child, he seemed to have visited almost every weekend.

He was sure that his memory was inaccurate, and that, because he had been a child at the time, the events - which were never particularly pleasurable to him - had grown by means of self-inflicted legend to have become an almost weekly torture. As the bus filled with the rich aroma of fresh coffee (Samuel obviously in an expansive, non-instant kind of mood) he was able to consider the lines of the building with fresh eyes. The negative sensation from his childhood amused him, and he found himself intrigued rather than daunted by his notion of the place.

'Intrigued?'

Samuel had come in on the end of his thoughts and was obviously interested in the line he had been almost unconsciously taking.

'Perhaps that isn't the right word, I don't know. But the fear has gone.' Neville smiled. 'I used to hate this place, just coming here. We lived quite nearby once - in Twyford, by the river - and my Aunt would insist on visiting regularly, normally on Saturdays when we came to town to shop. Even though she may have only been doing it for me, I was too young to protest, I suppose.'

'Or to know why you hated it?'

'Well, it wasn't the Cathedral I hated I guess; it was most likely the being dragged around, without the freedom to do what I wanted.'

'To stay at home and play with your model cars?'

Neville laughed.

'Something like that!'

Samuel placed a mug of coffee and a small plate of biscuits in front of him.

'And intrigue?' he said, as he resumed his own seat and began to much on a cookie.

'Interest; a lack of understanding, maybe. About what it stands for - the church, I mean. Church in the "big", general sense. Why is it here, the cathedral? What made - and makes - men build things like this?'

'Is it something you don't understand?'

'Something I don't think I comprehend, rather than fail to understand. Is there a difference?'

The square was quiet. Two old ladies left the Cathedral, walking arm-in-arm away towards the shopping centre. It was mid-week, mid-day, and the weather had encouraged the tourists to stay at home. Against the dull sky, the building - still impressive as a structure - seemed to blend its greyness in with the day itself. Neville looked for beauty and found none.

'Why now, Sir - if you don't mind me asking.'

'Now what, Samuel?'

'Why Winchester Cathedral now? Is there any reason for you to be here?'

Neville, still looking at the building and its square, tried to place it within some kind of context.

'I don't know. As we were passing, I thought it might be nice to see it again; to lay an old ghost to rest, if you like. And you said something about faith, too; do you remember? Perhaps there is a question there that I do need to answer.'

'About what, Sir; Christianity?'

Neville laughed gently.

'No, Samuel, I don't think so. My Aunt managed to put me off that very early on. Not that she was particularly devout, or tried to force it upon me - not that I remember anyway. I guess I saw her give a lot and receive nothing in return. Not as a child, anyway. So it has never appealed; nothing has, really.'

'And now?'

'And now I'm not sure if that's right. Or if it *is* right - right for me that is – whether or not I understand why that is. Do you see?'

There was silence as the two men drank coffee; a silence broken only by the occasional crunch of a biscuit, or the "clink" of mug on saucer. Neville, having finished first, rose from his chair.

'Are you coming, Samuel?'

Samuel smiled.

'I don't think so, Sir. I need to get one or two provisions. I thought it might be nice to have a bit of a picnic at Epsom, so I really ought to go and get the things we will need. So you go ahead. I will probably be back here before you, anyway.'

Neville imagined that Samuel could probably get all the shopping he needed without even leaving the comfort of the bus if he put his mind to it. In any event, having made the offer, he was quite pleased that Samuel had declined as he fancied seeing the place on his own. Returning to his compartment, he buttoned up his cardigan and pulled his overcoat from the cupboard. Momentarily, he toyed with the notion of wearing the flying jacket, but this seemed somehow inappropriate with a visit far removed from any idea of "action".

As soon as he had left the warmth of the coach, the wind - which was certainly stronger than it had appeared to be - bit hard into him, even into the fabric of his coat. In the grey sky, lumps of dense and threatening cloud chased in a hurry to get somewhere and wet someone. It did not seem like early June, and Neville - as he walked across the green - hoped that the weather would be kinder at Epsom.

He paused in the entrance vestibule and scanned the notices, including one for a local bell-ringing group, another proclaiming the advent of a bring-and-buy sale in Twyford in aid of the village school, and - largest of all - the rather imposing sign which requested (in a kind of demanding way) that visitors make a donation to Cathedral funds. Religion with menaces. Perhaps there was nothing new in that, but he was sure - all those years ago - entrance used to be free.

'But it still is free,' said a deep voice, surrounding him with a kind of quiet echo: 'free, free, free...'

Neville looked around and could see no-one. He checked the walls and the ceiling, but could find no indication of the source of the voice. Undaunted by something that might have struck terror into those instantly interpreting it as God, he pushed open the semi-glazed entrance door and walked into the cathedral proper.

His first footfall gave off a quiet echo of its own, and once inside, he stood still for a moment. There was no other sound. He could see that the small gift shop was closed and guessed that from the absence of any sound (except perhaps the occasional whistle from the wind outside) he had the place to himself. They had always walked the Cathedral the same way when he had been young, and now - habit still strongly in force - he began the same anti-clockwise rotation.

He had not gone far - past the first few stained glass windows - when he became aware that he was being watched. He paused by a memorial stone to an early Bishop of Winchester, stared up at one of the windows, and waited to see if the sensation would pass. It did not. Indeed, he now felt the feeling augmented by a sound which he could only identify as slow but deep breathing.

'Well, it has been a long time, time, time...'

It was the same deep voice, only now coming from behind him and within the body of the building. Neville turned expecting to find that he was being addressed by a member of the clergy, or a parish warden, or even the old pensioner who used to arrange the flowers; but still the Cathedral was empty.

'Here, here, here...' said the voice, the same slow echo bouncing off the pillars and pews.

A little over twelve feet from him was a monument to the crusades. On a stone plinth, was the figure of a Knight, one hand holding his sword, shield on his chest, dog at his feet; his other hand clasped with the hand of his Lady who lay at his side - except that the Knight was sitting half-upright, leaning on his right arm, and looking directly at Neville.

'I saw you come in, in, in... You haven't been here for a while, have you, you, you..?'

Neville took a pace or two forwards then stopped. The Knight slowly swung his legs over the side of the plinth, the movement of stone on stone making a deliberate and solid grinding sound. Lowering himself to the ground, the floor seemed to shake as he made contact with it, and Neville looked round involuntarily to see if the noise had roused anyone.

The Knight left his shield and the dog to guard his place and took two solid, heavy steps towards Neville.

'Shall we walk, walk, walk..?' There was the echo again, and now the breathing and the rather powerful sound of flexing stone.

'Do you remember everyone?'

'No, no, no...' said the Knight, ' but more than people imagine, imagine, imagine... After all, what else is there to do all day when you are lying there but look at people passing, passing, passing..?'

'And you remember me?'

They had started walking, still anti-clockwise and still slowly, their progress accompanied but the sound of the Knight's stiff movements across the stone floor.

'Yes, yes, yes... Of course I remember someone who I saw week after week, week, week... That was your mother who brought you, you, you..?'

'My Aunt. We lived nearby, in Twyford.'

The Knight looked puzzled.

'That is not a name I know, know, know...'

Neville chose not to elaborate; after all, it was quite likely that the Knight would be unfamiliar with many modern place-names, including, he guessed, even Winchester itself. It was not a subject about which he knew enough to do battle in. He returned to his previous theme.

'But I was only small then; and it was probably thirty years ago. How could you recognise me now?'

'Because I expected to see you again, again, again... Because I have come to recognise those who will cross my path at some stage in their own future, future, future...'

'So all those years ago, you knew that one day I would come back here?'

'Not one day, but this day, day, day... And I have been waiting - as I wait for all others - for you, you, you...'

They had walked nearly the length of the Cathedral and had reached the entrance to the crypt. Often, Neville had used to try and persuade his Aunt to let him go down into the crypt; more often than not she had refused. Neville paused, but the Knight continued in his slow pace, giving the impression that if he stopped once he would not be able to move again.

'You go down, if you want to, to, to... You can always catch me up, up, up...'

Neville thought for a moment, then decided to give the crypt a miss. He joined the Knight at his side.

'How do you find this, being -' Neville hesitated, thinking about using the word "stuck" but then deciding against it, 'being here after your exploits in the wars?'

'Wars, wars, wars..?'

The Knight's granite face showed little expression. Neville looked at it now, trying to find some degree of humanity in it, but there was none. It was a benevolent face, and not the face of a cruel man, but the Knight seemed to have lost any power of expression except in the resonance of his stony voice. Just now he seemed a little displeased.

'We were on a righteous and glorious crusade, crusade, crusade... We were fighting for God, God, God...'

Neville could imagine candles throughout the Cathedral suddenly bursting into flame with the power that seemed to underlie the Knight's last words. He was, however, undeterred. If recent experiences had taught him anything it was not to give in - and also that the Knight, whatever his own motivations or desires, was there for a purpose and there for him.

'But only your view of God, surely. Were you not fighting to impose your God on another race?'

'We were right, and we were chosen, chosen, chosen...' The Knight's right hand tightened its grip on his sword.

'But a lot of people died, didn't they?'

The Knight paused. His words, when they came, were filled with sorrow and grief.

'Yes, a great many died, died, died...'

'And for what? Things have moved on now.'

'Did we not win, win, win..? Were we not victorious, victorious, victorious..?'

And then it occurred to Neville for the first time that the Knight might actually have died during the Crusades and returned home a dead and unfulfilled man; that the sorrow he had just sensed, was the emotion of a man in part grieving for himself.

'They have a God there now; and they are a civilised people.'

'But the God they have is not our Master, Master, Master..?'

'Who can say?'

There was a brief pause. The Knight, now with his hand relaxed at his side, moved slowly on. They had reached the far end of the Cathedral and were walking behind the altarpiece. As they did so, the Knight turned his heavy head and looked directly at Neville.

'And what of you, you, you..?'

'Me?'

'You are embarked upon your own crusade, are you not, not, not..? That is why you are here, today, as God has willed it, it, it...'

Neville wondered about the Knight's assertion that he was expected to be here, and on this day too. How much of this was down to blind faith and an ignorance of the twentieth century calendar?

'I don't know about God's will, but I suppose you could say that I am on a crusade of sorts.'

'Ah, Ah, Ah...'

'But it's no holy war; not in my case.'

'Then you are seeking the Holy Grail, Grail, Grail..?'

The laugh escaped before Neville could stop it, and - although cut desperately short - it reverberated uneasily about the building. He sensed the Knight stiffen - if such a thing were possible - and saw his hand return to his sword once again.

'I'm sorry; forgive me.'

The Knight said nothing, and Neville tried to remember that he was walking with someone whose myths and legends were centuries older than this own, and untainted by decades of discovery, cynicism, and counter-truth.

'Yes. Yes, you're right; I suppose you could say that I am on a search for a Holy Grail of sorts.'

'For what do you search, search, search..?'

Neville paused. The answer was blissfully simple.

'For myself.'

The Knight lifted his left hand. Slowly it rose, the stone complaining with the stress, until it hung a little above Neville's head. Then, equally slowly, it began to descend until it was suddenly at rest on Neville's shoulder. It landed lightly, more as a feather than a ton weight. The Knight nodded.

'And God, God, God..?'

'God?'

'Have to come here to find Him, Him, Him..? Or to ask for his help on your quest, quest, quest..?'

Neville now wondered exactly why he had come here. Was there more to his decision than simply "looking up old friends", or because it was on the way to somewhere else? How much had Samuel's words influenced him, or was he simply looking for excuses?

'I don't think I have come to find God, or to get his help to be honest. I think I need to find myself first. Perhaps God comes later.'

'Then in what do you have faith, faith, faith..? In what do you believe, believe, believe..?'

'I think I need to believe in myself.'

They had reached the end of the Cathedral and were now only a few yards from the entrance and the Knight's resting place. He had removed his hand from Neville's shoulder and was looking up and along the nave to the altar. Slowly he crossed himself. Neville sensed that the interview was over.

'Now I must rest, rest...' said the Knight, the echo now weary and faltering.

'I may be back again,' Neville suggested, hopefully.

'I wish you well on your quest, quest... May you prosper, prosper...' And with that the Knight turned away from him and walked slowly back to his plinth.

For elsewhere in the Cathedral, Neville heard the sound of a door closing and then footsteps; sharp, quick, human footsteps. He looked towards the altar but could see no-one. Then there was the sound of another door, more muffled footsteps, then - for a moment - silence. Gradually, almost without beginning, the sound of the cathedral organ began to fill the Cathedral. Its notes were quiet and mellow, but all-pervading and peaceful. Neville looked back to the plinth. The Knight was at rest again, his dog at his feet, and again clasping his Lady's hand.

THIRTY TWO

Samuel was standing in the galley unloading two carrier bags of shopping when Neville returned to the bus. After the Knight had resumed his silent vigil on the plinth alongside his Lady, Neville had decided on another turn around the Cathedral, though this time accompanied only by the sound of the organ.

By the time he had gained the exit for the second time, the gift shop was open and a man was busy inside. Neville had decided to pop in for a quick look before returning to the bus. An elderly couple entering the Cathedral nodded to him. The gift shop was, like the very fabric of the place itself, little changed from his memory of it; the range of goods for sale was still the same - the bookmarks, the postcards, the imitation stained glass windows - though obviously of a higher quality than twenty-odd years before.

He had been uncertain as to his ground when he decided on the purchase of a small memento to remind him of his visit; uncertain because the rules of the game might not permit him such temporal fancies. Neville remembered how hesitant Samuel had been over the notion of a camera. Still, he argued, he had his suit and his flying jacket; were they not some form of rightful inheritance? So, when Neville emerged into the square, he began walking towards the bus with a small brass effigy of a Knight of the Crusades resting in the pocket of his overcoat.

'A bit nippy out there, isn't it Sir?' said Samuel looking up from his bags.

'I can't say I noticed it coming back.'

'Ah, well, perhaps that augurs well for Epsom then.'

Neville left Samuel with his bags and went to his cupboard to hang up his coat. As he did so, he noticed that the hangers that had held both his suit and the flying jacket from Binky's plane were now empty.

'Samuel.'

After a brief pause, the older man joined him.

'What is it, Sir?'

'My suit; it's gone. And the flying jacket.'

'Oh, yes. I meant to tell you. I thought your suit was looking a bit grubby - probably all that rushing around on the boat, I should imagine - so I thought I'd have it cleaned for you. And, while I was at the cupboard, I thought you might as well have the jacket tidied up as well.'

'I see. But there were things in...'

'In the pockets? Yes, Sir; I removed them. They're safe and sound.'

'Fine.'

'Would you like some tea?' Samuel had already turned and was on his way back to the galley. 'I was going to put the kettle on once I'd put the shopping away.'

'Thanks, yes,' Neville called after him.

He wondered where to put the small image of the Knight. Would it make sense to hide it away somewhere, just in case? He looked around and quickly came to the conclusion that, apart from beneath the mattress or under his pillow, there were no suitable hiding places. Perhaps it would be best left where it was; the coat was clean enough, and Samuel would be unlikely to make another trip to a cleaners in the immediate future.

'Has it changed, Sir? The Cathedral, I mean,' this when Neville re-joined Samuel in the galley.

'Changed? No, I don't think so. Not structurally anyway!'

Neville's small joke went unrewarded. Samuel, busying himself over the tea pot, continued with his predetermined line of thought.

'Same old faces, I suppose?'

'Sorry?' Neville thought of the Knight; surely not the face Samuel was referring to.

'You tend to get people working in places like churches and Cathedrals for years. Often until they are past working. You know, Sir; the little old lady who tends the flowers, or the old chap who sorts out the Bibles. That sort of thing.' He looked up, awaiting a reply. Neville thought of "the Old Boy who drives the bus", and wondered again just how long Samuel had been doing what he was doing.

'There was a chap in the Gift Shop. I didn't see him properly of course, but I guess he could have been an "Old Timer".'

The lie hung quite limply in the air, and for a moment Neville imagined that Samuel might simply swat it away and crush it against the wall. But he said nothing, nodded, and began to pour the tea. Neville wondered why he had bothered to avoid the truth, especially as Samuel could just read it from him if he wanted anyway. The Knight was no more fanciful than Mister Bossiman or "Bob", and yet he felt the desire to keep a hold of him, to retain the secrecy of their exchange and the privacy of his own response.

'We'll go for'ard, shall we, Sir?' Samuel, mugs of tea in hand, offered the suggestion in a now out-of-place nautical vernacular. He nodded too, offering his famous smile. Neville wondered if he might patent it - "Samuel's Soother", he could call it - and sell it to old Grandfathers and Uncles who needed a little something to keep young relatives in check.

As he followed him to the front of the bus, Neville wondered if, somehow, their relationship had begun to change; if his dependence on Samuel was beginning to diminish. As they sat down, Neville decided to try a little test.

'Can I ask you something?'

'Of course, Sir.'

'My suit; and that jacket.'

'Sir?'

'I'll never see them again will I?'

Samuel opened his mouth to protest, but immediately thought better of it. He looked out of the bus for a moment, then back to Neville.

'They have served their purpose, Sir. You wanted a tuxedo to wear to an expensive restaurant. You got a suit that served not only that purpose, but perhaps others too.'

'On the ship?'

'Indeed.'

'And now you're saying that I no longer have need of it, whatever happens?'

'You are going to the races Sir; to the Derby! You will need something much less casual.'

'And after the races? Are you telling me that you know I won't need them?'

'Perhaps an educated guess.'

Neville wondered how much of his experience - and those tangible things that went to make up that experience - were expendable. He wanted to go back to his compartment and check to see if the Croak guide was still there; if it were, he knew that he had at least one other lesson still to learn. But it went further than that. How much of this entire fabric - even down to incidents like the dog fight and, he could not avoid it, people like Mita - were there, invented almost, just to serve his purpose, to enable him to work things out for himself?

'What shall we do for the rest of the day, Sir?' Samuel called him back. 'I don't think that there is any point our heading to Epsom until sometime tomorrow, do you?'

'Sorry? I was miles away.'

Samuel smiled.

'I just wondered about the rest of the day; assuming we go to Epsom tomorrow.'

'Yes, of course. Tomorrow should be fine, don't you think?'

'And today?'

Neville, finally getting his mind to re-focus on his conversation with Samuel, took up his side of it.

'Today? I don't know, Samuel. Perhaps a lazy kind of a day. Things seem to have been so hectic. I think I might like to wander around the town this afternoon. More old memories, that kind of thing. And perhaps we could "eat in" this evening.'

'Or I could get a take-away, Sir. Do you like curry?'

Within a few minutes they had settled the plan. Neville was to take a stroll around the town (especially as the weather was beginning to improve) while Samuel took the bus off to check its water, fuel and tyres. Then they would have a Chinese meal to round the day off.

After a quick sandwich - rustled up by Samuel in a remarkably short amount of time - Neville found himself stepping off the bus, though this time without his coat and now heading away from the cathedral.

There was a small discrete exit from the square between two old cottages which led towards the town centre. Neville, emerging from the alleyway, found himself facing a scene which, it appeared, had changed little since his childhood. Indeed, the first of the small shops he came across - tucked away as they were, down this little back street - bore the same names and sold the same goods as he was sure they had all those years previously. Indeed, he even suspected that, on one or two of them, the paint work - which had been looking jaded even then - was still awaiting the touch of the handyman.

From one such shop - it sold trinkets, postcards, and sweets - a lady emerged as he was standing at the window. She nodded as she passed him, then walked off. Neville was struck, not by the fact that she chose to nod to him, but by her overall manner and demeanour which seemed strangely out of place. Then, watching her until she disappeared around a corner, he realised that the way she was dressed fitted, not his present time, but the past that he could remember.

Another figure crossed his line of vision. The old fashioned cut of the jacket, the hat - particular to a time when he was a child - all led weight towards a theory that he was in the process of forming. For an instant, he was gripped with panic, and, meaning it as some form of retreat, found himself inside the shop. The owner, standing behind the counter, gave his new customer a slightly wary look. Neville nodded, then pretended to look at the postcards. He glanced down at his own clothes. They were not ostentatious or outrageous certainly, but he was certain that they would appear so to a native of the nineteen sixties.

Deciding on a plan of attack, he pulled a postcard from the rack and walked with it to the counter.

'Hello,' he said to the man, attempting a fake and indistinguishable foreign accent, hoping that this would allow some explanation for his mode of dress.

The assistant smiled, and, in true British tradition, shouted "Hello" back, loud and slow.

As Neville reached for his wallet, he suddenly realised that although he was relatively "cash rich" at the moment, none of it would be of any use. He might try and palm the shop keeper off with fifty new pence, pretending it was Italian or something, but what if the Queen's head were spotted? He fumbled around and then, staring at the man waiting for the money, shrugged his shoulders, turned, and walked out.

A few yards further up the street he looked back. The shop keeper was standing in his doorway looking after him. Perhaps it had not been as convincing a performance as Neville might have wished.

In a way he was disappointed to find himself having regressed some twenty odd years, and to be walking the same Winchester streets as he had when a child. Part of him, on leaving the bus, had been looking forward to seeing how things had changed, so that he could compare and contrast; it was an opportunity to measure progress, to see how some other part of the realm had managed itself without his intervention. However, he was also acutely aware that, trick or no trick, there had to be a reason for him finding himself once again walking the same temporal streets as he had all those years ago, and staring in through the same shop windows at the same goods. Neville knew that this too gave him a sense of perspective, of measuring what happened with the passing of time. He was, of course - as he had already discovered - something of an alien being now; strange clothes, and money that wouldn't even buy him a cup of tea. At least the language was the same.

He had reached the end of the street and was about to turn the corner, when, from the direction of the bus station, he saw a woman and a child walking towards him. He stopped dead, causing a man who had been following him to bump against him heavily. The man muttered something indistinguishable; Neville failed to apologise.

It had been the woman he recognised first; or rather her coat. It was a little lighter than bottle green, with a dark brown imitation fur collar, and devoid of any semblance of "cut" or style. A little above knee length, he could see the muddy brown trousers and brown court shoes that, as an ensemble, came through those early years to symbolise his Aunt Maggie. And now here she was again, marching manfully towards him with those heavy Christian steps heading for the Cathedral. Neville realised that as well as marching *towards* him, she was also marching *alongside* him; for there, in those slightly ill-fitting corduroy trousers he always hated, *he* was walking too.

There was little harmony between these two figures - they were just across the road now, waiting for the traffic - and Neville could see, even now, the feelings he had had of prisoner and jailer manifested in physical reality before his eyes. He looked sullen, unhappy; reluctant to cross the road, reluctant to take his Aunt's hand when she insisted. As he watched, Neville caught the boy's eye. It was a dull stare he saw, without life, lacking any of the vibrancy he had always imagined that children had; indeed, that he thought he had been the proud possessor of. It was the face of child who was not interested, who did not care, and who - though without realising it - was letting his life slip by.

Margaret stepped into the street, dragging the boy - dragging **him** - after her. Neville stepped back a little, and they passed within two feet of him. Neither looked up. He caught the tail end of a sentence his Aunt was just completing but missed the words, though the tone and the manner of its delivery made his spine tingle. The boy ignored her, wrestling his hand free.

He had always imagined himself as a lively child (this as he followed both Margaret and himself back down the street towards the Cathedral). He could remember playing football in the playground, chasing the girls; he remembered snowball fights with Spotty Johnson and Big Jim, and how they used to beat him up if scored more goals than them at Subbuteo. He remembered how he liked to draw planes and build model ships from the plastic kits you could get, and how - despite years of trying - he was never very good at conkers. He thought the teachers liked him, even though he was never quite at the top of the class; and he knew his parents loved him. With this as a package, as the memory of himself he had chosen to take forwards into his adult life, Neville had imagined that he had been an OK kind of a kid; a solid foundation for the future. But now he had looked into those cold and empty eyes; his own eyes.

Neville allowed them to get a few yards ahead. Margaret, judging from her manner, was still talking - she could talk! - and occasionally pointing or pulling or tugging. The boy - **he** - was not responding. They passed the small shop into which he had so recently sought refuge; the boy tried to dawdle to look at the postcards, but Margaret was having none of it. In a whisker they were into the alleyway and through to the green.

As he reached the shop, Neville - perhaps it was habit from all those years ago - glanced in himself. It seemed a little changed from his recent experience of it. He stopped and stepped back. The paint work was a little different, a little brighter; and in the window, prices no longer bore labels marked up in shillings and pence. He looked through the archway. He could see no-one.

Stepping inside the shop, he received a cheery "Good Afternoon" from the man behind the counter. This was not the same man who had tried to serve him earlier. Neville looked at the postcards, at their quality, at the simple **difference** in them from twenty years previously. He picked one up and took it to the counter.

'Twenty seven pence, please Sir.'

Neville took out his fifty pence piece, handed it over and waited for the change. Twenty three pence was duly returned. He thanked the man and left.

As he walked towards the alleyway and the Cathedral green beyond, he knew that his Aunt and the boy would be long gone. In fact, as far as the boy was concerned, he was just about to walk through the alleyway once again, only this time carrying a small paper bag containing a postcard of Winchester Cathedral.

THIRTY THREE

Emerging into the Cathedral square, Neville checked first to see that the bus was there, rather than pursue any faint hope - if hope were indeed the correct emotion - that he might see his Aunt and the boy walking ahead of him. That the bus had moved he could be certain, as it was now parked facing away from the Cathedral; that his relations (if he could include himself in that family) were not there, was evidenced by the square being deserted.

'You were gone a while Sir,' said Samuel as Neville stepped on board the bus again.

'Was I?'

'A little over three hours, by my watch.'

Neville checked his own. It seemed like he had been gone no longer than fifteen minutes or so, but Samuel's estimate appeared to be pretty accurate. Did time to have a worth then, in the same way that money had? Something unconnected with its empirical, temporal measurement? If this were so, then the time he had left according to his watch might vanish in the blink of an eye.

'I was about to go out for the food, but thought I ought to wait for you.'

'Thanks, Samuel.' Neville moved through to sit on his bunk. Samuel followed him.

'Did you have any preference for dinner, or shall I get a range of dishes?'

'I don't mind. Go for the selection; that might be better.'

'I agree, Sir. I've opened a bottle of wine in readiness, Sir. It's breathing in the galley.'

'Fine.' Neville stood up again. 'I'm going to have a bath before dinner, if that's OK.'

Samuel smiled.

'I thought you might Sir, so I ran one for you. It may be a little hot still, but it's all ready.'

Neville nodded and began to pull off his cardigan.

'Well, I'll be off. Shouldn't be too long Sir. I've been recommended a suitable establishment in the town centre by a gentleman at the garage.'

Left alone, Neville removed the rest of his clothes and donned the blue and red striped velour dressing down that Samuel had laid out for him. Opening the top drawer of his small cabinet to retrieve some clean underwear, he saw the Croak guide still in its place, though he suspected that now - no matter how hard he might try - he would be unable to find the "Your Ship" guide to the S.S.Pilgrim.

Walking through the galley he could hear the laboured puffing of the bottle of wine as it breathed heavily on the work surface, readying itself for the meal.

'Evening,' it said as he passed.

'Keep it up,' said Neville encouragingly, then went through the door and into the bathroom.

The surface of the water was almost totally covered in suds from the bubble bath Samuel had obviously put into it. Neville pushed his hands through the bubbles to test the temperature of the water. It was a little hot, as Samuel had suggested, but nothing he couldn't stand. Disrobing, he placed his right foot into the bath, then the left; eventually lowering himself in.

'Hey! Careful, chum!'

From beneath the surface of the bubbles, a voice, followed by the yellow plastic duck, bobbed Neville's way.

'Sorry,' said Neville.

'Ain't I seen you before?'

'Yes, a few days ago.'

'Sure, I remember you. Never forget a face, know what I mean?'

The duck laughed its peculiar laugh.

'How are you?'

'How am I, mate? OK except for all these bleeding bubbles! I saw that geezer - Sam, in't it? - come in here with that bubbly stuff and I just knew he'd put too much in. Now look at me - friggin' stuff!'

'Can I help?'

'Na. I'll be OK, ta. It slips off after a bit; I got the right sort of skin, see?'

Neville picked the soap from the side of the bath and began to lather around his neck and arms.

'You rich?'

'Rich?' The question surprised him.

'Yeah, rich. Like most guys I only see once, but this is the second time I've seen you. Staying long in the 'otel, are you? Must be rich if you're still here.'

'I don't think I'll be here much longer, actually. Maybe another day or two, that's all.'

The duck bobbed off into a little circle, skirting the edge of the bubbles, while Neville continued washing. Having rinsed himself, Neville slid a little further down the bath and tried to relax. He listened for sounds from outside, but could only make out the faint puffing of the wine. With the water now up to his chin, the duck bobbed up closer.

'So, what you been up to then? Since I last saw you, I mean. Had a good time, eh? Seen the sights; that sort of stuff?'

'In a way, yes.'

Steadying himself about six inches from Neville's chin, the duck eyed him directly.

'What's the matter, mate? You look pretty pissed off, like you've lost a biscuit and found a bread crumb.'

Neville smiled.

'I like that, it's clever.'

'Clever; that's what I am see, though people don't pay be me no attention. Like they think that 'cos I'm just a duck all I do is float around all day, know what I mean? They don't give you credit, see?'

'I think I understand.'

'Sure, I ain't never gonna be no brain surgeon - ain't got the qualifications for that for a start - but that ain't the point. I know who I am, I know what I'm supposed to do; that's it. I just gets on with it, being a duck; but it don't mean I'm stupid!'

Neville watched the duck as it bobbed gently backwards, its big eyes unflinchingly wide.

'I don't think you're stupid; not in the least.'

'See,' said the duck, coming closer again, 'that's what I mean. You're all right. If you can take a guy for what he is, you know, and just let him **be**; shit, that's all there is to it!'

There was a slight pause as the duck quack-quacked gently away down the bath. Neville eased himself up in the bath, making slight waves as he did so.

'Hey, don't mind me mate!' said the duck, obviously happy that he had obtained some degree of respect from the bather, 'you make all the bleedin' waves you like, I'm OK.'

Careful not to hit his yellow companion, Neville raised his left leg out of the water and began to wash it. The lather from the soap had started to disperse the bubbles, and the surface of the water was now relatively clear. Having finished his left leg, he moved on to the right.

'Where you off to then?'

Neville paused.

'Next, you mean?'

'Yeah.'

'Actually I'm going racing, to the Derby.'

'That's horse racing, ain't it? I've heard of that.'

'That's right.'

'Yeah. 'Cos I've got a cousin who works on a farm near a place called Newcastle.'

'Newmarket?' Neville suggested.

'Sure; Newmarket, Newcastle - what's the difference? Anyhow; there's this horse riding place next to his farm, see. Sometimes - or so he says, anyway - he gets to hear things about the horses, and the races they're in like.'

'Really?'

'Yeah.' The duck bobbed closer and lowered his quacky voice to the equivalent of a whisper. 'Look; as you and me's mates, I'll have a word with him and see if he knows anything about this 'ere Derby thing. Might be able to tell you somethin', eh?'

'Indeed.'

Neville was uncertain how the duck might be able to communicate with his relative in Newmarket; but then, seeing as he had - in some sense or other - just managed to communicate with his own self from a generation ago, perhaps nothing was impossible.

From outside, he heard the sound of the bus door being opened, and immediately the smell of Chinese food came wafting his way.

'Heads up,' said the duck, 'it's Sammy!'

'It's only me, Sir!' Samuel called when he reached the galley. Neville heard him put a bag on the work surface, then a "sniff-sniff" as he checked the wine. 'Dinner shouldn't be long; I just need to put the plate warmers out. That sort of thing.'

'You'd better get goin' chum,' said the duck with a playful quack, 'else old Sammy'll be after you, and no mistake!'

'Samuel's OK, actually. Something of a gentleman to be honest.'

'That so?'

Neville nodded.

'Well, if that's what you says, then it's good enough for me.' The duck paused. 'But tell him to chuck a little stale bread my way, OK?'

And with the duck still cheerfully bobbing around at the foot of the bath, Neville hauled himself to his feet and reached for the towel. Within a couple of minutes he was standing by the side of the bath, once again in his dressing gown. He looked down at the bath and the duck still mobile within it.

The duck saw him looking.

'Hey, don't worry about me! Just pull the plug; I'll be fine!'

'Sure?'

'Sure I'm sure!' replied the duck, adding, just as Neville leant forwards, 'Listen; I won't forget about the horses, OK?'

'OK.'

'And take care of yourself.' And with those words the duck became rigid plastic once again, transformed as simply as if someone had turned out a light.

Neville left the bathroom and walked through the galley (where Samuel was sorting out plates and tin foil containers) and back to his compartment, where got he dressed. From that point on, the evening passed off without incident. The food was acceptable, without being exceptional (despite the King Prawns scoring quite well) and then, after dinner, Samuel suggested that they try a few hands of rummy to pass the time.

It had been a while since Neville had played rummy, but, apart from a few "local rules" as Samuel called them, they embarked upon a version of the game that was quite familiar to him. Familiarity was not, however, enough to triumph over Samuel's exceptionally strong play.

'I put it down to my memory, I'm afraid', he said, half way through the game, when he was leading by nearly two hundred points, 'I suppose it gives me something of an advantage, but I hope it doesn't spoil it for you.'

'Not at all; I actually enjoy seeing someone play the game well - even if I am on the receiving end!' Neville's complement was only half true: he did enjoy seeing the game played well, but as for being on the receiving end...'and anyway, it's only a game!'

After the second game, they decided to call it a day. Samuel went to make coffee while Neville cleared away the cards and - at Samuel's request - found a road atlas of Britain. As they drank coffee, they plotted the best route to Epsom, planning to arrive early evening, after the departure of that day's race-goers. Samuel had already phoned ahead to book their parking place - 'in the centre, near the fair', he revealed - so that was one thing they did not have to worry about.

Having chosen the route, and estimated both departure and arrival time - the duration between the two, suggesting to

Neville that Samuel would not be pulling any "tricks" the next day - they finished their coffee, chatted for a short while, then retired to bed.

Neville did not sleep well. His dreams were contorted with visions of himself as a young child merging into drowning at the hands of a malevolent duck who - as a bookie's runner - was getting revenge for an account that Neville had failed to settle. Having flitted in and out of sleep, at around seven Neville gave way to the inevitable, and decided to get up.

He drew back the curtains in his compartment to reveal that the weather was indeed on the change, and the day had dawned as all June days should dawn, bright and blue. Judging by the trees, the wind had not yet totally abated, but it was a step in the right direction. Driven by the need to go to the toilet as much as anything else, Neville donned his dressing gown and went to the galley where he put the kettle on. Then, while waiting for it to boil, he went into the bathroom.

As he stood urinating into the bowl, his eyes became focused on the mirror by the sink. There, in barely legible writing, was a message evidently meant for him. It took Neville a little while to decipher the rather strange script which, on reflection, was probably forced on someone with webbed feet, but eventually he made out the soap-scrawled note thus:

Mate, this durby thing. My cusin says that somefin called Restrant Rendevoos is the nag to be on, an no shit. OK?

Neville had yet to see a card for the race, and consequently had no way of knowing if "Restaurant Rendezvous" was a horse, let alone entered into the Derby. However, the duck appeared to have been as good as his word, and Neville - at this stage of the game - was not going to turn down anything that resembled a "hot tip".

THIRTY FOUR

Samuel appeared in the galley as Neville was making the tea, and immediately the day was begun. There was a strong air of routine about the breakfast performance that followed. Neville was beginning to get a handle on Samuel's way of doing things - like the sequence in which he made toast, fried sausages, and poured orange juice - and was able to augment the overall process so that the finished article materialised in double-quick time.

The breakfast ritual was, in Neville's case, not one borne from practice, but rather from an appreciation - inbred or developed, he could not say - as to how one should go about a cooked breakfast and what it should actually look like. His most recent prolonged domestic experience - with Mirelle – most resembled the attempt made by the hotel in Paris rather than anything an Englishman would want to own up to, so it was not from there that his notion of an ideal breakfast sprung. His mother had, at various stages, gone through phases of cooking "a proper breakfast". These usually coincided with either fits of depression or happiness and, as far as he could tell, were initiated by his Father rather than himself (though after his vision of himself in Winchester the previous day, he could no longer be truly certain of that).

The two men ate in relative silence, passing only the most superfluous comments on the state of the weather, the condition of the bus - which was, according to Samuel, far from excellent - and Neville's prospects for Epsom. He chose not to mention the duck's tip.

'What happens if I win, Samuel?'

'If you win, Sir? I'm not sure that I understand.'

'Well,' Neville put down the glass he had been holding, 'let's say I get lucky. I have a couple of bets and win a few quid.'

'I'm with you so far.'

'What happens to the money? I mean, I may well not need it.'

'In what sense?'

'In that - well, it depends on the outcome of Option 3, doesn't it?'

Samuel nodded.

'Yes, I see.'

'And secondly; if I've decided that money isn't as important to me as I once thought it was...'

Neville let the sentence finish itself there, confident that Samuel would be able to fill the blanks. There was a short pause, before Samuel responded.

'I would suggest - if I may - a slightly different approach, Sir.'

'Which is?'

'Firstly, maintain your new assertion that money is not as vital to you as you once imagined it was. That is important because - as I think you now see yourself - it is a healthy attitude to have.'

'And secondly?'

'Secondly, do not scorn it either. You cannot know what will happen to you in the future. If the goal you seek is achieved, then it may well be that money will be of use to you in the future. On that basis, I would not worry about being successful either. If you win - well, so much the better, whatever the outcome.'

'So, go prepared to lose, but try to win?'

'Indeed. I think that may well serve your purpose.'

Neville had heard his Uncle - Maggie's husband, who had been an inveterate gambler - advocating that same philosophy every Saturday morning before he left the house to make his weekly pilgrimage to Ladbrokes. 'My boy,' he used to say, 'I only go prepared to lose what I can afford, and if I win, well that's a bonus!' The problem had been that Freddie had, over the years, lost track of what he could actually afford to lose, driven on as he was, by an ever-inflating target of the actual amount he was trying to win. More than once - later, when he was older - Neville had accompanied Freddie on some of his last sorties to "church" (as he called it) and had discovered during those smoky afternoons that the "church" was filled with "Freddies", each being their own peculiar variety of the same fundamental strain. It had been enough to quash any inclination to become an addict himself, but he had learnt enough to know the difference between a "Yankee" and a "Canadian", and the pluses and minuses of a "Round Robin".

Mirelle had frowned on Neville's occasional flirtations with Lady Luck. The French enjoyed their gambling as much as any nation, but none of that spirit had been passed on in Mirelle's genes. For his part, Neville's tuition - as Freddie might have liked to call it - was, to some extent, proving useful now. In his immediate context, there was no way that Neville could fail to put money on "Restaurant Rendezvous" - a gambler's instinct for the coincidence, and his superstitious homage to such things, would not allow Neville to let it pass. The very experience he was actually going through had much in common with the craps player whose attitude was to throw the dice, say "to hell with it", and to ride his luck for as long as he could. It was difficult to know how benevolent Lady Luck was being just at present, but Neville felt willing to ride with her a while longer.

After breakfast they set off for Surrey. The route they had chosen allowed for a stop in Farnham for late elevenses and then a brief sojourn at a nearby beauty spot, Frensham Ponds. Here, despite the improved weather, Samuel chose to remain on the bus while Neville walked off the early lunch they had just consumed in the town. For an hour or so, he wandered around the lakes and paths, giving way to horses and their riders as they jogged along the bridle ways.

Samuel, who had been watching the general scene himself, suggested to Neville on his return that it might be a good idea if the horses he backed the next day went a little bit faster.

'But you don't know my luck, Samuel!' Neville had replied.

'Indeed. Perhaps that makes two of us!'

His laughter signalled that he was intending a joke, but Neville was still a little wary of Samuel's tendency towards the cryptic, and, as they drove away, the notion behind those last words remained with him.

The traffic increased the closer they got to their destination. Neville wondered if it might be the crowds leaving the course for the day, but Samuel's theory - and one, he maintained, that was based on hard experience - was that the volume of traffic increased in proportion with one's proximity to London in general, and the M25 in particular. Indeed, for a short while, the bus was actually stationary, a mere cog in a seized up chain.

Consequently, they arrived at the course a little later than planned. It was still light, but apart from a few cars belonging to course officials, deserted. Samuel pulled up alongside a man who appeared to be still patrolling one of the main entrances, and received directions to their overnight parking space. As he had promised, they made their way to the centre of the course, finally parking close to the running rail about two furlongs from the winning post.

Neville got off the bus as soon as they arrived in order to "soak up the atmosphere". Behind them, the fun fair - normally only seen as a bright, colourful and bustling arena - was quiet and dark, the only life it owned up to was in the occasional shadows of the stall holders and ride mechanics as they went about clearing up, checking equipment, and generally preparing for the next day. Across the other side of the course, the grandstand - itself in darkness - loomed high into the air. Tomorrow, it and the acres of space in front of it, would be a seething mass of spectators; a congregation that would come together and, as a single mass, rise up with one voice to provide the inevitable crescendo to the big race. Neville had never been to the Derby, but imagined how, after the race was over, the rest of the day could be nothing more than a gradual anti-climax.

He and Samuel had not talked about what happened after the racing was finished. Neville guessed that, if necessary, they might be able to stay another night; but if not, then he was fairly certain that Samuel would have something in reserve. If they were reliant on him coming up with their next destination, then Neville was at present in the dark as to where that might be. Perhaps he should trust to the luck that, as Samuel had suggested, he might not in fact be entirely familiar with.

THIRTY FIVE

The day of the race dawned bright and clear. Neville, once more beating the alarm clock and Samuel's call, was roused not so much by the light or the sounds of birds, but by a sense of excitement, of place, and the feeling that something was about to happen. His first thoughts were of Mita and the question that had been dogging him on and off over the previous couple of days: would she be there? Speculation was, of course, pointless, and he had been trying hard to adopt the stoic approached advocated by Samuel; if she was she was, and if she wasn't...well, something else might turn up.

Neville was conscious that this Micawber-like approach to life might get a little out of hand. He could see dangers in simply waiting for things to happen to him; perhaps he had been a little too much like this in the past, and now recognised that, by being a little more "pro-active" - and how many times had he heard that in his working life! - one was certainly in with a chance of gaining a degree of control, however slight, over one's destiny. Balancing all of this though, Neville still recognised that in the case of waiting for Mita, the "let's see what turns up approach" had its merits - if only in allowing him to water the flower of self-pity a little and thus the luxury of a little personal wallowing should he feel like it.

Samuel - obviously possessed by a sense of occasion as well - excelled himself at breakfast, and it was with a solid, if rather heavy, degree of well-being that Neville descended the bus and opened himself out onto the day.

All was much as it had been the night before: the fair still stood un-illuminated and motionless; the grandstand still loomed large, grey and empty. However, there was some activity to be witnessed, and this activity carried with it a sense of urgency and importance. Amidst the stalls and rides, men in lumberjack shirts and jeans could be seen hauling tarpaulin, pulling ropes, and carrying boxes; occasionally they would pass within feet of each other and share suitably cheery greetings. Across the course, others could be seen moving around the various buildings; occasionally a car would arrive in the officials' car park. Once or twice, thundering out of the quiet, a horse would gallop by, having its last work-out prior to the big race.

As he stood against the rails cradling a hot mug of coffee in his hands, an elderly gentleman in a bowler hat approached from the other side of the running rail.

'Morning, Sir!' he said brightly, his voice carrying a tone of the day's importance.

'Good morning.'

'Just walking the course, you know; checking it out. Going's a little on the soft side of good, wouldn't you say?'

Neville watched the man dig the heel of his boot into the turf, testing to see how easily the ground gave way.

'Presumably the rain,' Neville suggested.

'And just in time too! Last week it would have been bone hard; terrible, really. Watering every night; didn't make the slightest damn difference! Still,' he examined at his boot again, 'look at it now! Well, must get on. Good day, Sir; and good luck!'

Samuel joined Neville at the rails.

'Who was that Samuel; one of the Stewards?'

'I should think so, Sir. What did he say?'

'"On the soft side of good" apparently.'

'Perfect; just perfect!'

A new voice joined their conversation. A second man, who had evidently been walking just a few yards behind the Steward, now drew level with them. He nodded in greeting.

'That's what the Steward said.'

'Eh?' said the man, pausing.

'The ground; just about right.' Neville clarified.

'Ah, but it's perfect for my little beauty!' The man gave a slight wink in their general direction.

'You are hopeful of success today then, Sir?' asked Samuel.

'I am. But don't judge by the bookies. They don't think my little girl's got any chance in this kind of going. They think she needs to hear her hooves rattle. But mark my words, she'll prove 'em wrong!'

'Who was that?' Neville asked, once the man had resumed walking and was out of earshot.

'Harry Simpson,' said Samuel, 'or "Happy" Harry, as he's known. Local trainer. Doesn't have a big stable, but he's got one going in the race after the Derby; "Second Visit" I believe.'

'How do you know so much; I didn't realise you were in to racing?'

'I'm not, Sir. But as we were coming here, I thought I'd do a little checking up; research if you will.'

'Any "hot tips" then?'

Samuel laughed.

'Ah, that might be asking a little too much!'

For the rest of the morning, Neville wandered about the course watching as magically - like a photograph - the scene developed before his eyes. And with the changes that were visual came the additional sounds and smells that went with them. The rides in the fun fair were tested, lights flashing, music sounding out; then the hot dog and burger stands were prepared, with smoke rising from the early fries, cooked as reward for the hard-working men. Across the course, the tannoy blared out "One, Two; One, Two; Testing, Testing", and the huge television screen panned through an image of Tattenham Corner. Pulleys rattled as the numbers boards rattled up and down, finally raised with the names of the jockeys in the first race slotted into place; even the "Stewards' Enquiry" and "Weighed In" flags were run up and down.

The crowds began arriving early too, staking their claim for a place near the running rail or up in the Grandstand; marking out their territories, and always leaving either Granny or Granddad on guard while the rest of the family went exploring. Samuel had set up a couple of chairs in front of the bus near the rail, effectively sealing off a very small area, almost like a private enclosure. Neville had been a little surprised that they had not stayed in a hotel overnight, and then taken one of the better spots in the Grandstand, though he had chosen not to say anything to Samuel. Now however, with the atmosphere building, he was pleased to be in the heart of things, and near the people whose earthy attitude to the day seemed to make it even more real for him.

After lunch, Neville went off in search of a race card. He had decided that it was time to get serious and for that a list of the day's runners was needed. He found a man in a small booth selling the day's official programmes.

'How much are they?'

'Quid, mate.'

'Thanks.'

Neville went to his wallet to retrieve some cash only to find that it was strangely full. Opening it, he discovered that the reason for its increased size was that it now contained a large number of fifty-pound notes. Instinctively he checked his watch. The small display read zero.

'Quid, mate, please,' the man in the booth said, still holding out the small booklet.

'Sorry,' Neville smiled apologetically, found a pound coin, and took the race card.

Once away from the booth, he found a quiet spot and checked his wallet again. It seemed impossible, but there were eight bundles of fifty pound notes, each bundle with a little wrapper on which **£1000** was inscribed. In addition, there were some loose notes and his change. He replaced his wallet in his button-down pocket and contemplated the situation.

All he had in the world - apart from his clothes and things on the bus - was now there, resting in his back pocket. He had it all. He was free to do with it as he would. There could be no come-back if he lost every single penny on the first race; there was simply nothing else. The responsibility - and it was a responsibility for himself - seemed suddenly quite daunting. If he lost everything he would not be able to rely on Samuel to work some kind of miracle for him; perhaps there could be no more miracles. And what did this mean about what followed; about what happened tomorrow? Did it mean that he had no further use for money? That, somehow, his fate was sealed? Or was it that what happened there, on that day, was the key to his future?

He contemplated this last thought then rejected it. Money was not the answer. Even if he lost it all, it meant nothing - or at least not as much as he had once imagined. As he stood and thought, he felt a tug at his arm.

''Scuse me, Guv.'

Neville looked round. A man, perhaps in his late fifties (though it was difficult to tell) stood at his side. He was shabbily dressed in a torn jacket and with the souls of his shoes hanging from their uppers by a literal thread. The man was not particularly clean, and his fingers were stained with nicotine. But it was none of this which stunned Neville so much as the man's resemblance to his Uncle Freddie.

'Guv; ya couldn't spare an ol' hand a Sov', could ya Guv?' Not getting any response, the man lowered his demands. 'Or a few bob even. Just a few bob, God bless ya, Guv.'

As he stood looking at the man, he thought of Freddie's maxim about what you could afford to lose. He knew this man was not Freddie, but none the less, it seemed he now had a chance to give him a break; and if it was not his Uncle, that didn't really seem to matter. Neville thought about tomorrow, and he thought (all in a fraction of a second) about Mita, and about how he didn't have a clue what was going to happen. Much was unanswerable and out of his control; much, but not this.

He pulled his wallet from its pocket and opened it. Then, without a flicker of hesitation, pulled out one of the wads and handed it to the man.

'Here. It's a bit more than a few bob, I know; but that's just your luck, isn't it?'

The man stared at the twenty fifty-pound notes now lying flat in his dirty left hand, then looked up at Neville. His fingers gradually closed round the money until it was scarcely visible in his fist. Slowly he extended his right hand.

'By God, Guv, ya must be some fuckin' angel or somethin'; but, by Christ, I thank ya; by Christ I do...'

Neville smiled and shook the hand offered him.

'This ain't no joke, is it Guv?'

'No joke; no. Let's just say you remind me of someone, OK?'

'Whatever ya say, Guv. God bless ya. Jesus Christ!'

By now, tears had begun to well in the man's eyes and he relinquished Neville's hand in order to brush his grubby cuff across his face.

'I'm sorry, but I should go now.'

And with a final smile, Neville placed his hand on the man's arm and then left him. After he had gone thirty yards or so, he looked back over his shoulder. The man was standing in the same place, staring down at his still closed fist.

'There you are, Sir.'

Neville turned to find Samuel now beside him.

'Hello, Samuel.'

Samuel looked at the scruffy beggar.

'I saw that, Sir; and may I say how magnanimous a gesture it was.'

They began walking back towards the bus.

'Samuel, it was nothing. He reminded me of my Uncle Freddie. The poor bugger never really had a lucky break; I guess I was just trying to even the score a bit. And I don't need all this anyway.'

He felt Samuel's hand once again on his shoulder.

'Maybe so, Sir, but shall we see if we can find the winner of the first race and get your little donation back?'

Back at the bus, they settled in the chairs and began to study the form for the first race of the day. After a short while, Neville had narrowed his choice down to two; Thunderer, and Hard in Places. Samuel, having stated his intention to put a small wager on Dunmail, offered to take Neville's bet for him.

'It's OK Samuel; I'll manage. See you back here in a few minutes?'

The two men walked together to the bookmakers but were then quickly separated. Neville had decided on Hard in Places. Checking a few of the bookies' boards, his horse was generally quoted at four to one. However, one chap - an elderly man, in a rather dated tweed suit, and sporting the name "Dick Springs" -

was offering nine to two. Neville walked over to him and pulled a wad from his wallet.

'Can I have a thousand on Hard in Places, please.'

Neville expected to be turned away, or told that the amount was too great. Instead, Dick took the money, muttered "Four and a half grand to one, Hard in Places; ticket four one eight" to his clerk, and handed Neville an oblong card with "Dick Springs - 418" printed boldly in green. He then crossed out the nine to two offer and changed it to five to one. This was unusual. Neville would have expected the price of the horse to shorten having laid such a large bet on it. As he made his way back to the bus he checked the other bookies; sure enough, all were now offering Hard in Places at five to one.

Samuel was already back when Neville returned. He thought about describing what had happened, but decided that it might be best to wait for the outcome of the race first.

Having watched the horses gallop passed on their way to the five furlong start, Neville waited with mounting excitement for the start of the race. They could see nothing from where they were apart from a few hundred yards of the track and, given the angle from which they would be watching the majority of that, they were reliant on the racecourse commentator for a description of the action.

Within minutes "They're Off!" was called to great cheers. Hard in Places was apparently quite well away at the start, but soon faded from the commentary. Dunmail took up the lead at about half way and, as they sped by, Neville could see that a challenge was being thrown down by another of the runners. This turned out to be Thunderer who, having collared Dunmail in the final furlong, went on to win by two lengths; Dunmail was second, Hard in Places seventh.

'Any good, Sir?' asked Samuel.

'Afraid not. Did you back yours to win?'

'Each way,' Samuel smiled, 'so I should make a little bit of a profit.'

The second race followed a similar pattern to the first. Neville was torn once again between a choice of two and, having made his choice - Wood Kits - went off to the bookmakers. Again, Dick Springs was offering the best odds on his horse, and again, as soon as he had placed his bet, the odds on Wood Kits lengthened. However, with Samuel also putting money on Wood Kits, Neville felt a little more hopeful of his chances; but this time the horse made no show at all, and trailed in last.

Samuel was philosophical, but Neville was beginning to lose his "it doesn't really matter" attitude.

The third race was the one before the Derby. This time the winner looked clear cut to Neville, and, for the first time that day, his choice - True Mischief - was favourite. When Dick Springs was once again offering the best odds and, having placed the bet, the horse's odds lengthened to such an extent that it ceased being favourite, Neville assumed the worst.

For a while however, it appeared that things were going to change. In a muddling race, the field bunched as they came past the bus. Neville could see True Mischief's jockey flashing his whip, attempting to drive the horse through a gap on the rails. As they came towards the finish, the commentator suddenly announced True Mischief's arrival on the scene and, by the time they reached the line, its apparent victory.

Neville's excitement was short lived however. First the "Stewards' Enquiry" flag was raised; then the board containing the numbers of the first three horses was lowered. On the giant television screen, the replay of the race showed True Mischief barging two other animals out of the way as it forced its way through on the rails. The could only be one possible outcome; the horse was disqualified.

After three races, Neville had now lost three thousand pounds, and his wallet felt decidedly thinner. He had also lost much of his good humour, and the philosophy he had been in possession of before racing began - and which allowed him to give some of his money away - was now being put sorely to the test.

THIRTY SIX

'Next one's the big one, Sir,' said Samuel when he returned from the bookmakers. He had placed a bet on the horse which, with True Mischief's disqualification, was promoted to first place, and was consequently in something of a lively mood. Indeed, the entire crowd had been gradually building in anticipation of the next race, and the course was now a mass of colour and noise. Behind them the fun fair rides whirled and bucked, accompanied by screams and music, and in the grandstand the sea of heads bobbed continuously.

Neville was sitting in one of the chairs staring rather vacantly at the turf. He had seen Freddie in moments such as this, when, having backed three successive losers, he could feel himself approaching that point which he had defined to be "as much as I can afford to lose"; there was a moment of crisis and then - especially in the later days - Freddie would simply sail right across and into oblivion.

Despite the rather casual, if not cavalier attitude that he had displayed earlier with regard to the contents of his wallet, Neville was beginning to wonder if he shouldn't have set himself a limit beyond which he dared not cross. Perhaps he did not expect to lose. Given that he was here at the Epsom Derby meeting under less than normal circumstances, perhaps he had invested in himself - and quite wrongly it appeared - some form of divine right that he should win.

'Is something the matter, Sir?'

Neville looked up as Samuel sat down alongside him.

'Up? Not really. I just didn't expect to lose, I guess. And now I'm not sure if I know when I should stop.'

'Stop?'

'I can't blow all my money Samuel can I? And you do know that I have got **all** my money, don't you?'

Samuel nodded.

'Things haven't gone as I had planned, that's all. And maybe I don't want to take any more risks. Just in case.'

'"In case" what, Sir?'

'I don't know Samuel. Just **in case**. In case I need the cash tomorrow, maybe. Assuming that there will be a tomorrow, that is.'

Samuel leant across and handed him the race card.

'Why don't you just have a look at the runners in the Derby, Sir? I'm sure that you are quite all right at the moment.'

Samuel's words did not have the instant healing effect that they might have once possessed. However, Neville took the card and opened it up to the centre pages where the runners - all seventeen of them - were detailed.

Once upon a time, Neville would have studied form for an hour or so before a race like this in order to try and pick the winner, but not today. Indeed, after his experience in the first three races he was even tempted to close his eyes and just pick something at random; it was just as likely to be successful. However, a little over half way down the card he spotted Restaurant Rendezvous and remembered his tip. He wondered if the limited knowledge of a yellow plastic duck could be any better than him trying to glean the full benefit from years of experience - and then almost immediately decided that it could.

He stood up and threw the race card back onto his chair.

'Decided, Sir?'

'I have Samuel.'

'That was quick, if you don't mind me saying so.'

'A little inspiration, perhaps.' Neville had wanted to say "A little bird told me", but decided against it because firstly it would have required an explanation and secondly, the duck might well have objected to being referred to as "a little bird".

At the bookmakers, Restaurant Rendezvous was on general offer at ten to one. Neville spotted a couple of boards showing it at twelves, one at nines. He deliberately left Dick Springs to last, and, as he approached, hoped that this time Dick would not be offering the best price. The board showed fourteen to one. Neville's heart sank. For a moment he toyed with the idea of simply walking away, accepting that the outcome was already decided and that he must lose again. However, there were a number of forces at work inside him which prevented this: he'd had a "tip" for one, and Dick already had three thousand pounds of his money and he wanted it back. He pulled out his wallet.

'A thousand on Restaurant Rendezvous, please.'

Taking the money, Dick mumbled to his "Bag Man" and handed back ticket twenty six. Neville stood and waited, and - just as he expected - Dick rubbed out the fourteen currently against Restaurant Rendezvous and replaced it with the number sixteen. Neville remained motionless.

'Another thousand on Restaurant Rendezvous, please.'

'Sorry?' Dick looked at him eye-to-eye for the first time that afternoon.

'A grand on Restaurant Rendezvous, at sixteens. Please.'

'You sure?'

'Look, are you going to take the money?'

Dick held out his hand.

'Sixteen to one, the Rendezvous; ticket twenty seven,' he said over his shoulder, and handed Neville another green ticket, "027" the number brightly embossed upon it.

Neville, not caring what Dick did to his horse's price now, turned and made his way back towards the bus. He now had a little over two thousand pounds left. If he was unsuccessful this time then, he told himself, he had reached his limit.

It was difficult to walk anywhere in a straight line now, or without physically bumping in to people as you tried to do so. Things were beginning to reach fever pitch, and as he walked through the crowd his ears were assaulted by the names of horses just about to run, tips on their form, and fragments of stories relating how, "if only the jockey had held the whip in his **left** hand", a different animal would have won a previous race.

He realised how futile his suggestion had been to Mita that they should try and meet at the Derby. If she were here - indeed, if she were only a few feet from him - she would be impossible to spot, pink dress or no pink dress. He knew that he could hold out no hope of seeing her. If she were there, then perhaps she might get a message to him; perhaps Samuel might come up with one more trick.

Samuel was leaning against the rails when Neville reached the bus again.

'OK, Sir?'

There was a note of concern in Samuel's voice.

'If you've wondering whether I've bet all my money, Samuel, I haven't - though it did cross my mind, I have to say.'

Neville wasn't sure whether it had or not. In fact, he had been pretty uncertain about what he was going to do - anything except the horse which was to carry his wager.

Within a few minutes the horses emerged from behind the grandstand and began their parade. They would walk towards the two furlong post, then turn and gallop away to the start. It seemed as if everyone on the course was now crushed against a running rail. On both sides of their small area - where Neville and Samuel enjoyed the luxury of just a few feet to themselves - hundreds of people were craning their necks to get a glimpse of the horses.

As they came out in race card order, the first horse Neville saw was number one, which also happened to be the favourite. Samuel tapped his arm as the horse and jockey (the latter in bold black and white colours) came to a manned post placed temporarily in the centre of the course, walked round it, then headed off towards the start.

'That's my one, Sir.'

'The favourite?'

'I can't see it losing - not that I know anything about racing of course. And I met a gentleman a little while ago who put forward a most convincing case.'

Neville nodded, though he was not really listening. Across on the other running rail he could make out the green and gold colours worn by Restaurant Rendezvous. The horse seemed slightly smaller than the others; but then this seemed to be a fault Neville found in all the horses he backed, so probably said more about his perception of them than the horses themselves. It certainly seemed to move well (though how he could justify such a statement he wasn't sure) and as it turned at the post and galloped off, he had no reason to think any less of the horse compared to the others in the race.

There was a few minutes of hiatus now, as the crowd moved away from the running rail a little, some endeavouring to get to a position where they would have a better view of the race itself. On the large television, the picture showed the horses arriving at the start, having their girths checked by the green-uniformed handlers at the stalls, and then milling around, waiting for three forty to arrive.

The race course commentator describing the scene at the start elaborated on the pictures being shown on the giant screen. A great deal of attention was being paid to Thatched Twine, the favourite. On Dick Springs' board, Neville had noticed it being quoted at five to two, which seemed less than Dick's usual generosity. As he watched the television pictures, occasionally Neville caught a glimpse of the green and gold colours he was looking for, but the horse was denied any specific attention by either the camera crew or the commentator.

"They're going behind" echoing around the course raised the expectation level another notch. The horses were moving around to the back of the stalls and were beginning to be loaded. The electronic clock above the screen showed "3:39". Again the coverage of the loading process concentrated on Thatched Twine and another animal - Silver Madam - which was proving difficult to install. There was a moment's tension as a blindfold was applied, but then, on "3:41", the words "They're off!" were greeting with the cheers and shouts of the collective mass.

'Thatched Twine gets away to a good break on the inside, but its Zynman who immediately goes into the lead, with Sea Castle moving up on the outside.'

Neville listened to the commentary as he, like everyone else, became glued to the images on the huge screen. From what he could see, Restaurant Rendezvous was somewhere in the middle of the field which was being led by Thatched Twine's pacemaker.

The first few furlongs followed the usual pattern for the race: the runners sorting themselves out; jockeys finding their favourite position, trying either to get to the running rail or away from it - even, in some cases, trying to remember the instructions given to them by their trainers a few minutes before in the parade ring.

'Coming to the top of the hill and beginning the sweep down towards Tattenham Corner, its Zynman still with a commanding lead. He's followed by Sea Castle and Hokum; Silver Madam is improving after a slow start, with Thatched Twine tucked in nicely just off the pace.'

Neville could just see Restaurant Rendezvous a little way behind the black and white of the favourite. It seemed to be going quite well, but, as yet, had warranted no specific attention from the commentator. As the horses made their way to the home turn, the crowd once again pressed to the rail, forsaking the television screen in the hope of catching a glimpse of the live action.

'Rounding Tattenham Corner, and now Zynman, under pressure, is beginning to drop back, and Silver Madam has been rushed up on the outside to take it up. Hokum is trying to respond, and now Thatched Twine is being shaken up on the outside. Just in behind these, Restaurant Rendezvous is making a little headway.'

Neville wondered exactly what "a little headway" might actually be. As he leant over the rails - the horses now a couple of hundred yards away and racing towards him - he could see the black and white of Thatched Twine looming on the outside. He knew that Restaurant Rendezvous was there, but could see no sign of the green and gold.

'And Silver Madam is now coming under pressure as he's joined in the lead by Hokum. But here comes Thatched Twine, cruising on the outside! Two and a half furlongs out, and Thatched Twine now comes to challenge!'

With the horses now thundering towards him, Neville saw the favourite's black and white colours ahead of the field, the jockey waving his whip and urging his horse on. But there, just behind him, Restaurant Rendezvous was still in touch. As they flew by in a blaze of colour, Neville knew that the green and gold was on the move.

'And its Thatched Twine over two lengths clear. Hokum is second, with, on the outside, Restaurant Rendezvous moving into third and beginning his run. Just over a furlong to go, and its Thatched Twine still with a two length lead, Restaurant Rendezvous moves into second; Hokum looks beaten in third. These three are clear of the field. Coming to the final furlong, and its Thatched Twine now only a length in front from the Rendezvous in second. It's between these two. Thatched Twine is being challenged by Restaurant Rendezvous. Into the final hundred yards; Thatched Twine by half a length, but the Rendezvous is gaining. Coming up towards the line. Thatched Twine from Restaurant Rendezvous. They're stride for stride! Thatched Twine and Restaurant Rendezvous, neck and neck! At the line - they've gone past together!'

Neville closed his eyes.

'It's a photo finish, between Thatched Twine and Restaurant Rendezvous! Hokum is third, with Gold Cove running on to be fourth.'

Samuel tapped Neville on the arm.

'My, Sir, that was a close one! Yours nearly managed it, didn't it?'

'Do you think Thatched Twine has held on Samuel?'

'Don't you, Sir?'

Samuel seemed slightly surprised that Neville could contemplate any other outcome.

'Do you *know* your horse has won?'

'"Know", Sir?'

Neville knew very well that Samuel had caught his drift, but the latter had noticed that the giant screen was showing a replay of the finish. The two of them - along with thousands of others - watched as the colours of Restaurant Rendezvous clawed back the favourite. Fifty yards from the line there was still not doubt that Thatched Twine was in front; but on the line it was much closer.

'Perhaps you're right, Samuel - but would you want to bet on it?'

Samuel smiled, and gently shook his head. On the screen, the pictures showed a still frame of the two horses as they hit the line. For Neville, this result had suddenly come to symbolise something about his relationship with Samuel: specifically that here, for the first time, he might actually have the chance to **beat** Samuel at something; to get ahead of him, to be one step up.

The air was charged with the silence from the public address and the large black and white "P" hung in the frame. There was a crackle from the tannoy, and the "P" began to be descend.

'And the result.' Thousands of people were suddenly silenced; conversations chopped in half; drinks half-swallowed. Neville placed both hands on the running rail and stared down at the turf. This was it. It was victory he wanted; proof that he could be a winner on his own. He wanted to go back to Dick Springs and redeem his tickets - and in doing so, himself. It was not the money, it was more than money.

'First, number thirteen...'

The remainder of the announcement was lost as thousands of voices rose in one great "cheer" around the course. There were shouts, spontaneous bursts of applause; from those who had backed the favourite, there were harsher words.

Neville waited for a few seconds, then looked up. Samuel was smiling at him, his hand extended.

'Congratulations, Sir. Well done!'

THIRTY SEVEN

It took a few minutes - and the rather substantial feeling of holding thirty two thousand pounds in his hands - for Neville to realise his success. His appearance at Dick Springs' board, and the exchange of tickets twenty six and twenty seven for such a large amount of money, caused something of a stir. As he walked away, one or two people even raised a cheer in his direction, thankful that one of their own - the punting public - had managed to get one over on a bookmaker.

There was, he guessed, something of the heroic in what he had managed to achieve - or at least that was how it seemed to him when he re-joined Samuel at the bus. For his own part, Samuel had chosen to mark the occasion by producing a bottle of chilled champagne (from where, Neville had no idea) and filled glasses were awaiting the return of the victor.

'Do you want me to look after that for you Sir? I could put it somewhere safe on the bus.'

Neville contemplated the large wad. He counted five thousand off, and handed the rest over.

'I'll just keep this, Samuel; I feel that my luck may have changed.'

As Samuel disappeared into the relative security of the bus, Neville wondered if, considering that the champagne appeared to have been ready, Samuel had expected Restaurant Rendezvous to win all along. If so, Neville was uncertain as to where the blurred line that defined the border between Samuel's realm and - to put it bluntly - the "real world" might lie.

With the passing of the Derby, Neville was already aware that, for many, the drama of the day was now over and the anti-climax that he had suspected was now beginning to come into play. Indeed, it was only the announcement from the tannoy that the runners for the next race were coming out onto the course that prompted Neville to once again check his race card.

The sight of Second Visit's name towards the bottom of the list, reminded him of the brief encounter earlier that morning. Having had one successful tip thus far, the last thing he was going to do was to turn another one down.

Returning to the bookmakers on the rails, Neville made straight for Dick Springs' pitch: if he was set to duel with Mister Springs all afternoon, so be it; he had the upper hand now, and was determined not to relinquish it. However, arriving at his destination he found the place vacant, with only a small painted mark on the tarmac any indication that a bookmaker had once stood there.

The bookie next door eyed him nervously.

'You've cleaned him out, mate. 'E's buggered off; had enough.'

'I see,' Neville turned to the speaker, 'It was nothing malicious; just one of those things.'

'That's as maybe. We've got go to take our chances, ain't we?'

Neville began to look for Second Visit's price. Her trainer was undoubtedly correct in his forecast that, given the state of the ground, she would not be well supported. As he stood in front of one board, he heard another punter explaining to his companion that Second Visit needed firm ground or else she wouldn't last out the trip. Neville checked the distance of the race; it was nearly two miles.

The general offer on the horse was sixteen to one, but there were a few bookies offering twenties. Neville picked out five of these and placed a thousand with each of them; then, clutching five tickets, he returned to the bus.

'Feeling lucky then Sir?' said Samuel.

'I was just following the advice of that trainer we met this morning.'

'Harry Simpson?'

'That's the one; Second Visit he said.'

Samuel checked his own card.

'What price did you get, Sir - if you don't mind me asking?'

'Twenty to one.'

The race started right over the far side of the course, a little beyond the Derby start. A little after four fifteen the commentator announced "They're Off!", and once again another small drama began to unfold.

Neville watched the beginning of the race on the giant screen. Second Visit - it appeared - was a confirmed front-runner, and bounced out of the stalls to build up an immediate five length lead. The remainder of the pack seemed quite content to settle in behind, and let her do most of the donkey work. As they turned into the straight, Second Visit was still clear in front, but the remainder were beginning to prepare a challenge.

As he leant over the rail and stared down the straight towards the field, Neville asked Samuel which horse carried his wager.

'None, Sir. I feel I've had my share of the day.'

Neville glanced at him, then back to the horses as they drew ever closer. The scarlet of Second Visit was still visible ahead of the field, but her jockey was beginning to work hard.

'And it's still Second Visit in the van, four lengths ahead of Ernest's Story and Nunnery who are making a move on the outside. As they come towards the final furlong, Second Visit still leads but by only three lengths now from Nunnery who goes second. Its Second Visit into the final furlong, being driven hard in the lead. Nunnery is closing in second. There's about a length in it. Second Visit from Nunnery. The leader's beginning to fade, but still has the upper hand. Its Second Visit from Nunnery. Nunnery's not going to get there. At the line, Second Visit's the winner, Nunnery second, Gallic Crunch third.'

After the horses had gone passed the post, Neville, fist clenched in victory, looked at Samuel.

'How much Sir?' Samuel asked.

'Did I win?'

Samuel nodded.

'It's not how much really, Samuel; it's the fact that I won that matters. Somehow that seems the most important.'

Samuel's smile showed that he accepted Neville's words, but at the same time indicated a desire to have his question answered.

'A hundred thousand. That's the answer to your question. Why do you ask?'

'No reason, Sir.' Samuel paused. 'There's one race to go. Are you stopping now, or have you had a tip for that too?'

All the way to the bookmakers and all the way back (this time clutching an ever larger bundle of winnings) Neville tried to answer that single question. He had won a hundred and thirty thousand pounds in two races, but he knew he couldn't kid himself: the reason he had been successful was because of information he had received from different of sources; it seemed almost like cheating. This time he was on his own.

He thought of quitting. When Samuel held out his hand for the portion of the money to be secreted in the bus, Neville paused, uncertain how much - if any - he should keep back. He thought about looking at the card first, deciding on his horse, getting a "feeling" for it, then deciding on the wager; but this seemed out of spirit with the day. He kept ten thousand back, handed the rest to Samuel, then picked up the race card.

The last race was for two-year-olds having their first run in public, consequently there was no form for Neville to go on. In races like this either you knew something or you didn't; and if you didn't, you either followed the market, or had a favourite trainer or jockey. Neville was inclined to disregard all three of these factors, which left him, he knew, with nothing to go on but the horses' names.

He was beginning to think that there might be something in the fact that his success had come with horses called "Restaurant Rendezvous" and "Second Visit", and having registered the possibility that their names might be significant, was allowing the idea to sit quietly at the back of his mind. If he was right, then there would be something in the last race - a five furlong sprint, with eight runners - that should also fit the bill.

On the card, the eight names appeared baldly in front of him, unembellished with the addition of form figures or handicap weights:

1 - Dance Rail

2 - Flying Fashion

3 - Go Candidate

4 - Gurl Burl

5 - Harawa

6 - Mareda

7 - Pharaoh's Tomb

8 - Return to Work

There a great deal of money on Harawa which, Neville knew, would start a very short priced favourite, but - using his rule that the name must be significant - could be ruled out as far as he was concerned. He was also able to rule out nearly all of the others immediately, and left himself with Return to Work as the only possibility.

Despite the apparent logic he had applied to making his selection, Neville was disappointed with the outcome. He had been expecting to find something that would be more **obvious**; in fact, he was expecting to find something called "Mita's Message" running! Return to Work was hardly inspirational. And what did it mean? Was this, the name of a racehorse in a small newcomers event at Epsom, telling him what to do with the rest of his life?

As he walked towards the bookmakers - and the five new vacant spots he had created as a result of the last race - he began to doubt that Return to Work would even win, never mind the rest; if it failed to win, then there was probably nothing in it after all.

Return to Work was generally quoted at six or seven to one, along with a number of others behind the hot favourite. His presence amongst the bookmakers had been noticed, however, and -having seen six of their clan wiped out by him already - a number of them had placed hastily-written signs saying "£100 max." on their boards. The consequence of this was that Neville was unable to get a decent price about his horse - and a decent wager - so he decided to try the Tote.

He knew that this was another risk; that he was changing something else, and moving away from the pattern: first it was a different bookie, and now it was the combination of a different bookie and not being able to rely on any tip. If he were to win, he knew there was more of his own decision making behind this than anything else he had tried to-date.

There was a slight delay at the Tote window when Neville announced his bet, "Ten thousand on number eight". The staff there were only used to dealing in five or ten pound units, and it required the personal attention of the manager to produce a ticket to the required value. Wandering back through the rails bookmakers, Neville noticed that Return to Work's price had now fallen to five to one, and wondered if that might be in part due to the interest he had shown in the horse.

Many people around the bus were beginning to gather up their picnic things and assorted belongings in preparation for a speedy departure after the last race. Samuel was sitting in one of the chairs reading.

'Should we think about packing up, Samuel?'

He looked up.

'Is there any need, Sir? I wasn't aware that we had anywhere to rush off to, and on that basis assumed that we might let the crowds disperse first.'

Neville remembered that, as yet, he had not decided their next destination, and that the decision appeared to lay entirely with him. Samuel was giving no hints.

Their conversation was interrupted by the commentator's announcement that, for the last time that day, the runners were on their way. Neville went to the rail and leant over, staring at the specks of colour half a mile away. He had been unaware that the runners had even come out onto the course, let alone gone down to the start and been ready to race.

From the first strides, the race appeared to be between Harawa and Return to Work. After a couple of furlongs - and nearing the place where Neville was standing - Go Candidate flattered on the outside, but that effort was short lived. Class appeared to be telling, and as they flew passed him, he could see both jockeys at work on their horses.

The commentary seemed a little low key compared to previous races, and the cheers and encouragement of the crowd - especially when Return to Work got its nose in front - were the most muted of the day. For the first time, instead of leaning over the rail and trying to follow the horses all the way to the line, or standing head down and eyes closed, Neville watched the conclusion of the race on the big screen.

He felt a kind of numbness spread over him during those closing moments as he watched Return to Work - in slow motion almost - just get the better of the favourite and pass the post first. He wondered if he had always known that his horse was going to win; and then imagined that if there had been a horse called "Mita's Message" in the race on which he would have placed his money, that Return to Work might still have won. What would that have told him?

'Any good, Sir?' Samuel asked from the chair.

'Afraid so, Samuel; my luck really does appear to have taken a turn for the better.'

There was a slight delay at the Tote window when Neville returned with his ticket. The manager, who seemed to spend much of the time on the telephone, was apologetic about the delay, and it was some ten minutes later when he was able to place a cheque for seventy thousand pounds in Neville's hand.

Walking to the bus, Neville was surprised to see how quickly the course was beginning to empty. Apart from a few punters collecting their winnings, the rails bookmakers' area was now a desert of torn-up tickets and crushed plastic beer glasses. There was litter everywhere, and all across the course, lines of cars had begun to edge and honk their way out of the various car parks. In the fun fair, a few families were still making the most of the day, giving the children one last ride before they fell asleep on the long and tedious journey home. The tannoy limped out one final message about the Tote Placepot and was then silent. The numbers board showed the "8", "5" and "3" result from the last race, but there was nothing else; the

"Weighed In" flag had been taken down. Suddenly the day was over.

Samuel was pouring tea as he got back to the bus.

'So, what was the final tally then Sir?'

Neville sat down, feeling suddenly tired.

'Another seventy thousand there. I guess that makes about two hundred - though it doesn't seem particularly real, or particularly important.'

'I had a feeling you might be that lucky,' Samuel smiled.

'That lucky?'

'Win that much. Or I hoped you would, Sir, let's put it that way. I wanted you to be successful today.'

'Whatever happens?'

Samuel passed Neville his tea.

'Have you decided where you want to go next? We could stay here overnight if necessary, I believe.'

Neville took a sip of tea and looked out across the course to the grandstand. A number of men in overalls had already appeared, and were beginning to sweep up the debris of the day. He wondered if any fortunes had been won or lost over there, and then remembered the man - "Freddie" - to whom he had given the thousand pounds. How had he managed? Did he have any of the money left? Had he gone away a new man, to start a new life? It would have been nice to think so, but Neville knew that it was out of his hands; the man would decide for himself, it was up to him.

Picking up the race card, Neville flicked through its pages, pausing at the last three races, and staring at the names of the animals which had provided him with a considerable expansion of his personal wealth. He thought of Mita suddenly, and looked up, half expecting to see her suddenly walking towards him, her flamingo pink dress startling against the lush green of the turf. She was not there of course, and, he suspected, she never had been. He thought of asking Samuel if he "knew" anything, but decided against it. There seemed little point.

Restaurant Rendezvous had, he realised, triggered this particular thought. He had hoped that he might get some clue as to his future rather than a reflection of his past, and the name appeared to be nothing more than that; but then he turned the page. Second Visit. What if he were to combine to two names? What if "Mita's Message" was in fact an amalgam of these two? He stiffened slightly in his chair. Samuel looked his way. Was he to meet her once again at the restaurant?

He felt an urge to leap from his chair and demand that Samuel get him there immediately, so that he could be there for that evening's meal; but logic and a surprising degree of self-control (coming from where, he was uncertain) kept him in his chair. If this was Mita's message, she would surely not expect to see him at the Restaurant for a couple of days, so it would be ludicrous to rush off immediately. And, in any event, there was one slightly more pressing reason to wait.

Neville decided that, the only way he would be prepared for such a Rendezvous would be if it could be undertaken on his own terms, and with all the unknowns about his own future resolved. He did not want one fleeting evening with Mita, and then oblivion. It would not be fair to either of them. He knew he had to resolve his own future first.

'Samuel, we're going to Birmingham,' he announced.

'Birmingham, Sir?'

'Back to the restaurant.'

Samuel nodded, slowly.

'Do you want us to leave now, Sir?'

Neville looked down at his race card.

'No, there's no hurry. There's something I have to do first.'

And from the last page of the booklet, he stared at the words "Return to Work".

THIRTY EIGHT

It was a little later, as Neville sat at the front of the bus watching its headlights carving their way through the darkened countryside, that he checked his watch.

After his decision to return to Birmingham, and to go back to the place where, just a few days previously, he had been a conscientious employee, he and Samuel had discussed their departure time. Neville had been adamant - though without knowing why - that he did not wish to re-enter the building during the working day. It was not confrontation he was looking for; not in the sense of meeting again those people who had once been his colleagues but had become his usurpers. There was nothing to be gained from that. What he was searching for, and what he wanted to experience again was the **place**, the atmosphere; he wanted to be able to re-evaluate an environment which, for so long, had been almost more of a home than his domestic dwelling with Mirelle.

Since he had left the firm, he had been given the chance to come face to face with his feelings about money - amongst other things - and, having done so, had discovered nothing but self-delusion in the past and what amounted to a new-found independence in the present. He suspected that there were other things, those taboos related to work for instance, which needed re-examination too. It was, he sensed, a time for cleansing.

They had debated travelling the next day, but Neville was keen to strike while this particular iron was hot - and, if he was honest with himself, while he felt his luck was in. Samuel was of the opinion that, provided they made good time, they could be in Birmingham around three in the morning. Given such an estimate, Neville suggested that they set off at once.

Having delayed their departure for a brief snack (Samuel was unwilling to undertake the journey on an empty stomach, and had suggested that it might be wise if they **both** ate something before getting started) they eventually left Epsom a little after eight o'clock. The course was still, the queues had gone, and rumbling out of a deserted car park, they found their way onto relatively quiet roads.

They talked little during the first part of the journey. Samuel had passed a few comments on the day's proceedings thus far, and they had joked, in a quiet, understated kind of way, about how Neville had seen his luck change to dramatic effect. The amount of money he had won was never mentioned, and Neville knew that somewhere on the bus it was safe enough.

Gradually the light had begun to fade, and on the horizon the sky deepened to a soft red glow that leant itself to optimism about the following day's weather. The presence of sun shine was, however, the last thing on Neville's mind as he stared out of the window, watching the ever-darkening houses and trees go by outside, occasionally lit by the head lights of a passing vehicle. Samuel had earlier suggested that he try to sleep, and now - roused by a bump over an uneven piece of road - Neville realised that it had grown quite dark, and could only assume that he had indeed slipped into a brief but restful slumber. Without thinking, he raised his wrist to check the time.

It took a few seconds for him to realise that in staring at a watch showing a fraction before one, he might not be registering the actual hour.

'What time do you make it, Samuel?'

The other man checked his watch.

'A little after eleven thirty, Sir. We're making quite good progress.'

Neville looked down again, saw the second hand sweeping slowly backwards, then remembered. Surely this could not be right. The last time he had looked, his watch had said at least four o'clock, and now it was telling him that he had entered his "last" day.

'Samuel?'

Samuel turned briefly, put on alert by the rather tremulous tone Neville had used.

'Sir?'

'My watch. It says twelve fifty three, Samuel. I have less than a day to go; **less than a day**!' Neville's voice had found a degree of fear which had now supplanted its apprehensive quality. He had not expected this. Although he had no concrete plan, he had wanted to allow himself a little contingency; to "go back" early, to give himself some time to get it "right". But now it appeared that there was no time to be had, and that - like it or not - he had embarked on perhaps his final journey.

'Where has it gone, Samuel? Where has all the time gone? I've lost days. Gone. Why?'

Samuel put his hand to his driver's mirror and adjusted it so that he could see Neville in it, rather than the road behind. Neville watched those old eyes in their new rectangular frame as they flitted between his face and the road ahead.

'Sometimes it just goes. Time passes. We are never in control of it; there is nothing we can do about it. Today it may drag, tomorrow it may fly...'

'But I've less than a day! This is it; now, here. By this time tomorrow... And I'm going back to an empty building in Birmingham. Should I be? Shouldn't I be somewhere else, doing something?'

Samuel's eyes showed the offer of a consoling smile.

'"Doing something", Sir? I think you are doing something. And if you are going back to an empty building, as you say, then perhaps that is what you were meant to do all along.'

'But I've so many unanswered questions. A day! There isn't time to answer them all!'

'But at least you have them, Sir. And perhaps there are only one or two you really need to answer just now. Do you expect to solve them all; to have **all** the answers?' Samuel paused, to allow Neville the chance to speak. He did not. 'No-one has all the answers, Sir. Indeed, no-one knows all the questions. You have your set, you say. They belong to you; they are yours to live with, to work at. Perhaps - perhaps, mind - there will be others; perhaps not. Who can say? I know you cannot. And I? I know nothing...'

Neville watched the headlights paint splashes of colour on the night, then saw the colour swallowed again by darkness. He had less than a day, and that without knowing what would come of it. The roller-coaster he had been riding had suddenly taken a sharp turn - just when he thought he knew where it was going - and was plunging down towards the water splash at the bottom; it was gathering speed, and there was no way off.

Had it been like this for Mita, he wondered? Had the end come suddenly upon her and caught her unprepared to deal with it? Neville remembered her note; there had been a degree of calmness about it, as if she knew what might be round that final bend, and what she expected of herself. He had the impression that nothing had been sprung on her - but who could say, now? He wanted to ask Samuel, but his last words - "I know nothing" - implied for once a kind of impotence, the suggestion that his power - whatever it might be - had gone, was used up, and could affect nothing else.

Suddenly tired, Neville tried to sleep. Debate, with either Samuel or with himself, would get him nowhere; there was, he supposed, something climactic ahead.

He slept fitfully, occasionally waking to find Samuel still intent at the wheel, the bus still pushing its wedge of light along the road. Breaking from sleep, he would look out of the window almost unconsciously, attempting to catch a glimpse of a road sign to give him an indication of where they might be. The journey seemed to take forever. He remembered, as he tried to sleep, the journey to Paris; how it had been over in an instant. And how they had returned from Paris almost as quickly. Things had been taking longer recently, and Samuel's twenty seven miles per hour had become nothing more nor less than that.

Samuel announced their arrival on the outskirts of Birmingham a little before three. Neville roused himself and tried to place them in his old home town. This was never easy in the dark; but as they drew closer to the centre, the lights and shapes of familiar landmarks offered certainty. Samuel requested directions when they reached the centre, and Neville - feeling himself involved once again - began to perk up a little. This was no time to be passive.

The block Neville had inhabited was twelve storeys high; a large square monolith. As the bus came to rest in the car park outside, Neville looked up with something of an air of expectation - and of the unknown. The building was in darkness, apart from a small light visible in the main entrance lobby.

'How will you get in, Sir?'

'I know the Porters. I'm make up some cock and bull story; there shouldn't be a problem.'

Samuel scanned the building.

'Do your firm own all of it?'

Neville laughed.

'No. They lease floors seven and eight; that's all.'

There was a brief silence as the two men contemplated the structure ahead of them.

'Would you like some coffee, Sir?'

Neville shook his head.

'No thanks. I just want to get this - whatever it is - over and done with.'

'I understand, Sir.'

Neville rose from his seat and move to the top of the steps where he paused. Samuel, pushing a button, opened the door for him.

'Samuel?'

'Sir?'

'When I come out - and I am assuming that I will come out of course!', Samuel gave an encouraging laugh, '- will you still be here?'

'I fully expect to be, yes.'

As he made his way the short distance from the bus to the building, Neville guessed that Samuel could probably offer no more of a guarantee than that. He had given him an opportunity to challenge the assumption that he would even emerge from the office, and Samuel had let that slide too. Things had certainly turned around.

The Night-watchman had evidently seen him approaching and was unlocking the front door as Neville mounted the three large flat steps that led up to it. He could sense in the posture of the man - and in the way he carried his torch - that he was not immediately inclined to niceties; perhaps he had been trained for the moment when, out of the blue at three in the morning, he would be accosted by the ultimate villain.

As Neville walked into the light cast by the lobby, the Watchman visibly relaxed, pulling the main door open wider than he had allowed it thus far.

'Hello, Sir! I wouldn't have expected to see you here; certainly not at three in the morning!'

'Hello, Cliff.' Neville offered his hand, which was taken warmly.

'I was sorry to hear they chucked you out, Sir; and after all these years too.'

'One of those things Cliff, I'm afraid.'

Cliff ushered him into the lobby, locking the door behind him.

'That's as may be, Sir; but it's still a bastard thing to do to a bloke. How's it going, anyway?'

Neville stood by the front desk, waiting for Cliff to join him there.

'Oh, so-so. You know how it is. Takes a little bit of time to adjust to things. As you said, it's been a long time.'

Resuming his seat behind the desk, Cliff glanced out to the car park.

'So what are you doing here then Sir; at this time of night - if you don't mind me asking.'

'Well, it's actually quite a long story.' Neville leant on the reception desk with the air of a man about to tell a story, or to let someone in on a great secret. 'Let's just say that my friend and I - that's my friend, out there in that old bus; Samuel his name is. Nice bloke; you'd like him Cliff, really.' Cliff nodded. 'Anyway, Samuel and I are actually on our way back from the Derby, believe it or not.'

'Have any luck, Sir?'

Neville smiled.

'Managed to get the winner actually.'

'Get away! Have a few bob on it, did you?'

'A little tickle, yes.'

'Well good on you, Sir; that's what I say!'

'Thank you, Cliff. So, anyway. Samuel and I were on our way home, when I realised that we'd be passing through town and that I'd left one or two things in my old office. I'd thought about coming back during the day, but, well, that might prove to be a little awkward; you know what I mean?'

'Awkward? Yes, Sir; I can see that.'

'So I said to Samuel that we'd try and stop by here. I was sure I'd see someone I knew on duty - and I'm pleased it was you Cliff - and that I'd be able to get the rest of my stuff.'

There was a pause as Cliff wrestled with the decision.

'I'm not sure, Sir. I mean, it's not exactly regular.'

'I was thrown out in a bit of a hurry, that's all. Look, Cliff; you can search me if you want to - just to make sure I'm not carrying a bomb.'

Neville pushed his hands into the air and spread his legs wide, making himself ready for an American-style body search. Cliff laughed.

'That won't be necessary Sir! Lifts one and two are out of action tonight, so if you'd like to take lift three.'

'Thanks Cliff.'

'I'll be on my rounds in about forty minutes; so if you could be down here before then I'd appreciate it.'

'I'll see what I can do.'

It took Neville just a few seconds to reach the lift and then a little longer before - with the sound of a "ping" as the door opened - he stepped out onto the seventh floor. The hallway was in darkness, but knowing where the light switches were - years of familiarity here - he had soon illuminated the hallway leading away from the lifts and down to his old office.

Once through the open plan section, his boss's office was the first door on the left. There was one door next to that - his old room - and two corresponding doors on the other side of the short corridor. As he passed the first of these, he noticed David's name in bold letters upon it; next to David's office was Colin's, his name also similarly garish in large red script. Turning then and coming to a halt, Neville faced what used to be his own door. Brian - to whom he had never given much credit on the simple basis that the man lacked talent - was evidently now the proud owner of his old desk and filing cabinet.

He took one step forwards, then placed his fingers on the familiar door handle. He paused, looked back down the corridor, then twisted his hand. The door eased open with all its old accustomed fluency.

THIRTY NINE

The room was dark. Neville's fingers felt along the wall for the light switch, which they found with accustomed certainty. He pressed, but nothing happened. He knew that a little further into the office, there was a white board on the wall, and a small strip light above that. Provided Brian had moved nothing, the cord-pull for that was just two paces away.

Neville, as he edged forwards, knew that Brian was a man unlikely to make major changes to the office layout, so the chances of him running into an out-of-place chair was remote. Indeed, Brian had been praised - more than once, Neville could remember, and within his earshot too - for his methodical approach to his work; the boss liked the way he ordered and filed things, everything cross-referenced, and all within a finger tip's reach. Neville argued to himself that this was the approach of a man frightened that his limitations might become exposed, and who chose to conceal them behind a facade of order.

His fingers found the wall, then his arm brushed the cord. He traced the small plastic knob at the bottom of the cord and tugged. There were one or two pulses of light from above which threw a strange and inconsistent strobe effect across the room. It was not much to go on, but Neville was sure - even in these temporary flashes - that he had spotted something different.

With a hum, the white board light fairly popped into action, illuminating the office. As Neville had surmised, the desk and its chair were in the same location as he remembered them. Indeed, he would have sworn that they were in **exactly** the same places as when - on his last day - he had picked up his briefcase, loaded it, and walked out; along the corridor, passed the Boss's office (with its now open door), and to lift two and the car park. It was as if Brian had moved neither of them an inch.

For a split second, this was Neville's impression of the room - partly because that was what he expected of Brian. The desk however, became insignificant - **invisible** almost - when he noticed the far wall. The filing cabinet had gone, and in its place, Brian had erected shelving from floor to ceiling. Each shelf was around two feet deep and some fourteen feet long - and each one was filled with lever arch files.

There was not a single inch of shelf space free. The first file in the top left corner was neatly labelled "CD-CH" in bold, over-large Dyno-tape; the one next to it "CI-CN" and so on throughout the entire alphabet. Neville bent to check the bottom right-hand corner; sure enough he found "ZO-ZZ". Each spine also carried the initials "BJF" - Brian's name - and the year. Neville knew the Boss would love it.

Along the far wall, the long window looked out onto the car park, and beneath this, another single shelf ran its full length. This shelf was not home to more binders, but to an assortment of books, mainly paperback. Neville walked to the window. The bus was just visible in the car park, a small glow coming from the window of Samuel's compartment. That made him feel better.

Curiosity forced Neville to pull a few books from the shelf. There appeared to be nothing these had in common apart from their alphabetic ordering by author. Thus, a DIY Manual by a chap called "Griggs", was preceded by Graham Greene's "It's a Battlefield" and followed by "The Return of the Native". They seemed a strangely apt trio considering his present circumstances.

As he slid the books back - in reverse sequence, just as a small joke which would piss Brian off no end! - Neville remembered that the files had begun with "CD". He checked the walls of the room again; there was no other shelving, and the desk - not surprisingly - was tidy to the point of being spartan. Where then, were the volumes that contained "AA" through to "CC"?

It was precisely at this moment that Neville noticed the narrow door in the corner of the room between the window and the shelves. There had not been a door in the office during his period of habitation, and, as far as he was aware, there was nothing the other side of this particular wall at all; it was the end of the building. He knew he might be mistaken and, as he was there, could only find out. He tried the handle, but the door was locked.

Undaunted, Neville went to the desk. Brian was a creature of habit. The key to the door would be in his desk drawer, but his desk drawer would be locked. Neville tried; it failed to move. The key to his desk drawer was always stuffed down the seat cushion of his chair - and on the left-hand side, as Brian was left-handed. He felt between the cushions and sure enough his fingers found metal. Neville unlocked the desk drawer, and pulled the key from the small desk-tidy compartment reserved - according to the advertising material - for paper clips. To someone who didn't know Brian, this might seem like a diversion from his regulated personality, but it was not. Brian did not believe in paper clips; things could become detached, lost, and in consequence would never find their true place in the ordered and documented scheme of things. So, paper clips were banished from Brian's world - which left a nice little slot in his desk tidy for this small key.

Neville slid the key into the lock and it turned with a positive "click". He pushed the door open. In the half-light cast from the white board, Neville could make out some sort of cupboard beyond and felt for a light switch on the wall beyond. There was nothing on the wall, but as he was withdrawing his hand, his fingers brushed another cord. He pulled it. Again there was the strobe pulse as the neon was kicked into life; in front of him Neville caught a glimpse of more binders and the letters "ERG-AL" caught his eye. Confident he had found Brian's secret store, he took a step forward, found there to be no floor beneath his feet, and suddenly tumbled forwards.

He came to rest against the bottom shelf, partly on his back. The impact with the wall had dislodged two of the files which now lay by his feet. Neville looked to the doorway and the two small steps leading immediately down from the office that he had missed. He felt a slight twinge in his left side, but apart from that seemed unharmed.

Picking up one of the volumes, he checked the spine: "BT-BZ". Opening the cover, he revealed a number of index cards inserted throughout the folder running from BT and BU, in sequence to BY and BZ; he could have expected nothing else. Loosening the folder's document grip, Neville pulled back the BT partition and revealed the first paper. It was a letter from a firm of solicitors relating to a complaint from a member of the public who had tripped in the car park and was suing for damages; apparently they had torn their trousers. Neville read the letter, then, having done so, realised that there was no obvious reason why this had been filed under BT, even though it had "BT" scribbled in the top right hand corner. He turned to the next page, only to discover that it was blank. The next page was blank too, as was the one after that. Indeed, all the pages were blank except those that immediately followed an index card. BU heralded a gas bill; BV, a summons from the County Court; BW, a shopping list.

For years Brian had been peddling his "method", displaying his "system", and all the while it was - as Neville had constantly suspected - nothing more than a sham. He had always been vaguely suspicious of things displaying such rigour so baldly and dubious about any straightjacket offered as a means of doing things, despite a secret envy and regard for the order they imposed. He had never been particularly organised himself, but had sometimes felt a craving to be almost robotic. However, since his recent experiences, he had come to realise that, although there was a place for some consistency and system in the world, one could not be a slave to it. Brian had evidently sold himself to his "method"; a system which had ceased to function as anything other than a cover for randomness.

As he stood, the two files in his hand ready to replace them, Neville noticed a small spiral staircase about six feet in front of him. He restored Brian's folders - again in an incorrect order - and made for the stairs.

They wound their narrow way upwards towards a hole in the ceiling, and - Neville could only assume - to the eight floor. As he ascended, he tried to remember what had been directly above his office. One of the lavatories thereabouts, and a store room. He hoped the stairs led to the store room.

On the bannister a few steps from the top, there was a small light switch. Neville pressed it and light flooded down to him from above. It appeared too dark in the room above for him to be heading for a porcelain-filled cubicle - unless the toilets had been recently decorated in something akin to Royal Blue mixed with Earth Brown.

With his head a little above the level of the floor, Neville found himself in a cavern of boxes; brown and blue boxes stacked floor to ceiling, at least eight deep. On each of the boxes was a small label, with an untidy scrawl on each; often the scribble had been crossed out and written over. Once fully upright in the room, he pulled a box from the top of one tower. The label had "April 1991" written in blue ink; but this had been crossed through in red and "January 1992" annotated above. Neville flicked off the lid. Inside was a pile of papers. He pulled a few sheets off; they were badly aligned and had been stored messily. Browsing through the first few, he could see no connection apart from the date.

'Had to come back, didn't you?'

A voice, not without anger, assailed him from the far corner of the store. Neville dropped the papers in surprise.

'Had to come back, eh? Why? Why d'you come back? To find me out, eh?'

From behind one pile of cartons, Brian stepped half into the light. Neville moved a pace backwards, stepping on the dropped papers as he did so.

'Come to find me out, eh? To prove that you were right all along? I heard the stories and rumours you used to spread about me in the canteen, you bastard!'

'Brian?'

'I've been waiting, see. I knew you'd be back. I knew you'd try and get your old job back by trying to get me kicked out.'

'Brian.'

'Well you can't, you bastard! The old man loves me, see. He thinks I've got it licked. He likes to see my files; he thinks I've got all the angles covered, and I'm not going to let some little shit like you spoil it for me.'

Brian moved forwards. In his hand he held a large four-hole punch with which he appeared intent on doing some damage. Neville took another step back, his foot finding the top step of the staircase.

'Brian, I don't want my job back. I don't want to get you kicked out. I'm happy now.'

The last words escaped from him. There was not reasoning behind them. Brian scoffed at him.

'How can you be happy, you miserable shit! You were never very good at anything; how can you be happy out of here? How can you function without this place? Don't give me that crap, OK?'

'I mean it,' as he spoke, Neville moved down a step; Brian was gradually approaching across the room, 'I don't care about this place. You can have it. Keep my job; keep it, I don't want it.'

'Fucking bollocks!'

'Look,' another step, 'I'm sorry about the things I've said about you in the past. Really. We each have our own ways of dealing with things, that's all.' Neville cast his eyes over Brian's crates; the summation of his professional career. 'You have your system; it works for you...'

Brian suddenly let fly with a scream. The hole-punch missed Neville's head, becoming embedded in a carton labelled "May 1991".

'You sarcastic shit! "Works for me" does it?' Brian was now wild-eyed; he cast about, picking up the nearest crate. 'Works for me, eh? Of course it doesn't work! Look!' And with that, he tipped the entire contents onto the floor.

Neville found another step.

'Perhaps if you spent a little time - sorting things out...'

'The only thing I'm going to sort out is you!'

As Brian made a lunge across the store room, Neville turned and bolted down the stairs. A carton - still fully laden - followed him down, catching the back of his legs three steps from the foot of the staircase. He missed the final eighteen inches in consequence and landed with a thump on his knees. He could hear Brian beginning his descent.

'Come here, you little shit! You were never any good at anything! I'm not letting you spoil my fucking pension!'

Neville got to his feet just in time to avoid another box as it flew towards him. As he reached the door, Brian's legs were just visible coming down the steps. The time for negotiation - had it ever been available - was now over. Neville leapt up the two steps, tugged on the light cord, and dashed into the office. Closing the door behind him, he locked it and threw the key into the waste paper basket.

There was a bang on the door the other side. Neville heard Brian turn on the light.

'You wait 'til I get out of here, you shit! I'll be after you, mark my words!'

Neville waited, not sure what to expect. There was an unnatural pause, then a howl from the other side of the door.

'My files! My files are out of order! You've put my files out of order, you bastard! I'll get you, you sodding bastard! You sodding...'

Brian's anger suddenly gave way to the sound of sobbing. Neville waited. There was nothing else except quiet sobbing. Brian moaned "my files" once or twice and was then silent. Neville guessed that whoever had locked him in would, in due course, return to release him. Perhaps he should mention it Cliff on his way out. But then again - this thought as he turned out the white board light - perhaps he shouldn't.

FORTY

There was a question in Neville's mind, as he stood once again in the corridor, regarding his next move. The encounter with Brian actually amounted to something of a close call, and with Colin and David's offices still ahead of him, he recognised a desire - which was growing in strength - to simply turn around and leave. He checked his watch. It was now around twelve fifteen; he had hours left, at best.

As the lift had risen to the seventh floor, he had tried to understand exactly what he was doing there; why had he returned, and what he was to do. The decision to invade the offices of the three men who had replaced him had only been made as he had walked towards them. If he had been looking for retribution or revenge, then he could simply have ransacked his old boss's office; but Neville knew that there was nothing to be gained from that beyond an exceedingly temporary element of satisfaction. In any event, he had learned much about himself recently and concluded that he had been ousted from his job because these three juniors had, together, been able to offer the company something that he obviously lacked. It felt - and all of this rationalised within a few paces too - as if he, in now going into their domain, was facing head-on an earlier insufficiency in himself. If anywhere, that was where he needed confrontation.

The theory was fine; it fitted nicely, and gave him a degree of comfort knowing that his action might be justified - or at least rationalised. Perhaps he was looking for something he could justify to Samuel too, for even now he could not but believe that Samuel still held at least one ace in that invisible hand of his.

He paused before Colin's door, staring hard at its name plate, almost trying to see through it and into the room beyond. He had not been prepared for Brian, though the nature of the office and the encounter failed, on reflection, to surprise him. Colin was a character of order too, though not in any mechanistic sense. He was - to use a popular consultant's term - something of a "Starter-Finisher"; he was definite and precise, liking things to be procedural, ordered, black-and-white almost. Neville knew that Colin regarded himself as an intellectual, and that he tried to play up to a kind of quiet "boffin" image; it was not an impressive piece of role playing, but had proven to be sufficient to dupe the boss.

Neville expected to find the office in darkness, as Brian's had been. He had sufficient recollection of Colin's room to be able to undertake a similar - if less confident - negotiation of the furniture in darkness had he been required to do so. However, this was not necessary on two counts: firstly the light was on; and secondly, because he appeared not to have entered an office at all.

The door had opened out into an incredibly small, almost square room devoid of any furniture. There were one or two pictures on the walls - Colin liked to display a taste in art and expostulate about music, much as Brian talked about books - but apart from these, there was nothing to break the monotony of the box except another door in the opposite corner. There was just room for Neville, once inside, to close the first door behind him and open the second.

This anti-chamber was evidently new. Neville, his capacity for surprise now almost worn entirely away (except when accosted by a maniac wielding a four-hole punch) could see no reason why Colin should arrange construction of such a useless buffer between himself and the outside world - and then wondered if this was related to Colin at all, having been provided instead as a one-off for his visit. There was a degree of hesitation in Neville's opening of the second door, but this was so marginal as to be imperceptible.

Neville was half-expecting to find darkness beyond this second portal, but again he was wrong. The presence of light, however, was the least of the things to surprise him. He appeared to have stepped out onto a pavement. Beneath his feet, grey and uneven paving stones stretched the width of the office. On both end walls, murals had been painted to give the illusion that he was standing on a public highway between a milliners and a jewellery shop. If this were not surprising enough, ahead was the facade of a shop selling musical instruments. He had been convinced that there would be no more tricks; he had sensed reality beginning to encroach on his immediate experience again, and this - which was certainly **not** Colin's day-to-day office environment - was possibly a retrograde step.

From the shop ahead, he heard vague strains of music. In the window - which was only a window in name, as there was no glass in evidence - two rows of cellos hung, three to each row. They were brightly illuminated by individual spotlights, and, alongside them, a large double Bass made up the display.

The music, which had been vague and indistinct, suddenly rose in volume; the tune - immediately familiar - blasting out an accompaniment of bells of various kinds. Neville had not heard the theme for ages, but it was something not to be forgotten. As it echoed around the small room, the sound of applause joined it, the six cellos and the Bass began to fidget on their stands. Neville leant back against the wall, preparing for what was apparently going to be some kind of show.

The Bass made a stiff attempt at a bow, and the music began to subside.

'Hello, good evening, and welcome.'

The words were delivered in a deep and resonant voice, the cellos all leaning towards the larger instrument.

'This evening we have the first semi-final in Symphony Challenge, with the French Violas taking on the Dutch Cellos.'

Neville recognised that the instruments on the upper row - the violas - were slightly smaller.

'First the Violas.'

'A above middle C,' said the first smoothly, 'reading Nardini's Violin concerto in E flat major.'

'G above middle C,' said the next, 'reading Bach's Violin concerto number two in E major.'

'E above middle C, reading Grieg's Holberg suite.'

'C above middle C, reading Rimsky-Korsakov's Symphonic Suite, Opus thirty five.'

As the violas introduced themselves, they did so in gently rising voices as they moved up the scale from G, through D and A, and onto C. There was a small ripple of applause as the introductions ended.

'And the Cellos,' said the Bass.

'E below middle C, reading Mahler's Symphony number five, in C sharp minor.'

Neville noticed the very different tone of the first cello.

'G below middle C, reading Elgar's Cello concerto.'

'A below middle C, also reading Elgar's Cello concerto.'

'C below middle C, reading Vaughan Williams' Sinfonia Antarctica.'

As Neville listened to the applause, he noticed how the tone of the cellos had fallen during the introductions, their overall mood seemingly more serious and determined. The Bass waited for the applause to die down.

'Well, there they are and here we go. A starter for ten, with a bonus of ten to follow. Which Polish composer died in 1849?'

A bright, clear note rang out from the upper row.

'Viola, D,' prompted the Bass.

'Frederic Chopin,' came the reply from the said viola.

'Correct. Your bonus for ten; you may confer. When was Anton Bruckner born?'

The violas leaned together, a strange, inharmonious combination of four notes rising from them as they conferred. After a few seconds there was silence.

'1824,' came the reply from Viola A.

'Correct. Another starter for ten, a bonus of twenty to follow. Which conductor became the biographer of Delius?'

There was a pause, and then a hesitant note from a Cello.

'Cello, C.'

'Sir Thomas Beecham?'

'Correct.'

The contest continued in this vein for a few minutes. Occasionally, the Bass would remind the teams of the scores, which, although never very divergent, were beginning to suggest a win from the Cellos after the Violas had taken an early lead. The questions, although demonstrating a rather heavy musical bias, also strayed into other areas of the arts, particularly painting. When this happened, one of the Cellos - C - was particularly outstanding and, had he been counting, Neville felt certain that he would have found this one contribution the key difference between the teams.

With the scores at 145 to 125 in the Cellos' favour, Cello C, in making a rather over-hasty attempt to jump in on a question, sounded an unhealthy "Twang" rather than its customary professional note. There was a gasp from the invisible audience as the strings of the instrument snapped and the cello fell lifelessly forwards and onto the pavement.

'Where is the substitute, please,' said the double Bass, evidently unruffled by the incident. The three remaining cellos hummed slowly and nervously to each other; above them, the violas were showing signs of excitement, sensing their chance to get back in the game.

'The substitute, please,' said the Bass again, and with those words, Neville felt the sudden heat of a spotlight on him. He stood away from the wall stiffly.

'Come on then,' said the Bass.

'Not me,' said Neville.

'Who else?'

'But I know nothing about music.'

The viola's now chattered with even more excitement on hearing this news.

'Please,' said the Bass, insistently, 'take your place.'

There was applause from somewhere as Neville, sensing he had little choice in the matter, moved forwards. There was a small ridge upon which the fallen cello had been resting, and Neville perched himself on that as best he could.

'And you are?' The Bass leaned his way, wanting an introduction.

'Neville.' He looked apologetically along the line of the three remaining cellos.

'Reading?'

'Reading?' echoed Neville.

'Reading, yes. What are you reading?' The Bass was beginning to get a little cross that his show seemed to be getting out of hand.

Neville tried to think quickly.

'Rhapsody in Blue, by George Gershwin.'

It was all he could think of. The audience greeted the news with a gasp; his team mates could only moan.

'On we go then. A little over ten minutes to go, and here's a starter for ten.'

The competition continued, but with the initial questions majoring on classical music and Neville's team effectively being outnumbered four to three, the gap in the score began to diminish. As it became even more evident that Neville was unable to contribute anything, his team mates began to ignore him.

The violas had established a fifteen point lead, when the Bass asked:

'Which mythical game is played on a number of levels with an infinite variety of pieces and moves?'

There was silence from the instruments.

'I'll have to hurry you,' hinted the Bass.

Neville wondered what noise he needed to make that was comparable with the instruments. Giving in, he faked a cough.

'Cello, Neville.'

He felt the pressure of expectation upon him.

'Is it "Croak"?'

'Correct.'

There were murmurs of approval from the three other Cellos, and, although Neville could not answer the follow up question, he felt had made something of a contribution.

A few minutes later, Cello E had correctly answered a starter, but the subsequent question - "Who played in both "Genesis" and "Mike and the Mechanics" - had them flawed. Neville leaned towards them.

'Mike Rutherford,' he whispered.

The cellos were instantly silent. They conferred briefly again, then all leant his way. He was evidently expected to offer the answer.

'Mike Rutherford.'

'Correct,' agreed the Bass.

With the cellos still fifteen points adrift, the Bass announced that they were entering the final round. There was to be a starter question, and then three follow up questions, all worth five points. If Neville's team were to win, they must answer all four questions correctly.

'What do Vaughan William's and the song "Cry Me A River" have in common.'

He had not wanted to say anything. He did not want to be responsible for the outcome of the contest; but as the word "London" suddenly slipped from his lips, he knew the die was cast.

'Correct,' said the Bass, 'the symphony by Vaughan Williams, and the singer, Julie London.'

Assuming Neville's intervention had sealed their fate, the cellos groaned a discordant and low moan. Above, the violas suddenly let fly with a volley of cheery notes.

'Quiet, please,' demanded the Bass. 'Here is your bonus, three questions worth five points each. Remember, no conferring. You are ten points behind. Good luck.'

Neville prayed that there would not be any music questions.

'These questions all relate to lessons learned in modern mythology. Firstly, what was the purpose behind the General's purchase of the motor car?'

Unsure that he had heard the Bass correctly, he asked for the question to be repeated. The Bass did so. As he had suspected, the question was related directly to himself. Was this to be another reason for his return?

'To illustrate the value and worth of money.'

There was a pause.

'I'll need a little more,' said the Bass.

'In buying the car for an inflated sum of money, the General displayed that money has both an accepted value and an intrinsic worth. The value is a universal norm, accepted by all; it's worth is related to an individual, and cannot be measured except by that individual in their own particular circumstance.'

'Correct.'

There was a small ripple of applause, and the cellos let out a low note. Neville knew that if he were able to answer the next question, then at least they would not lose.

'Second. What was the purpose of the excursion in the painting in the Musée d'Orsay?'

This was a question he could never have expected. Neville remembered how the experience had developed, moving from the pleasurable to the nightmarish, but had not - until now - ever been forced to consider it. He wished he had taken the opportunity to discuss it with Samuel after all.

'I must hurry you.'

'It was an illustration of the relationship between life and art.'

It was desperate, but all he could think of.

'Go on.'

'Well. It showed how life and art are different things. How art can imitate or depict life, but that it is something else.' Neville paused, unable to tell if this was enough for the Bass. 'And that one cannot live one's life through art. Art is a part of life, not vice versa.'

He had said it, but was unsure that he understood it, let alone believed it. The Bass appeared to be thinking.

'That's not quite what I wanted, but I'll take it.'

There was more applause, and the cellos sounded their own harmonious note of congratulation. Overhead, the violas were beginning to sound a little nervous.

'And finally - with the scores level -' the Bass allowed a little pause, to heighten the tension, 'describe the game of Croak.'

He did not know what he had been expecting, but this final question came as something of a relief. He smiled a little, relaxing as best he could on the small ledge.

'Croak does not exist.'

It was the most confident he had sounded about any of his answers. He was convinced that, if he had learned anything, he knew this much. There was a brief pause. Neville waited for the announcement that he had just won the match for the cellos.

'I'm sorry, that is incorrect. The match is tied.'

The Bass' words were greeting with a whole cacophony of sound: the viola and the cellos sounding forth, either celebrating that they had not been beaten, or lamenting their failure to win; applause - mixed with a few quiet boos - echoed around the room again; and Neville, trying to remonstrate with the Bass, slipped from his perch and fell crashing down onto the prostrate cello whose place he had taken. At that moment, the lights suddenly went out, and all was silent.

Overtaken by circumstance, Neville lifted himself to his feet. He remembered where the door had been, and made his way towards it, his hands out in front of him. He had expected to find the broken cello beneath his feet, but encountered nothing. A pace or two further on than he expected, he found the door. His search for a light switch was unrewarded, and he settled for opening the door.

Instead of facing the ante-room, he saw the corridor, and - looking back over his shoulder - saw nothing more exceptional than Colin's empty office. There was no street, no murals, and no broken cello.

FORTY ONE

Having regained the corridor and closed Colin's door behind him, Neville was suddenly thirsty. He was tired too, he realised, but there was nothing he could do about that. He had no opportunity to rest or take a break; Cliff, due to start his rounds soon, had given him a time limit, and Neville was certain that this had nearly expired.

He ignored David's door for the moment - the last of his challenges, it made him feel like Hercules - and walked to the open-plan end of the corridor and the vending machine. He selected a coke (the machine was never switched off) and waited as it dropped, through to the perspex compartment from which it could be retrieved. The can popped open with its customary "hiss", and Neville raised it to his mouth.

After the encounter with Brian, he was surprised that the version of University Challenge he had just participated in had been so personal. It had been "set-up" for him; he could not think otherwise. The collapse of the cello, his presence on the set, and those final questions; it was not a situation over which he had any control. All he had had to do was to walk through the door.

Coming within range of David's office, he wondered if he were about to engage in another act in the drama; if, once he had crossed the threshold, the parts would be played out as if already scripted. He thought back to his answer of the penultimate question. Surely it might have been any question; there were dozens he had already been unable to answer, and the guess of "London" was nothing more than a thought somehow escaping verbally. He had no knowledge that Vaughan Williams had written a symphony called "London", and so how could it be possible for the scene to have been scripted elsewhere?

He felt caught between impotence and complete power. When he walked into David's office - or, rather, into that which lay beyond the door - presumably he could either play along with whatever transpired, or he could kick hard against it, determined to buck the system and assert himself. The latter was an attractive option, but how could he know if that wasn't precisely what had already been laid out for him?

He drained the last of the coke and walked back to the bin by the vending machine. The can gave out a hollow rattle as it hit the bottom of the empty receptacle. The rattle sounded like the note of a feeble bell, and he imagined, somewhere, a lone bell tolling in an empty and echoing chamber; was it calling him? For whom did that particular bell toll?

Despite his uncertainty and this rather romantic sense of foreboding, the one thing Neville was not experiencing was fear. He had come too far for that, and his new attitude - more stoic and relaxed than any he would have previously owned up to - allowed him to contemplate this immediate future with a degree of calm. So, when he returned to David's door and pushed it open, he did so with something of an air of conviction and determination.

Expecting either bright light or - and this was favourite - darkness, he walked into neither. Expecting either a conventional office, or something that failed to resemble any space that might be recognisable in that context, again he was surprised. The room - for it was a conventional room, about the size of David's office as he remembered it - was rather dimly lit from a number of wall lights, with, at its centre, a few brighter lights embedded in the ceiling. The sense that it appeared to be something of an arena, was heightened by the fact that it was bare of furniture - with the exception of a large chess board laid out in its centre.

The board began about a yard into the room, and filled it completely with the exception of the little skirt around the edge in which Neville now stood. The squares - approximately a yard in width - alternated a pale yellow and an inoffensive brown.

Neville's arrival, and the closing of the door behind him, triggered (as seemed the norm) activity elsewhere; and, from another door in the opposite wall, a number of chess pieces made their entrance. He watched them as they walked (in the case of the Kings, Queens, Bishops and Pawns) to their respective squares, the Knights trotting in behind them. Neville waited for the Rooks but there were none - and then he realised that they were in the middle of a game, and were playing from an established position.

His own role was initially unclear. He had begun to reflect on David's character, on the rather scheming intellectual he had often seemed, and realised that the scenario - a chess game - was entirely in keeping with the theme thus far. Of course - and this he realised with something of a shudder - if the same theme from Colin's room was to be followed, then this game also had something to do with him.

The Knights were small but intensely realistic horses mounted by well-armoured figures. Consequently, when a white horse appeared from the second door but without its rider, Neville's question as to his role in the pageant was answered. The horse made its way over to him, and, breathing a little heavily, came to rest at his side. Without hesitation, he lifted one leg over the horse's back and eased himself into the tiny saddle. Once there, the horse - with a surprising degree of strength and agility - lifted Neville's feet from the ground, and carried him to a square on the board. They stopped, and as the ceiling lights became a little brighter, a solo and slow drum beat began to echo around the room, and a thin layer of fog drifted across the board.

From what Neville could see - and he was no expert - the two sides appeared to be even: apart from the Kings, both Queens were on the board as was a White bishop, another white Knight and three white Pawns. The white pieces were opposed by black's three Pawns, two Bishops and a Knight. It seemed that white had lost his traditional advantage and had been pushed back onto the defensive, with the black pieces threatening to overrun his position; however, all was not lost, and Neville felt his own position - in the centre of the board - could be critical.

On the edge of the board to his right, a black Pawn took a step forwards. Against the backing of the drum beat, Neville tried to get a grip on the position.

'A little tricky, isn't it My Son?'

Neville looked over his shoulder to the source of the voice. The white Bishop - bearing a remarkable resemblance to Samuel - stood just behind him.

'It would appear so, yes.'

'A tactical error in the early part of the middle game, I'm afraid; and now it's touch and go.' The Bishop paused as a white Pawn moved up to block the most recently advanced black piece. Neville was suddenly relieved that he was not expected to make all the moves. The Bishop pushed his mitre forwards in the direction of the black Queen. 'Watch out for her.'

Following the line of the Bishop's gaze, he noticed that the black Queen - Mirelle to a "T" - was bearing down on him. Luckily the Bishop was, at present, offering some protection. The black King moved to a square at the corner of the board, tucking himself away. From his present range, Neville could not make out the face on the black King, but had begun to realise that most of the major pieces seemed to bear a likeness to people he knew.

There was a sudden and familiar shout of "Tally-Ho" from nearby as Neville's compatriot Knight - "Binky" Bingham, complete with armoured flying suit - charged at a black Bishop, leaving the latter prone on the board. Two tiny figures suddenly scuttled across to the Bishop and dragged it away. The Knight's joy was short-lived however, as the exchange was completed by the black Queen simply marching forward and somehow propelling both horse and rider clean from the board. She now stood within two squares of Neville, but - owing to his movement restrictions - not within his present compass.

'Not expecting to win, are you?' The Queen taunted him in a slow drawl, reminiscent of Mirelle's non-English accent.

Elsewhere a white piece moved, and this was followed by the black Knight - David, of course, lording it as if on home territory - galloping to the Queen's side. Both now threatened Neville.

'Hello, Darling,' the Queen said to the Knight, as the latter pranced alongside her.

'My Queen,' came the reply, and the Knight bowed low.

Neville wondered just how closely this game was meant to be a mirror of his own life; was this an infidelity he had long suspected being played out in front of him?

'Better move back,' the white Bishop suggested from behind, 'just by me should be OK.'

With the smallest tug on the reins, Neville's horse responded, immediately travelling to the square in question. As they came to rest, he was still uncertain as to the degree of control he was supposed to have over the game. A whole series of moves was now played out which seemed not to involve him. Two pawns on each side were exchanged - the tiny figures running on to the board to drag off the stricken - and various positional adjustments were made. From behind him, the white Queen -

Neville was confident that this was Mita - made a significant move forwards.

'It won't be long now,' hinted the Bishop.

'Long?'

'Before the decisive stage of the game. Look. The Queens are beginning to eye each other up. I can keep an eye on the Knight - he's all show, that one - but you'll need to get that last pawn.'

Neville looked across to where the remaining black Pawn - a small, faceless piece - stood unguarded. He could not reach it in one move, but could see a way across.

'When should I make my move?'

'Await my signal.'

There was a brief lull before the black Queen moved towards the white camp. Neville could understand the Bishop's logic; things were going to get a little hot. By making the last move, the black Queen had removed some of the pressure on Neville. He wondered if this were to be his cue, but the white Bishop moved a single square behind him. It seemed little had changed.

Gaining in confidence, the black Queen called her Knight forwards. They were now very close to the King, with only the white Queen directly in their way.

'Prepare to meet thy doom, Usurper!' cried the black Queen.

'You are an evil woman,' came the reply, 'and I have Right on my side!'

As the black Queen began to laugh, the Bishop banged his mitre on the board and pointed towards the pawn.

'Now, My Son; now!'

Neville tugged the horse towards the pawn which he immediately threatened. In doing so, he realised that he had allowed a discovered attack by the Bishop on the black Queen.

'Now, Madam,' cried the Bishop, 'as God is my witness, the Righteous shall have the day!'

The black Queen could do nothing in the face of the attack by the Bishop; she could only retreat, leaving the Pawn at Neville's mercy. He pulled the lance from his holster on the horse's tack, and levelled it at the Pawn.

'Charge!' shouted the Bishop.

Neville looked back. The black Queen was now threatening the Bishop; surely either it should move, or Neville should try to protect it.

'But...' he began to remonstrate.

'Charge, My Son! Have faith! Charge!'

Levelling his lance, Neville turned to the Pawn again and drove his horse forwards. The lance landed high on the pawn which spin out of its square, and fell to the side of the board. As the small retrievers came for the corpse, Neville heard a scream from the centre of the board. The black Queen was bearing down on the Bishop.

'Now I have you! Die!'

And in an instant, the black Queen was in possession of the Bishop's square with no sign of its former occupant. The victor let out a manic laugh. It seemed to Neville for an instant that white was about to be overrun, then there came a rallying cry from his Queen.

'Now the black Knight; the Knight!'

Neville turned to see that his opposite number was now within his sights and preparing for an attack. The black Knight raised his lance.

'Try your luck, you imbecile! I've defeated you before, and I can do so again! You used to think that you were so smart, but all the while you were blind; dumb and blind!'

'Not anymore, my friend; not anymore!'

With a dig in his horse's ribs, Neville made for the Knight. There was a clash as lance hit shield, but the black Knight did not fall. Instead he prepared his own assault. This did not appear to be following the strict rules of chess. Neville raised his own shield just in time to deflect the oncoming lance, and though rocked back by the impact, remained steady on his horse.

The black Knight prepared to charge again. Neville dropped his lance and removed his sword from its scabbard, preparing it beneath his shield. As the black Knight charged again, Neville, in raising his shield, was able to deflect the powerful lance upwards, and then drive his sword beneath the shield and into the armour of the black Knight. The latter stopped suddenly. There was a scream from the black Queen as her consort felt to the ground.

'You scum! You'll pay for this, like you've never paid before!'

She moved towards Neville, preparing her assault. Neville could see no way out. Then, from behind, he heard the sound of rushing footsteps and turned just in time to see his own Queen flying across the board to his rescue. The black Queen had forsaken all control of the game and was now lost.

The two Queens met head-on in the centre of the board. As they struggled, their robes flying in the fray, coronets and chains broken and torn from their apparel, still the drum-beat sounded out its accompaniment. Was this the battle that would decide the result of the contest?

For a moment it seemed as if the white Queen was in the ascendant, then, without warning, she was thrown to the ground where she lay helpless, the black Queen threatening above her. Neville tugged at his horse, but nothing happened; it was not white's move, and the horse would go nowhere. Resolved to do something, he threw his leg over the horse's back and slipped to the ground; then, sword in hand, he made for the black Queen.

She was about to strike when Neville got to her. His approach had been swift but not quite silent. She turned to see him just as he was raising his sword, her face suddenly a mix of fear and bravado. Beginning a wild and loud laugh, she managed but a few sounds before his arm swung and the sword severed her head from her body.

The drum beat stopped. On the board, the face of the black Queen became lost in the layer of fog. Neville could hear the scampering of the two salvagers but could not seem them. The white Queen was getting to her feet.

'The King,' she whispered, 'you must get the King!'

Neville looked to the corner of the board where the black King now appeared to be attempting to make his escape. The rules of the game now in tatters, Neville walked to the edge of the board and within a yard of the defeated monarch.

'Now,' he said, knowing that this was his victory and his day, 'show yourself!'

The black King stood still, straightened himself and stared at his vanquisher. Neville, still with his sword at his side, stood looking at an image of himself: but it was not the Neville he knew, the Neville he had now become; this was the Neville he had been, the one who had lost his wife, his job, and his life. Was this what the game had been about and the end to which he had been destined? In order to regain himself did he need to slay himself first?

From behind, the white Queen whispered to him.

'The King; you must slay the King.'

Neville took a step closer. He was expecting a plea, almost waiting to hear some argument to justify mercy; he was staring at his own death, and his own life. There was nothing. Not a murmur. The drums were silent, and the room echoed to nothing more than the fog. He raised his sword.

'Farewell.'

And with a single movement, Neville plunged the sword into the heart of the black King.

For a moment nothing happened, then the King buckled at the knees and fell to the ground. Neville looked down. All that remained were the robes he had been wearing and his broken crown; the body was gone. And then, in that split second, Neville felt a searing pain in his chest and collapsed to the ground.

FORTY TWO

When he regained consciousness, Neville found himself lying prostrate on the floor. A little time had evidently passed, though he had no idea how much. He waited for a few moments, allowing himself the luxury of a little re-orientation, then with care, raised himself to a sitting position and looked around the room. It was deserted; the fog had gone and, in the dim half-light, the chess board appeared much as when he had first seen it. All was silent.

He was sitting approximately where he had struck out at the black King, though no evidence remained of this encounter. Involuntarily he rubbed his chest, remembering the sharp stabbing pain that had rendered him helpless. For a moment he wondered if he might be dead. Indeed, if this were not the case (and he felt reasonably alive) then a secondary issue might well be his location, as he felt uncertain that he was still in situ in David's office.

Pulling himself to his feet, Neville walked to the door nearest to him, the one the chess pieces had used as an entrance. He tried it, but it was locked. He retraced his steps to the first door and turned the handle. Outside in the corridor, all was silent. He stood there for a moment, contemplating the offices, half wondering if he was now meant to try his boss's, but knowing in his heart that it was all over.

He made his way back towards the lifts. There was a welcoming "ping" as the doors of lift two slid open (it had evidently not moved since he last used it) and the comforting and familiar sensation of falling as he descended. As he walked towards the reception desk he realised that he did so empty-handed. He had told Cliff that he was going to collect some things and now appeared patently not to have done so.

Cliff was sitting at the desk when he reached it.

'Hello, Sir! That didn't take you long. I was going to ring up in a few minutes, just to make sure that you were OK.'

'I'm fine thanks, Cliff.'

'Get what you wanted?' Cliff looked towards Neville's empty hands.

'Yes and no, actually. I found what I was looking for, but then, having found it, discovered that I didn't need it anyway. You know how it is with old papers and office mementoes.'

'If you say so, Sir, yes.'

Cliff rose, pulling his keys from the desk.

'I'd better let you out, Sir.'

They walked together towards the door. Cliff unlocked it top and bottom, then pulled it open.

'You look all in, Sir.'

'Do I?'

'Must be the excitement, eh?'

'Excitement?' Neville was a little surprised.

'The Derby, and all that.'

'Yes, of course,' Neville had forgotten about the events of the previous day.

Cliff held out his hand.

'Well, at least your friend has waited for you.'

In the car park, the old bus still kept its lone vigil.

'Yes,' said Neville, realising that this had been by no means a certainty, 'of course.'

'Well, good luck, Sir. And take care.'

'Thanks Cliff.'

The two men shook hands. As Neville walked down the steps he heard the sound of the locks turning in the door, and waved back to Cliff. The security man offered a kind of half-salute then disappeared back into the building.

Neville had debated, for a fleeting moment as the lift had descended, whether or not the bus would still be there. After the bizarre events in the office - and the finality of their climax - Neville had wondered if he were to be alone once again. He was uncertain how his story would end; when, for example, would he be told of the ultimate decision? If he were heading towards the unwanted outcome of option 3, then surely he would, at some stage, feel vaguely suicidal?

Sleep, however, rather than anything more permanent, was the only thing really on his mind as he opened the door of the bus. There was that particular smell he had grown accustomed too over the previous few days, and, along with Samuel's smile, was a good a welcome as he could had wished for.

'There you are, Sir. Are you all right? You look a little bit done in, if I may say so.' Samuel had walked towards him and was standing in Neville's compartment.

'Hello, Samuel,' Neville sat on his bed, 'to tell you the truth, I'm completely knackered.'

'Would you like some tea, Sir?'

'No thanks. I think I'd just like to get some sleep.'

'Very good, Sir.' Samuel seemed on the point of leaving him, but paused. 'Did you find what you were looking for, Sir?'

Neville looked up and offered a tired smile.

'I'm not sure, Samuel; perhaps I did. I'll let you know later.'

Samuel nodded. It was a slow, knowing nod; the kind of a gesture that, amid his vast repertoire of wise gestures, fitted uncommonly well. Neville, as he began to get undressed, wondered how much Samuel knew about events so recently passed, and - if he had been right about him having one last ace in his hand - whether or not he had yet played it.

He was in bed when Samuel returned with a mug of cocoa.

'Just in case, Sir, I made you this.' He set it down on the bedside cupboard.

'Thanks, Samuel.'

'If you don't mind me asking, Sir; but where did you want to go next?'

'Go?' Just at that minute, Neville struggled a little with the concept of "going" anywhere. He remembered his plan. 'Anywhere you like, really. I just want to be at the restaurant in the evening.'

'Very good, Sir. Now you get some rest.'

Samuel's words were already beginning to blur before he got to the end of his last sentence, and when he awoke some time later, Neville found the cup of cocoa still full by the side of the bed. It was cold.

The bus was moving but the curtains were drawn. It appeared to be light outside, but Neville refrained from opening them to find out. He was not much interested in where they were, only where they were going. Consequently he rolled over, and offered himself up again to the arms of Morpheus.

Drifting in and out of sleep occupied him for the majority of the day. In his waking moments, Neville imagined that he was recharging some internal battery that had been run-down over the previous few days to near exhaustion; when asleep, his mind flitted in and out of dreams where his escapades were reordered and recreated; where the most frequent image was of Mita saying "Kill the King", and then witnessing his own demise.

When he did finally manage to rouse himself, he drew back the curtains to find that they were in the country, stationary in a lay-by. Samuel, who had evidently heard or sensed Neville's awakening, came back from the front of the bus.

'Good day, Sir. I would say "Good Morning", but as it's mid-afternoon, I don't think that would be appropriate.'

Samuel's smile enhanced Neville's feeling of being relaxed. He suddenly realised that he was hungry.

'It may not be morning, Samuel, but any chance of a little late breakfast?'

'You don't want to spoil your meal, Sir, but I think I might be able to rustle something up.'

A few minutes later, the two men were installed at the front of the bus, one reading, the other tucking in to a bacon and egg sandwich. Steam rose from mugs of tea, and the sun filtered in through the windows.

Samuel had asked nothing further of the visit to the office, and Neville had chosen to volunteer nothing either. He had come to realise - perhaps as a result of his dreams, or perhaps because it was a logical conclusion - that soon he and Samuel would be parting company. Whichever result, that conclusion was inevitable. He had considered divulging the events of the various episodes as he remembered them - especially the game of chess - with a view to receiving Samuel's gloss on them; but he now knew that his own interpretation was the one that mattered and, he guessed, he already had that.

They talked for a while; conversations about inconsequential things - the weather, even cricket. It transpired that Samuel had been something of a star bowler when young, but that an injury had forced him to change careers. Neville made some joke about the "magic" he could probably spin with a googly, and they laughed together.

Later, when Neville had finished eating and "breakfast" was over, Samuel returned to his seat and turned the key in the ignition. Despite its customary struggle to rouse itself to life, Neville sensed a degree of willingness in the old engine - and, with almost an echo, he was suddenly possessed with the knowledge that he would never again hear that distinctive sound. This - undeniable as it was - pierced him suddenly. He had not expected it, and, to be honest, had not looked for it either. From staring at the floor of the bus (from whence the grinding had emanated) he looked up to his pilot.

'Samuel.'

'Sir?'

The old boy turned to look at him, still full of acres of wisdom and good sense; still kind and unswerving and loyal.

'I'd just like to say "thank you", for helping me through all this.'

Samuel nodded, silently; smiled; then slipped the bus into gear.

By the time they had reached the restaurant, the day, although still bright, was beginning to show signs of giving way to evening. The shadows had lengthened, and the air - which boasted a kind of balmy stillness - carried the trace of a mist and the hint of cut grass upon it.

Theirs was the first vehicle in the car park. Neville, leaving the bus to stretch his legs, walked over to the restaurant. It had not yet opened for the evening.

'I'd just relax if I were you, Sir,' Samuel suggested as Neville returned to the bus across the tarmac. 'Perhaps a nice bath.'

Taking a bath seemed to be one of those tasks in Samuel's armoury - like drinking tea - which was undertaken in order that one might relax. Neville's bath time experiences had proven to be enlightening and entertaining, but, as usual, Samuel's suggestion was a sound one - if not, in this case, wholly necessary.

As he closed the door behind him, Neville hoped to discover the yellow duck bobbing in the water awaiting him; but he was disappointed. As he lowered himself beneath the bubbles, he remembered how this was the second time he had hoped for such company and been disappointed; only when he did not expect it, did the duck appear. This seemed a little fable in itself, and, as Neville had begun to collect such things - in order, as he imagined it, to collate some kind of personal philosophy - added the thought to his growing stock.

When he emerged some time later, he did so to discover that the evening was indeed beginning to descend, and that the car park was no longer empty. Samuel had laid out some of his casual clothes, and as he began to dress, Neville remembered how on his first visit, he had been resplendent in Mister Bossiman's suit. Through the open door of the small wardrobe, he could see that the dancing shoes had gone the way of the suit, and all that remained was his original and somewhat dull selection of attire.

'I feel a little under-dressed, and a little tatty,' he said to Samuel as he stood at the front of the bus, ready to leave.

'You look fine, Sir.'

'But everyone was so smartly dressed last time, Samuel. They might not let me in.'

'They always welcome old customers, Sir,' and Samuel gave him one of his "don't worry about anything" winks.

Neville paused on the steps of the bus.

'Samuel?'

'Sir?'

'Do you know? Am I going to be disappointed? Is this all just a waste of time?'

Samuel stood above him and placed a hand on Neville's shoulder.

'How do you feel, Sir?'

'A little nervous? A lot uncertain.'

The older man smiled.

'But does it feel "right"?'

Neville looked at the building, then back. He nodded.

'Well then; just have faith, Sir. And enjoy yourself.'

Half-way to the restaurant, Neville paused. Samuel, still standing on the steps of the bus, offered him a little wave. Neville nodded, then walked on.

On the threshold, the Maitre was manning his bookings podium like a Vicar about to preach a sermon. He smiled when he saw Neville approach and offered his hand.

'Good evening, Sir. And welcome back.'

'You remember me?'

The man gave a professional laugh.

'Of course, Sir! We remember all our old friends.' He turned towards the entrance to the dining room. 'Gustav! You are lucky Sir, we have just the table for you.'

Gustav appeared and offered Neville a smart bow.

'Please, follow me Sir.'

They were within two paces of the dining room when Neville stopped. He was suddenly scared. He had no desire to turn into the room and be disappointed. For a moment there was almost something he did not want to see, something he would have preferred not to know. Samuel's voice "have faith" echoed in his mind, and Neville knew that he would never be able to face himself if he did not go on.

Gustav had waited. Neville smiled and walked on.

Turning the corner, Gustav paused to signal to another waiter. Neville scanned the room in an instant, hoping for nothing more nor less than a flash of flamingo pink. There was none. The room was busy and with an abundance of colours, but there was no pink. Another waiter joined them.

'Michel will show you to your table, Sir,' and bowing, Gustav moved from Neville's line of sight.

In the corner of the room, at the same table he had occupied before and towards which he was once again being led, the smiling face of Mita waited to greet him.

FORTY THREE

By the time Neville reached the table, Mita had risen to greet him, tears already beginning in her eyes. They met as friends who were more than that, and their embrace was natural and unconstrained. Several conversations stopped; there was even the muted sound of soft applause from one table.

They stood, hugging, feeling the presence of the other, their physical reality, the certainty of life. Nothing was said, for there was nothing that needed to be said; words would have been inadequate for the moment and all that it embraced. Neville, his eyes closed, wondered if this was how it was to end; was his journey now over, or would there be one last step to take?

Mita eased herself away, and kissed him gently.

'Hello,' she said, a coy girlish playfulness in her voice; her eyes sparkling and radiant, 'you made it then?'

He sat beside her.

'Have you been waiting long?'

'Oh, just a couple of days!' She laughed, waving her free hand in the air in a gesture of supreme ease. 'I wasn't sure that you would make it. I mean, make it here; or how you would know where to meet me.'

'There were messages.'

'Messages?'

'Aren't there always?'

This struck a chord, and she laughed. They were like children who belonged to a private gang; a gang with its own rules and history; a gang with its own secrets too.

'I went to the Derby,' she confirmed.

Neville nodded.

'Busy, wasn't it? I knew that even if you were there, I wouldn't be able to find you.'

Michel brought the menus and Mita asked him to fetch some champagne.

'They've had it ready for me - just in case.'

'I'm pleased to be able to not disappoint them then.'

She gave him a soft dig in the ribs.

'Was it at Epsom you got the messages?'

'Partly; but it was there I put them together. The names of the horses, of course.'

'Restaurant Rendezvous! Did you back it?' She smiled mischievously, and immediately Neville could tell that she had done so.

'A little. It was too good to miss, wasn't it?'

They joined hands, still ignoring the menus that lay on the table before them. Michel came over with the champagne, preparing to open it.

'There was another message too...'

'Stop,' she was still smiling, but insistent, 'does it relate to what happened afterwards?'

He nodded.

'Well, there's plenty of time for that; let's not spoil the evening.'

The champagne popped loudly, and Michel filled the waiting glasses. When he had gone, they prepared to toast.

'What do we drink to?' Mita asked, glass suspended in mid-air.

'How about tomorrow?' Neville suggested.

'How about today and tomorrow?'

There was some satisfaction in the clink of the glasses as they came slowly together. It seemed like a contract, a pact almost; Neville - though still harbouring a sense of doubt, a concern that, in the end, there might be some wicked twist in the tail - felt satisfied and victorious, more than ever before.

Mita caught a trace of the thought on his face as he sipped the wine.

'You're not sure?'

'Sure?'

'If it's real, all of this. I wondered too; perhaps I still do, just a little. But we're here, and after all we've been through - well, that has to be some kind of miracle.'

Gustav had moved to the table and was waiting for them.

'Would you like to order, Madam, Sir?'

Neville glanced at Mita.

'Whatever we like?'

'Whatever we like!'

'We should have different things, just to prove...'

'And no monkfish!'

Their laughter caused a little concern with Gustav who immediately protested that the monkfish was excellent, and that they should not be put off at all. Neville assured him that it was a private joke and had nothing to do with the restaurant. He seemed satisfied. Nevertheless, they both avoided the monkfish and, as they had agreed, chose different things from the menu, though what they ate seemed of little importance.

As Mita handed back her menu, she noticed Neville looking over her shoulder.

'What is it?'

'The fish.'

She turned. The open-mouthed blue fish stared inertly past them and into the room; the eyes remained as Neville remembered them, and he half-expected one of them to suddenly wink at him.

'Friend of yours?' Mita asked, a wicked inflection in her voice. Neville could not tell if she was asking from full knowledge or partial guesswork.

'Kind of. That's Bob.'

Mita looked back at the fish.

'Bob, eh? Nice to meet you Bob; any friend of Neville's is a friend of mine.'

He could never have had a better invitation to spring into life, but Bob remained still and lifeless. Neville was a little disappointed, part of him would have liked to share this return with him, but presumably his day would come again.

They ate between conversation; mouthfuls of salmon and pate, trout and lamb, mixed with a bubbling but understated excitement at what had passed and - but this was unuttered - what might lay ahead. It took them a long time to get through the first two courses, but time seemed not to be a problem. Gustav asked them if their food was acceptable - it was of course - and Michel kept them topped up with champagne. There was no pressure to get a move on, and Neville - when the dessert menu appeared - breathed a sigh of relief that here was another sign of normality onto which he could hang.

Having placed their orders for dessert, Neville rose and excused himself. At the dining room door he asked Gustav for the direction to the gents toilet.

'Through the archway, Sir, and left at the bottom of the corridor.'

Neville paused, remembering his most recent experience of doors off of corridors and, for the briefest moment, considered leaving the building and trying to find a suitable bush around the car park. However, sanity - which appeared at last to be on the way back - prevailed, and a few moments later he walked in to the lavatory.

There were no urinals (which immediately struck him as slightly odd) but rather two cubicles facing a wash stand and mirror. Both cubicles were empty. Neville chose one, closed the door behind him, and - in something of an automatic way - was soon seated on the mahogany-topped pedestal.

He had been there only a few seconds when he heard the door open, and someone enter the other trap. He waited for the sound of the seat being raised or lowered, or the sound of a trouser fly being unzipped, but there was nothing. It seemed a little odd that there should be such silence. And then he heard Samuel's voice.

'How is it going, Sir?'

'Samuel, is that you?'

'Yes, Sir.'

Neville made preparations to rise, but was immediately halted.

'I'd hang on just a minute if I were you, Sir.'

'Hang on?'

'We won't be disturbed, and there are a few things I really think we ought to clear up.'

Neville froze. He felt a sudden chill grip the nape of his neck and then flood down his spine. He shivered, hard. Was this it? Was Samuel's last trick to be the one that sent him into oblivion? If he had been shown just a glimpse of happiness only for it to be snatched away...

'Sir?'

He chose not to reply.

'I know what you're thinking, Sir; but really, you've nothing to worry about.'

'What do you mean?'

'What time is it?'

'Time, Samuel?'

'Please, Sir. What time is it?'

Neville looked at his watch. It was nearly ten o'clock - a little later than he had expected, but time seemed to be passing quickly this evening. And then he realised that the second hand was moving clockwise and that his watch was back to normal.

'It has been like that for a little while now, actually. You are back in the "real world", as it is known.'

'Since when? I mean, when was it all over; when was everything all right?'

'Last night; probably just before you returned to the bus.'

There was a brief silence. Neville thought about the climax to the chess game; his hand went to his chest.

'Something significant happened, I take it?'

'You might say that, yes,' Neville paused, 'but then presumably you know all about it?'

'Some, Sir. Some things I guess from you.'

Again there was a tiny lull, then Neville realised the simple question he had yet to ask.

'Why are you here, Samuel?'

'As I said, Sir, we've got a few things to clear up. Like this, for instance.'

An A4 brown envelope was slid part-way under the door. Neville picked it up and opened it. Inside was all the money he had won at Epsom, including the cheque from the Tote.

'All my winnings?'

'And the little bit you had left over, yes Sir. That - as I suggested at the time - is now yours; please use it wisely.'

Neville laughed a little; his first moment of relaxation since the bizarre interview had begun.

'I think I have learned a little about money recently.'

'And a few other things too, I trust.'

'Indeed Samuel, yes.' Neville waited for something else to be forthcoming. 'You said there were a few things to clear up. What else is there?'

'Well, nothing terribly tangible, I'm afraid. I've packed your things, and they are in your bags by the entrance.'

'You're going away?'

'Indeed Sir, yes. As soon as I have finished here.'

'But this is absurd, Samuel; we shouldn't part like this! I want to shake your hand; to thank you. Really.'

'Ah, I have thanks enough Sir when I see you and Miss Mita together. Audrey tells me that she had a rather difficult time of it - as you did too, of course. I am pleased she is well; please take care of her.'

Neville was thrown by Samuel's use of the word "well", which seemed strangely out of context. He could not debate it, however.

'You said "my" things. Not, presumably the suit or the flying jacket?'

'Indeed not, Sir. I'm afraid certain things were - how shall I put it - repossessed. I hope you understand.'

'I'm not sure I do, Samuel. Indeed, there's much I don't understand.'

'Ah.' There was a brief pause from the other cubicle. 'The only other thing I have to do, is to give you a chance to ask me - well, whatever you like, really.'

'"Have to do", Samuel? It sounds like some kind of rule.'

'Well, in a way it is Sir, yes.'

'And presumably you mean about the last few days, about what happened to me?'

'Indeed; though I must warn you that I may not be in a position to tackle everything.'

Neville considered the whole gamut of his experience and wondered where to begin.

'Do I have a limit?' It was just a hunch, but the sort of thing he expected to apply. He was right.

'Yes, Sir; time or the number of questions - I can't say which.'

'OK. Take Pierre, the Pierrot in Paris. Was he on your side?'

'On my side, Sir?'

'Yes; part of the set-up, part of the plan. Was I supposed to find him because that was all in the game? Did everything I experience belong to some prearranged sequence?'

'Sir, there's more than one question there!'

'OK. Take the rescue of Mita on the boat. Was that part of your plan, or was it really me living out a fantasy, just like the Pilgrim advertised?'

'Or was it you living out one of Mita's fantasies, Sir? That could be a possibility.'

'But do you know?'

'Does it matter?'

Neville banged his fist against the cubicle wall.

'Damn it Samuel, yes it does! It matters to me!'

Samuel said nothing. Neville knew he was still there; he could hear his breathing - though a little laboured now - through the thin veneer.

'Sir; does it really matter? *Really*? You know what matters *now*; you have learned what matters - and are still learning. Remember you said that you had lots of questions to ask, and that I told you that it was a good start to at least have the questions? That is still true. If I told you that it was your fantasy, or Mita's fantasy, would that make any difference? Would it matter if you knew how much of your experience was pre-arranged, or how you managed to find out the winner of the Derby? Does any of that matter? Is it important to you, Sir, now, with Mita waiting for you in the dining room? And yes, she will still be there waiting when you get back. Today and tomorrow, Sir; just like you said.'

His voice was beginning to sound a little thick and his breathing a little heavy.

'Are you all right, Samuel?'

'I should be going, Sir.'

'One last question?'

'Quickly then.'

'How much choice did I have in all of this? I mean, when was I actually making any decisions that changed it all around? Or was it planned - in the smallest of details - and all I was doing, decisions and all, was acting out my part, like an actor in a play?'

There came a throaty laugh from the other cubicle.

'That old question? Always the same, in the end.'

'So?'

'There are two possibilities: it was all a plan, or you made it happen yourself. Presumably there may be shades in between. But you want to know which is true?'

'Yes.'

'Then again I say, does it really matter? Really? Perhaps it is one, perhaps the other. Perhaps there is a combination of things, so complex that one cannot comprehend it. But who cares, if it really doesn't matter? What happened, happened; do you complain at the outcome? People are so lucky, and yet they fret over such impossible things.'

'But people need to believe in things.'

'Indeed. Have faith, yes; but have faith in yourself. Forget those theories, the philosophers' stones. People give names to big things that cannot be explained. If you want to believe in something, then call it "The Big Frog Theory"; it's as good a name as any other, and there might just as well be a frog deciding the outcome of the universe as anything else. But, above all; faith in yourself.'

The monologue ended in a splutter of coughing and then, for a moment, silence. Neville noticed a strange, but vaguely familiar smell. He rose, half expecting to be told to resume his seat. There was nothing. As he placed his hand on the door latch, he heard a single and distinct sound - the croak of a frog - and then nothing.

The cubicle was empty when he finally managed to get the door open. There was no trace of Samuel, or of anything else come to that. Neville turned and looked in the mirror. All he could see was himself; but it was the new Neville, not the one he had slain on the chess board. He thought of a quote he had heard a long time ago: "the King is dead; long live the King!".

He was uncertain of its origins, but just now it seemed remarkably appropriate.

As Samuel had said, his bags were waiting for him to pick them up in the hallway. He checked each in turn. They simply contained the clothes with which he had begun his adventure - except for the smaller bag which, hidden between two shirts, concealed his copy of the rules to the game of "Croak".

Walking back to the dining room he thought of Samuel and smiled. There were many pieces to be reassembled before he would understand much of his own version of the jigsaw, but at least he would not be facing it entirely alone.

EPILOGUE

They approached the town from the hills. The weather had broken during the night, and the bright day had given way to heavy summer thunderstorms. By the morning, these had begun to fade and now, in early afternoon, the clouds - white and unthreatening - were in retreat from the bright blue sky.

It had been a long time since Neville had walked the hills; so much so, that his walking boots had felt vaguely uncomfortable at first. There had been no real need for boots - they had hardly strayed from recognised paths after all - but even so, first thing in the morning they had stopped in Worcester to buy Mita her own pair.

The remainder of the previous evening and much of the night had been spent in discussion. Neville had said nothing of his final experience with Samuel, but Mita - who was shrewd enough to notice a subtle change in his demeanour - gathered that something had happened.

'The icing on the cake?' she had said, when he returned to their table. He had simply smiled.

It would have been easy for them to launch into vague and outrageous plans for the future, but the next day and a walk on the hills - this at Neville's insistence - was as distant as they had managed. There had been vague references to the recent past, as was inevitable, but they had managed to stop at allusion on most occasions. Neville had talked about tangible things - his old job, his previous life with Mirelle (the coincidence of name making Mita laugh) and his old Sierra - and Mita, less forthcoming, had left hints of her past like a trail she was inviting him to follow.

He had not told her why he had wanted to walk the hills: there had been some excuse; a little romantic embroidery, perhaps. They had eaten their picnic reasonably early (despite the meal the previous evening, they were both hungry) and when Neville suggested taking an early tea in the town, it seemed a natural suggestion.

As they turned the corner into the street on which his tea shop stood, Neville did so without the slightest doubt that it would still be there, and that the last thing he would find would be the remnants of the place strewn in diverse piles of rubble across the street. So it proved to be. He had suggested it to Mita as "a little place he knew" which "had fond memories for him". She had shot him a quizzical look, wanting a little more but aware that more would - one day - be forthcoming.

He opened the door and the bell gave a ring. Pausing on the threshold, he gave his boots - which despite their route, still carried a little debris - a vigorous wipe on the doormat. Mita did likewise. His memory of the tea shop was a little hazy, but the sight of the counter, the layout of the tables - even the geese on the wall - reinforced all he had retained.

The table near the window - **his** table, and the one he had secretly been hoping for - was occupied, as was the one next to it. Mita, who had overtaken him by now, made for a location at the back of the shop. One of the waitresses, in prim black and white, gave her a brief nod. Neville joined her.

'This is nice,' Mita said, 'quite plain, but perfectly charming.'

Neville was amused by the sense of the place being plain, but fell unready to explain.

They ordered tea, and the waitress asked them if they would like anything to eat.

'A little gateau?' Mita suggested.

Neville ordered two scones.

The Proprietress - still as large as, but not larger than, life - emerged from the back of the shop and prepared their tea. As they waited for the waitress to return, Neville relaxed and surveyed the place again.

There was little, he realised - beyond perhaps the ducks on the wall - that he could recall. The lady who ran the cafe was, by her bulk if nothing else, quite unforgettable. But in truth, as Mita had said, it was indeed quite plain.

They were half way through their scones - and through a discussion about the route they should take to return to Mita's car - when Neville caught a glimpse of an old bus rolling by outside. It was a blue bus, and quite dissimilar to Samuel's vehicle, yet its presence - even briefly - was sufficient to unnerve him slightly. He scanned the room again, his mind only half attending to Mita's conversation.

At the table in the window, a solitary man sat staring out into the street. On the table cloth in front of him was a cup of filter coffee. As Neville watched, a waitress took a slice of gateau to the table and left it there. The man appeared not to notice. Voices from the next table - two ladies, one with well coiffured hair - rose and caught his attention. It was not the Conservative Lady - not **his** Conservative Lady - but near enough.

And then the blue bus pulled up on the opposite side of the road and the driver stepped out.

Mita had stopped talking, her attention grabbed by the sudden change in Neville's attitude. She looked to where he looked, but without comprehension. She squeezed his arm.

'Are you OK?'

Neville said nothing; his eyes were fixed on the bus driver as he walked towards them. He was hoping - and not hoping - that it was Samuel. The door opened and the man, certainly past his prime, entered. He nodded to the man at the window seat, and then to all in turn. His eyes rested for a moment on Neville. It was not Samuel, but there was something there...

'I think we should go,' he suddenly said.

'I've a little tea left.'

'Mita,' he had turned to her now. She could see that he was serious. 'Do you trust me?'

She laughed a little uneasily. There was in his voice and in his eyes, a strange mix of fear and sublime joy; simultaneously, he seemed both possessed yet full of self-awareness.

'Yes.'

'There is a little part of my story I must tell you - but not here,' he took her hand and rose, 'perhaps outside, as we're walking.'

As they walked through the shop, Neville nodded at bus driver. By the time they reached the street, he was smiling blissfully to himself. They walked a little way then Mita stopped him and kissed him.

'And do I get you little story now?'

Neville placed his arm around her shoulder.

'Where shall I begin?'